2016

# Jacob's List

# STEPHANIE GRACE WHITSON

Jacob's List

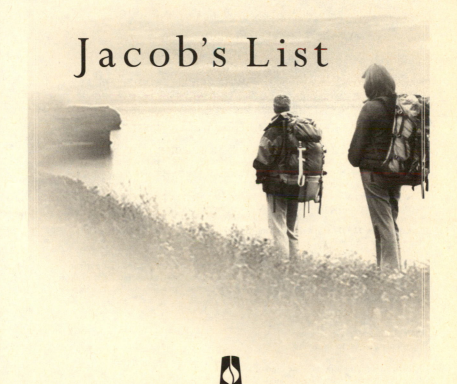

**BETHANY HOUSE**
MINNEAPOLIS, MINNESOTA

For Daniel

who had the idea and gave it away

# BOOKS BY
# STEPHANIE GRACE WHITSON

*A Garden in Paris*
*A Hilltop in Tuscany*
*Jacob's List*

## PINE RIDGE PORTRAITS
*Secrets on the Wind*
*Watchers on the Hill*
*Footprints on the Horizon*

## PRAIRIE WINDS
*Walks the Fire*
*Soaring Eagle*
*Red Bird*

## KEEPSAKE LEGACIES
*Sarah's Patchwork*
*Karyn's Memory Box*
*Nora's Ribbon of Memories*

## DAKOTA MOONS
*Valley of the Shadow*
*Edge of the Wilderness*
*Heart of the Sandhills*

## NONFICTION
*How to Help a Grieving Friend*

{about the author}

A NATIVE OF SOUTHERN ILLINOIS, Stephanie Grace Whitson has resided in Nebraska since 1975. She began what she calls "playing with imaginary friends" (writing fiction) when, as a result of teaching her four homeschooled children Nebraska history, she was personally encouraged and challenged by the lives of pioneer women in the West. Since her first book, *Walks the Fire,* was published in 1995, Stephanie's fiction titles have appeared on the ECPA bestseller list and have been finalists for the Christy Award and the Inspirational Reader's Choice Award. Her first nonfiction work, *How to Help a Grieving Friend,* was released in 2005. In addition to serving her local church and keeping up with two married children and three college students, Stephanie enjoys volunteering for the International Quilt Study Center and riding motorcycles with her blended family and church friends. Widowed in 2001, Stephanie remarried in 2003 and now pursues full-time writing and a speaking ministry from her studio in Lincoln, Nebraska. Learn more at *www.stephaniewhitson.com* or write stephanie@stephaniewhitson.com. U.S. mail can be directed to Stephanie Grace Whitson at 3800 Old Cheney Road, #101–178, Lincoln, Nebraska 68516.

## {one}

"I CAN'T BELIEVE I'm doing this." Motioning for the black dog at her side to jump into the back seat of the blue convertible, Pamela Nolan climbed in beside her best friend.

Rainelle peered over the top of her sunglasses. "What's to believe?" she teased. "We always do comfort food on Father's Day. It's our traditional antidote for 'dysfunctional dad brooding.'"

Pam tucked her hair up into a baseball cap as Rainelle backed the car toward the street. "I wasn't talking about the food and you know it. I was talking about the rest of the morning."

"You mean the watching-my-baby-boy-jump-out-of-a-perfectly-good-airplane thing?" Rainelle shifted into first gear and headed up the tree-lined street.

"Yeah. That thing." Pam paused. "He was so disappointed when I said I just couldn't bear to watch. It'll be fun to surprise him now, but—" She cleared her throat and laid an open palm across her midsection.

"Butterflies?"

"I wish," Pam replied. "Try an entire flock of birds—and they're trying to claw their way up and out." She grimaced. "Let's just head on out there. Now that I've decided to go, I want to get it over with. And I don't think I can eat, anyway."

"Oh, no you don't." Rainelle glanced at her watch. "You said they were scheduled for nine this morning. It's only seven-thirty. I can just see you chewing your nails down to stubs while we wait and you imagine all kinds of things going wrong." She pulled to a stop at a red light. "Listen, honey. You yourself told me all about how Jacob had convinced you that sky diving is safe. Statistically safer than

9

driving a car, if I remember correctly. And I do. So settle back and leave the whining to him." She pointed at the dog in the back seat. When he sat up and chuffed softly, Rainelle laughed. "Sorry about that, Rambo. Aunt Rainelle knows you're not a whiner."

"*Aunt* Rainelle?" Pam protested. "What would Cicero think if he knew you were kissing up to a poodle?"

"Let me tell you something, girl friend," Rainelle said as the light turned green and she shifted into first gear. "That may *look* like a dog, and heaven knows it *smells* like a dog sometimes, but that's all part of a very clever disguise." She peered in the rearview mirror. "I know the truth, Fur-face. Underneath the raggedy black coat there resides a very large cat."

Rambo chuffed again and shook his head.

Pam laughed. "Raggedy is right. He's overdue at the groomer." She glanced back. "Personally, though, I kind of like the look."

"I'm with you on that one," Rainelle agreed. "The pom-poms-on-the-derrière thing never did work for me." She whipped into a parking space at the diner.

Pam got out, but when Rambo started to follow she held up a hand and said quietly, "No. You stay." Another gesture and the dog sat. Pam reached to the floorboard and grabbed her purse. "Let's go," she said and headed inside.

"What was *that*?"

"Jacob taught me a few hand signals when he was home on spring break," Pam said. "I just told Rambo to stay put." When Rainelle hesitated, she motioned. "Come on. He'll be fine. Trust me."

"Are you kidding?" Rainelle cast a doubtful glance toward the car. "Shouldn't we at least attach a leash to a door handle or something? What if a cute little thing named FiFi saunters by?"

Pam shrugged. "Jacob says Rambo is bulletproof. That means 'trustworthy' in human." She motioned for Rainelle to follow her. "So let's go."

"Is Jacob gonna be home all summer?"

"At least until he and Andy head out to do the next thing on the list." She grimaced. "Rock-climbing, I think he said. Somewhere out west. Some really, really high, difficult-to-scale rock." She shivered. "Why?"

"Because," Rainelle said as they stepped inside the diner and plopped into a booth. "I'm gonna see if I can get him to spend some time with Cicero—who has taken to late-night chases through the condo. The other night he landed on the pillow next to me. I was half asleep—but I still managed to launch his furry little tush across the room. He's still mad at me about that."

Pam picked up the menu. "How can you possibly tell when a cat is mad at you?"

"You don't want to know," Rainelle said and squeezed her nose between her fingers.

Pam gave an *I see* nod. "I don't think Cicero would take well to obedience training."

"Oh, he would," Rainelle joked. "He'd have me fetching his catnip mouse in no time." She chuckled and peered out the window at Rambo. "Such a perfect gentleman. If only the rest of the men in our lives would follow his example."

"Amen to that." Pam glanced over the menu before putting it down with a huge sigh. "Really. I don't think I can eat."

Rainelle handed the menu back. "You are going to eat a real breakfast like any self-respecting woman with realities to ignore and things to forget." She smiled. "I will *not* have you reverting to the good old 'albino pole bean' days."

"Relax." Pam forced a chuckle. "There's no chance of the albino pole bean *ever* making an appearance around here." She sighed. "For all my efforts not one single thing in my closet is too big . . . and I can't seem to get past level four on the recumbent bike." She shook her head. "Hard to believe the two of us used to run six miles three times a week."

"Yeah, well, at least we gave up *that* nonsense at the same time. I don't think I could stand hearing you talk about your umpteenth marathon over cocktails." She chuckled. "It's thin ice for you and me as it is, what with you all rich and me all normal."

11

"Oh, yeah," Pam teased. "It's just paycheck to paycheck for you these days." She pointed out the window to the car.

"The deal of the century on eBay. Couldn't resist." Rainelle put the menu in her friend's hands. "Come on, now. I know how you are. You'll feel better with something in your stomach."

"All right, Counselor. You win."

"Usually do."

"But when all those trans fats show up on the backside I've been trying to downsize, I'm blaming you."

"I thought you were going to quit the gym," Rainelle said.

Pam shook her head. "I just started going in the afternoon so I don't have to witness my gorgeous husband and his little bevy of pre-dawn Spandex Rangers." She fluttered her eyelashes and struck a pose. "'Oh, Dr. Nolan, could you help me with this machine?' 'Oh, Mikey, could you help me rack these weights?'" As she talked, Pam mimed the flirtatious stretches she'd witnessed, thrusting out her chest and sucking her gut in while she ran her open palm over her rib cage and abdomen.

Rainelle clamped her hand over her mouth, snorted, swallowed, and coughed. "Never do that when I have a mouth full of water—unless, of course, you *want* a free shower." She wiped her mouth with a napkin. "So—" her voice lowered—"has Dr. America of the six-pack noticed?"

"Noticed what? That I noticed his flirting, that I'm not going to the gym the same time as him, or that I've lost five pounds?"

"Either. Any."

Pam shrugged. "I made up some lame excuse for why I didn't want to go so early in the morning. He didn't protest. And he'd only notice the weight loss if we were actually—" She stopped herself. "Over sharing," she said. "So . . . how's Malcolm?"

"Guarding his heart like it was the National Archives. I can't get him off home base. We have coffee twice a week at The Mill. Other than that, our relationship amounts to longing looks across the law library table."

"Holding pattern?"

"Holding. But not each other," Rainelle said, regret sounding in her voice.

"Maybe you should bring out Diva-Ray for him," Pam teased. "She usually gets her man."

Rainelle shook her head. "I'm tired of the kind of men Diva-Ray can get." She looked toward the kitchen. "Where *is* that waiter?" She called out to a waitress headed toward the kitchen with a tray full of dirty dishes. "Would you track down our waiter and have him hustle his cute little buns over here?"

When the waiter arrived Pam ordered, then settled back to enjoy yet another performance by one of Rainelle's many alter egos. As expected, the one who surfaced was the one Pam called Diva-Ray—an incorrigible flirt with a remarkable ability to get whatever Rainelle wanted. A nearly faultless judge of people, Rainelle had long ago developed the talent to become whatever was required to achieve her goals. It had served her well in life and in the courtroom. Over the years Pam had seen her friend be gracious, loud, sophisticated, down-to-earth, charming, pushy, and a dozen other things in between. This morning, Rainelle's goal was to talk the waiter into bringing her real cream for her coffee, Tabasco sauce for her hash browns, real butter for the pancakes, and to make sure her eggs were cooked according to her own very specific definition of "over easy." Enter Diva-Ray.

"You are amazing," Pam said when the waiter left.

"*Moi?*" Rainelle spread her fingers and pointed all ten of her elegantly manicured nails toward herself in mock surprise.

Pam laughed and shook her head. "It would take years of therapy to meld all those personalities in your head into one persona."

"What do you mean 'all those personalities'?" Rainelle feigned offense.

"Let's see," Pam said, counting on her fingers. "There's Diva-Ray, the goddess of 'have it your way.' Then there's Ray-Ray the party girl, Ellie the Innocent, and my own personal favorite, Tough Mama."

"When have you *ever* thought of me as a tough mama?" Rainelle paused. "Oh, all right. But that was junior high and you know that situation required one tough mama."

Pam nodded agreement. Transferred into a nearly all-white school, Rainelle Washington had walked the halls of Clark Junior High with her head held high and her true self hidden behind a bawdy persona who seemed willing to be everyone's token black acquaintance. Referred to—behind her back—as the African Queen, Rainelle revealed not one flicker of her real self to anyone. It was a long time before Pam realized how much the supposedly "only in fun" daily jokes about her skin color and afro hurt and how much Rainelle resented the girls who made them.

"And besides," Rainelle said, leaning forward with a smile, "I may have been doing Tough Mama back then, but you had an act, too."

"Don't I know it. That school could have been Darwin's proving ground for survival of the fittest."

"Speaking of survival," Rainelle said, twisting around and peering toward the kitchen, "does breakfast seem to be taking longer than usual?" Without waiting for a reply, she scooted out of the booth and headed off in search of the waiter. Once she'd located him, she gave Pam a thumbs-up and extended each finger of her right hand in a silent count. It would be five minutes and they'd have their breakfast. With a grin, Rainelle struck a Diva-Ray pose and then headed off down the hall toward the women's rest room.

While she waited for Rainelle and breakfast, Pam reminisced. Her own skin color might not have put up the barriers Rainelle's did in junior high school, but Pam's shyness, athletic ability, and intelligence did. And if that weren't enough, Pam held everyone at arm's length lest they discover the truth about Dottie Fletcher's drinking. Fifteen-year-old Pamela Fletcher would never be accepted by her peers, and she told herself she didn't care. She excelled academically, played tennis like a future champion, and was several inches taller than everyone in her class—until the arrival of Rainelle Washington.

When Pam and Rainelle passed in the corridor, they eyed one another with a wariness borne of their competition on the tennis court and their latent suspicions about just how much of the other girl's personality was fake. In the lunchroom, each girl sat alone. And then one day for no particular conscious reason—although as an adult Pam would come to realize it was an action motivated by desperate loneliness—Pam slid her lunch tray into place at the opposite end of Rainelle's table.

"What you think you're doing?" Rainelle said.

"Eating lunch," Pam said.

"This table is reserved."

Pam looked around her. Shrugged. "Doesn't look to me like the reserves are gonna show today." She paused. "And even if they do, what are *you* gonna do about me sitting here? It's a free country last time I checked."

Rainelle shrugged. "Who said I wanna do somethin' 'bout it? I don't see any reason to pick a fight with a pole bean."

Pam stabbed a piece of the lime Jell-O on her plate with a fork and said nothing.

"That's what you are, you know," Rainelle prodded. "Jus' a albino pole bean."

When Pam said nothing, Rainelle slid her tray closer and continued the soliloquy of insults. Pam listened, regretting ever making the first move toward what she had hoped might be . . . what? Friendship? She chastised herself. So much for thinking they might have something in common. "Suppose you just hush that big mouth of yours," she said, and threw a piece of green Jell-O Rainelle's way.

It landed in Rainelle's afro. Pam stifled a smile and looked away. The Jell-O came back at her, followed by a green bean. Pam answered with a French fry. Aware that the lunchroom had grown quiet and that she and Rainelle were the center of attention, Pam stood up, her hand on the carton of milk on her tray. Rainelle didn't wait to see what Pam was going to do before acting, and two minutes later the entire lunchroom was bedlam. When order was finally restored, half a dozen students had been dragged to the principal's office and a dozen more assigned detention to help with cleanup.

Pam and Rainelle sat next to each other just outside the principal's office while Mrs. Jeffers called their parents.

"Won't do any good," Rainelle muttered under her breath. "My foster parents don't care one way or the other what I do as long as I get home on time to do dishes and laundry and baby-sit."

Pam slouched. "Won't do any good for her to call mine, either."

"Why not, pole bean?" Rainelle chided. "Your daddy too busy at the country club to take calls?"

"That just shows what you know."

"I know what I know." Rainelle lifted her chin and looked down her nose at her.

"My daddy's dead," Pam blurted out.

Rainelle's dark eyes showed surprise.

"And if my mama's even home," Pam added, so quietly only Rainelle could hear her, "she's probably drunk." She looked out of the corner of her eye at the girl sitting next to her. "So don't tell me your sob story, 'cause I've got one of my own. And by the way, you're no different than all those girls you hate for believing the African Queen bit. You just look at someone and think you know what and who they are. Well guess what, you don't know anything about me."

Rainelle fidgeted. After a minute she said, "I know you've got a great right hook. For a pole bean."

Pam turned to look at Rainelle, who had raised her palm to her face and was slowly rubbing her jaw. Her mouth didn't smile, but her dark eyes did. She winked. Pam nudged her arm with her elbow. "That's *albino* pole bean to you."

And so began the friendship that got Pam through junior high school and beyond. It was Rainelle that Pam called when her mother finally landed in the hospital and the doctors said she would die of liver disease; Rainelle who stood beside her at her mother's funeral and dragged her back to college and insisted she get her nursing degree; Rainelle who arranged her blind date with a cute medical student named Michael Nolan; Rainelle who served as her maid of honor when they married; Rainelle who was godmother to Jacob. And today it was Rainelle who would get her through witnessing number six on Jacob's infernal list.

# {two}

SOME DAYS IT SEEMED like God took things a little too far. Stan Novac was all about doing good to his fellow man and being a good testimony on the job and all that, but he had been on the police force for nearly thirty years, and he had seniority, and for crying out loud, it was Father's Day. Did it matter that he had six kids who actually *liked* him and *wanted* to celebrate Father's Day with him? No. Did it matter that he'd worked overtime last week as a special favor to the captain? No. Did it matter that his only son, Andy, and Andy's best friend, Jacob, had actually decided to do something on their list locally and the day was going to be about as perfect weather-wise as a Nebraska day could be? No. All that mattered was Pete had sliced his hand open on his day off, and somebody had to pony up and fill the slot. And of course since Stan was the nice guy, everyone figured he wouldn't mind skipping church and filling in.

*Man, it is hard to be me some days.* Grousing to himself, Stan slipped his dented pickup into his parking place, got out, and headed for the precinct door. Halfway there, he stopped. Turned around. Scanned the parking lot for his partner's car. And when he realized Ken Randolph hadn't arrived yet, smiled. Heading back to his truck, Stan opened the door and reached for the bag on the floorboard. If he couldn't have fun with his kids today, he might as well have some fun with the new kid at work.

————

Even the most whiskey-fogged male brain heard authority in the nether regions of The Voice. Stan seldom had to resort to physical compliance techniques. Not that he minded physical compliance techniques. As far as he was concerned, punks who misread gray hair as a synonym for old and weak were fair game. Stan loved the look in their eyes when they realized that what they thought were extra pounds on "the tall dude" had been won at the gym—not over a bowl of potato chips.

But this morning he didn't need anything but his voice—well, The Voice and the gun in his hand (which was a toy but Ken didn't seem to know that)—to keep the blond-haired kid rooted to the locker room floor. Stan took The Voice a notch lower, into what the guys called Darth Vader mode. He waggled the gun up and down as he spoke, drawing out each word for emphasis. "Bee . . . cauzzz . . . GOD told me to!" And he pulled the trigger.

The rookie staring down the barrel of the gun jumped back—too late to avoid being baptized.

Laughter broke out in the locker room as Randolph sputtered and swiped the water out of his eyes.

"You guys," he said, feigning anger, "you guys are gonna be the death of me." He looked at his partner. "Did that really ever happen?"

"Did *what* ever really happen?" Stan asked and tossed the water gun in a high arc over Randolph's head and into a trash can waiting at the end of the long row of metal lockers.

"Some psycho taking a bead on you and saying God told him to shoot a cop." Randolph shrugged out of his wet shirt and reached for a fresh one.

"That's not the point," Stan said. "The point is it *could* happen. And from what I just saw, if it ever *does* happen, all that self-defense stuff you learned from our hotshot trainer will fly right out the window." He tapped his temple with his index finger. "Training's no good if it stays in here, kid." He reached for his duty belt. While he buckled it on, he grinned at his new partner. "Okay, Randolph. Happy Father's Day. You're in. No more initiate-the-rookie jokes." He raised his voice and boomed out, "Right, guys?"

A chorus of *Right*s answered back.

Randolph muttered doubt as he tucked his dry shirt into his uniform pants and reached for his own duty belt.

"No, really," Stan insisted. "You are officially welcomed into the brotherhood and forthwith entitled to all the privileges of your fellow police officers."

"What privileges would those be?"

"Day-old Krispy Kremes!" a voice from the opposite side of the row of lockers yelled.

"Low pay!" someone else added.

"No respect!"

"Long days!"

Half a dozen voices took up the chant. "Krispy Kremes, low pay, no respect, long days. Krispy Kremes, low pay, no respect, long days. . . ."

Ken shook his head. "I'm beginning to think I should have been a fireman."

"What?" Stan grinned. "And miss all this?" He gestured around him at the pale green room filled with battered lockers and worn wooden benches. Closing his locker door, he ran his hands through his curly hair before donning his uniform hat. "You ready?"

"Ready as I'll ever be."

"Relax," Stan said and slapped Ken on the back. "The answer is no. I didn't *really* ever stand at the wrong end of a gun with a crazy perp saying God told him to kill somebody. Things are comparatively run-of-the-mill in our little corner of the U.S. of A."

"Compared to what?"

Stan shrugged. "Compared to LA, Lincoln doesn't even *have* crime." He looked down at his watch. "Besides that, it's Sunday morning. The worst thing we're gonna face this morning is a few speeding grandmas worried they're late for church."

———————

Andy Novac had laughed when Jake had first showed up with a bumper sticker that read *Always late but worth the wait* on his brand-new Chevy S–10. But he wasn't going to laugh today. He'd checked his camera equipment a dozen times. Talked to the guy who'd packed Jake's chute. Convinced the pilot to wait just a few more minutes before taking a run with a few of the dozen or so weekend sky divers waiting near the tarmac. And still . . . no phone call. No excuse. No word from Jacob Nolan.

As he began to pace back and forth in front of his car, Andy's frustration mounted. How hard could it be to be on time, anyway? Andy had five sisters to fight for use of the shower. Was he ever late? Nope. Andy had to ride his bike to class. Was he ever late? Nope. But Jake . . . the only child of wealthy parents, who could wallow in his king-sized bed until noon if he wanted to, who had his choice of five—count them, *five*—bathrooms, who had his own brand-new pickup . . . Jake Nolan acted like being late was his own special brand of performance art.

*I should make my own list*, Andy thought as he paced. *Jacob's Top Ten Excuses*. A late meal. A last-minute phone call. A malfunctioning alarm. The dog. The dog next door. Andy paused and looked toward the road. The entire morning was turning into one huge fiasco. First there was The Look from Mom as she herded the girls out the door for church this morning. About the only thing Betty Novac could accept as a bona fide excuse for missing church was illness or having to work. Andy's argument that this might be the only chance the dads would have to witness "the list" didn't sway her belief that both Andy and Jake—and the dads, for that matter—belonged in a church pew this morning and anything else could wait.

Mom's disapproval wasn't the only thing that threatened to ruin the morning. Dad had been called in to work. And no sooner had Andy arrived at the drop zone than Dr. Nolan called to say he was stuck at O'Hare, Jacob wasn't answering his cell phone (now *there* was a surprise), and they should go ahead without him because the airline wasn't saying anything about when things would get straightened out.

*Finally*. There was a trail of dust rising from the gravel in the distance. But even as Jake was coming up the road, Andy heard the

Cessna's engines rev. The pilot was getting tired of waiting. Great. Just great. All the planning Andy had done to make sure he had the right settings on both cameras was a waste. By the time they got in the air—now what? The dust plume wasn't being raised by the pickup after all. It was Jake's mom and her lawyer friend . . . and Rambo. And still no word from Jake. Andy looked down at his watch. Was the entire morning going to go down the tubes?

———————

"You know what to do."

At the sound of her son's cryptic message, Pam flipped her phone shut. "He doesn't even have it *on*." She ran her hand through her hair and gazed toward the road, then back at Andy. "Listen," she said. "He's bound to show up before too much longer. Even if he was already at the Lincoln airport before Michael got hold of him about being stuck in Chicago."

"Jake was headed to meet his dad at the airport?" Andy said. "He didn't say anything to me about that."

"He thought if he snagged Michael as soon as he got off the commercial flight and they headed out here together that it would save time." She didn't say the rest of it. That Jacob had probably gone to meet his dad just to be sure Michael didn't come up with yet another excuse for why he couldn't keep a promise.

Andy shrugged. He glanced toward the runway and back at Pam. "I don't know what to do. I suppose I could do a jump without him. Check the camera settings." He smiled. "You could ride along. Watch from the sky. People do it all the time." He glanced toward the plane. "The pilot might even do it for free. As a favor."

"No thanks. I'll keep trying to get hold of Jacob. And keep an eye on Rambo."

"Rambo," Rainelle said, "has about six avid admirers out here already." She pointed toward the group of young people gathered near the plane. "Any one of those kids would be glad to dog-sit while you ride up with us. And you know how Jacob is. Always late—"

"—but worth the wait." Even as she echoed the mantra, Pam shook her head. "I'll stick around and watch, but no way do I want to go up in that tiny little thing." She nodded toward the Cessna, then grabbed Rambo's collar and hung on. "But you go ahead. You'll probably love it."

"Probably?" Rainelle grinned as she linked her arm through Andy's. "Come on, hotshot. Lead the way."

Pam watched the plane buzz down the runway and take off. As it lifted its nose toward the sky, she inhaled sharply, realizing she'd been holding her breath. Rambo whined and pulled against her hold on his collar. When she let go he meandered into the grassy field, sank down, and rolled in the grass. Pam reached for her phone and dialed Jacob's number again. When he still didn't answer, she leaned back against the ridge of the picnic table, wishing she'd taught Jacob to be more reliable. *Like father, like son.* With a sigh, she realized the truth of it. *But you can't blame mechanical failure in Chicago on Michael.* And, she thought, there was probably a good explanation for Jacob's being so late, too.

She was glad she'd come. Especially now that Michael wasn't going to be here. Looking skyward, Pam began to watch for parachutes even as she remembered the day Jacob had presented his now-infamous list a couple of years ago. They'd been having a rare meal together—burgers Michael had grilled—out back by the pool.

"You want to *what*?!" She and Michael had blurted it out in unison as they stared down at the typewritten list.

"Do those things before I settle down." He weighted the piece of paper down with the ketchup bottle and then took another bite of burger, talking while he chewed. "Actually, I want to do a lot more— but I narrowed it down to ten for now."

Pam set her own sandwich down and read the list again with a combination of anger and terror. *Hang gliding. Rock-climbing. Sky diving.* "Isn't there something you'd like to do that *isn't* potentially lethal?"

"Hey," Jacob said with a grin, "if it can't kill you it isn't really a sport." He made a face then and said with emphasis, "Kidding."

"Ha. Good joke," Pam said in a tone that reflected anything but good humor. She skimmed the rest of the list, settled back in her chair, and glowered at her husband. "This is your fault."

"My fault?" Michael protested. "How do you figure that?"

"*You're* the one who had to show him you could still ski the back bowls at Breckenridge. *You're* the one who bought a Harley. *You're* the one who took him up in a hot-air balloon when he was nine. *You're* the one who did that bungee jumping thing at the mall." She paused to take a breath. "*You're* the one who arranged that trip rafting down the Colorado River." She reached for her glass of iced tea, took a swig, and sat, her legs crossed, her foot bobbing up and down as she tried to control her emotions.

Jacob spoke up. "I *loved* that trip!"

"So did I," Michael agreed. "Until I ended up *in* the river instead of *on* it." He and Jacob began to reminisce about Michael's falling overboard and the subsequent adventure after he collided with a rock and was carried, unconscious, down the river for nearly a mile before his life vest was snagged by a low-hanging tree branch.

"You think that was fun?!" Pam said, glaring at them both.

"It sure made for a great story when we got home." Michael glanced at her. "And I was never in any real danger." He tapped the tip of her nose. "That trip was nothing compared to a certain young woman I know backpacking the Appalachian Trail right out of high school."

"You can't get killed hiking that trail," she said. "And I only did part of it. It's not the same thing at all." Michael had never quite gotten just how terrified she'd been when she saw his still form in the water. And that wasn't the only reason she didn't like remembering that trip. She'd found the lump right after they got home.

People celebrated breast cancer survivors a lot these days. As if they were warriors who'd conquered the foe. Maybe they were, but Pam didn't feel like a conqueror. She identified more with the kitten in the poster—the one clinging to a limb by the tips of its claws. Michael had said all the right words in the days before and after her surgery, but as soon as she was back on her feet he'd started working longer hours. Pam had slowly shifted the center of her daily life from her marriage to other things. She'd joined a couple of civic organizations and indulged her love of flowers by creating a garden the local club once called the jewel of its spring tour. By the time Jacob started high school, she and Michael were two strangers living polite—but very separate—lives.

When Jacob presented his list the summer after his sophomore year of college, Pam didn't know whether to be afraid for Jacob or upset with Michael for *not* being afraid for Jacob. Extreme hiking was one thing. But Jacob was taking the word *extreme* to a ridiculous . . . extreme. *Rock-climbing*. What if he slipped? *Cave diving*. What about sharks? *Hang gliding*. What if he lost control? *Kayaking*. Michael's vest had snagged on a branch and kept him from drowning. What if Jacob wasn't so lucky? She felt like a giant fist had closed around her chest and was squeezing off her air supply, and all the while Michael was agreeing that everything was "cool."

"It's not so bad, Madre," Michael said, turning to Pam and patting her hand. "He's done his homework."

"Knock off the comforting it'll-be-all-right-just-trust-your-doctor routine," Pam snapped. "I'm *not* an overprotective mother and we are *not* in your office." She spoke through clenched teeth. "This is different. This is our son we're talking about."

He had the nerve to agree with her. "Yes. Our son. Who will soon be twenty-one and who doesn't really need our permission to do any of this stuff. So . . . let go, Madre mia."

She wanted to smack him. "I *am* letting go. He practically lives at Andy Novac's house when he's supposedly 'home' from school on weekends. But do I complain? Nope. And why not? Because *I'm letting go!*"

"Hey," Jacob pleaded. "Don't fight. Please."

The plea deflated her anger. Looking across the table at Jacob's scruffy beard and clear blue eyes, Pam wondered where time had gone. Wasn't it just about a month ago he was in kindergarten? Wasn't it just last week *she* was the one whispering *don't be afraid* while she talked *him* into petting the goat at the children's zoo? Where on earth had this six-foot-two-inch macho outdoorsman with shaggy black hair and a half beard and blue eyes that still made her heart stop . . . where had he come from?

With a sigh, Pam forced a smile. She made nice, looping her arm through Michael's. "It's not that I don't want you to grow up and do your own thing, honey. It's just . . ." She picked up the paper with her free hand and looked at the list again. "Isn't there *something* you want to do before you settle down that isn't so . . . so . . . dangerous?"

"If it's any help, I won't be doing this alone. Andy's going to come with me."

"Andy?" Michael pulled away from Pam as he protested, "I won't have you paying Andy's way."

"I'm not," Jacob said. "He wouldn't let me, even if I offered." He leaned back in his chair and frowned at Michael. "Gee, Dad. When have you ever known the Novacs to be freeloaders? They won't even come and swim in our pool without buying their way in with Betty's kolaches."

"No one said they had to do that," Pam protested. "We want you to share your home with your friends." She frowned. "Is that why they never come over? Have we made them feel unwelcome?"

Rambo got up from where he'd been curled up in the sun and came to sit by Jacob, who began scratching behind the dog's ears as he said, "No, Mom. No one's made them feel unwelcome." He looked away. "It's just weird for them, that's all."

"Which is why it's best to have friends from your own neighborhood," Michael said.

"Yeah," Jacob said. "I'll have to remember that. Dad's List. Item one: Only make friends with kids whose fathers earn six figures. Item two: Make sure they live in south Lincoln and have a pool."

"Jacob!" Michael barked.

"Okay," Jacob retracted, "scratch item two."

Rambo whined, looking earnestly from face to face.

Pam could see Michael's jaw muscles working. The last thing she wanted was for these two to fight. She liked being able to brag about Michael and Jacob's closeness to her friends. It was the perfect thing to hide behind when the girls were gossiping about whose marriage was in trouble and whose divorce was final. So she did what she always did when the air was getting too thick with testosterone. She joked about Rambo's part in the conversation and tried to make peace. "Where did all this come from, anyway?" she asked her son. "Do you know anyone who sky dives? What's the Papoose? And—abseiling? What the heck is abseiling?"

Jacob smiled. "Yes, I know people who go sky diving. There's a club at school. The Papoose is a wreck off the shore of North Carolina. And I have some articles about abseiling in my room." He grinned. "'A picture's worth a thousand words.'"

"But you don't know how to *do* any of this stuff," Michael said.

"I know how to swim. I can get certified to dive while I'm at school. And I can do serious conditioning for everything else while I'm at school, too. We've already talked about it. We'll spend winters training and then use spring break or summer vacation to do the deeds." He looked from Pam to Michael. "And the rest of the time I'll be working my tail off and living as cheaply as possible like a good boy. And getting A's." He held his right hand up and closed his eyes as he vowed, "All A's. I promise."

"Back to my original question," Pam said. "Where'd this come from? Obviously you and Andy didn't just cook this scheme up yesterday. You've done some research."

"Last semester Dr. Romani—you remember him. Psychology?"

"The professor you loved to hate?" Pam said. "The guy who nearly ruined your 4.0 over a run-on sentence?"

Jacob nodded. "The critical word there being *nearly*." He pretended to wipe sweat from his brow. "He had us do this stream-of-consciousness thing one day in class. A list of twenty things to do before I die. I was surprised at some of the things that came out when I did it. But it didn't stop there."

"Clearly," Michael said.

"Andy got the same assignment in *his* Psych class up here at UNL."

"Is his list this scary?" Pam asked.

Jacob shook his head. "But we talked about it, and the more we talked the more we realized our lists could go together." He paused. "When I started talking about the things I wanted to do, Andy started getting excited about it, not because he wants to jump off a cliff or anything—"

"Of course not," Pam said. "Andy's still got a brain."

"Mo-om," Jacob sang.

"Sorry." She raised both her hands. "Just thinking aloud."

"Andy wants to go to film school in California. And he thinks it would make a cool documentary."

"What would make a cool documentary?" Michael asked.

"My list," Jacob said, holding up the piece of paper. "It's the story of a college guy who decides it's time to stop talking about all the things he wants to do . . . and do them."

Pam groaned. "Don't tell me. He's going to title it 'Just Do It.'" She drew a swish in the air.

Jacob grinned. "That's been used." He leaned forward and said in a stage whisper, "'The Xtreme Ten of Two Good Men.'" His eyes sparkled with enthusiasm. "Only we'll spell *extreme* with an X—you know, like in the X Games."

"What's extreme about making a video?" Michael asked.

"Andy can't exactly get footage of me scuba diving if he doesn't jump into the water with me."

Michael nodded. "Okay. I get it. In fact, I think it's kind of gnarly."

"You do?"

"Sure I do. I can't tell you how many of my generation made great plans they never realized. Life has a way of interrupting 'the best laid plans.'"

Jacob grinned. "Right. Exactly. I mean, I'm not exactly planning on settling down anytime soon, but when I do, I don't want to be looking at my wife thinking, 'If it hadn't been for her I'd be . . .'" He paused. Looked away. Shrugged. "You know what I mean."

*Oh yes*, Pam thought. She knew. How could she forget? A person could have hot-wired a car with the electricity in the air between her and Michael that day. Thinking back on it still hurt. Did Jacob know what he was saying? Had Michael told him that an unplanned pregnancy was what had propelled his parents into marriage? Was part of Jacob's determination to follow through with this list because his disappointed father had told his son to learn from his dad's mistake? After they were married, Michael had stopped talking about serving through Doctors Without Borders or some other humanitarian organization. He'd settled into practice with his father, and whenever Pam brought up the old dream to help in a third-world country, Michael muttered an excuse.

Now as she watched for parachutes to appear in the sky, Pam wondered again if Michael had just been pretending to be surprised that long-ago morning on the patio. Maybe he and Jacob had rehearsed how the conversation would go, manipulating things so that Jacob's dreams would come true. *It doesn't matter. You did the right thing. You always said that mothers aren't supposed to smother their children's dreams. They're supposed to give them wings. And here you are, and . . .* there they were. One—two—three parachutes. Two round, one arched. Andy had explained the difference before he climbed into the plane with Rainelle, and as the chutes came closer, Pam was able to find Andy's. She watched, her hand to her throat, her heart pounding—with something besides fear, she realized. She was glad she'd come. Michael was going to miss something wonderful this morning.

———

"Whoa!" Stan put a hand out to brace himself against the cruiser's dashboard as he glanced at his partner. "You trying to win the Winston Cup or something? Slow down. Those are brake lights up ahead."

"I see them," Ken said. "And it's the Nextel Cup."

"Huh?" Stan leaned to the right trying to see around the semi in front of him.

"It's not the Winston Cup anymore. Nextel's the sponsor now."

"Whatever. I lost interest when number three hit the wall." Stan motioned at the traffic. "Pull over, hotshot. I'm too close to retirement to die of a coronary brought on by a rookie driver. I'll take over."

Before Ken could comply, the radio crackled with news of an accident. Stan radioed in. "We're there," he said, flipping on the cruiser's lights and sounding the siren. Ken guided the cruiser into the left lane and sped to the scene, swearing under his breath as they stared down an embankment where a rusty Blazer was crumpled nose first into a tree. In the distance—also at the bottom of the embankment—a semi had come to rest against a stand of pine trees that had probably kept it from flipping on its side. The driver's door on the cab was open. Stan glanced back at his partner, whose pasty white face reminded him of the geisha on the cover of a book Betty was reading at home.

"Is this gonna be a problem?" Stan asked. "'Cause we don't need any more problems right now."

Ken cleared his throat. "Nope."

"Good." Stan opened his door. "You decide to throw up whatever your mommy made you for breakfast, you do it where nobody sees you, you got that?"

"Got it."

Stan pointed to where a woman and two young girls stood huddled beside the Blazer. "From the way they're just waiting outside the car, it doesn't look like anyone's hurt down there. Go talk to them." He took a deep breath. "I'll take care of whatever's up ahead." He slid out of the car and headed toward the spot on the shoulder where a few people stood huddled together beside a minivan. A motorcycle was parked just past the minivan and beyond that—beyond that the worst part of his job.

The murmur of voices stopped as Stan got closer. Eyes focused on him and the group parted, forming a gauntlet he walked to the spot in the grass where someone had spread a frayed blue blanket over a body. He looked back down the hill at the truck with the open cab door. He'd worked a lot of accident scenes, and something about the position of the truck in relation to the victim's body didn't seem right. He couldn't quite picture how the guy could have been thrown out.

Lifting one edge of the blanket, he fought back the physical response to what lay beneath. Obviously no need for CPR. Still, he automatically put two fingers to the side of the guy's neck, knowing there would be no pulse. He guessed the victim was male, but beyond that—he'd leave it to the coroner. He didn't need any more fodder for nightmares.

As he dropped the blanket, a burly guy sporting a day-old beard walked over. "Would have started CPR right away. But—" He shook his head. "I don't think the poor kid knew what hit him." He gestured down the embankment. "It's a wonder the truck didn't roll, the way he came barreling down on them. Didn't slow down at all. Just plowed into them and kept going. Never touched his brakes." He swallowed. "Clipped the Blazer and sent it down there"—he gestured—"then swept the pickup in front of it clean off the road. Pinned it between his trailer and those trees."

"Did you see him get thrown out?" Stan demanded.

Obviously confused, the guy looked from Stan to the truck, then back again. Finally, with an almost imperceptible shake of the head, he said, "That isn't the truck driver." He looked toward the semi. "Don't know what happened to him. Maybe he ran." He pointed to the blanket. "I was busy parking my bike and running over to help him."

Hysterical crying drew Stan's attention away from the witness. Ken was walking the woman and the two girls toward the cruiser. With both arms outstretched he reminded Stan of a sheep dog herding its charges toward shelter. Once up the embankment, Ken opened the cruiser's back door and the trio climbed in. As Stan watched, Ken pulled a blanket and two teddy bears out of the cruiser's trunk and, returning to the opened back door, crouched down and distributed bears and blanket. *Good*, Stan thought. *Good job*. The woman was calming down, swiping the tears off her cheeks as she talked to Ken.

The ambulance arrived, followed by a state patrol car. Adrenaline kicked in. While the EMTs did their job, Stan did his, walking down the hill to where the state trooper was searching the cab of the truck. As Stan approached, the trooper held out the trucker's mileage log. "I don't get it. Unless there's another log—but if there is, I can't find it." The guy shook his head. "Looks legal to me. He was pushing the limit, but he didn't go over his hours."

"So—not asleep at the wheel?"

"Hard to say. Could be other stuff involved besides needing sleep."

"Well," Stan said, tipping his head toward the body being loaded into the ambulance. "He's gonna need some really good answers."

"When we catch him," the trooper agreed.

"Can't be far."

The trooper nodded. "K-9's on its way."

---

How anything that tiny could have such power over a grown man was a miracle, but Eddie Lee Monroe had come to believe in miracles in recent years, so when the nurse lifted one of the bundles with a blue cap and carried it to the window and pulled down the white blanket so that Eddie Lee could see his son, he didn't even try to keep the tears from falling. He knew he must look a fool, standing there in the hospital corridor with his two-day beard and wrinkled clothes. Maybe more than a fool, he thought, remembering the muddy cowboy boots and his stained straw hat. But Eddie Lee didn't care. Sleeping on the other side of that glass was the finest of all the wondrous things that had happened to the Monroes in the last year, and for Eddie Lee, it might be the last. And so he'd run through a couple of fields and then hitchhiked across town to the hospital, where two human beings were the only proof in Eddie Lee's life that sometimes good things do happen to bad people.

The baby stretched. One tiny fist emerged from the blanket.

Eddie Lee counted fingers. Five. Five perfect little fingers on a hand that would someday wind up and throw a baseball, or strum a guitar, or maybe even write a book. The idea that he wouldn't be around to see those things caught in Eddie Lee's throat. The idea that he couldn't walk down the hall into Lisa's room and tell her how he felt about this miracle in the blue cap did more than catch in his throat.

*Time to go.* Through his tears, the rumpled trucker nodded at the nurse. Waved at the baby. He eschewed the elevator for the stairs, stopping at the street level, where he pulled a crumpled piece of paper out of his jacket pocket and, with a pencil, scribbled a note. With only his knee for a writing surface, and with his hand trembling so, the paper ended up punched here and there with a lead-rimmed hole. There was so much he wanted to say. So much he wished could happen. But he was fresh out of miracles today. God had allowed him to get here and see his boy. Which was more than he deserved. He wouldn't ask for anything else, because he'd already drawn more than his share from the well of mercy.

Back inside the hospital, he gave the note to an old woman sitting at the information desk who promised to see that it made its way upstairs to Lisa Monroe in room 426. The old woman's face was lined with a lifetime of laughter, and the puff of white hair that framed her face had the odd effect of a halo. For one brief moment Eddie Lee was tempted to tell her why the paper was rumpled and why he couldn't deliver it himself, just so she would understand how important it was that the note be hand carried upstairs as soon as possible. But he didn't say any more than a cursory thank-you.

"Is everything all right, young man?" the old woman asked.

*No, ma'am. Everything is about as wrong as it could be.* The sound of a lullaby drifted into the foyer.

"Another little angel just arrived," the old woman said and smiled up at Eddie Lee. "Isn't that just wonderful? Another little miracle from heaven."

Eddie Lee nodded and turned to go. He paused just outside to look back to where miracles in the form of newborn babies happened several times a day. Eddie Lee didn't know what the rate was outside these walls. But he knew one thing for certain. Eddie Lee Monroe had used up his quota of miracles. His knees wobbled a little as he headed for one of the taxicabs waiting in line just past the entryway.

———————

As the ambulance faded into the distance and Stan listened to the witnesses tell their stories, he made certain they realized how grateful the victim's family would be for their testimony.

"I'll do anything necessary," one said. Her voice wavered as she looked in the direction the ambulance had gone. "That poor boy. His poor mother." She shivered.

Another witness pointed toward the truck and swore his way through a sentence that generally said the felon should have to pay for what he did with various parts of his own body.

Stan might not have expressed himself quite that way, but he agreed in principle. The guilty should be punished. In this case, he felt it even more intensely than usual. A do-gooder had stopped to change a flat tire for a stranded mother and her two kids and gotten killed for his trouble. His pickup wasn't even visible from the road anymore. Witnesses had described how the semi trailer had swept it off the road and down the embankment, pinning it between the semi and a stand of trees.

The witnesses had also seen what happened to the victim. A young guy with his whole life ahead of him. As Stan thought about it, the familiar tension headache began. This was one of those times when he couldn't help asking God, *I know you know what you're doing . . . but are you* sure *you know what you're doing?* Sometimes when he questioned the Almighty this way, Stan wondered if this would be the time God would weary of his doubting and just squash him flat. So far, though, he was still breathing, still blessed. As he stood on the roadside surveying the accident scene, he couldn't figure out why.

# {three}

THE SKY DIVERS landed one, two, three—the last one showboating, coming in low and fast, lifting his legs to get the most distance possible before landing. When his feet finally touched the ground, he let out a whoop, released his rig, and spun around to gather up the yards of fabric that had brought him safely back to Earth.

"Rambo!" Pam called as the dog danced and pranced around Andy and his parachute. "Rambo, come!" Hearing his name, the dog paused, looked Pam's way, and with a disappointed whine, padded his way back to where Pam and Rainelle stood beside Rainelle's car. But as soon as he reached Pam's side, he darted away again, this time ignoring even Andy, and began a frantic kind of search in the pasture where the sky divers had just landed.

"Maybe Andy dropped something," Pam said.

Rainelle eyed her doubtfully. "And Rambo would *know* that?"

Pam shook her head, mystified by the dog's odd sniffing-running-spinning antics. Occasionally, Rambo paused and lifted his snout to the air, but after one quick sniff he'd lower his head again and return to the spin-run routine.

"Rambo," Pam called, walking toward him. "You smell a rabbit or a skunk?" She patted the side of her leg.

Instead of obeying the unspoken command to come, Rambo stuck his nose into the air and adopted the regal pose Pam had come to think of as 'Czar Rambo Impresses the Peasants.' But it only lasted a moment before he began to howl.

"Rambo!" Pam repeated, "come!" The dog looked at her, but instead of coming, he lay down in the grass, planted his nose between

35

his forepaws, and moaned with a misery that sent chills up her spine.

"What's wrong with him?" Rainelle called, hurrying after Pam.

Andy came out of the hangar and looked their way. Dropping his camera bag, he came running. "What's up?"

"I don't know," Pam said. "Could he have gotten into something when we weren't watching?"

"I can't imagine what," Andy said as they both crouched down beside the dog, running their hands over his torso and down each leg.

"Roll over, boy," Pam said, examining his underbelly, then each paw. Nothing seemed to be hurt, but the dog was trembling all over. She hooked a finger through his collar and urged him to get up. He did, but before she could stand up he pressed the top of his head against her chest and moaned. "What is it?" she whispered, then looked up at Andy. "Maybe he's chewed on some noxious weed. . . . I just don't know."

"What about a toxic spray?" Rainelle offered.

"Whatever it is, I'm taking him to the vet," Pam said. "You'll tell Jacob I came to watch?"

"You bet." Andy glanced toward the hangar. "If I can get hold of him, I'll send him your way or would you like me to come with you?"

Pam shook her head. "We can handle the dog." They walked back to the car. Rambo jumped into the back again, huddling down on the seat, shivering and moaning.

"That's the most pathetic thing I've ever heard," Rainelle said, reaching down to pet the dog. "Don't you worry, Rambo. Aunt Rainelle's gonna take you to the doctor. It'll be all right."

"I'll call you," Pam promised Andy and climbed into the car for the trip back to Lincoln.

---

Traffic was almost normal again, and the other cruisers had left the scene when Stan picked his way along the deep furrows carved by the semi's tires. As he walked the path the truck had followed when it left the pavement, Stan decided he probably just looked like he was talking to himself. At least he hoped that was what Ken thought he was doing. Sometimes it was easier to be thought eccentric than to try to explain.

"You wait here," he'd said. "I just need to work it through. Walk it out." He wasn't about to tell a brand-new partner about his personal ritual of praying for the people involved in the accident scenes he worked. It had taken years to gain the respect of the precinct after their hard-drinking, skirt-chasing sergeant got religion. Guys had actually taken bets on how long it would be before Stan-the-Man Novac fell off the "righteous wagon" and got back to normal. When they finally realized Stan was on the wagon to stay and wasn't going to be an obnoxious in-your-face kind of religious nut, the guys backed off. And Stan liked it that way.

So, as Ken Randolph sat in the cruiser, Stan walked the furrows. He put his hands on his hips and pretended to examine the tire tracks. *I've got no use for this guy.* It was a personal triumph that he actually referred to the trucker as a *guy.* His mind had other words. Which, an inner voice reminded him, could have been applied to Stan Novac for the first three decades of his life. *Yeah. I remember.* He took his hat off and raked his hair with one hand. *So maybe you have a plan. I hope you do, 'cause this idiot's going to end up serving some serious time over this.* At least Stan hoped he would.

He looked down the embankment trying to muster up compassion. Where was the driver, anyway? Crouching in some ravine just past that stand of pine trees? He had to know K-9 would find him. And it wouldn't take long. He had maybe a half hour head start, but it wouldn't be enough. His face would be plastered all over the five o'clock news. So why had he run? Why hadn't he just stayed put and faced reality? Stan really didn't even know how to pray about this one. Sometimes he thought the prayers were more for him than anyone else. Certainly they helped him let go of things so he wasn't a walking open wound when he got home.

He walked back up the embankment to the spot where the blanket had covered the do-gooder's body. *Some mother's going to feel like she's in hellfire in a little while. Send someone to comfort her.* He didn't like the next thought that came to mind, which was relief that his kids were all safe and healthy. Something felt wrong about that. *Forgive my selfish thoughts.* A tow truck was backing down the embankment now. The driver climbed out and went to the back of the semi trailer to check things out. Stan headed back toward the cruiser to tell Ken Randolph he'd done a good job that morning.

"Hey! Officer!"

Stan made his way down the hill.

"Just wanted to be sure I got this right. I take the semi. Union Towing is sending trucks for the pickup and the Blazer. Right?"

Stan nodded. "Sounds right."

"You told them to bring a winch, didn't ya? Because it's definitely gonna take a winch to separate the pickup from the tree this bozo wrapped it around."

"Let me take a look," Stan said. "I was busy interviewing—" He got to the edge of the trailer and peered at the do-gooder's pickup. Sweat broke out on his forehead. He leaned against the tractor-trailer and bent over, his hands on his knees while he tried to suck in some air.

"Hey," the driver said, putting a hand on his shoulder, "you having a heart attack or something?"

As the driver opened his mouth to yell for help, Stan managed to put a giant hand on his shoulder. "Don't," he gasped. "Don't call. Just . . . just give me . . . a minute." He willed himself to inhale. Exhale. Breathe. He unbuttoned the top button of his shirt. His mind was numb. He kept looking at the smashed pickup . . . the license plate . . . the pickup . . . the tree . . . the plate. *XTRM10.*

If he never worked another accident scene, it would be too soon.

———

"You're kidding, right?" The cabby looked at him in the rearview mirror.

"Nope." Eddie Lee shook his head.

The cabby pulled off the road. "I've dropped fares off at weird places before, but out in the middle of nowhere? That's a new one."

Eddie Lee handed a bill across the back seat. "Keep the change," he said and let himself out of the cab. He pulled the straw cowboy hat on and watched as the cab made a U-turn and headed back in the direction of the city. Then, turning toward the emergency lights in the distance, Eddie Lee broke into a cold sweat. *Help.* As if God was going to listen to him, anyway. His feet felt like they weighed two tons each. It was all he could do to get across the road. All he could think about was Lisa. How he'd failed her. How he'd ruined her life. And what he wouldn't have given to have felt her arms around his neck right then. To hear her say she loved him. *Too late.* His eyes intent on the flashing lights in the distance, Eddie Lee took a deep breath and headed out.

———

"Doesn't he know hitchhiking is illegal?" Ken said, nodding toward the guy walking in their direction.

"Let's go," Stan said wearily. "We have to drive right by him on our way back to the station. It's not the ride he wanted, but it's the one he's going to get."

Ken reached for the radio. "I can call this one in. You've got more important things to do right now."

Stan put his hand out to stop Ken from grabbing the mike. "No big deal. We can just warn him. It'll only take a minute . . . and besides, I could use the time."

Ken shook his head as he watched the hitchhiker. "Nobody can be this stupid. He just walked right by the sign that *says* it's illegal to hitchhike, and unless he's blind he knows the flashing lights mean there's a cop in his future."

Stan snapped his seat belt shut. "Yeah, well, welcome to your new job, where the level of human stupidity is exceeded only by the capacity of humanity for cruelty to its own kind."

Ken turned the ignition and guided the cruiser onto the road. "I thought you'd have something more . . . religious . . . to say about all of this."

"Really? Why?"

"Because the guys said—" He shook his head.

"The guys said what?"

"They said you're one of those born-again types."

"Yeah," Stan muttered. "I am."

"So . . . where was God when this all went down?"

Stan was silent as Ken drove toward the hitchhiker, who didn't seem to notice the police car headed his way. He was walking head down, his straw hat pulled down nearly over his eyes, his hands in his pockets. Just like they all did. Pretending not to be hitching a ride, hoping the cops would keep going.

"He'll probably change direction in a minute," Stan said. "Amble off like he's headed for that acreage. Give us an excuse not to stop."

"You going to answer my question?"

"What question?" He was doing his best not to break down. So far all Ken Randolph knew was that Stan had asked to notify the kid's next-of-kin because he knew the family. And that was all Stan wanted him to know. For now. All he wanted to do was get back to the station and get on with what was going to be one of the worst days of his life. But the dumb hitchhiker wasn't changing direction. He was headed straight toward them.

"Where was God when that whole thing went down?"

"Pull over," Stan said. "Turn on your lights and flip the siren a time or two." As Ken obeyed, the hitchhiker came out of whatever haze he'd been in and looked up.

"Where was God?" Ken repeated.

Stan released his seat belt and opened the door. He got out without answering the question.

———

Eddie Lee Monroe was shaking so badly he could barely walk when he heard the crunch of tires on loose gravel. Before he could look up, a blast from a police siren nearly scared him out of his patched jeans. The guy who climbed out of the police cruiser was a giant who could likely win the arm wrestling championship in any state in America. But it wasn't the arms that worried Eddie Lee. It was the look on the guy's face.

"Where do you think you're going?" the guy asked, and hooked his thumbs in his belt loops so that Eddie was reminded of Sheriff Buford T. Justice in his all-time favorite trucker movie, *Smokey and the Bandit*. Except Eddie Lee doubted this guy fumbled any plays.

Eddie Lee cleared his throat. "I was . . . uh . . . headed . . . uh . . ."

"Suppose you take your hands out of your pockets so I can see 'em," the officer said, and as he spoke he unsnapped the strap holding his revolver in its holster.

Eddie Lee snatched his hands out of his pockets and held them out toward the officer, palms up.

The officer nodded. "All right." He pointed. "That sign says hitchhiking is illegal."

"Yes, sir. I'm not." Eddie Lee cleared his throat and croaked, "I'm not hitchhiking, sir."

"Really."

"No, sir. I'm . . . uh . . ." He couldn't make himself say it. He didn't even know what to say. While he bumbled around and the officer waited, the tow truck hauling the semi rolled by. White cab. *LCC* painted on the cab door, the letters slanted toward the back of the trailer. Wavy lines streamed off the red letters, giving the subliminal message that Lincoln Carrier Corporation equals speed. Eddie Lee watched it go by.

He swallowed. "That's my truck." His voice caught and for a minute he remembered the blue knit cap and the tiny waving fist behind the window at the hospital and he almost lost it. Almost. Finally, he held his hands out again, this time with his wrists together like he'd seen in the movies. "That's my truck being towed," he said again, "and I guess I'm under arrest."

———

41

"Where are you, son?"

"Just leaving the drop zone," Andy said. "And in case you're wondering, the morning was a waste. Well, all right. Not a total waste. Mrs. Nolan came out. Her friend Rainelle rode up with us and thinks she wants to sky dive. Which is very cool. But Rambo got sick, Dr. Nolan cancelled, and Jacob never showed up. Can you believe it? He won't even answer his phone." He paused. "I'd be worried if this wasn't only about the thousandth time something like this has happened. But darn it, Dad—"

"I need to see you," Stan said. "Meet me at that little wayside picnic area just before you get into town. You know the one I mean?"

"I know it," Andy said, his voice wary. "But—what's wrong?"

Stan tried to force nonchalance into his voice. "You're not in any trouble or anything. But there's something we need to discuss. Before you go home. So just meet me. Okay?"

"Okay." Andy's voice sounded doubtful. "But, Dad—"

Stan hung up and called his pastor, who immediately suggested he wait for Stan and Andy at the entrance to the Novac's neighborhood. "Thanks," Stan said. "I don't want them to hear this in a phone call, but I've got to get to the Nolans' as soon as possible. Having you there with Betty and the girls will make it easier to do that."

"I'll do anything I can to help," Pastor Garrison said. "Are you driving right now, Stan?"

Stan cleared his throat. "Uh . . . yeah. I've got a call in to Andy to meet me."

"Well, then I won't pray with you now . . . while you're driving," the pastor said. "God's grace and peace, Stan. God's grace and peace."

Most people would say it was by chance that the sixth grade teacher at Edgemont Elementary School had made her students sit in alphabetical order. But Stan didn't believe in chance. He believed God controlled everything, even details like seating arrangements in classrooms that put a Nolan and a Novac together and birthed the friendship of a lifetime. The memory of Andy and Jacob bonding over hot dogs and s'mores at Boy Scouts brought more tears to Stan's eyes. It wasn't the first time in his career he'd been the bearer of this kind of news. But it felt like it. With a sigh, he forced the memories out of his head and concentrated on what he was going to say to Andy.

*Help. God. Help.* It was as close to prayer as Stan could come.

———————

Pam had turned around in her seat and was trying to comfort Rambo when Rainelle turned onto the broad street that led to what she called Pamela's Estate.

"That neighbor of yours is having some shindig today," Rainelle said.

Pam looked up. Lots of cars. And Stan Novac's old truck parked in her driveway. As Rainelle drove up, Stan and Andy got out. Pam sat up straighter, frantically searching the street for Jacob's pickup. She clutched Rainelle's forearm.

"Now, listen, honey, don't worry before there's something to worry about."

As Rainelle pulled up next to Stan's truck, Rambo leaped out of the car and ran to Andy, who crouched down in a pretense of playing with the dog, then slumped onto the lawn and pulled Rambo as far into his lap as he could. He bent over, his shoulders shaking, muffled sobs rising as he buried his face in Rambo's fur.

Stan Novac looked haggard.

Pam climbed out of the car. *Jacob.* She stopped, resting her hand on the front fender for a minute trying to control her quaking knees.

Stan walked up to her and said quietly, "There's been an accident." His voice was gentle, but the words grated.

"Take me to him," Pam said. "Take me now."

Stan hesitated just long enough for the reality of what she was being told to hit full force. She groped for Rainelle and clutched her arm. "Take me to my son," she repeated, willing her mind away from the words she could not hear.

Rambo pulled away from Andy, started for her, looked back at

Andy . . . sat down, his attention focused on Stan. When Andy got up and came toward them, Rambo followed, positioning himself next to Pam. She could feel his breath on her hand.

Reaching down to pat the dog, Pam began to ramble. "He's been acting so weird," she said. The minute the topic became Rambo, the knot in her gut loosened a little. She could breathe. All right, then. If she talked, no one else would be able to say what must not be said. She forced a weak smile at Stan. "I decided to surprise the guys. We went out to the drop zone. We saw Andy make a jump and then Rambo—we thought he was sick. He was charging around, sniffing and searching—you'd have thought he was in an obedience trial or something, and then he just stopped and howled his heart out—I shushed him up but then he just curled up and—and—" She stopped talking. She'd heard of things like this. Unexplained instances where when people di—She covered her mouth with her hands and squeezed her eyes shut and tried not to scream. Her stomach lurched. Rainelle tried to hug her, but she struggled, breaking free and then stumbling. The porch railing kept her from taking a nose dive into the flower bed. The door was locked. She'd left her purse in the car.

Stan followed her onto the porch, his soothing voice explaining. "Jake stopped to help a stranded mother with two kids change a flat tire. A trucker lost control—we think he fell asleep at the wheel—and there was an accident." Stan's voice didn't change. Pam would later think it should have taken on the sound of something being hurled through a giant storefront window for the effect the words would have on her life. But it didn't change. The voice that shattered her life was gentle, the words simple. "Jake didn't survive."

As she looked down at the flagstone porch, Pam would not have been surprised to see her own bleeding heart lying at her feet. For a split second, everyone stood motionless. Pam heard a strange sound— like a grunt from a linebacker who'd been hit on the field and was about to go down. When she realized the sound had come from her, when she felt her throat tightening up and her midsection refusing to respond when she tried to breathe, terror flitted through her mind, but only for a second.

She gasped for breath and caught enough to blurt out, "That's ridiculous." She looked at Stan. "I don't care how bad it is. You have to take me to see him." When Stan didn't answer, she plunged ahead, "That's it, isn't it? He's hurt. Really, really badly hurt. And you don't want me to see him until Michael—until Michael—" She gulped. "Is he paralyzed? I don't care. Is he unconscious? That doesn't matter. Just take me—"

"I wish with all of my heart that I could take you to the emergency room at Bryan West right now, Pam. But I can't because Jake isn't there."

She pleaded. "Please. Stan. Don't do this. Let me see him. Let me see my baby."

Stan nodded. "Of course you can see him. You should. As soon as they tell us they're ready. I'll drive both you and Michael over myself. But first," he motioned toward the front door, "first we should all go inside for a little while."

"Come on, honey," Rainelle said. "I've got your keys now." Just as Rainelle cupped Pam's elbow with her hand and gently pressured her to move toward the door, Pam caught a glimpse of movement out of the corner of her eye. Don and Helen Wilson. Headed this way. Their faces masks of . . . *concern.*

"You go on in," Stan urged. "Let me do my job, Pam. I'll handle the neighbors."

Pam allowed herself to be led inside, across the entryway, beneath the balcony, down the hall into the family room at the back of the house. Andy Novac followed with Rambo crossing the family room and plopping down on the hearth, his back bent, his face hidden in his hands.

*Poor Andy.* A boy needed his mother at a time like this and Betty Novac was nowhere in sight. Pam went to him. She put her palm on the top of his shining red curls, and when she did, his entire body shuddered with emotion. When he looked up, his tears carried Pam out of her own tragedy. Here was a boy who needed a mother. Meeting that need helped Pam retreat from the edge of the precipice yawning before her. Dry-eyed, she put her arms around Andy and murmured comfort while he cried like the brokenhearted boy he was.

When Stan came back in and saw Pam sitting with Andy, he went to the phone. Rainelle, who didn't even drink coffee, was trying to make some. Andy's tears had subsided enough for Pam to let go. And Rambo . . . where was Rambo? Looking toward the stairs that led from the kitchen up to Ja—toward the bedrooms, Pam realized the dog must have gone up there. Someone should go to him. He was a sensitive dog . . . intuitive . . . almost telepathic at times. He had to be miserable up there all alone. But she couldn't go there. Not yet. She asked Andy to go after Rambo and joined Rainelle in the kitchen.

Opening the cupboard was the big mistake. There was that stupid coffee cup with the hula girl staring her in the face. Pam reached for it, and, once it was in her hand, she froze.

"What is it?" Rainelle was at her side, her voice gentle, her hand warm on Pam's shoulder.

"I always . . . hated this ugly thing. The boys brought it back after that first trip. Surfing. I think that was the first thing on Jacob's list. Maybe it was the second. . . . I can't quite . . ." How she could be confused about something that had dominated her emotional life as much as Jacob's list, Pam didn't know. She wasn't thinking straight. Maybe that was normal. Maybe that was just how some people reacted. She stopped. Bit her lip. Frowned. The coffee maker gurgled. "He . . . liked . . . such . . . strong . . . coffee." The words warbled as they came out. Her voice shook, and then it wasn't just her voice shaking, but her entire body. Rainelle reached for her, and if it hadn't been for those strong arms around her, Pam might have slumped to the floor. As it was, she leaned against her friend, sobbing the last name even she would have expected. *Michael.*

"I JUST STEPPED OUT onto the patio so I could talk," Stan said, switching the phone to his other ear. "I need you here. Dr. Nolan still isn't answering his phone, and I'd feel a lot better about going to look for him if you and the girls were here for Andy."

"Sweetheart. The girls are in various stages of deconstruction. They aren't in any mood to—"

"This is about doing what's right," he snapped. "Whether we're in the mood or not."

"Fine," Betty snapped back. "Give us twenty minutes."

He could hear her telling Rachel to help the twins gather up Legos, coloring books, and crayons . . . telling Suzanne to get Reba's pull toy and some pigs' ears . . . directing Emily to sack whatever preparations for dinner she must have had out.

"I love you," he said, his voice dangerously close to a tear-laced warble. "And I'm sorry about the Robocop thing. I just—I just—"

"I know."

"Yeah." He broke off and took a deep breath. "But I shouldn't pull that on you and the girls."

"Talk to me," Betty said.

Turning his back to the house, Stan walked to the edge of the patio. "Pam isn't going to call anyone until her husband gets here. She's not catatonic, but close to it. Mostly she's sitting on the couch with a death grip on Andy, staring out the window. Waiting."

"Surely Michael's flight will—"

"The plane landed over an hour ago." Stan hesitated, then said, "I think I know where he is. But I don't feel right about going after him unless—" He broke off. "Please, baby. I need you. I love you."

"I love you, too," Betty said, "and if Robocop helps you do your job I'll put up with him. He's not a bad guy once you realize there's a heart beneath the titanium skin."

"A heart that belongs to you."

"I know," Betty said, and hung up.

***

Stan was out the Nolans' front door almost before the minivan's wheels stopped turning. Yanking open the driver's side door, he swept Betty into his arms and held her close, drawing strength from her presence, inhaling the fresh scent of her lavender shampoo. Finally, he let go and went to Rachel, who slid out of the passenger seat and threw herself into his waiting arms. She'd been so convinced she would marry Jake some day. All Stan could do was hold her while she cried.

Twelve-year-old Emily came next. Emily, so recently in the throes of her first honest-to-goodness crush, so often at odds with her older sister, who had no patience with what she called Emily's "childish behavior."

Six-year-old twins Madison and Megan had at first hidden their adoration for Jake behind fluttering eyelashes and bashful grins, but Jake's tickle-me-tickle-you game quickly dispelled their reticence. When Stan crouched down on the drive, they clambered to him along with four-year-old Suzanne.

"I'm counting on you to be good helpers," he said to them. "Even if Mommy doesn't ask, you can watch Reba and Rambo." The girls nodded, and with a last hug Stan let them go. Watching his children follow their mother up the walk toward the house, Stan wondered anew at the impossible task ahead. How did one explain death to a four-year-old? Would Emily and Rachel comfort one another, or would grief pull them apart? And what about Andy . . . Andy who publicly complained about being lost in a sea of ruffles and lace, but who privately adored his status as big brother. Andy's life would be impacted more than any of the other Nolans. What, Stan wondered, would happen with Jake's list?

He was lost in thought and halfway to the street when Betty reached around him from the back. She hugged him fiercely, then stepped around to look up at him. "I needed one more hug," she said, tearing up. "This is awful."

"I'm so sorry I couldn't protect you from this."

"Stop." Betty reached up and laid her palm against his cheek. She glanced at the house and the children huddled on the porch. "Maybe we're the best ones to be here, after all." She swallowed. "No one loved Jake more than we did."

———————

It felt as if the people around her were paddling their way through the air in slow motion, swimming through time while she stood apart watching. Pam sat quietly, trying to remember what it reminded her of. Yes, that was it. They'd gone with Michael to a convention in Chicago . . . stayed at the Palmer House. She'd taken Jacob to the aquarium. They'd arrived just in time to see the divers feed the sharks. But Jacob wasn't nearly as enamored with the sharks as he was with the sea turtle hovering just on the other side of the glass.

"Too-tle," Jacob had said, pointing wide-eyed at the creature.

Closing her eyes against the tears that threatened, Pam spun on the bar stool . . . away from the kitchen . . . toward the family room, where the Novac children had taken refuge. It was amazing how they had settled in. How well behaved they were. Why hadn't she noticed that before? Suzanne was sitting on her brother's lap while Maddy and Megan lay on their stomachs in front of the bay window coloring. The twins had sent Rambo and Reba outside to snooze in the sun. Rachel and Emily sat on either side of their brother.

And here in the kitchen, Betty had taken charge. She and Rainelle were sitting at the table right now, silent chefs filling a baking pan with meatballs formed from the mound of ground beef in the stainless steel bowl between them. That was something, Pam thought. Instead of taking over, Rainelle was taking orders. Obviously there was more to Betty Novac than met the eye.

Pam got up and crossed the room, still thinking of the aquarium, feeling like she was wading against an unseen current of water. When Rainelle scooted over, she sat down.

"I know you can't imagine eating," Betty said, "but—"

"I'm glad you thought to do this." Pam nodded toward the family room. "The children will need supper."

"And," Rainelle offered, "it won't hurt to have something for any-one else who drops by later."

Pam frowned. "I don't want anyone dropping by."

"You don't have to talk to anyone you don't want to talk to," Betty said.

When the phone rang, Betty answered. "Nolan residence. This is Mrs. Novac speaking. May I take a message?" When the caller answered, she covered the mouthpiece with her hand. "It's the Wil-sons from next door," she said. "Wondering if there's anything they can do."

Pam shook her head.

Betty walked toward the front of the house, talking in low tones.

"She's good," Rainelle said.

When Betty returned to the kitchen, Rainelle repeated the praise. "You're a good friend in need, Betty Novac."

"Thank you."

The three women finished making meatballs. When Betty had put them in the oven and began to peel potatoes, Rainelle got up. "I can do that," she said, and reached for the potato peeler.

Betty surrendered it and sat back down at the table.

"Thank you for coming," Pam said.

"We wouldn't want to be anywhere else."

"You don't have to lie," Pam said, and brushed her forehead with the back of her hand. "It's a very safe bet you'd rather be just about anywhere else on earth than right here right now." Her voice warbled and wobbled as she spoke, and although she thought she surely must have shed all the tears possible, more threatened to spill out. Betty reached across the table and took her hand. Pam didn't pull away. Looking out the window to where Reba and Rambo lay curled up in the sun, she said, "Rambo knew. He howled. A sound I've never heard before. Unearthly. Soul-splitting." She paused. "How could he have known when I didn't? Shouldn't I have *felt* something?" She swiped at the tears. "Michael should have at least called. I don't understand why he hasn't called. His plane has to have landed by now." She pulled her cell phone out of her pocket and handed it to Betty. "Can you check? It was—I think it was United."

"Stan's gone to get him," Betty said. "I'm sure they'll be here soon."

Pam frowned. "*Stan's* gone to get him? Is Michael in some kind of trouble?"

"No. Of course not."

"Then why do the police have him?"

"Stan's not going as a policeman. He's going as a friend."

Rainelle spoke up. "How about I make us a couple of margaritas and we go out on the patio?"

She made a great margarita. That sounded good. And that, Pam realized, as she got up and headed outside, seemed horribly, horribly wrong.

---

As he headed north toward the Highlands development, Stan switched on the radio, hoping to lose himself in a country ballad about something totally unrelated to his life at the moment. What he got was a song about arriving in heaven and riding raindrops. He changed the station. More country music, this time a song about living like you were dying. He almost had to pull into a parking lot after that one. The next song wasn't a new tune, but it was one of his favorites. Alan Jackson singing about teaching his girls to drive. Maybe it didn't matter what was on the radio. Maybe he just needed a minute. He pulled into the parking lot of a strip mall, all the businesses closed for Father's Day.

He took a deep breath and spoke aloud. "If you had to take somebody from Lincoln today, why'd you pick the all-American-loves-his-mom-and-no-holds-barred-live-like-you-mean-it kid?" He shook his head. "I don't exactly expect an answer. But I had to ask the question." He totally identified with the guy who'd once told Jesus, *Lord, I believe,* and then immediately begged, *help my unbelief.* Putting the truck back into gear, Stan pulled back out onto the street, wishing he didn't know where to find Dr. Michael Nolan.

Stan's heart rate accelerated when he pulled into the neighborhood, mostly from anger as he remembered the night shifts when he'd seen Nolan's black BMW parked in places no man with a family should be. *Don't be so self-righteous. When it comes down to it, the only difference between Nolan and you is you aren't a practicing jerk when it comes to other women.* Of course he was still a practicing jerk in other areas. Like his temper. He could sense an almost dangerous level of anger bubbling just beneath the surface right now. *Lord, I believe.* He was supposed to be doing this. It was a good thing. *Help my unbelief.* Guys like Michael Nolan weren't the type to react well to being found out.

What made things even worse was that Stan had learned to like Jake's mother. If it weren't for the good doctor's penchant for putting his nose in the air, the four of them might even have found a way to be friends. The dads could have been cheerleaders for Jake and Andy's list. But Dr. Nolan always had an excuse for why he was too busy to get involved, even in a minor way. When Stan discovered one of the things that kept the doctor so busy, he'd given up on the idea of friendship. He hadn't confronted Nolan. He'd just stopped trying to plan stuff and hoped the brilliant but stupid doctor would wake up before it was too late.

A garage door a few houses away started going up. *The* house. But there was no sign of Nolan's BMW. Relief flooded in, only to be squashed when, as a silver Chevy Cavalier started backing out, Stan saw the other car parked in the garage. A black Beemer. *The* black Beemer.

---

"What the——?" Michael twisted his head around to stare at the pickup blocking the driveway. He honked once, then whipped his head back around and closed his eyes, swearing softly as Stan Novac climbed out of the truck. Things went from bad to worse when Kim opened the front door and called out a last minute addition to the carryout pizza order.

"Don't forget the artichoke hearts, babe."

With an open palm, Michael beat on the steering wheel. Could it look any worse? His car in the garage. Him at the wheel of Kim's car. Her calling him babe? Shifting the Cavalier into park, he got out.

"Hey, Officer," he said. "I hate to tell you, but you're illegally parked." He grimaced even as the words fell flat. Bad joke. Bad time to joke. Wrong person to joke with. Saint Stanley Novac, the champion of all fathers, the supreme husband of the ages, the wondrous example of manhood, would never understand Kim. Heck, he hardly understood Kim himself. Glancing back at her now, Michael wondered what had possessed him to get involved in something this obvious. *Psychoanalysis later. Damage control now.*

He decided not to explain or make excuses. The best defense was usually a good offense. "What are you doing in this part of town?" he asked.

"Looking for you."

"Well, you found me."

"There's been an accident."

Novac's expression put a halt to any more attitude. "What kind of accident?"

"A bad one."

"What hospital?" Michael asked.

"What?"

53

"What hospital is she in? Is she all right?"

"It isn't your wife," Stan said. "It was Jake. And he's not in the hospital."

Michael looked back toward the front porch, where Kim stood watching the two men talk. He waved her inside and then returned to the conversation at hand. "So if Jake's all right, why all the dramatics?"

"He's not all right," Novac said. "Betty and the kids are with Pam. And her friend Rainelle. But she's asking for you."

"You're not making any sense. If Jacob's not all right, then what's Pam do . . . ing . . . at . . . the . . . housssssss." As reality broke over him, Michael could hear his voice wind down. Leaning against the car door, he reached for the handle for support.

———

It was like watching a blow-up doll be punctured with a pin. As Nolan began to grasp the truth, his speech slowed, his shoulders sagged, and he ended up leaning against the car with both hands over his face. "No," he moaned. "Oh, God. No."

"I'm here to take you home."

"But—" Michael waved his arm at the garage.

"Go sit in my truck. I'll take care of it."

As Michael wobbled off toward the pickup, Stan opened the Cavalier's door and turned off the engine. He went to the front door. The woman must have been watching from inside, because he didn't have to knock. When she opened the door, he said, "I'm taking him home. There's been an accident. His son's been killed."

Some part of him took relish in crashing this world with abrupt language. But whatever Stan expected, it wasn't this. The young woman's hand went to her heart as she gasped, "Jacob? Jacob's . . . dead? Oh no." Tears spilled down her cheeks as she glanced out the window at Stan's truck where Michael sat, head down. Silent tears spilled down her cheeks. She swiped them away and looked him in the eye. "Is there anything I can do to help?"

He thought for a minute. "Are you going to be here later?"

"If you need me to be here, I'll be here," she said. "I'm supposed to work an extra shift but I'll find someone to sub for me." She filled in the blanks for Stan. "I'm an ICU nurse."

Stan nodded. "Can I come back later and get his car out of your garage and drive it home?"

"Of course. Or—wait—" She extended her hand. "I could drive it to work and leave it in Michael's parking spot at the hospital. Leave the keys under the floor mat. No one would—" She cleared her throat. Looked away. "No one would need to know."

"If you're okay with that—"

"I'm okay with anything you say. Anything that will help."

Stan frowned. This was getting more confusing by the minute. She was nothing like he would have expected. She was educated. Articulate. "All right then." He handed her the car keys. "I'll leave it to you. And I'll tell him he can find his car at the hospital." He turned to go.

"Wait—" the woman said, and headed down the hallway. She ducked into one of the rooms at the end of the hall and emerged with a man's suit coat in hand. Shaking it out, brushing off an imaginary piece of lint, she folded it carefully and handed it over. "Tell Michael—" She broke off and shook her head. "Never mind." She stepped away and opened the door for Stan. "In case you wonder later about someone seeing me with Michael's car . . . my shift won't start until after midnight. I'll be discreet."

"Good," Stan said.

"And—" she reached for a purse on the pass-through to the kitchen and pulled out a business card—"in case you need to reach me."

Stan stared down at the card. Simple. Straightforward. *Kim Silevan. Image Consultant.* Pretty grandiose title, Stan thought. Betty wore that brand of makeup and from what Stan remembered of the little gal who sold it, there wasn't much image consulting that went on.

"More of a hobby than a job," Kim said with a weak smile.

Stan shoved the card in his pocket and headed for his truck. This was definitely right up there with one of the weirder experiences he'd ever had. He'd expected a sleazy black nightgown, too much makeup, and dyed hair. Kim Silevan was workout sweats and what appeared to be natural blond hair. And kindness. None of it fit. He was still trying to figure it out when he got into the truck and handed the suit coat over.

"How'd you know," Nolan croaked, "where to find me?"

Stan put the truck in gear and pulled into the woman's driveway, then backed out and started back up the street. "You don't actually drive a run-of-the-mill car." He paused. "And this part of Lincoln has been on my regular beat for months. Which you probably didn't know. But the car. You might have given that a little more thought."

Nolan stared out the window. "Maybe part of me was wishing Pam would find out."

*Maybe you'd better change the subject.* Stan could feel his blood pressure rising as the guy whined. "Ms. Silevan said she would drive your car to the hospital. Said to tell you she'd leave the keys under the floor mat."

Nolan nodded. As they drove past the university stadium and into downtown, a sob racked his body. "Do me a favor," he said.

"I won't say anything to your wife. And that's not a favor. It's what needs to happen right now. For her sake."

"That's not what I was asking," he said. "Take me to the morgue."

Stan didn't know what to say to that, so he just kept driving south.

"There are certain things I want to make sure get done right. Before Pamela sees him."

"She's wondering where you are," Stan protested.

"So you call her and tell her we left my car at the hospital and we'll be home soon." He cleared his throat. "I want to make sure things are right. For her. Before we go over there together."

"She should hear that from *you*," Stan said. "Right now, she needs you at home."

Nolan disagreed. "Pamela's a survivor. And not that it's any of your business, but my wife hasn't needed me for a very long time."

"She's been asking for you."

"There's nothing I can do for her your family and Rainelle aren't already doing. But I *can* do this. And no one else can." He insisted, "So take me to the morgue."

As they pulled into a parking place at the morgue, Nolan cleared his throat. "Thanks for doing this." He hesitated. "Look. I know you've never had any use for me, but I'd appreciate it if—" He broke off.

Stan turned to face him. "Listen up," he said. "I've been where you are right now—as far as that house in the Highlands is concerned. And I was a really good liar. Gifted. But I don't lie now. For anyone. So here's how this is going to work." He paused. "How you handle the questions about why you didn't answer your phone or your pager is up to you. As far as I'm concerned it's the truth when I say you were at the hospital tonight." He gestured toward the building. "Because here we are." He glared at Nolan. "This subject is closed unless you choose to open it again. Ms. Silevan seemed to indicate she would play this any way you need it played. And the truth is, you have much bigger problems to face in the next few days."

Nolan nodded. "Whatever you may think of me, you should know that Kim can be trusted."

Stan resisted the urge to point out the obvious inconsistencies in the logic. "So can I. But don't push it. And don't have any doubt about whose side I'll be on if sides ever have to be chosen. I've always liked your wife."

"Got it," Nolan said and got out of the truck.

THEY LAY SIDE BY SIDE in the dark and did not sleep. Rainelle had said they shouldn't have to answer the door or the phone. Betty agreed and suggested they take some time to be alone together. Betty and Rainelle would take turns calling friends and extended family. Stan would keep trying to reach Michael's father, who was aboard a cruise ship somewhere in the Caribbean. Andy and the rest of the Novacs were out back with the dogs. And so Michael and Pam had come upstairs where they could escape the ringing phones and the doorbell, but where they could not escape the truth.

At the moment, Pam wasn't sure which truth was worse, the fact that Jacob wasn't coming home or the fact that, left to their own devices, the last thing Michael and she would have sought out tonight was each other. Asking for Michael earlier had surprised even her. She'd given up leaning on him years ago. Rainelle knew that, of course. Apparently Stan and Betty did not. Pam took a strange kind of comfort in the idea that however close he might have been to the Novacs, Jacob had apparently never mentioned his parents' troubles to them. Maybe, Pam thought, Jacob himself wasn't aware of just how close to the edge of divorce his parents were walking these days. She liked the idea of his not knowing. After all, her unwillingness to cause Jacob pain was the main reason Pam had stayed in the marriage. *There's nothing stopping you now.* She closed her eyes. Where, she wondered, did that thought come from?

She'd had all kinds of crazy thoughts since coming home today, beginning with her initial refusal to believe Stan Novac. Jacob couldn't possibly be gone. Even in the midst of all the tears around them during the rest of this never ending day, the idea that Jacob would never walk in her front door again was unfathomable. But now, as she and Michael lay side by side in the quiet room, the truth fell around her like a concrete cloak pressing her into the bed, threatening to squeeze every last bit of air out of her. Struggling to inhale, she could only manage a strangled sob.

Michael hadn't moved since they'd come to the bed, but at the first sound from her, he slid his hand across the bedspread. "You're cold," he said the moment their fingers touched. He got up and covered her with an afghan from the love seat by the fireplace, then perched on the edge of the bed next to her, his profile barely visible in the darkened room.

"I want to see him," Pam said.

"The funeral home will call when they're ready."

She sat up. "But you've seen him. I want to see him. Tonight." Throwing off the afghan, she slid to the edge of the mattress. Careful to leave space between them, she insisted, "I want to see my baby."

Michael took her hand. He started to speak, but then the sound of laughter from the neighbor's backyard pried its way into the room. Pam curled her fingers against her husband's palm and gave up the demand she knew he was about to deny again.

"How can they do that?" she asked.

"Do what?"

"How can they just go on as if nothing happened? Stan *told* them what happened. How can they . . ."

"We can't begrudge the Wilsons the use of their backyard for a family gathering."

Pam made a fist. "Yes. We can. They should—just—stop. They should be *quiet*." Standing up, she crossed to the French doors leading out onto the private deck that ran the length of the suite they'd created by knocking out the walls between three smaller bedrooms in the elegant French country style manse. She opened the door and stepped outside onto the deck. And then couldn't remember what she'd intended to do, why she'd gone out there. Something about the Wilsons. Something—

"So do you think Jake's sky diving in heaven?"

The voice was young. Pam hesitated, then stayed put so she could hear a little more. When Michael came to the open door, she held her finger up to her lips, then motioned for him to join her out on the deck.

" 'Course not," a voice answered. "You can't sky dive in heaven. You're already up there. And why'd you want to come back down here anyway? Jake's busy meeting Moses and King David. He doesn't care any more about sky diving."

"You think you know *everything*."

"Do not."

"Do too." There was a pause, and then the voice said, "I bet he's met Jesus already."

"Of *course* he's met *Jesus*!" Annoyed.

"Well, smarty pants, do you think he's met Davey, too?"

"Yeah. Daddy said he thought Jake would meet Davey right away. He said Jesus prob'ly took him right over."

Maddy and Megan's voices faded as they went back inside. Pam followed suit. When Michael moved aside to let her in, she murmured, "They were talking as if he isn't gone. As if he's just—changed addresses."

"Children their age can't grasp the meaning of death," Michael said in the "doctor voice" she despised.

"They were visualizing our son talking to Jesus," Pam said. "And meeting their brother, who died before they were even born. I, for one, find that very comforting. It's as if they believe Davey and Jacob are just on the other side of some unseen curtain. I think it's beautiful."

He picked up the bottle of pills that was on her dresser and checked the label. The pharmacy had dropped them off at the house earlier. "Rainelle and Betty were right," he said. "You need to rest."

How could he think she could sleep? She moved to the window and looked down on the yard. Rambo must have heard them talking. He was standing in the patch of light spilling out of the family room windows, looking toward the balcony, head up, ears alert. Reba stood beside him. The breeze had cooled. The moon was coming up on the horizon, casting soft light on everything in the garden. "I didn't finish weeding," she murmured.

"What?" Michael moved closer.

"My back was hurting yesterday," she said. "I didn't finish weeding. I should do that tomorrow." She made a noise, a brittle, mirthless sound meant to be a chuckle at the irony of her statement in light of the madness of the day. "I'll finish the weeding after we get back from the funeral home tomorrow." She turned and looked at her husband. "Is that . . . wrong?"

"Is what wrong?"

"To think about gardening when—whe—" The words caught in her throat.

"Who can say right or wrong when it comes to things like this."

Michael stood looking at her, his hands at his sides. When the moonlight spilled over the tops of the trees in the backyard and illuminated his face, Pam could see evidence of his pain in the deep shadows lining his face. In this light, what the women at the office called laugh lines had nothing to do with laughter. The dark spot that was the cleft in his chin somehow made her think of a bleeding gouge. When she raised her eyes to meet his, she saw unspilled tears glimmering in the moonlight, transforming his deep blue eyes into dark pools of pain.

He opened his mouth to speak. Stopped. Shook his head, reached out to her. "Come lie down. Please."

The party next door was breaking up. Murmuring voices and the scraping of chairs on the patio tile seemed harsh against the stillness around them. Disoriented for a moment, Pam hesitated.

"Please," Michael repeated. "Please, sweetheart."

*Sweetheart?* He hadn't called her that since—since the days when her body was whole and he actually slept here in the king-sized bed. Lately endearments surfaced only when he wanted to manipulate her reaction to something. Or when Jacob was within earshot. At least that's how it seemed. Could she have been wrong about that? Did he still feel something? As he stood with his shoulders bowed and moon-silvered tears spilling down his cheeks into his day-old beard, Pam couldn't bring herself to be angry. It was silly to take issue with a pet name in the context of the pain in their lives. Let Michael call her what he wanted. She wouldn't mind. Let him give her sleeping pills. She would take them. Let him tell her what to do. She would obey.

He led her back to the bed and told her to lie down and she did. For the briefest moment she expected—almost wanted—him to lie down beside her. But he didn't. Instead, he put two pills in the palm of her hand. Gave her a glass of water. Watched as she took the drugs. Covered her with an afghan. Kissed her cheek. And went alone to the love seat . . . facing the fireplace they hadn't lit for a very long time.

As she lay quietly contemplating Michael's profile in the dim light, Pam could feel whatever drug he had given her take effect. The tight bands that had made breathing so difficult all evening long began to loosen.

Rambo came into the room. He paused at her bedside to kiss her hand before walking slowly to where Michael was sitting. Pam was groggy by the time the odd thing happened, but not so groggy that she didn't wonder at it. Rambo had always seemed to sense that Michael tolerated his presence because of Jacob and that, without Jacob, there would be no dog in the Nolan house. He always kept his distance from Michael. But not now. Now, deep in his throat sounded a half moan, half whine, half something indescribable as he moved toward the love seat. When Michael ignored him Rambo moved closer and rested his snout on Michael's knee. Just as Pam drifted into blessed oblivion, Michael reached over and rested his open palm atop Rambo's head.

———

The rest of the week was a Valium-assisted blur. Rainelle drove them to the funeral home and waited in the chapel while Michael and Pam went into an adjoining room for what the funeral director called "the viewing." Reality sliced through her wall of denial and Pam collapsed against Michael, hiding her face in the crook of his neck, digging into his back with her nails, wondering later how he had withstood the pain of her clawing attempts to escape reality. She wailed as she clung to him, and he was strong. She could feel him trembling, but he didn't cry.

Later, when they met with the funeral director and Pam was overwhelmed by the questions, Michael and Rainelle took over. Who should perform the service? *Does it matter?* Would it be at the mortuary or at a church? *Does anyone care?* What music would they like? *Like? What music would anyone* like *at such a time?* Did they want to purchase a family plot? It was more financially wise. *Bargains at the burial ground. Do you give green stamps, too?* Where should people send memorials? Did they want a family car? What kind of flowers should be included in the casket spray? Michael and Rainelle came up with answers, and Pam remained silent. As they rose to go, she made one request. She wanted someone who knew her son to say a few words at the funeral.

"You mentioned that your son didn't attend your church," the funeral director said.

Pam nodded. "He'd been going with his best friend."

"Well, perhaps the pastor of that church—"

"Absolutely not," Michael interrupted. "I won't have some Bible-thumper turning this into something our friends will snicker at over drinks."

"If they do that," Pam said, "they aren't our friends."

"Nevertheless—"

Pam bit her lip. "All right." She pondered for a moment. "What about Stan?"

Michael frowned. "Stan Novac?"

She nodded. Lifted her chin. Insisted. With a sigh, Michael relented. They drove home in silence. Pam didn't even realize she'd done it, but by the time they turned into the driveway at home, she had reached out to Michael. And he was holding her hand.

# {six}

IT WAS HARD TO BE twenty-five years old and realize your life was over. You started out wrong somehow and whether it was because you never knew your father or your mother didn't love you or for whatever reason you could muster, the truth was that you just flat out started wrong. You didn't try at school, and you were friends with the guys who thought it was funny to blow stuff up and trash the neighborhood and write cuss words on the sides of the garages. And you felt yourself sinking, but you didn't think you could do anything about it and what was the use anyway because when you applied for a job, The Suit on the other side of the desk took one look at you and smirked and said he'd call, but you knew he wouldn't call and one day something just clicked and you quit trying.

That's how it had always been for Eddie Lee Monroe, and as he sat with his back to the jail cell wall trying not to cry, trying to think about something besides Lisa and the baby and, please God, whoever it was he'd killed out on that highway—as he sat trying to hold his stuff together, Eddie Lee thought that maybe it was time to flip the switch again and just go back to being what everyone had always told him he was. A loser. With a capital *L*. No one was going to care that he'd worked day and night cleaning toilets and mowing lawns and picking up trash at the stadium and doing any other odd job he could find to pay his way through school to get his operator's license. No one was going to care that he'd landed a job and kept his driving record clean and married a girl and settled down. Shoot, he was even registered to vote. Wasn't that something? Eddie Lee Monroe, a registered Independent. It made him feel like a real person instead of the cockroach someone had once called him.

Lisa made him feel like a real person, too. That day in the truck stop when some guy twice Eddie Lee's size started talking smack, and Eddie Lee nearly got himself killed by intervening and trying to get the guy to lay off—which he did until he met up with Eddie Lee in the parking lot. That day Lisa smiled at Eddie Lee like he'd done something amazing. She brought him ice for the black eye and a piece of pie he didn't even order.

It took three months for Eddie Lee to get up the courage to ask her out. When she said yes, he nearly fainted with surprise. A year later, when he stuttered a proposal and she said yes again, he felt as happy as Coach Tom Osborne when the Nebraska Huskers won the National Championship back in the day. And it just got better because it wasn't long before he was coming home to a trailer, where the woman he loved met him at the door with a big smile and a beautiful white stretch of pregnant belly peeking out from beneath her shirt.

Eddie Lee Monroe had never expected to be loved, never expected to have anything, never expected to be happy. And now, as he sat staring down at the gray floor of his jail cell, he had to fight to keep fear from crushing him. He was going to lose it all, just like that. Should have known it was all too good to be true. Too good to last. He didn't mind so much for himself. What broke his heart was thinking about Lisa. Clutching his sides, Eddie Lee leaned forward pressing his chest against his thighs and looking at the floor and wishing it would open up and swallow him so he wouldn't have to face the look in Lisa's eyes when he next saw her.

At least he didn't have to listen to her voice. They'd told him he could make a list of folks who could call. He didn't write any names down. He didn't want to talk to anybody. Especially not Lisa. If there was one thing he would not be able to stand it was her voice on the phone. That would break his heart. It would be bad enough when she showed up in court. And she would. Lisa Monroe was not a woman to go easily. She was the original "stand by your man" kind of girl.

He'd have to find a way to get her to change that. Not talking on the phone was the beginning. Maybe his lawyer would be able to make her stay away from court. Maybe he'd get free season tickets to watch the Cornhuskers play football. It could happen. They'd only been sold out since before he was born. The voice in Eddie Lee's head that sounded a lot like the last guy who lived with his mom started up again. He managed to silence it. For a while.

The truth was, Eddie Lee Monroe wouldn't have hurt a fly yesterday morning. He wasn't hopped up on anything legal or illegal and he hadn't even driven more than he should. He had been tired, and he should have stopped instead of pushing to drive that last stretch of road. But it was only ninety more miles, and he had a son and all he wanted to do was go see that baby boy and hug his wife, and then he would go to bed so he could get up Monday morning and get back on the road. It didn't even seem like that much of a risk. Ninety extra miles.

Eddie Lee shivered. One mistake and life as he knew it was over. And that wasn't the worst of it. More than one life would never be the same again. From the cop who'd worked the scene . . . to the EMTs . . . to the witnesses . . . to the family—oh, God. The family. Hiding his face in his hands, Eddie Lee let the tears stinging the backs of his eyelids slide out. He cried soundlessly. No need to let the entire jailhouse know Eddie Lee Monroe was a wuss.

*"It's your fault. Doesn't matter whether you meant it or not, it's your fault. What do you think now of all those great ideas of yours? You think you can be something you ain't? The acorn don't fall far from the tree, kid. Like I always said. You always was too big for your britches. Now look what it got you. Just like that—"*

With the word *that* sounding in his head, Eddie Lee could almost see Rico snapping his fingers right in his face. He could almost hear the voice, smell the beer-tainted breath. He closed his eyes and sat back, arguing with the memory. *You're wrong. A man can be good. He can decide. He can choose. I made a mistake. That doesn't mean I'm a bad person. I'm not a bad person. I'm not.*

Shackled and dressed in the same blue uniform as the rest of the jailbirds, he was going to his arraignment. He'd met with someone called an indigency screener and answered a long list of questions about where he worked, how much he made, and whether or not he could afford a lawyer. *Not in this lifetime.* Then he'd met with a paralegal who worked for the public defender. The courtroom was small and crowded and almost as claustrophic to Eddie Lee as the jail cell. As he entered he thought he saw a flash of blond hair. *Lisa.* No, Lisa was still in the hospital. Even so, his heart began to pound even harder from a confusing brew of emotions that ran from guilt to dread to fear to hope and back again.

"Eddie Lee Monroe," the jail employee said as they stood in front of the judge.

"Are you Eddie Lee Monroe?" the judge asked without looking up.

"Yes, sir."

The judge scanned the sheet of paper in front of him. "Public defender appointed. Mr. Ambrose."

He nodded at another lawyer, and this guy faced Eddie Lee and said, "Mr. Monroe, you have been charged with motor vehicle homicide in that on June 19, 2005, you did cause the death of Jacob Michael Nolan unintentionally while engaged in the operation of a motor vehicle in violation of the law of the State of Nebraska, to wit, a violation of Nebraska Revised Statues . . . blah blah blah blah . . . up to a year in jail, a thousand dollar fine or both such fine and imprisonment."

Even on a good day it would have been hard to follow the legal language, but today Eddie Lee's brain only processed part of what he was hearing. *Jail. Fine. Imprisonment.* He could feel droplets of sweat on his forehead.

"In court two," the guy continued, "you are charged with leaving the scene of a personal injury motor vehicle accident in violation of . . ." Once again, Eddie Lee listened for the part that mattered most, and although he'd heard it from the paralegal earlier, hearing it here in public made it sound even worse. ". . . five years in prison, a ten thousand dollar fine or both . . . suspend your driving privileges . . . pay restitution. Do you understand the charges against you?"

"I'm guilty," Eddie Lee blurted out as he swiped his forehead with the back of one hand.

The judge ignored him. "Do you understand the charges against you?"

"I said I'm guilty," Eddie Lee repeated. "I just—I just want this over with."

"You may not enter a plea in this court," the judge said, scowling. "Do you understand what you are charged with?"

He swallowed. "Yes, sir, I do, and I'm guilty."

The judge leaned forward and said distinctly, "You *cannot* plead to these charges in my court. You should talk to your public defender about your plea. Now answer the question. Do you understand the charges?"

Eddie Lee bowed his head. "Yes, sir."

When the topic of bail came up, the public defender said, "Your Honor, Mr. Monroe has no prior failures to appear. He has lived in Lincoln all his life, is married and has a newborn child, has been working at the same trucking company for the past five years, and does not have twenty-five thousand dollars to post bond. He surrendered himself to authorities. We recommend a twenty-five thousand dollar percentage bond."

Which, Eddie Lee knew, was meant to help out, except it didn't make any difference—unless the guy could get him out for about thirty bucks, because that's all he had and he wasn't going to take a loan even if a bail bondsman would give him one.

Just as he was wishing everything could move along faster, there was a stir at the back of the courtroom and a voice blurted out, "We can't afford to pay twenty-five thousand dollars, Your Honor."

Lisa? Here? Out of the hospital? How . . . ? Eddie Lee glanced behind him just long enough to see a deputy leaning down to talk to her. She was dressed in a pink sweater with a baby carrier draped over her shoulder and . . . Eddie Lee wished the floor would open up and swallow him even as his heart began to thump with love for what she'd done. How'd she get the doctor to let her come here? A million new worries settled on his shoulders. She shouldn't have come. It wasn't good for her. She should be in the hospital healing up instead of arguing with the deputy, who was trying to get her to quiet down.

"But we don't have the money," she said, "and everything that law-yer said is true. He works hard and we have a new baby and—" She broke off, and Eddie Lee didn't have to look to know the deputy was getting tougher. "All right, all right," Lisa said. "I'll be quiet. Just—don't make me leave." Her voice quieted. "Please. I won't say another word."

Once Lisa hushed, things moved along fast, with Eddie Lee being told he'd enter a plea on August 2. None of that mattered, though, because as he was being led away, Lisa said real loud, "I love you, darlin'." He would replay that memory in his mind a million times. Lisa had called him *darlin'*.

————

The only thing good about the rest of the third week of June in Pam Nolan's life was the hope that in due time she wouldn't remem-ber much of it. She'd always been that way, coping well in the midst of a challenge and avoiding clinical depression later by letting the gory details be absorbed into the murky past. Even the things she couldn't forget—like the night her mother vomited all over her prom dress half an hour before her date was to pick her up, or the look on Michael's face when she woke from the mastectomy—even those things were never allowed to come to the surface often. She hoped the same would hold true for this, the worst week of her life. With one excep-tion. She never wanted to forget the reappearance of the Michael Nolan she'd fallen in love with.

Maybe it was only a short-term miracle. Maybe with time the

chasm that had stretched between them for years would open again. But for now—for this broken time—the old Michael was here. He'd gone in to the office just long enough to dictate a few files and leave orders for two patients who had been admitted to the hospital over the weekend. And then he'd told his father, who was also the senior partner in the medical practice, that he'd have to find someone to fill in—indefinitely. Other than a couple of phone calls conducted while he paced the patio out back, Michael had been at Pam's beck and call. He was even sleeping in their bedroom again, albeit on the pullout love seat.

And then Rainelle stopped by with news that sent the gentle Michael Nolan back into hiding. "A misdemeanor?!" he shouted, leaping out of his chair and beginning to pace back and forth in front of the family room window. "You cannot be serious."

"I don't understand," Pam said, clutching the arms of her wing-backed chair as she glanced across the room at Michael. "What—what does that mean?"

"It happens all the time," Rainelle said without answering Pam's question. "The booking officer automatically called it a felony because there was a death. That's motor vehicle homicide. But after looking at the facts of the accident . . ."

"Facts," Michael spat out. "What facts would those be?"

In the face of Michael's barely controlled rage, Rainelle affected a subtle but complete transformation. Reaching for the slim leather folder she'd brought with her—a deep red color that matched her current manicure—Rainelle withdrew a single sheet of paper. When she spoke next, she was no longer a friend talking with friends. She was a prosecutor doing her best to explain the legal system to a victim's family.

"I'm not saying it will happen, I just wanted you to know that the public defender's office has already brought it up. It's an unusual situation. Monroe left the scene, but then he came back and turned himself in. Ambrose wouldn't be doing his job if he didn't try to get this pled down." She paused and glanced down at the sheet of paper in her hand while she explained. "According to the blood samples taken when the accused was arrested," she began, "there were no drugs or alcohol involved. The investigator saw no indication of excessive speed. And while Monroe's hours behind the wheel are barely within legal limits, they are within those limits. He didn't falsify his driving record. His employer has volunteered information via the public defender that presents the image of a hardworking, honest guy." When Michael opened his mouth to protest, Rainelle shook her finger at him. "Let me finish," she said. "He has no criminal history—"

"—except that he left our son to bleed to death on the side of the road while he took off."

"That's not what the evidence indicates," Rainelle told him. "Monroe says he knew there was no chance Jacob was alive. He stated that clearly in the initial interview with the defender's office, and we have testimony from a witness and the coroner that upholds his testimony. Even Stan Novac's police report indicates that—" She paused and glanced from Pam to Michael and back again. Her voice was maddeningly reasonable, even gentle, as she said, "Everything corroborates Monroe's testimony that he definitely saw enough to know Jacob was—that he hadn't survived. That's part of why Monroe ran. He knew he was going to jail, and he wanted to see his baby."

"What baby?" Pam asked.

"His wife gave birth early. That's why he was pushing to get back to Lincoln. When he realized what he'd done, he was determined to see the baby. But as soon as he did, he returned to the scene and turned himself in." She paused, moistened her lips, and went on. "Which is what we call mitigating circumstances."

Michael had stopped pacing and come to stand beside Pam's chair. "I sense more bad news," he said. "Just get it over with."

"If the charge for leaving the scene is dropped it's more likely that the other charge will be pled down to vehicular manslaughter." She glanced at Michael. "Which is a misdemeanor, not a felony."

Pam frowned. "But he's still in jail—right?"

"Yes. And it doesn't look like he's going to fight for himself. But

Ambrose is an excellent public defender and—"

"Wait a minute," Pam said. "He's not getting his own lawyer?"

Rainelle shook her head. "No money for a lawyer. No money for bail. He'll be in jail until trial."

"If he's pleading guilty, why would there even be a trial?"

"The plea won't officially be entered for a couple of weeks. A lot could happen between now and then."

"Like what?" Michael asked.

"If he were my client," Rainelle said, "I'd do my best to get him to enter 'no contest' instead of 'guilty.'"

"The guy is guilty," Michael said. "He says he's guilty. Why would anyone try to talk him out of that?"

"It's complicated," Rainelle said.

"I'm all ears," Michael demanded and sat down in the chair next to Pam.

With a sigh, Rainelle explained. "If Monroe enters a guilty plea, then it's basically over. He's thrown himself on the mercy of the court. There's very little bargaining to be done on his behalf, and a judge doesn't have much leeway when it comes to sentencing."

"Good," Michael said.

"But the system guarantees him proper representation," Rainelle said. "And 'no contest' is the better plea. Because that means 'I'm not saying I did it, but I don't want a trial. I agree to let you find me guilty.' In the long run, this is a better plea for Monroe, because now the judge can take into account the mitigating circumstances. His boss will want him to plead 'no contest,' too."

"What does his boss have to do with it?" Pam asked.

"Do you really want to get into all of this right now?"

Pam looked at Michael and back at Rainelle. "Yes," she said. "I think we do."

"There is going to be a lot more going on with this case than just Monroe being punished for Jacob's death," Rainelle began. "There will be other civil suits." She peered at Michael. "Have you gotten in touch with your attorney yet?"

Michael shook his head. "He left a message. Said he'd heard. Said we need to talk. I haven't returned his call."

"You should talk to him as soon as possible. He'll explain it when you're ready, but there will be negotiations between the trucking firm's insurance company and you."

"Why?" Pam asked.

"Because you'll be suing them."

"We will? Why would we do that? Did the truck have defective brakes or something?"

"There's no indication of anything like that playing a role in this. Still, there's going to be a lot of back and forth between your attorney and theirs, and when all is said and done, you will be receiving a check."

"A check?" Pam repeated.

"Remuneration for the loss of your child. From Monroe's employer's insurance company." Rainelle paused. "Monroe himself doesn't have any assets beyond an old pickup truck."

Pam sat back. Swallowed. "I don't want to ruin his family. What good would that do? It won't bring Jacob back. But . . . these insurance people . . . they're going to try to *pay* us for Jacob?"

Michael covered her hand with his. In the silence that ensued, Pam tried to make her sluggish brain work through what Rainelle was saying. She returned to an earlier topic. "If he's admitting his guilt, then why do we care if it's a felony or a misdemeanor? I don't even know the difference."

"You care," Rainelle explained, "because it will affect the sentencing. If the case is pled down, that could give the judge leeway to sentence Monroe with probation instead of jail time."

"Probation?" Michael's voice rose again. "Are you saying that our son's killer could walk?!" He leaned forward. "Tell me that's not going to happen."

Rainelle laced her fingers together. "I cannot begin to imagine what the two of you are going through right now, Michael. I know that. But—" She paused. Took a deep breath. "There's tragedy on both sides of this issue."

"My dead son is not an *issue*." He jumped out of his seat again.

"I cannot believe I'm hearing this," Pam said, fighting not to cry.

"You asked me to see what I could find out about the case," Rainelle replied. "Well, here's what I found out: The Monroe story is a 'pull yourself up by your own bootstraps' kind of thing. Broken home, school dropout, minor trouble with the law—"

"What kind of minor trouble with the law?" Michael asked. "You said he didn't have a criminal record."

"Nothing that will have much bearing on this case. A couple of things when he was a juvenile. He did community service, got his GED, put himself through the SCC Driver's Training Institute and has the best safe driving record in the company—or had, until—" Rainelle looked up at Michael, who was still standing. "I know you want to hate him. No one can blame you for that. It's a perfectly natural response. But from everything I've learned, Eddie Lee Monroe is not the bad guy." She looked at Pam. "And he's got a wife and a new baby who are going to be in real financial trouble if he ends up serving time."

"*If* he ends up serving time?" Michael barked.

"Look, you both need to prepare yourselves for the possibility that a judge may not see jail time as having much purpose in this case." She leaned toward Pam. "I know you. You are not a revengeful person. Think about it, honey. Do you really want another child to grow up fatherless like you and I did?"

Michael interrupted her. "That's enough. How dare you sit in our home and take the side of the man who killed our son?"

"I'm not taking his side," Rainelle protested. "I thought it would help if you knew—"

"What would help," Michael said, "is for you to leave now. You've said what you had to say. We asked you to investigate for us and you did. From now on we'll be talking to the prosecutor's office through our own attorney." He picked up Rainelle's red leather folder and handed it to her.

Sliding the piece of paper she'd brought with her into the folder, Rainelle stood up. Pam could sense that she was expected to intervene, but she had neither the strength nor the interest. Weariness washed over her.

Rainelle paused. "I love you, Pam. You are my dearest friend, and my heart is broken for you. But revenge won't bring Jacob back. There is no sense in ruining Lisa Monroe's life because her husband made a mistake he's willing to pay for. All that accomplishes is another child growing up without a daddy."

"*We* aren't the bad guys in this," Michael said.

"I didn't mean to imply that." Rainelle sighed. "Look, after you two have had a chance to think more about it, if you have more questions, you call the office. But—I think you've got the right idea, Michael. Malcolm Sutter's been assigned prosecutor for this case, and from now on you should talk to him. Through your own attorney."

Michael nodded. He put his hand on Pam's shoulder.

"I'll walk you out," Pam said, and got up. At the front door, Rainelle hugged her. "You know I didn't mean—"

"There's no right thing to say or do right now," Pam said, although she didn't feel or sound convinced.

"I love you," Rainelle said.

Pam nodded.

"Is there anything else you want me to do tomorrow?"

"Betty's church ladies offered to serve a lunch after." Pam's voice wobbled. She cleared her throat.

"That's nice. The Novacs are good people."

After Rainelle left, Pam returned to the back of the house, where Michael was staring down at Rambo, who was sitting by the back door.

"No," he said. "You can't go out there." He tilted his head toward the windows. "Hear that yapping? The Wilsons have let Freaky

Freddy out. And you know how he is. He'd just love to have a serving of poodle canapé."

Pam chimed in. "We could go for a walk instead."

*Walk.* Rambo did a 180 and headed for the laundry room. He soon reappeared with leash in mouth.

"How much of what we say does he understand, anyway?" Michael wondered.

"You can put that down, Fur-face," Pam said. "We haven't decided for sure."

*Down.* Rambo deposited the leash on the floor and lay down, front paws stretched out before him, ears alert, head cocked to one side. He whined softly and wagged his tail as he looked from Michael to Pam and back again.

"Okay," Michael said. "That is beyond weird." He looked down at the dog.

Rambo chuffed.

"All right," Michael said. "You win. We walk."

# {s e v e n}

THE GRIEVING PROCESS could take many forms. Today it was yelling. Stan could hear the argument from the front gate. Reba was standing at attention on the porch looking at Andy's bedroom window. When Stan unlatched the front gate, she jerked her head around and wagged her tail, then went back to studying the window with canine concern.

As he stood beside Reba listening, Stan heard Rachel yell, "*Give me that! If you don't want it I do. You can't just throw—*" Then her voice broke off and she wailed, "*An-deeeeee!*" A door slammed. Music blared.

Out of habit, Stan glanced toward the kitchen as he stepped inside. The white board displayed a message. "Grocery shopping with 4." That meant the four youngest were with their mom. Sort of good. Sort of bad. Stan adored his kids, but he was better at showing it with camping trips and fishing adventures. Bared souls and heart-to-heart talks were Betty's territory. Maybe he could pretend he never—

He squashed the temptation to run the other way at the same instant Andy's bedroom door flew open. Dressed in a gray T-shirt that touted the names of several famous movie directors—the only name Stan recognized was Coppola—Andy sauntered toward the kitchen with little more than a nod and a "Hey, Dad."

"I could hear you two yelling at each other way all the way to the street."

"The Drama Queen was having a moment," Andy said, opening the refrigerator and pouring himself a glass of milk.

Rachel's door opened, and she came into the living room, her arms encircling the black Nascar trash can that had been Andy's since he was ten years old.

"He can't just throw this away," she said.

"I can do whatever I want," Andy retorted. "It's mine." He turned to Stan for support. "Tell her, Dad. It's mine."

"I don't *care* if it's technically his. He can't just toss it out." Rachel's lower lip trembled. She sat down on the couch and, putting the trash can before her, drew out a piece of paper. "Jake wrote this." She held it out to Stan, who took it and read, *I didn't have any idea where this list would take me. It began as a way to live large. But I've figured something out along the way. There's more than one way to be extreme.*

Rachel pulled another crumpled paper out of the can and smoothed it on her knee. "And this." She took in a deep breath. "Wouldn't his parents want it? Someday? Shouldn't they at least see it?"

"There's nothing to see," Andy said as he put his glass down on the counter separating the kitchen from the living room. "It's over. It was our project and it's over." He flicked the air with one hand. "No big deal." He pointed at Rachel as he said to Stan, "Except for the Drama Queen's performance, here."

"Stop calling me that!" Rachel protested.

Andy rolled his eyes and mimicked her voice, "My beloved Jake wrote this, Jake's in that. Oh, I can hear his voice. . . . Oh oh oh—"

Rachel's cheeks blazed with color. She glowered at her brother and blinked back angry tears.

"That's enough, Andy," Stan said. "You know your sister loved—"

"Yeah," Andy interrupted. "The whole wide world loved Jake." He paused. "He was certainly the star of *my* life." Turning his back on the living room, he opened the refrigerator again and stood staring at the contents while he spoke. "Well, here's a news flash. He's gone. End of story. End of documentary. No big deal," he repeated, bending over to rummage in the refrigerator.

"That's baloney, and you and I both know it," Stan said. "'Xtreme

Ten' has pretty much defined your life for the last couple of years, and—"

"Well, it's over now," Andy almost shouted. He finally stood up, took an exaggerated bite out of the apple he'd pulled out of one of the refrigerator drawers, and slammed the door shut.

"So . . . maybe we should talk about it," Stan said. "We've all been so busy trying to be there for the Nolans that we haven't really talked to each other about it. Maybe we need to do that."

"Why?" Andy said. "Nothing you can say is going to make any difference." He chomped on the apple and chewed noisily while he mumbled, "Just let it go, Dad. It stinks and that's that." Tossing the remains of the apple into the kitchen trash, he raised his hands toward heaven, "So let's just praise Jesus and move on."

"Don't blaspheme," Stan snapped.

"Afraid lightning will strike?"

Both his attitude and his mouth had taken Andy light-years across the line that usually earned one of Stan's kids a serious grounding. Painfully aware that Rachel had sunk into the old chair where she'd been perched defending her right to the trash and was now staring in disbelief at her mouthy brother, Stan resisted the temptation to order the kid to his room. In that moment of hesitation, he saw the tears glimmering in his son's anguished eyes. Swallowing hard and forcing his own anger into retreat, Stan tried to reach the pain behind Andy's words.

"If you mean that talking about it won't resurrect your project, you may be right," he said. "But if you mean it won't make a difference in how you feel about it, I think you're wrong." He crossed the room and sat down on the couch. "So how about you come over here and have a seat, and let's give it a try." He forced a joke. "If you obey now I won't have to force compliance later by four-pointing you until you talk."

Andy made a face that said *pathetic joke*. But with a scowl in Rachel's direction he came back into the living room. Dropping into the recliner he folded his arms and sat staring toward his bedroom door.

"Tell me how all this stuff got in here," Stan said, motioning from the pile on the couch to the trash can at Rachel's feet.

"It levitated and inserted itself," Andy quipped. "What do you mean how did it get there? I tossed it." He bent over and picked at an imaginary fleck on the carpet.

Stan suppressed the urge to bodily lift the brat out of his chair and escort him to his room with orders to stay there until he was ready to talk. Forcing calm into his voice, he said, "It seems a little early to be giving up on it."

Andy frowned. "Really? Just how do you think I'm going to be able to finish it? Because if you've come up with a way to resurrect the star of the production, I'd sure like to hear it. My entire future was dependent on winning a scholarship with that documentary, and now it's a worthless piece of trash. Which is why I put it in the *trash*."

As he talked, he picked up steam. Days of pent-up emotions poured out in a stream of invectives, first against Rachel for intruding where she didn't belong, and then backward to the trucker who'd caused the accident, the witness who couldn't keep Jake alive until the EMTs got there, fate, and finally, God. Having begun to cry partway through the diatribe Andy finished by leaning forward in the recliner and choking out, "And what kind of lowlife scum cares about stuff like this, anyway?" He motioned at the crumpled papers. "My best friend is dead and all I can think about is my movie?" He scrubbed at his forehead with his fingertips. His voice broke and he hid his face in his hands as he began to sob. "How can I even think about that, Dad? How can I?"

"Oh, Andy," Rachel said and went to him, putting her hand on his shoulder. "I'm sorry, Andy. I'm so sorry. . . ." She began to cry, too.

Andy threw his arms around her and wept on her shoulder while Stan knelt beside them trying to keep his own emotions in check. When Andy and Rachel had finally calmed down enough to listen, he said, "Somewhere in this mess there's a plan. We can't see it, but it's there." He looked at Andy. "Rachel's right. You shouldn't throw everything away. Even if you don't use it in a film, the Nolans might want it. Maybe that's what God wants you to do with it. Maybe that's why Rachel had to throw a fit and intervene."

Andy shook his head. "Naw. That wasn't God. That was just Rachel being Rachel."

She popped him on the arm, but it was a gentle hit. "I just didn't want you throwing it all away. That's all." She smiled sadly. "And for whatever it's worth, I've had some of the same feelings. About being selfish. I mean, all I've been thinking about is me and how awful it is for me."

"That's human," Stan said. "Not evil. None of us is thinking straight. Grief does that. You've both had a terrible shock. So cut yourselves some slack. And above all, stick together. Help each other."

Andy patted his sister's shoulder. "I'll try to do better." He got up and began to gather crumpled papers and torn magazines. Taking one of the top papers, he handed it to Rachel. "Here. If you go to those Web sites you can see some of the stuff we were going to do." He turned around. "Thanks, Dad."

Stan nodded.

"Thanks, Daddy," Rachel said and headed for her room.

Andy looked down at the stuff in his arms. "I just don't see how this can possibly be worth anything now. I mean—it's such a mess."

"I'm not sure of this," Stan said, "but it seems to me that somewhere I heard that there's a job in the film industry that requires taking bits and pieces of stuff and making sense of them. You know what I'm talking about?"

Andy made a face. "Yeah, Dad. That's the director."

"Um-hmm. And what was it you wanted to be when you grow up?"

"I get the point," Andy said. At the door to his room he paused. "Thanks again."

Stan nodded. He moved to his recliner and picked up the remote. As he pointed it at the television, he realized that he didn't really care all that much about the news today.

He would rather be at the wrong end of a gun than sitting in this pew. Well . . . maybe it wasn't quite *that* bad. Betty was on his right, Suzanne in her lap, the twins next to her. Andy was on the left, his arm draped across the back of their pew so that Emily and Rachel could have a sense of their big brother's protective love. Stan would have known Betty was trembling even if they weren't sitting close enough for him to feel it. Jake's death had resurrected plenty of ghosts from their past. It might be over twenty years since Davey died, but the grief had come roaring back for both of them as they tried to help the Nolans. Having lost a child might make them more able to empathize . . . but it was also making Stan shaky this morning. Of course, there was more to it than that.

First, there was the church itself. The Nolans were prominent members of one of the grandest churches in town. The physical space wasn't all that much bigger than the Bible church the Novacs attended, but that's where any similarities ended. From the ornate carvings to the stained glass windows and the marble floors to the pipe organ in the balcony, the building was breathtaking—and intimidating to the simple man about to stand behind the massive pulpit.

But even more intimidating than the church was the size of the congregation gathered this morning. In theory, the numbers weren't surprising. Stan had expected that. After all, Michael was the heir of a medical dynasty that went all the way back to the founding of the city of Lincoln. His great-grandfather had been one of the first presidents of the first medical society in the state. His father had been in practice for longer than Stan had been alive. The Nolans were members of the oldest and most prestigious country club in Lincoln. Dr. Nolan Senior was known for his generous support of University Foundation projects and civic causes. Both he and his son were such enthusiastic boosters for UNL that they had their own reserved parking places about five feet from the stadium entrance for football games. Okay, maybe not exactly five feet, but Stan knew what those parking places meant in donations, and it was more than he made in a year.

But Pam Nolan had asked. "Your family meant so much to—" She'd stopped short of saying Jake's name, which was more than a little worrisome. "Please." She looked up at him with those eyes. Stan doubted that the Michael side of the couple really wanted him speaking at their son's funeral. But Michael played the winning card when he said Pam deserved to feel like the service was a proper tribute to Jacob, and if she wanted Stan to speak . . . please. So here he sat, staring up at a carved altar and stained glass, wishing the whole thing was over.

*It's not about you.* That was how one of his favorite books started, and Stan was thankful he believed it, because he was probably about to make a complete fool of himself in front of some of the most educated minds in the city. Who knew who might be sitting behind them. Certainly every other physician in town would be here. Hospital administrators. Judges. Lawyers. Maybe even the mayor. He just knew he was going to make some stupid grammatical mistakes.

Somewhere between the last high note of the soprano who was doing an operatic version of the Lord's Prayer and the reading of the obituary, Stan thought back to those late night discussions he and Andy and Jake had had in the last few weeks. If it hadn't been for those, today would have been impossible. But those conversations had happened and decisions had been made that reassured him. This might be the hardest thing he'd ever done, but it was also one of the more right things he'd ever done. He'd just have to pretend to be the tough cop people seemed to think he was.

He looked down at the book in his lap and the color-coded sticky notes jutting out from the pages. He'd numbered them in case he got nervous and forgot. He didn't even have to look up from his notes if he didn't want to. Maybe he wouldn't.

A soft nudge from Betty brought him back to the present. Glancing around him, Stan saw expectant eyes focused on him. He hadn't heard a word of the obituary. He was glad. He thought they were stupid, anyway. Anyone who cared already knew everything written in an obituary. Wasn't it torture for people who loved someone to have to sit there and listen to all that formal gibberish? Speaking of torture, it was time for him to do his part.

Clearing his throat, Stan stood up. He snagged the toe of his dress shoe on the edge of the pew support in front of them and stumbled his way into the aisle. *Klutz.* Taking a deep breath, he stood for a moment looking at the casket. Big mistake. Tight throat. Scratchy eyes. He looked away from the casket, up at the pulpit, and then higher to the cross hanging above the altar. Shrugging his right shoulder, Stan tilted his head in the characteristic gesture of a body builder trying to loosen up. It didn't do any good, but it got him moving. Slowly he walked around the casket, among the dozens of floral arrangements banking the entire front of the church, up the stairs, where the pastor nodded and stepped back, giving Stan access to the massive mahogany pulpit.

When he looked at the crowd, Stan's knees went weak. It was one thing to know the church would be full of educated, wealthy people and another to be up here looking at pews that were crammed full and a crowd of mourners standing shoulder-to-shoulder in the back. Standing room only. And he'd been right: the mayor was there. And the head football coach. And Senator Nelson. This was worse than he had anticipated. He'd barely gotten through high school. What had he been thinking when he'd agreed to "say a few words"? What a joke.

*It's not about you.*

Grasping the sides of the pulpit, Stan stared past the crowd at a spot of color on the stained glass window in the balcony and began. "Betty and I lost a son once." *Oh brother.* Here it came. He could feel his throat tighten up. Sense tears gathering behind his eyes. He cleared his throat. *It's not about me it's not about me it's not about me it's not it's not it's not . . .* "Betty and I lost a son once," he repeated. "And I just wanted to share the reason we survived."

There. The rest would be easy. All he had to do from here on was read. Without looking up again, Stan turned to the first place marked in his Bible. "The Gospel of John. Chapter eleven. Verses twenty-five and twenty-six. 'Jesus said to her, "I am the resurrection and the life; he who believes in Me shall live even if he dies, and everyone who lives and believes in Me will never die."'" Stan paused before repeating the last phrase, "'Everyone who lives and believes in Me will never die.'" He read what he'd written on the bookmark inserted in the pages of the Bible. "Jacob Michael Nolan is no longer here with us, but because he believed this, he is alive. He is not here, but he is alive."

Turning to the passage marked by the big number two written on electric orange paper, Stan read, "The Gospel of John, chapter fourteen, verses one through six. 'Let not your heart be troubled; believe in God, believe also in Me. In My Father's house are many dwelling places; if it were not so, I would have told you; for I go to prepare a place for you. If I go and prepare a place for you, I will come again and receive you to Myself, that where I am, there you may be also.' Jacob Michael Nolan is not with us now. He is with Jesus. And Jesus has promised all of His children a reunion."

He reached for the marker with the big three on it and read, "Paul's first letter to the Thessalonians, chapter four, verses thirteen through eighteen. 'But we do not want you to be uninformed, brethren, about those who are asleep, so that you will not grieve as do the rest who have no hope. For if we believe that Jesus died and rose again, even so God will bring with Him those who have fallen asleep in Jesus. For this we say to you by the word of the Lord, that we who are alive and remain until the coming of the Lord, will not precede those who have fallen asleep. For the Lord Himself will descend from heaven with a shout, with the voice of the archangel and with the trumpet of God, and the dead in Christ will rise first. Then we who are alive and remain will be caught up together with them in the clouds to meet the Lord in the air, and so we shall always be with the Lord. Therefore comfort one another with these words.'

"Jacob Michael Nolan is alive. We grieve, but we also have hope."

He looked down at the casket. "Jake. We miss you. But we'll see you soon."

Closing his Bible, Stan tucked it under his arm and made his way back to his place beside Betty. Suzanne climbed into his lap. Betty slipped her arm through his. He looked down at her. Her eyes were shining with love and pride, and in that moment Stan realized that it just didn't matter what anybody else thought about what he'd said or how he'd said it.

# {eight}

IN THE DAYS THAT followed the funeral, Pam began to feel like the victim of a haunting. Nightmares ruled her sleep, and no part of the day was safe. Just walking by Jacob's empty room could bring on an attack of vertigo until Pam learned to remind herself to stop holding her breath. It was odd to have to script the day with things like *Remember to breathe*. She never knew when something unexpected would shatter the protective layer she tried to erect around her sanity. Jacob's picture on the mantel in the family room was comforting one moment and the cause of a crying jag the next. One day she used Jacob's favorite coffee mug and felt better; the next she had to shove the same mug to the back of the cupboard. The day she put her hands into Jacob's old hunting boots and sat on the laundry room floor sobbing was one of the worst.

Leaving the house was no help. Everywhere she went there was something to remind her of Jacob. The school where he met Andy. The curb that had sent him flying when he was learning to in-line skate. The park where they used to meet other young mothers with their kids for play dates. And the grocery store. Pam had to flee the cereal aisle when, reaching for a box of bran, she could almost hear Jacob's voice teasing her. *"Eating kitty litter again, Madre?"* His absence seeped into the nooks and crannies of her life until Pam felt like someone who'd gone swimming in the ocean with an open wound. Everything hurt.

And then there were the people. She did go out to weed the garden after the funeral . . . and saw Helen Wilson next door hurry inside. The obvious avoidance bothered her, but not nearly as much as the well-meaning but clueless friends who seemed to think comfort clichés helped. If every cloud had a silver lining, why couldn't she see it? And, no, she wasn't glad Jacob was in heaven. She wanted him back. Here. Grieving was all that Betty Novac had said it would be— and worse.

"Will it ever end?" she sobbed one day when Betty called.

"Not entirely," Betty said, then apologized. "I don't mean to frighten you, but this isn't called 'the worst loss' for no reason."

Through her tears, Pam said thank-you. "At least I know I'm not going crazy. The way I'm acting, sometimes I wonder."

"Oh, hon, of course you're going crazy. But it's an understandable kind of crazy." She paused. "I wish I could promise you things will be better soon. What I can promise you is that you aren't alone. When I said you could call and I would come any time, day or night, I meant it."

"I know," Pam said. "And I'm grateful. So . . . grateful."

Somehow she and Michael made it to the second weekend. He'd crawled into bed beside her a couple of times in recent days, and she'd been glad, even though she was unable to respond beyond a surface appreciation for another human to share the space that had ceased to feel like home. He made no demands on her. This morning he was sprawled on the pullout love seat. She didn't know when he'd come upstairs. He was having his own emotional struggles. She'd witnessed them and been saddened by her own inability to reach out and offer comfort. Betty said that was normal. That they might not be able to help one another, at least for a while.

She sat up, dreading the day. It surprised her when she walked by Jacob's room and the emotion assaulting her wasn't sorrow. This morning she was angry. Angry because Jacob should be home for the summer. He should be sound asleep behind a closed door. But his bedroom door stood open, his bedding rumpled only because Rambo had taken to ignoring the "No dogs allowed on the bed" rule.

She was angry because the kitchen counter shouldn't be clear. Late-night snack dishes should be piled right there above the dishwasher. How many times had she hassled Jacob about that? *How hard could it be to open a dishwasher*, she'd grumbled. Well, now she had her pristine kitchen. And she was mad.

As she poured coffee—thank goodness for programmable coffee makers and caffeine—she sat down at the kitchen island, suddenly aware of the stacks of envelopes, stamps, and pens on the table. And the wicker basket overflowing with sympathy cards. Anger off. Sorrow on. Tears flow.

Bare chested and bleary-eyed, Michael descended the stairs, pausing to kiss her on the cheek before he headed for the coffeepot. He froze in midstride, looking at the table. "That's today?"

Pam nodded. "I want to get it over with."

He poured coffee and took a sip. "You told me something about this, but I can't remember what it was."

"Probably that Betty and Rainelle are coming over to help," Pam said. "It won't take long."

He disagreed. "It'll take most of the day." He shook his head. "I wish you'd listened to me and just let Laura at the office do it. She'd welcome the extra income."

"I can't farm it out. It's—I can't explain it. I just need to do it."

"You don't have to pour your guts out as an offering to every single person who showed up and wrote a check." Michael's voice was laced with bitterness. "They're all playing golf this morning. Or shopping. They've written a check or sent a card that says how bad they feel and now they're off living their lives without another thought of Jacob. Or us." He pulled the cell phone out of his pajama pocket and laid it on the counter. "I offer exhibit A. Hasn't rung in days. Unless you count my father's twice daily checking in and hinting that it's high time I came back to work."

Pam resisted the urge to expound on her father-in-law's insensitivity, opting instead for a simple "I hope you told him no."

Michael shrugged. "I told him." He grimaced and rubbed one hand across his forehead. "Although my terms were a bit more colorful than a simple no. Dear old Dad is likely a bit more disappointed than usual with his son at the moment."

"Good. It wouldn't kill him to show some genuine compassion—and to think of you first." She swallowed the urge to add *for a change*.

"He cares, Pam. He just doesn't know how to show it."

There it was again. The defensive attitude about his father. Pam poured more coffee and refilled Michael's while she thought back. If she'd known when they were dating what she knew now—but no. She couldn't go there. She'd made her bed and she would lie in it. In the last few days she'd begun to value her marriage more than she had in a long time. The long and short of it, as her mother used to say, was that she'd lost enough. She might have been toying with the idea of divorcing Michael as soon as Jacob graduated college, but since the accident, the old Michael had begun to make brief appearances in their lives. This morning, as he stood here in the kitchen with his scruffy beard and his rumpled hair . . . *Stop it. Are you out of your mind?* She was losing it. The kitchen table was covered with sympathy cards and her libido was kicking in? She shook her head and forced a smile. "I'm sorry. What were you saying?"

"That my father does care." He scratched one eyebrow. "Or at least I think he must." He took another drink of coffee. "Come to think of it, I guess he hasn't really been engaged in the event, has he?"

Michael Nolan Senior's detached way of looking at life had very nearly scared Pam out of marrying Michael. *"You won't have to worry,"* he'd promised her when she'd broached the topic once. *"I take after my mom."* Pam had expected the birth of a grandson to break through her father-in-law's reserve. She was disappointed. Michael Senior rarely came to any of Jacob's sports events and showed up for birthdays and anniversaries clearly uncomfortable and visibly relieved when he could make his exit. When it became clear that Jacob wasn't going to become a medical doctor, Senior withdrew even more. Pam learned to walk a tightrope, showing respect for him as her father-in-law and her son's only living grandparent even as her dislike for the man grew.

In recent years Michael had started giving in to his father's demands to work longer hours and to center his life more around his busy medical practice and less around his family. He traveled more, and sometimes Pam wondered if he really spent every night in every hotel alone. She wondered, but she didn't know. She'd convinced herself it was better that way. For Jacob's sake.

Turning her back on Michael, she opened a cupboard, pulled out a loaf of bread, and began to make toast she didn't want. "Want some?" she asked without looking Michael's way.

"No, thanks. Think I'll take the dog out."

The toast popped up. Grabbing a piece, she slathered it with butter and sat down at the breakfast bar, watching as Michael halfheartedly tossed a Frisbee for Rambo. The grass needed to be mowed. And her flower beds were looking raggedy again. She hadn't deadheaded anything in over a week. *I really do have to get back into the yard. Unless I want an entire field of dandelions.*

Rambo barked, and Michael got down on all fours and started a wrestling match. He really was a beautiful man. How had the wall between them started, anyway? She blamed her breast cancer. But maybe that was oversimplifying. Maybe she'd given up too easily. Certainly she had shrunk away from confrontation—building a different kind of life than the one she wanted, immersing herself in community causes, learning to garden, and more recently, doing research for Jacob and his list.

She smiled wistfully, realizing she'd been digging dandelions the day Jacob had dragged her old backpack out of the loft . . . and his mother into helping with his list.

"Mom," he called from the back door. "What's this?"

"Oh my gosh," Pam said, shading her eyes with her hand and peering at the mildewed backpack. "Where on earth did you find that?"

"Loft of the garage," Jacob said. "I was looking for my dragon kite. Thought I'd take it over for Maddy and Megan."

"Well," Pam laughed, "you've unearthed a relic. You remember your father teasing me about my hippie days?" Jacob nodded. "Well, if that thing could talk . . ." She chuckled and shook her head, grateful it couldn't. There were some things about a parent a child should not know, and her days of hiking and camping included nights around campfires best forgotten. "Let's just say it's seen a lot of wilderness."

"Can I use it?"

"Suit yourself, but I'm telling you there are much more well designed backpacks available today."

"Oh, but they don't have the aura," Jacob said as he pulled the pack across his shoulders.

"Or the aroma." Pam wrinkled her nose and made a face. "You really should get something new."

But Jacob was adamant. He would have the backpack cleaned and repaired for next summer's llama trek in the Hoover Wilderness.

"Llama trek? Hoover Wilderness? I don't remember that one from the original list."

"Google it," Jacob said, then joked, "maybe you'll want to come along."

"All in the past, kiddo. All in the past."

"Come on," he urged. "At least think about it."

Pam smiled. Put her hand to her right shoulder. "Not to be a wimp, hon, but what the surgeon did made it pretty unlikely I could haul fifty pounds of equipment these days. You can't strengthen what isn't there anymore."

Flustered, Jacob looked down at the ground. "I'm sorry, Mom. I . . . I forgot."

She felt a hand on her shoulder. Michael's voice. "Earth to Pam," he said.

When had he come back inside? He was . . . nuzzling her neck? What was going on? Even as she wondered, she caught her breath and tilted her head just the right way. What was she doing . . . encouraging him? But it felt so good. Wasn't this how it was supposed to be? Shouldn't they be reaching for one another? She spun around on the barstool and leaned into his embrace. When his body began to respond, the doorbell rang.

"Company's coming," he whispered and stepped back, but not

before tracing the line of her neck down toward her scar. She instinctively pulled away, but he held her against him with one hand pressed to the small of her back while he stared into her eyes. The doorbell rang again. Michael backed off. "Your public awaits," he said.

"It's just Rainelle." Reaching for her coffee, she knocked it over instead. As she grabbed a kitchen towel and blotted it up, she muttered, "I hate that. She's started ringing the doorbell. Ten years we've lived in this house and she's always just tromped in. . . ." She finished mopping up and shouted, "It's open! Come in!"

Michael headed for the stairs. "You girls have fun," he said, then stopped short. "Nothing in the English language makes sense anymore." He shook his head as he recited things they'd both heard in recent days. "What a *nice* service. He looked so *natural*. You girls have *fun*. As if you were planning a Mary Kay party."

Pam looked up. "Since when do you know anything about Mary Kay parties?"

"Hey, baby. I'm in touch with my feminine side." The doorbell rang again and he shrugged and headed for the stairs. "Tell Rainelle and Betty I said thanks for helping."

He was almost flirting with her. What was going on? "What are you going to do today?" she asked.

He paused on the bottom stair. "Oh, I've got a full calendar. Walk the dog. Swim some laps in the pool. Watch 'Trading Spaces.'" He faked a smile and looked away. "I'm sorry about—" He motioned toward the table. "I just can't face the outpouring of required sympathy from people who—" He shook his head. "I just can't, that's all."

"I told you it's all right," Pam said. Now Rainelle was knocking. "Why doesn't she just come in?" Michael retreated up the stairs as she headed for the door.

"I was beginning to worry," Rainelle said.

"I hollered twice for you to come on in. Didn't you hear me?"

"I guess not."

"Michael said to say thank-you for helping."

"Isn't he going to be here?"

Pam shook her head. "I see that look," she said.

"What look?"

"That arched eyebrow disapproval thing you do," Pam said.

"I'm not disapproving. But if I were, it would only be because you don't need it all dumped on you."

"Thank you, Counselor," Michael said from the balcony above. He looked down at Pam. "If you want me to help, I will. I didn't think it would matter with Betty and Rainelle coming over."

"I said it's all right," Pam said.

Michael looked at Rainelle. "She says it's all right."

"And you just go on believing that," Rainelle retorted. "Like you believe everything else she says that makes life easier for you."

"Whoa," he said, raising both hands. "I confess, Counselor. Guilty of taking advantage of the best wife in the universe. Not to mention her two incredibly gifted and gorgeous friends." He lowered his hands. "Does that make you feel better?"

"It would if you meant any of it," Rainelle answered.

"Point taken," Michael said and retreated toward the bedroom.

Pam hurried into the kitchen and began to unload the dishwasher. Noisily.

"I'm sorry," Rainelle said. "I shouldn't have hassled him. But the way he treats you just rubs me the wrong way."

"Back off, Rainelle. For your information Michael has been treating me like a queen."

"Hey, I was just—"

"You were just being Tough Mama. Well, put her on ice. Okay? Michael's got enough people pressuring him, and the truth is neither of us needs to be scolded right now," she said, her voice wavering. "We're doing the best we can."

"Who else is putting pressure on Michael?" Rainelle asked.

"Just guess."

"You're kidding me. His *father*?"

"Um-hmm. Thinks Michael should be back at the office. Stiff

upper lip. Keep up appearances, never let anyone know you aren't superhuman and all that."

"I've always thought someone needed to create a skylight into that man's ego so he could see where the rest of the world lives." She mimed taking a chain saw to one of the countertops.

"Hmph," Pam snorted. "Not going to happen. At least not in my lifetime." She closed the dishwasher. "Truth be told, Senior isn't the only one worried about Michael. The guy you just scolded is someone I've never really seen before. He's always been so in control—even when we faced my cancer."

"Make that controll*ing*."

"Yes. All right. Controlling. But that's not always a bad thing. You and I both know that if he hadn't taken charge when I was sick and demanded we get some second opinions, I might not even be here." Was she really doing this? Defending Michael? Well, so be it. What she was saying was the truth. He might have been less than under-standing about the psychological effects of losing a breast, but he'd been amazing in the way he'd managed her medical care. She forced herself back into the moment. "These days he doesn't even want to decide what we have for dinner. If I didn't think he would snap out of it, I'd be really worried."

Betty arrived, and in the flurry of greetings and concerned ques-tions, no one heard Michael come down the front stairs. But there he was, standing at the end of the hall, Rambo at his side. After saying hello to Betty he announced, "We're going for a walk," and headed out the front door.

"Yes," Pam said in answer to Betty's unspoken question, "the man who has barely tolerated the family dog for years now treats Rambo like he's the most important creature in the world."

Betty smiled. "That's not too surprising. Rambo is a living, breathing connection to Jake."

"So am I," Pam said. "But he doesn't spend that much time with *me.*" *Unless I count those nights when he's crawled in beside me. And this morning.* She could feel her cheeks flushing at the thought.

"That's not necessarily bad," Betty said. "Remember when I told you both not to expect the other to be your counselor?"

"And Rambo is the answer?" Pam frowned and looked at Rainelle, who appeared just as dubious. "What can Rambo do?"

"Listen," Betty said.

"I would listen," Pam protested.

"Yes, but then you might try to help. Maybe Michael's way of grieving is just to be near the people who loved Jake. Maybe he needs someone to listen *without* answering back."

"Michael Senior is throwing a fit about what he calls 'Michael's need to get back to work instead of moping about doing nothing.'"

"Grief is the hardest work a person can do," Betty said. "I hope Dr. Nolan Senior will let him do it his way."

"I hope we all will," Pam said, with a pointed glance in Rainelle's direction.

"What's wrong?"

Instead of answering Rainelle's question, Pam handed her the piece of paper. "Read it," she said and got up to get a glass of water.

Dear Mr. and Mrs. Nolan,

I don't expect you will believe me or even want to hear this. Eddie Lee Monroe isn't a bad man. He made a mistake but he made it because of love. He was worried and he only wanted to know that the baby and me was all right. If I could make things different I would and so would Eddie Lee. We are parents too. If we could do something to change it we would. Someday I hope you will find it in your hearts to forgive us. We are so sorry.

The note was from Lisa Monroe. "What am I supposed to do with that?" Pam asked. She touched the edge of the note card. "And how did it get mixed in with the things from the funeral home?"

"I suppose she could have slipped in and out before the viewing times that were listed in the paper," Betty said. "She could have left this without anyone even seeing her."

"But why?" Pam reached for the note and stared at it.

Rainelle spoke up. "I think it's just what it appears to be—an apology and a plea for forgiveness." She took a deep breath. "Look, honey. I know we agreed to leave this between you and Malcolm, but I think you might want to ponder the idea that in some ways Eddie Lee Monroe is a victim of this situation, too."

Pam glared at her. "Really. Where's *he* buried?" Her eyes glimmered with angry tears as she crossed the kitchen to the back door and stood looking out.

"I'm not trying to hurt you," Rainelle said. "But the more Malcolm has worked on this case, the more evidence he finds that supports what I said before: Eddie Lee and Lisa Monroe are good people. Monroe has accepted responsibility for what amounts to a terrible mistake, and he doesn't want any legal maneuvering done on his behalf. He's much more concerned about his wife and baby than he is about himself." Rainelle paused. "And they're going to have a tough time of it without Eddie Lee's income."

"Is that supposed to bother me?" Pam's voice was shrill.

"It isn't supposed to do anything. All I'm saying is, don't paint monsters in your mind, because these people aren't monsters." Rainelle sighed. "I can't help it. As much as I hurt for you and Michael, I feel bad for the Monroes, too."

Pam inhaled sharply. She glanced at Betty, who was looking at Lisa's note, her expression indiscernible. "Excuse me if I can't call up sympathy for Eddie Lee Monroe's *life*. Why should he have any life at all? He took my—" Her voice broke and the tears came. "He took my *baby*, Rainelle." She murmured it again. "He took my baby. How can you sit there defending him? How can you?" Grabbing the box of tissues sitting in the middle of the kitchen table, she headed out the back door.

Rainelle's hand on her arm woke her up. After storming around the garden for a few minutes, Pam had been overcome with weariness and flopped onto a lounge chair by the pool fuming . . . crying . . . angry . . . and tired. Exhausted. Again. She must have dozed off. Her life these days was a weird combination of furious activity and fatigue from the third ring of hell. The fatigue was a good thing. Sleeping more than usual was better than staggering around the house like Michael.

"I'm sorry," Rainelle said as she settled on the lounge chair next to Pam's.

Pam sighed and squeezed her hand. "I know. You were just doing what you've always done."

"And that would be . . ."

"The Mother Teresa thing. The caring thing."

"But I hurt you," Rainelle said. "That's not very Mother Teresa-ish. I'm so sorry. I should have let it go when you reacted that way before. But I thought maybe since a little time has passed—" She ran her hand over her hair. "Obviously I don't really know *how* to help."

"You're here," Pam said and reached out for her, forcing a weak smile. "And you've addressed a lot of envelopes today."

"I blew it with Michael, too." Rainelle forced her own smile—big and fake. "At least I didn't mess up with Rambo. That's something."

"It's nearly impossible to be my friend right now."

"Difficult, yes. Impossible? Never." Rainelle squeezed her hand. "I'm not going anywhere."

"Good." She looked toward the house. "We should go in."

"Betty's cooking some pasta. She'll holler when it's ready." Rainelle settled back in the chair. "She's a gem, by the way. I'm glad you have her."

"I was worried you might be a little jealous."

"Oh, I didn't say I'm not a little jealous. But I'd be an idiot not to be grateful that you have someone who can honestly relate to what you're going through." She paused, then said, "So tell me about Michael."

"Tell you what about Michael?"

"How he's doing. You were really defensive in there. What's up?"

Pam sighed. "Nothing's up. Michael's . . . not doing well."

"Not doing well . . . how?"

"Not doing anything." When Rainelle didn't respond, Pam continued. "You think I'm joking. I'm not. He sleeps in. When he can't sleep anymore, he shuffles to the kitchen for coffee and then takes Rambo for a walk. I have no idea where they go, but they're gone for a long time most mornings. When he comes home, more often than not he goes into the media room. Sometimes he turns on the TV. Sometimes he doesn't. But he almost always ends up asleep on the couch by lunchtime. If we eat at the same time, it's torture because we just sit across from each other staring out the window. Sometimes we pretend to read the paper just to make it look like we aren't in a stupor.

"Then I head out to the garden—but I wander around more than I garden—and Michael takes Rambo for another walk. By evening I've either ordered food in or we rummage in the refrigerator." She paused. "We still have a freezer full of casseroles. We don't even *like* casseroles. But we eat them. It doesn't matter. And then the evenings." She took a deep breath and let it out slowly. "As early as possible I head upstairs and hope for an old movie to stare at. Once or twice Michael has come in and watched with me. But usually he falls asleep in the media room watching TV." She lifted her hands in a frustrated gesture. "And that, my dear friend, is the pathetic truth of things at the Nolans right now. The doctor is definitely *not* 'in' . . . in any sense of that word."

"Have you two been able to talk about—"

"About Jacob?"

"Actually," Rainelle said, "I was thinking more about the two of you. I mean . . . facing something terrible together could be healing."

Pam just stared at her. "Betty says a huge number of marriages get in trouble when a child is lost." She sighed. "Which, I suppose, means Michael and I are a shoo-in for divorce court, because we were already in trouble before this happened." She paused. "Funny thing, though, part of me is starting to rethink all of that. For the three minutes a day when I can really think." She told Rainelle about the nights Michael had crawled into bed beside her. And his hug.

"Really," Rainelle said.

Pam shrugged. "It was nice to be reaching out to each other instead of just coexisting. Even for a minute." She pulled her knees up and got comfortable again. "I know you don't approve of Michael, but—"

"I *love* Michael," Rainelle said. "I introduced the two of you. Remember? And if *that* Michael would come back, I'd think you were crazy *not* to be crazy about him."

Pam looked up toward the second story bedroom suite. "Even before this morning there have been glimpses."

"Good."

"I think so. But it's kind of scary in a way, too."

"Of course it's scary, girl. Just when you'd figured a way to cope with Michael barely being *in* your life, things look like they could change. But your guard is up, and you don't want to risk being hurt again. Especially now."

"I'm barely maintaining status quo in the sanity department as it is," Pam said. "Any other waves breaking on this shore, and I'm pretty sure you and Betty will have to cart me out to the Regional Center."

"You listen to me, Pamela Nolan. I know you feel shaky. But the truth is they could put a picture of you next to the word *survivor* on the Wikipedia Web site."

Pam shook her head.

"You don't believe me?" Rainelle began to count on her fingers. "The late George Fletcher. The dumpy neighborhood called SunnyVale. Dottie Fletcher's retreat from your life. Working your way through nursing school. Childbirth—*without* an epidural, as I recall. Michael Senior. Michael Junior. Cancer. Jacob." Rainelle raised both eyebrows and peered at Pam. "And there you sit, still clothed—in a size ten—and in your right mind."

"Size fourteen," Pam corrected her.

"Whatever. You are a winner, Mrs. Nolan."

"If you're going to be my cheerleader you're going to need pom-poms."

Rainelle jumped up and strutted around leading an imaginary cheer.

"I love you," Pam said, swiping at tears even as she laughed. "Everyone should have a Diva-Ray to cheer them on." She looked back at the house. "And all my poor husband has is his father ragging on him."

"What do you mean 'your poor husband'? He has *you*."

"You heard Betty earlier. I'm too deep in my own 'Slough of Despond' to help Michael."

"Well," Rainelle said. "Betty's there for you. Maybe her husband could talk to Michael."

"I thought about that. For about three seconds. Michael and Stan aren't a good match."

Rainelle nodded. "I can't say I'm surprised to hear you say that. Stan is biscuits and gravy, and Michael is sushi and—" she shrugged—"and he's a snob. Now I admit he's a foxy snob, but—"

"I get it," Pam said. "And you're right. But there's more to it than that. It started when I said I wanted to ask Stan to speak at the funeral." She quoted Michael. "'We don't need some self-righteous, right-wing Bible-thumper standing up there and telling us how Jesus can make it all better.'"

"I didn't hear Stan say anything like that. As I recall, he just read the Bible. And Michael objected to that because . . . ?"

"Oh, forget it. *I* thought what Stan said was comforting. I even asked him for a copy of what he read at the service. I've read over it more than once."

"And?"

"I want to believe what it says about heaven. I want to believe Jacob is there. Sometimes I picture him sky diving, or rappelling down a wall, or shooting some heavenly rapids, and for just a fraction of an instant it helps." She smiled. "I mean, sky diving in heaven doesn't require a reserve chute, does it? It's all perfectly safe there. And

I do think Jacob's there. I'm not sure what it's like, but he was a good kid and there's just no reason he wouldn't be in heaven."

"Jacob was as good as they come." Rainelle laughed softly. "I like the idea of him shooting some heavenly rapids." She grinned. "Do you think they use kayaks or can they just body surf over the rocks?"

Betty opened the back door. "Spaghetti's ready, girls," she called out.

Rainelle extended her hand. "Let's get you something to eat."

As they headed for the back door, Pam gave Rainelle a hug. "You're the best, girl friend. Simply the best."

"True, dat," Rainelle said, opening the door and bowing low to sweep Pam into the house. While Betty dished up spaghetti, Rainelle explained what she and Betty had done with the sympathy cards and memorial gifts while Pam napped by the pool. "They're all addressed and ready to go. There's a list of who donated how much and, believe it or not, the unsealed thank-you cards are alphabetized so you can find them easily if you want to insert a personal note."

"You've got a very generous group of friends," Betty said. "You'll be able to do something very nice in Jake's memory."

"The best friends are right here in this room," Pam said, her eyes filling with tears. "What would I have done without the two of you these past two weeks?"

Betty waved the compliment away. "You're welcome. Now let's eat."

"Amen, sister," Rainelle said. "Dessert awaits."

"Dessert?"

"We're going out for hot fudge sundaes."

"I can't," Pam said, putting her hand to her rear and patting.

"Of course you can," Rainelle said, inspecting Pam's derrière. "Those pants are loose, girl. Time you filled them back out again."

Michael came in, inhaling with relish. "Smells good. Is there enough for one more?"

"There's enough for an army," Betty said. "I'll never learn to cook for two when the kids are gone." With a pained expression, she turned away. "Open mouth, insert foot," she said, reaching for another pasta bowl for Michael.

"Welcome to my world." Michael sprinkled grated Romano over the unadorned pasta. "Thank you for coming to help Pam." Grabbing a fork, he headed for the media room.

After dinner, Pam flipped through the envelopes on the table, set aside half a dozen, and handed the rest to Rainelle and Betty. "Seal and stamp," she said. "We'll mail them on the way to get ice cream."

"I'll put these in another envelope," Betty said, picking up the pile of checks. "You can think about that another time."

*Another time.* Would there ever come a day when Jacob's death didn't hover over time?

––––––––

She must have been crying in her sleep. She didn't always know when she was doing that, but often when she started awake in the night her pillow was damp with her tears. More than once, when she woke up, Rambo was standing by the bed, his chin resting on the mattress. When she opened her eyes, he'd whine softly and kiss her hand. Once or twice she had even invited him to crawl up on the bed. But tonight it wasn't Rambo beside her.

"Shh," Michael whispered. "It's all right." Sitting down on the edge of the bed, he began to stroke her forehead and temples, following imaginary lines back through her hair, gently massaging her scalp. Closing her eyes, Pam relaxed as Michael combed the tension out of her body.

"That's better," Michael said when her sobs had quieted and her breathing evened out. He raised her hand to his lips and began to kiss the tip of each finger.

As Pam opened her eyes and looked up into his face, Michael slid to his knees beside the bed and held the palm of her hand to his cheek. He'd been crying, too. She reached for him, ignoring the flicker of an inner warning light. She'd been so lonely for so long . . . and so empty.

Backing across the bed, she pulled Michael toward her. "Hold me," she whispered. The words were barely intelligible, but when Michael responded and pulled her close, the emotional barriers she had erected over the past few years came down. As she gave herself to the moment, Michael answered back. They clung to one another and began to cry again, sharing a sorrow born of grief for Jacob that quickly became a keening about much more than their lost son.

"I'm sorry," Michael whispered through his tears. "Oh, my love. I am. So. Very. Sorry." He kissed her cheek, her jaw, the side of her neck, her collarbone. When he encountered the lace trimmed neckline of her nightgown, he pulled it aside and pressed his lips against the tip of her mastectomy scar.

Instinctively, Pam raised her hand to shield it, but Michael denied her, planting kisses along the ridge of the scar as he cried and whispered how beautiful she was . . . how terrified he'd been of losing her . . . how lost he had been when she pulled away . . . how much he loved her. "You're so beautiful . . . don't you know how beautiful you are . . . how you shine," he murmured, "how you shine . . ."

Longing to cross the abyss of brokenness in her life, desperate to have at least some part of the darkness healed, Pam unlocked the part of herself she had guarded carefully for so long. Her hands and then her entire body remembered and responded to her husband, transporting her past the pain into a place where none of the brokenness existed, a place where they were once again in love—where nothing had happened to harm that love. Together they mourned heartbreak and found joy, lamented separation and discovered reunion. Finally, as their breathing evened out and the room grew quiet, Michael curled himself around her and cradled her in his arms, and they slept sweet, sweet sleep.

# {nine}

PAM WOKE TO THE SOUND of Freaky Freddy yapping next door. She wrinkled her nose. *Coffee.* Images from the night before flashed in her conscious mind evoking an array of confusing and conflicting emotions. And then . . . the crushing weight of loss descended. And guilt. She had known *pleasure.* She had not thought of Jacob. Even when she woke just now, her first thought hadn't been of Jacob. How could that be? How could she have forgotten, even for a moment? With a groan, she sat up. She reached for the bathrobe that lay on the floor and headed out into the hall. Michael was standing just a few feet away, a coffee mug in each hand. Apparently he'd paused to look into Jacob's room.

"Good morning," he said and held a mug out for her.

"Good morning." She was blushing. Or hot flashing. Either way, she knew her face had to be red. She was embarrassed. *Guilty is more like it. How could last night have happened? How could we have been so . . . selfish?* Intending to retreat downstairs with her coffee, she took a step around him, but as she did so, Michael reached for her. She shied away, looking pointedly into Jacob's bedroom and then toward Michael as she shook her head no.

"What? I can't put my arm around you?"

She cleared her throat. She couldn't look at him, so she took a sip of coffee instead. "I can't just go back in time and ignore—" Helplessly, she gestured toward Jacob's empty bed.

Michael's voice was strained. "Were you in the same room with me last night? Because it didn't seem to me that we were ignoring anything. We cried halfway through it." He paused. "I thought we

107

were helping each other. I thought maybe we were going to get past—at least part of the past."

She didn't even realize she was doing it, but apparently as he talked, Pam had raised her hand to cover the place where her breast had been, because the next thing she knew Michael was grabbing her hand and almost shouting, "What do I have to do to prove to you that I don't *care* about that!"

"It's not . . . that. Not entirely. Things just aren't that simple. And it's not just about Jacob." She could look him in the eye now. "And you should know that."

She started to walk away, but he put his hand on her shoulder. Angry, she spun back around and stared up at him. Expecting defensiveness, she was surprised. The sadness in his eyes was almost palpable.

"All right," he said. "You don't have to draw me a picture. I understand." He looked down at the cup of coffee in his hand. "I suppose I should apologize, then. For last night." He cleared his throat. "I—I thought maybe we were on the same page about trying to—" He broke off. "Never mind. My bad."

As he turned around and retreated down the hall, Pam argued with herself. Part of her wanted to call out to him. Part of her wanted to try to build on what they'd experienced last night in the dark. They'd clung to each other, whispered their hurts, comforted each other, and for a few hours they'd remembered love. But she was wide awake now, and one night of reunion simply could not erase all the other nights when she'd heard him come home late and prayed he wouldn't bother to make excuses. If she allowed herself to hope for better things, and Michael went back to his old ways . . . No. She couldn't knowingly risk more pain. Not now. Better to leave things as they were than to hope.

She could hear Michael banging around in one of the guest bedrooms where he'd been sleeping for nearly a year—except when Jacob was home. They'd kept up appearances for Jacob. What if he wasn't only angry? What if he was hurt, too? Well, what if he was? He deserved it. Did he really expect one night of lovemaking to heal the chasm between them?

*Healing.* Back in her room Pam started to get dressed, then paused to look at herself in the full length mirror. He'd said it didn't bother him. But if he really didn't mind what the cancer had done to her body, then why hadn't he fought harder to prove it to her? Why hadn't he insisted they go to counseling together before things got out of hand?

*Would you have gone?* She honestly didn't know. It seemed so long ago now. And so . . . minor compared to what they were facing now. Clutching her shirt in one hand, she slumped down onto the bench in her dressing room. Was he sincere? Was there still a glimmer of real love between them? Did he really want to try to find it? The idea was terrifying. Terrifying and . . . Pam looked at herself in the mirror and shook her head. Too much. She couldn't deal with it now.

Downstairs she saw that Michael had scrawled a note on the white board in the laundry room. *Gone to retrieve Rambo.* What a relief. Betty had taken Rambo home with her last night for a "play date" with Reba. With any luck, by the time Michael got back with the dog, he would have had more time to think things through and to realize that now was not the time to try to fix their marriage.

---

*Great. Just great.* Betty's minivan was gone. Michael pressed the brake and prepared to turn around. He should have called before coming over to get Rambo. Glancing down at his watch, Michael did a double take. *Duh.* It was Sunday. The Novacs were at church. The dogs must be inside. He'd head back to the "community" entrance— "trailer park" wasn't a politically correct term anymore—and drive over later.

His foot still on the brake, Michael looked the place over, wondering if it made Saint Stan feel better about himself to call the oversized camper a "modular home." He didn't know how they stood it, all those kids crammed into a three-bedroom trailer. He would have thought Betty crazy if he didn't know her better. She'd planted flowers all along the chain link fence. Some kind of vine that was blooming bright blue and white and purple. A huge vegetable garden started on one side of the place and stretched out of sight around the back. How could she possibly be happy living here? He could remember his mom sweating over a pressure canner when he was little. No woman should have to do that. Green beans were only fifty cents a can. Novac should be ashamed of himself.

*Perfect. Just perfect.* The front door was opening and here was Rambo bounding across the yard barking his head off. And Saint Stan himself, yawning and stretching. Must have worked the night shift. The guy was ripped. Michael put his hand on his own former six-pack. He had to get back to the gym. He had to get out of here. After what he'd just been through with Pam, he didn't need a one-on-one with Saint Stan.

"Sorry," he said as he got out of the car and walked toward the gate. "Didn't mean to wake you. I didn't think about Sunday—and church."

"I worked until about four this morning," Novac said. "Catching a nap before I head over for the ten o'clock service."

It probably made the guy feel great, standing out here in his muscle shirt, looking down his nose at Michael, knowing what he knew, talking about going to church. Why hadn't Michael just waited until after lunch? One more stellar example of his thought process these days. And now here he was staring up at a guy who was about five inches taller than him. Which had nothing to do with why he felt so uncomfortable around Novac. Maybe he should just get it over with.

"Look," he said, "about that day when you came and got me—"

Stan interrupted him. "I think it'd be best if we both forgot that day. Don't you?"

"I just didn't want you to think—"

Novac's hand rested on the gate latch. He didn't open up. "Like I said, Doc. No need to bring it up. I've had to keep a lot of secrets."

"I know what you must be thinking." *Why am I doing this? Why do I care?* "Kim's a nurse at the hospital. She has a niece with a rare endocrine disorder. I helped out with some referrals to a specialist in Omaha. A guy I went to school with. Our friendship just happened. I didn't plan to—I didn't mean for it to—"

Novac interrupted him. "You didn't *un*plan it, either."

"Look," Michael said. "I'm a big boy. I don't need a caretaker and I most definitely do *not* need a judge." What was it about this guy that made him feel so defensive, anyway? Why did he care? *Because of Jacob.* Jacob had spent a lot of time here. The idea that Jacob might have known about Kim put a knot in Michael's gut. What was it about these people that drew Jacob—and now Pam—into their circle, anyway? He looked up at Novac. "Can I come in?"

Stan opened the gate and waved him through. Michael was glad Rambo was around. It gave him something to do while he tried to talk his way out of the hole he'd dug for himself. Walking over to the stoop, he sat down and began to pet Rambo while he spoke, but the dog wouldn't hold still. Finally, Michael let go, and Rambo and Reba ambled off around the back of the trailer and out of sight.

"I know it isn't right," he said, "and I'm not going to defend myself. It was a mistake, and I will end it." He paused. "But I can't exactly do it over the phone." He glanced at Novac, expecting some level of understanding. Maybe just a nod. But Saint Stan could have been made of marble at that moment, standing there, his arms crossed, his feet about a foot apart. "Believe me or not," Michael said and stood back up, "I will do it. I just don't have the energy for that kind of confrontation right now." He forced himself to look Novac in the eye. "I'm sure you can understand that this kind of thing could be devastating for Pam right now. She doesn't need any more pain in her life."

Finally a reaction. Novac unfolded his arms. "You are a real piece of work, Doc."

"I beg your pardon?"

"You can sell that pile of stuff about being concerned about your wife somewhere else, because I know it's a bunch of—" He broke off.

Swallowed. Took a deep breath. "If you were really concerned about Pam, you could end this other thing in about—" he snapped his fingers—"that much time. So let's be real. Your wife deserves about a thousand percentage points better than you've been giving her."

"What would you know about what I have or have not given my wife?" Michael snapped. He looked around pointedly, angry at the guy's holier-than-thou attitude. "My wife gardens because she enjoys it. She doesn't have to dig in the dirt to keep from going hungry."

Novac's face flushed. He put his arms behind his back, looking even more like a drill sergeant about to lose it. But when he finally spoke, his Darth Vader voice was calm. "You're way ahead of me in the 'stuff' department, Doc. Always will be. But answer me this: can you name the ten richest people from 1980?"

"What?"

Stan waited. "Can't do it, can you?" He continued, "Answer me this: does having all that stuff make *you* happy? Because I seem to remember Jake spending more time here than at home with all that stuff you're so proud of."

"Thank you, Dr. Phil. You've been great. I've taken stock of my poor performance as a human being and resolved to make some changes." Michael shouted for Rambo and headed back toward the gate. As Rambo bounded up, he turned around. "One thing, though. You forgot to bring God up. I'm disappointed in you, Saint Stan. I really expected you to preach a little more. It is Sunday, after all." He opened the gate and headed for the car.

"You've gotta hate what you're doing to her," Stan blurted out, closing the gate so Reba wouldn't follow Rambo out.

"I came for my dog, not to audition a life coach."

"Look," Stan said. "If I gave you the impression I think I'm better than you, that was wrong. Betty and I wouldn't even be married today if she hadn't stuck by me when I didn't deserve it. And beyond. Which is probably why I react the way I do when I'm around you. You think I'm jealous about the money? Well, I don't expect you to believe me, but I'm not." He put his hands at his waist. "It just makes me mad to see someone as smart as you being so dumb."

Michael didn't know what to say to that. He opened the back door for Rambo to jump in and then walked around the car and slid in behind the wheel. He started the engine and pulled away without looking back. The guy had a lot of nerve calling him dumb.

Instead of driving home, Michael headed across town to Holmes Park. Parking the Beemer where he could look across the lake, he sat for a long while thinking. Rambo lay quietly stretched out on the back seat while Michael stared at a flock of ducks paddling around. Everyone thought his odd behavior these past few weeks was all about Jacob. Michael knew better, and this morning as he stared at the state capitol building just visible in the distance, he faced the other reality he'd been trying to avoid. He had the right house, the right car, the right friends, the right wife. From the outside looking in, Dr. Michael Nolan was at the pinnacle of his life. Only from his side of things, he felt like he was looking up into the opening of a tunnel he'd dug. Because if Jacob was gone and Pam didn't care about their marriage . . .

His mind went back to the image of Stan Novac standing in the yard of his glorified trailer. Michael didn't like him one bit. But he did have to give the guy credit for one thing. He was a good judge of character.

---

On a Sunday evening a little over four weeks after Jacob's funeral, Dr. Nolan Senior arrived uninvited at the front door. When Pam told him Michael was resting, the white-haired patriarch growled, "That's the problem," brushed past her, and headed for the stairs.

"In the media room," Pam said and Senior detoured toward the back of the house. She looked down at Rambo. "There's going to be shouting." She turned the opposite direction toward the laundry room. "Time for a walk," she said.

When Pam and Rambo returned, Michael was just descending the stairs. He'd showered and shaved and put on a sports coat. "Dad needs me to do rounds for him tomorrow morning," he said. "So I'm meeting him at the hospital tonight to go over a few charts."

"You're not ready," Pam said.

"Well, he made it clear that I'd better get ready if I don't want to get booted out on my ear."

"He wouldn't do that."

"Probably not. But he's right about one thing. It's not doing any good for me to lay around here all day." He shrugged. "So here I go."

"He doesn't understand," Pam protested.

"Is this the same woman who was telling her friends I'm practically catatonic not long ago?"

"But I don't think—"

He held up his hand and pressed his fingertips against her lips. "It's my job, Pam. It's time I tried to do it." He touched the tip of her nose lightly. "But thanks for the show of concern. It's very touching— in a controlling, motherly sort of way."

Michael came home late. Very late. Rambo hurried out into the hallway to greet him. He said no very firmly, and then Pam heard the guest room door close. Rambo came back to her side and lay down with a gentle sigh that portrayed what sounded like disappointment. Lying in the dark, Pam stretched out her hand and stroked the dog's head.

---

For a split second Michael doubted the old code would work. Certainly he wouldn't have blamed her if she'd changed it. But then the garage door began to lift. He closed the little door on the touch-pad and retreated to the car. As the door closed behind him, he hesitated, looking down at his hands resting on the steering wheel while the garage door wheels squealed their way along the track, slowly shutting out the daylight. He sat for a moment in the darkened garage. This was how things felt most of the time now. Like he was in a room where things wouldn't quite come into focus.

At the office, his father had acted like nothing had changed. *Just do the work*" was the only advice Senior had given him that first day when he encountered Michael standing outside a patient's room staring at the unopened chart in his hand. Senior had read the body language and known Michael was "having a moment." When he walked by he didn't even pause before saying, "Just do the work, *Doctor.*" And Michael obeyed. Somehow he made his brain work when he was in the office. Most of what he'd faced this past week was routine. The nurses and PA's didn't expect him to talk much, and he was able to keep blundering through. He rarely knew what time it was until someone reminded him he hadn't had lunch. He had no appetite, so instead of eating he drove around aimlessly, listening to the radio, waiting to go back for the afternoon.

Things had been no different only a few days ago. Malcolm Sutter had said Michael and Pam absolutely *had* to be there when Monroe entered his plea. And so they went, clutching each other's hands as they listened to the judge ask Monroe an agonizingly long set of questions, commiserating later and agreeing that it felt like the judge didn't *want* Monroe pleading guilty. But by the time they were back home, the gulf between them had yawned open again.

Pam obviously thought he was working the old long hours again, and she didn't question his not being home for dinner most nights. Most days he thought up excuses to stop at the hospital instead of going home. Or he stopped at the cemetery. Pam left cryptic notes on the refrigerator like she always had. The name *Novac* appeared far too often. It was just like old times again except for Rambo being happy to see him when he was home.

He'd made a couple of lame attempts to spend time with Pam, but she obviously was doing it out of duty rather than desire. *Desire.* Funny choice of words. He knew better than to approach Pam in that way again, and yet he couldn't forget that night. He'd told her—again—that he didn't care about the changes in her body, and he'd meant it. He'd never stopped wanting her, but now he was faced with the possibility that she might never want him again. He wouldn't blame her. Still, the thought sent him into that downward spiral where occupying the spot next to Jacob didn't seem like such a bad idea.

If she was home, Pam spent the daylight hours in the garden. After sunset she headed upstairs to the master suite. Michael spent his time hiding out in the media room. As far as he could tell, neither of them had been in Jacob's room since the funeral. He'd stood at the door once or twice, thinking about what to do with all of Jacob's stuff. Both times he'd gone back downstairs and tried to distract himself with a football game or movie on TV.

Sometimes when he walked by Jacob's room, Rambo was curled up on the bed. Sometimes he hopped down and followed Michael to the guest room. Michael liked that. He hated everything else about his life. He began to think about Kim again. Her acceptance. Her warmth. Her laugh. But every single time he thought of Kim, he also saw Stan Novac snapping his fingers.

Today when he'd run out of things to do at the hospital, he'd headed home, but at the last minute he'd taken an extra lap on a roundabout and reversed his direction. Almost as an afterthought. Right this minute he just couldn't face the thousands of reminders at home of what a failure he was. Of course this was wrong, too. He could still hear Stan Novac's voice in his head. But here he was and Pam didn't care anyway. So he got out of the car, went inside, and sat down to wait. He told himself he would do the right thing. He would end it. His mind kept creating scenarios, and then he must have fallen asleep, because the next thing he knew Kim was kissing his cheek.

She must have been home for a few minutes because she'd changed out of her scrubs and into jeans and a cropped T-shirt that showed off the best part of her anatomy—although he could have done without the piercing. At least she'd chosen a simple white gold ring instead of some fake jewel. She'd teased him a while back about buying her a diamond for her belly button. "No one would have to know," she'd suggested. "But it would be kind of fun to have a secret reminder that I'm yours when I pass you in the hall."

"You're not mine," he'd said and pulled away from her. He'd

avoided her for weeks after that, but he'd eventually come back. She was bright and easy to talk to. There wasn't any negative history to try to fix. No dark cloud loomed above the dinner table when they ate together. She wasn't judgmental, and she didn't second-guess him. "No strings attached," she'd promised. He chose to believe her.

If he expected recriminations because he'd been incommunicative for over a month now, he was surprised.

"Hello, stranger." She went to the couch opposite him and sat down, curling one foot beneath her and stretching one tanned arm out across the back of the couch.

"I thought you might have changed the garage door code," he said, pushing on the footrest of the recliner so he could sit up.

"Why?" she said. "I didn't think you'd be giving it out to serial killers or anything."

He shrugged. "I thought you'd be upset." *End it now. End it. Now.*

She leaned forward, her lovely face a mask of concern. "In case you haven't noticed, I'm not really into making things harder for the people I love. I missed you, though. And I'm glad you're back." She paused again. "How are you, Mike? And don't give me the automated response. I really care, and if you want to talk, I'm here to listen." She slid to the floor, crawled across to where he sat, and put her hand on his knee.

It was a simple gesture. But when he looked down into her sweet face all he could think of was Pam and how much he wished that she would do something like this. Just ask how he was doing.

"You don't have to feel sorry for me," he said gruffly. "That's not why I'm here."

"I don't feel sorry for you. Not the way you mean. I hurt for you. It's all right to hurt, you know. To be human. You don't have to be Super Doc when you're with me."

When her eyes glimmered with tears, he almost lost it. "I should go. I shouldn't be here. This is—"

She raised up on her knees and put her arms around him.

That simple gesture of caring broke him, but not for the reason Kim assumed. He broke down because of guilt. He'd made a mess of his life, and now he was doing the same thing for this young woman who thought she could make it all better. He could almost hear Stan Novac snapping his fingers, saying *just like that*. He had intended to make it short and sweet, but somehow it didn't work out that way. It ended up long and emotional and disconnected.

"I need to go now," he finally said and started to get up.

"Get some rest first." At his questioning look Kim lifted her shoulder in a half shrug. "Look. I'm a smart chick, Michael. I knew this was coming." She blinked a few times and looked away. "And honestly, it's for the best. But you're a wreck. You can't go home like this, and I don't want to have to worry about you stopping in some bar and having one too many and *then* driving home." She stood up and grabbed the afghan. "So stretch out for a little while." She covered him with the afghan, kissed his cheek, and left the room. He fell asleep. Some time in the wee hours of morning, he started awake. The house was quiet. He sat up and looked around him. How could someone sleep that many hours of dreamless sleep and still feel exhausted?

As quietly as he could, Michael backed his car out of the garage, grateful that it was still dark. Just as he headed back to the car after entering the code to lower the garage door, a police car turned the corner about a block away and headed in his direction. His heart lurched. He broke out in a cold sweat. His hands started to shake. The car slowed, and the officer—who was not Stan Novac—nodded and kept going. Inside the Beemer, Michael leaned forward and rested his head on the steering wheel until he stopped shaking.

---

"I wish you hadn't said we'd do this," Michael groused as he drove past the trailer park gatehouse and up the gravel road toward the Novacs' fenced lot.

"Well, then you should have answered my page last night and told me so," Pam snapped. "I certainly hope your father appreciates your agreeing to be on call at the last minute like that. I would have hoped he'd let you get back into the swing of things a little more gradually."

"Are you going to nag me about going back to work again?"

"What do you mean 'again'? I haven't nagged. I've been concerned, but I haven't nagged."

"Not with words," Michael said. "But you have a real talent for letting me know what you think of my decisions. At least the ones you don't approve of."

"It's not that I don't approve. It's just that I wanted it to be your idea. Not a response to your father's bullying. You haven't been sleeping well, you've lost weight, and now you're on call and gone half the night. It worries me."

"Right," Michael said.

"You don't have to be sarcastic. I *have* been concerned." *Why is he so angry? Lately it seems like he's angry all the time.*

"Well, you can stop being concerned. I'm getting along all right. So let it go." He peered straight ahead as he said, "In case you've forgotten, I'm the one who earns the living, and our lifestyle isn't cheap—to put it mildly. We need the money. Unless, of course, *you* want to try your hand at the pleasures of double-wide living, too."

"All I'm saying is you need time to heal. Surely your father can understand that."

"He's not a monster, Pam. And he made some good points. As far as my needing time to heal, hanging around the house answering the phone and pretending things are fine isn't going to heal anything. Things aren't fine, and I can't seem to do anything about it. But I *can* do something positive at work, where people depend on me and where, once in a while, I actually have an answer to a problem. That's a good feeling. I want it back."

"I want to feel better, too," Pam said. "Which is why I told the Novacs we could come tonight. I know you don't exactly click with Stan. But I thought maybe you could get past that and appreciate being around people who loved him—who knew him—I thought maybe somehow it would help."

Rambo moved forward and rested his chin on the back of the seat. When Pam glanced at him, his dark eyes were alert and his tail wagging as he peered through the windshield. At least Michael had seemed to care about *him* recently. "Look at it this way. Tonight will be good for Rambo. Look how excited he is. He's been so sad since Ja—since the accident. But he always perks up when he's with Reba." As she reached over to scratch behind the dog's ears, Michael spoke up.

"Jacob," he said.

"What?"

"You did it again."

"What are you talking about?"

"You didn't say his name. Our son's name. It's Jacob. Stop avoiding it."

Pam concentrated on looking out the side window of the Suburban and didn't reply.

"And what's this about doing it for the dog?" He was almost sneering.

"His tail started wagging the minute we turned in at the gatehouse." She scratched behind Rambo's ears as she spoke to him. "You know where we're headed, and you like it."

Michael made a face. "You talk to him like he's human."

"And you don't?" She tapped Michael on the shoulder. "He's found ways to scale the walls of your fortress recently. Or was that your twin brother tossing the Frisbee around in the backyard with him last weekend? Don't look now, Dr. Nolan, but I think there's a latent dog lover somewhere inside you."

He snorted a protest.

"You have to admit Rambo's been good company lately."

"If he's such good company, maybe I should just let the two of you have fun at the Novacs' and I'll bow out. I didn't want to come anyway. You were the one who pushed for it."

"I didn't push for anything," Pam said. "I thought you said I should stop hibernating at home. I thought you'd understand my wanting to make my first night 'out' with someone who's been through what we have and survived. Someone who wouldn't treat us like we have leprosy. And besides that, I didn't want to hurt Betty's feelings."

Michael pulled the Suburban over to the side of the road and put it in park. "Now we're getting somewhere." He mimicked her voice. "We mustn't offend Jacob's *other* family. We wouldn't want to hurt their feelings. We can't act like we think we're too good to have dinner at the trailer park."

Pam glowered at him. "You sounded like your father just then." She took in a deep breath. "Look. This isn't getting us anywhere. I know you never approved of the friendship between the boys. I know you think we're somehow above all this." She gestured around her, for the first time noticing the window boxes filled with flowers on the trailer across the street. "But can't we just for tonight be two people who lost a son accepting comfort from two other people who also lost—"

"I hate it when you do that," Michael snapped.

"What? When I do what?"

"We didn't *lose* Jacob. He died. He didn't leave us. And he sure as heck didn't 'graduate to heaven,' as the Novacs are so fond of saying. I cannot believe there are people who talk like that. But what I really can't believe is that *you're* starting to do it. As if that makes it all better. Why can't you say the word *dead*? It's a clinical reality. Why do you have to use stupid euphemisms? The next time some idiot says they're sorry I lost my son, I think I'm going to ask them to help me look for him." He took a breath before saying, "And why can't you ever say his name?"

She'd listened to the diatribe with her gaze fixed on the window box of flowers. Rambo had sidled toward her. She could feel his breath on her shoulder as she sat trying to keep from bursting into tears. Finally she said what he wanted to hear. "Jacob. Jacob Michael

Nolan." Her voice wavered, and she put her hand to her chest. "I don't say it because when I do it hurts. Here. A physical pain." She cleared her throat and fought against the looming tears. "I didn't know it would actually *hurt* like this." In the silence that followed, she studied her lap, wishing for all she was worth that Michael would just let go of the steering wheel and reach for her hand. If he did that, she'd be able to get past everything else he'd said.

"Yeah, well . . . get used to it," he said, biting off the words with masochistic pleasure, "because this is your life now."

She stared at him in disbelief. He wasn't even looking at her. He was looking straight ahead at the road. "I won't," she replied. "I refuse to get used to this—this broken life." She put her hand on the door handle. "If this is all there is, Michael—if this is it, then—" She shook her head and opened the car door.

"What are you doing?" Finally he looked at her.

"I'm going to dinner at Betty and Stan's. In the middle of all of this, they are the only people we know who seem to have some kind of perspective that's gotten them through. Even Rainelle doesn't know what to say—how to be around me anymore. But Betty knows when to talk, when to be quiet, when to pour coffee. She's helping me cope."

"Poor Pamela, stuck with a big bad husband who doesn't understand. And as for coping, of course she can cope. We didn't bury *her* son six weeks ago."

Weariness settled over her. What was the use, anyway? It must have been her imagination, thinking she'd seen flickers of the old Michael recently. Maybe grief could make a person see things that didn't even exist anymore, just because they wanted them so desperately. Right now, she could almost imagine he felt sorry for what he'd just said. He'd let go of the steering wheel and dropped his hands into his lap. His face was slack. Almost like he was ready to say something nice. But she didn't care anymore. Whatever he said, it would probably just be another lie.

"Congratulations, Dr. Nolan," she said. "After twenty-five years I thought I knew all the good, the bad, and the ugly there was to know about you. But you've just managed to shock even me. I had no idea you could be so insensitive and cruel."

"Life is cruel. And we had both better get used to it."

His tone of voice wasn't so much bitter as it was despairing. But that didn't matter, either. She didn't have the energy to try anymore tonight.

"No," she said. "I won't." Calling Rambo to her side, Pam closed the car door and headed up the road toward the Novacs'. What she was longing for didn't happen. As she walked away she heard the gravel crunch beneath the Suburban's tires. Michael was leaving.

---

"No Dr. Nolan?" Betty asked as she opened the door.

Pam shook her head and hoped Betty wouldn't ask for details.

"Well, tell him we missed him," Betty said, stepping onto the concrete stoop to pet Rambo. "The girls took Reba for a walk. They meant to meet you at the gatehouse, but—"

Rambo interrupted Betty's explanation with a flying leap off the stoop. Charging to the fence, he danced back and forth, wriggling with joy as Reba came into view at the opposite end of the lane, practically dragging Megan and Maddy toward the yard.

Betty laughed, "Well—there you have it. Come inside and help me get a salad together, would you? Stan should be home from work soon. He's gonna be sorry Michael didn't come. Are you sure we can't lure him with meat loaf and potatoes?"

They stepped inside, Pam grateful for the air-conditioning and almost glad Michael wasn't here. He would have thrown a fit later about sitting outside to eat in the July heat. And he would have definitely complained about the dining table and chairs—two picnic tables.

"Mom makes the best meat loaf in the universe," Andy said, coming out of his bedroom.

The sight of him brought tears to her eyes. Jacob should have been right on his heels.

"Andy," Betty said, "why don't you set the table." She opened a cupboard and began to count out plates and glasses. "Pam'll have the salad ready in a minute." She handed Andy a stack of plates and shooed him out the door, then came back to stand beside Pam at the kitchen sink. "It'll get easier."

"It had better or I'll never be able to go anywhere again."

"It's too soon. Give yourself some time. I was surprised you said you'd come over. Glad—but surprised."

"Michael—" Pam started to tell her, then stopped and just shook her head. "We had a fight. That's why I was walking with Rambo."

"We'll take you home whenever you're ready. Even if it's in five minutes. You give me the high sign and we're out of here."

Pam nodded and whispered her thanks just as Stan came in the door, hugged his wife, said hello, and headed down the hall to change out of his uniform. He didn't ask about Michael, and when he came back into the living room, he said, "Any time you want to get away from the madness here, you just say the word, and we'll get you home." He headed outside. From the kitchen window Pam could see him swinging the twins on an antique A-frame swing set painted bright orange.

When Pam opened the refrigerator to collect bottles of salad dressing, Betty rattled off, "The twins are in that 'nothing green' phase of life, so they won't eat any, ranch for Andy and Rachel, poppy seed for me, Italian for Stan—and whatever else you can find if none of those suit your fancy." She opened the oven door to pull out the meat loaf. While she was slicing it, Pam piled baked potatoes in a bowl.

"Ketchup," Betty said. "They'll all want ketchup for the meat loaf." She lifted her hands. "I know, I know . . . it's an insult to the chef. We're plebeians, what can I say."

Pam grinned. "I always used to put ketchup on my mom's meat loaf."

"Because you liked ketchup or because you hated meat loaf?" Betty teased, heading for the door.

"The latter," Pam said, following her with the salad bowl. "But I outgrew that fault in my taste buds." She stepped outside. "I'll come back for the dressing."

"The girls can get it," Betty said.

A secret sign must have somehow been communicated, because as soon as the screen door closed, children began to appear from every corner of the yard and house, and after a few moments of "I-want-milk-not-water-where's-my-napkin-do-I-have-to-eat-the-beans-this-is-too-hot" bedlam, everyone sat with their plates filled and their heads bowed while Stan said grace.

"Thank you for our friends the Nolans, Father. Bless our time together this evening. Show us ways to love one another better."

Stan had just started to say the amen when a childish voice piped up. "And please tell Jacob and Davey hi and we're having chocolate pie."

Things got unnaturally quiet around the table. Pam could feel several pairs of eyes on her, but then Stan cleared his throat and said, "And help Mama's meat loaf to be just meat loaf this time."

Everyone laughed nervously. Pam opened her eyes to see Betty hiding her face behind a napkin. Megan and Maddy giggled and began to pick through the meat loaf on their plates with exaggerated care. Maddy looked at Megan and said, "Nope. No ninjas."

"You two"—Betty waved her napkin at the girls—"cut that out." She shook her head and chuckled. "My family. Comedians. Every last one of them." She glanced around the table. "Is anyone going to explain what we're talking about to Mrs. Nolan?"

Rolling her eyes, Emily spoke up. "It's not even that funny. Mother likes to add 'nutritional benefit' to our meals. Without us knowing. And sometimes she gets a little sneaky."

"I get it," Pam said. "Ninja food. No one knows it's in there."

"Well, that's the general idea," Betty said. "Although they've learned to check the meat loaf."

"Only after you tried to put broccoli in it," Andy said.

"And carrots," Megan added.

"And beets," Rachel chimed in.

"That doesn't sound so bad," Pam said.

"In the *same* meat loaf?" Emily said. "There was about a half pound of meat and the rest was . . . well, we don't even know what all the rest was."

"Okay, so I got a little carried away. But you don't have to worry today. The salad is *salad*. And the meat loaf is *meat*, except for an egg and some bread crumbs to hold it together, and my secret spices."

"Secret spices, eh?" Stan lifted his gargantuan slab of meat loaf with his fork and peered under it suspiciously.

"Misty's," Betty said quickly. "Misty's Seasoning. That's it. I promise."

The subject went from meat loaf to Emily's summer school and on to a dizzying array of topics. Pam couldn't keep up, but she didn't have to try. She was helping Betty wash dishes when it hit her. She'd been surrounded by Jacob's absence this evening, and yet, somehow, it hadn't been agonizing. With this family, death wasn't the monster in the room everyone tried to ignore. More than one member of the family had teared up over the course of the evening, but they hadn't felt compelled to hide it or to go off by themselves. Instead, they'd stayed and cried their tears with the people who loved them.

While the children dried the dishes, Stan settled onto a wood bench near the storage shed and called the dogs. He sat alternately brushing one, then the other, while Betty and Pam shared an old porch swing hanging from yet another brightly painted metal A-frame.

"I had my doubts about coming tonight," Pam told Betty.

"Perfectly natural. As I said earlier, I was actually a little surprised that you showed up."

"And now that I did . . ."

"You're dreading going home."

Pam nodded.

"The silence looms large," Betty said and patted her hand. "That will get easier with time."

"That might work if only—" She stopped. Closed her eyes.

"If only what?"

"No," Pam said. "Not tonight. Tonight was nice. I don't want to ruin it." She cleared her throat. "Michael's gone back to work." It was ridiculous how saying that seemed to open the dam that had been holding back her tears. Betty reached into her apron pocket and pulled out a small packet of tissues and handed them over.

"Will I ever get over this?"

"No."

"He asked me to make chocolate pie that day. I told him I wasn't in the mood. I wish—I wish I'd done it."

"You didn't have to make Jake a chocolate pie for him to know you loved him."

"I don't think I can stand any more losses right now." Pam bent over and hugged her knees. "I don't think I can do it."

"What are you afraid of?" Betty put her arm across Pam's shoulders.

"Michael," she said, her voice breaking. "I'm going to lose him, too, and . . . oh, God . . ." She wept for a few minutes with Betty holding her. Finally, she quieted and sat back up. As she sniffed, she said, "I wish I had your faith. So it wouldn't hurt so much."

After a moment, Betty said, "My faith was strong when Davey died. But it didn't make losing him hurt any less. I was devastated. Stan would come home and find me on the couch with my eyes closed. The drapes drawn. The house quiet. No dinner. It looked as if I hadn't done anything all day. And some days I hadn't. He'd try to come and hold me, and I'd push him away. He started staying at work, volunteering for extra shifts. After a while, he just stopped trying to touch me altogether."

"How did you get past it?"

"One day Stan knelt beside the couch and told me that he loved me and he needed me, but that if I didn't find a way to come back to him, he was leaving. I was terrified. I spent that entire day crying—about a lot more than Davey. It was probably the worst day of my life—after the day Davey died. It took every ounce of strength I had, but while Stan was at work that day, I showered and washed my hair. When he got home, I had set the table and made macaroni and cheese. It was just opening a box and boiling water, but it was a major accomplishment. I focused on just those things for a long time. Get up. Get dressed. Do your hair. Make dinner. And then one day I realized that I was carrying my grief. It wasn't carrying me."

"How long?"

"How long what?"

"How long was it before you could carry—"

"My timetable has nothing to do with your reality, Pam. It's a very individual thing. And you can't know what's best for Michael, either, at the moment. Even if the two of you had a great marriage before the tragedy, you still wouldn't know. Maybe going back to work is what he needs right now."

"What about what *I* need?"

"He can't give it. It's not a character flaw. It's reality. 'You can't lean on something bent double from its own burden.' That's a quote from a book I read the year after Davey died. Another bereaved mom gave it to me. I thought Stan and I were going to break up, when what was really happening was he was doing grief the only way he knew how—and that was working. Our house had become a symbol of his loss to him, and for a long time he just had to avoid it. He wasn't avoiding *me*. And he came home in time. Michael will, too."

Pam sighed. With all of her heart she wanted to believe Betty, but there was more to her problems than the recent past. Her marriage was a wreck. The screen door opened, and Maddy and Megan came bouncing out with Rachel in tow.

"The dishes are done, and Rachel's gonna swing us," Maddy giggled.

"I should head home," Pam said.

"There's no hurry," Betty protested.

"I don't feel hurried. But I'm exhausted, and apparently I'm not the only one." She pointed to where Rambo and Reba lay entwined around each other, sound asleep.

"I'll get the van keys," Betty said just as Andy came out on the porch.

Reba and Rambo snapped to attention, tails wagging.

"I was going to take the dogs out to Pioneers Park for a run," he said.

"What about the leash law?"

"Don't ask, don't tell," Andy said and grinned. "Can I drop you off on the way?"

"Last I knew, my house wasn't on the way to Pioneers Park from here."

"Buy me an ice cream cone at Zesto on the way, and I won't complain."

So she did. Only it ended up being four ice cream cones because the "kids" in the back of the truck just plain deserved it.

## {t e n}

"SO THERE I WAS," Pam said as she and Betty walked the neighbor-hood with Reba and Rambo in tow, "tomato in hand, and the vendor is asking me if I'm all right, and I can't take my eyes off a little boy at the far end of the row of booths, because I know it isn't and I know it can't be, but it looks like Jacob." She cleared her throat. "I'm going nuts. Certifiably insane. I never did answer the poor man. Just put the tomato down and headed for Rainelle's car. Thankfully she had the top up. At least my wailing was muffled." She rubbed her neck. "The only thing that's certain these days is that nothing's certain."

"How'd Rainelle handle it?" Betty asked.

"Okay. I don't think anything I could say or do these days would surprise her." Pam sighed. "But it sure ruined what was supposed to be a nice morning at the farmers' market. I thought that would be safe. Jacob hasn't gone there with me since he was in junior high."

"Memory is a mysterious thing. Sometimes you know when a cer-tain event or location will have land mines everywhere, and you avoid it. Other times when you think things will be all right—wham. I never knew when the sound of a crying baby would send me over the edge."

"So what can I do short of hibernating for the next—oh, I don't know—twenty years?"

"Buy stock in Kleenex but don't hibernate." Betty smiled. "You'll find your way to the balance that's right for you."

"Balance? You're talking to a crazy person about balance?"

"You'll find it," she repeated. "I can't tell you where that is for you. No one can. Be gentle with yourself, and try something brave once in a while. And *brave* might mean something as simple as shopping for groceries or setting the table for a nice dinner."

Pam told Betty about the near panic attack she'd had in the cereal aisle at the grocery store.

"Come to Compassionate Friends sometime," Betty said. "Every parent there would nod with understanding if you told that story. They've all had something similar happen."

Pam shook her head. "Michael would be mortified if word got out that his wife can't cope. The neighbors have already expressed concern that I spend too much time hiding at home not facing reality."

Betty put her hand on Pam's arm. "You cannot be bothered by the opinions of idiots."

Pam forced a laugh at the abrupt reaction from someone she thought of as soft-spoken.

"I mean it," Betty said. "You just have to stay away from the idiots for a while—and that's most people when it comes to the topic of grief. And on the days when you feel especially fragile, hide out with the people you know best. Like Rainelle."

"Even though she wasn't too freaked out at the farmers' market after I told her why I fell apart, things are still weird with her—and part of that is my fault."

"Why your fault?"

"Well, my reaction to the way her office is handling Eddie Lee Monroe, for one thing."

"After all the years Rainelle has been a prosecutor, I doubt she was surprised by that. She's had plenty of experience dealing with victims' families."

"Exactly what she said. But that's not the only thing that's caused fireworks between us lately." Pam pointed to two water fountains up ahead. "Let's get these two a drink." She led the way and unfolded a collapsible water bowl she carried in her fanny pack when she took Rambo for long walks.

While the dogs lapped up water, Pam explained. "Rainelle has a nephew about two years younger than Jacob. He's been giving

Rainelle's sister a bit of trouble. Nothing serious—just teenage boy stuff. Missing curfew, a speeding ticket or two. That kind of thing. Rainelle's sister uses her for a sounding board, and sometimes Rainelle bounces stuff off me. I've always taken it as a compliment—the idea that Rainelle wants my opinion. But the other day I lost it with her. She was going on and on about Richie, and while I can understand the stress he's putting on the family, I just couldn't take it. 'If Merril is so fed up,' I said, 'you tell her to send Richie over to my house. I'd give anything to have a son again.'" She folded up the damp water bowl and they set off again with the dogs in tow.

"I remember feeling just about the same way when one of the young moms at church complained about a rough night with a fussy baby."

"So you're telling me that was normal?" When Betty nodded, Pam said, "Rainelle apologized all over herself."

"God bless her. And God bless you, too. It was brave of you to speak up like that. Better that than silence and avoiding Rainelle. Honesty like that will strengthen your friendship in the long run."

"At the moment all it's done is make things awkward. Between the fit at the farmers' market and the fit over Richie, I've pretty well succeeded in making my best friend feel like she's walking on broken glass when she's around me."

"Is that Rainelle talking or you interpreting her?"

"Me interpreting," Pam admitted. "But I hate the way June 19 looms over every relationship I have. Rainelle and I have been like this since junior high." She gestured with her free hand, two fingers pressed together.

"It'll be that way again. Give it time."

Pam sighed. "Rainelle loves me, but there are parts of this she just can't understand no matter how much she cares. I mean, I just learned to put the words *Jacob* and *died* in the same sentence without hyperventilating. There is no way Rainelle can understand that. I have definitely crossed over into some weird part of the twilight zone where she can't follow." Pam paused. "I hope you're right about our friendship."

They walked along for a few minutes in comfortable silence. Finally, Pam forced a low laugh and said, "So . . . now that I've gotten that off my chest . . . let's arrange for world peace."

Betty chuckled. "What a superb idea. My kids will be so impressed when they see their boring mother on the news."

"How are the Novac kids doing with all of this? They seemed okay when I was at your house for dinner the other night, but how are they *really* doing?"

"The Novac kids are going to be just fine."

Pam turned to face her. "Please don't just give me the answer you think I want to hear. I know a comfort cliché when I hear one."

"Hey," Betty protested, "no fair using my own material against me."

"So . . . how are the Novac kids?" Pam repeated and led the way to a bench, where the two women sat down, chuckling when both Reba and Rambo flopped over on their sides with grateful sighs.

"Suzanne's too little to understand much—other than the fact that her family is sad right now. Maddy and Megan are playing hide-and-seek with the dogs again. For a while they said they couldn't play Jake's game without Jake. But Andy finally got that going again the last time Rambo was at our place, and somehow that seems to have helped them. Emily has been writing long, sappy, really awful poetry. But she's let me read it, which is a good sign. It will take longer for Rachel and Andy. Rachel's talk about someday marrying Jake was more than just talk. She has an entire scrapbook full of wedding gowns, wedding flowers, wedding cakes." She reached over to squeeze Pam's hand. "She loved him as much as any sixteen-year-old girl can love. And of course Andy—" Betty paused and shook her head. "At least they've quit yelling at each other."

"I thought they got along great."

"They did," Betty said. "But the stress had to come out, I guess." She related the battle over film materials.

"Poor Andy," Pam said.

"He'll be all right. Although now that his dad gave him the challenge to work on it, he's gone to the other extreme, organizing to the point that he's just shuffling stuff around. Of course he's discouraged."

"He can't let this make him give up on film school."

Betty shrugged. "He won't. Although without a finished product he may have to delay a little while. He was hoping for more than one scholarship as a result of that piece. He may not be able to head west as soon as he'd like, but it'll work out, and in the meantime he's taking some classes here, and he's applied at a nursery and a couple of other places that hire seasonal help."

"I thought he already had a job."

"He does. But he doesn't think he'll get enough hours, so he's devising plan B. His dream is an expensive one."

"Which is why God invented student loans," Pam said.

"Not for the Novacs of the world, He didn't. There is no way Stan is going to let Andy graduate thousands of dollars in debt. He's a pay-as-you-go kinda guy."

Pam sighed. "It just doesn't stop."

"What doesn't stop?"

"The avalanche. The dominos. Whatever you want to call all the negative effects of one person's bad decision." She put her hands up to massage her temples and muttered, "Thank you, Eddie Lee Monroe."

Betty was quiet for a minute, then said gently, "That's an honest reaction, but we've been trying to help Andy look at it a different way."

"What other way is there to look at it?" Pam asked. "Monroe did it."

Betty stood up. "Let's walk some more." As they walked, Betty talked. "A few years ago we had a young couple in our church facing the wife's terminal illness. I've never seen anyone so calm and at peace. One Sunday Stan and Bill were talking after church, and Stan just blurted out, 'I don't know how you're doing it.' I've never forgotten

Bill's answer. 'Well,' he said, 'I've decided to take life as a multiple choice test. A. God's in control. B. He's not.' And then Bill got this amazing smile on his face and said quietly, 'I choose A.'"

Pam frowned. "What's that got to do with Andy?"

"This is Andy's time to choose. A. God's in control and there is a way to finish Jacob's list and the film, or B. God messed up, the entire thing is a fiasco, and 'The Xtreme Ten of Two Good Men' will never be completed." Betty paused. "It's a defining moment for Andy. Stan and I both believe *A* with all our hearts. We don't have any doubt that God is in all the details of our lives. He isn't looking at the pieces of Andy's unfinished film thinking, 'How do I get this kid through college *now?*' But belief doesn't get passed on to our kids like hair color and height. Andy can't live his life on our faith. He has to get his own. He has to find his own way."

Pam reached down to pet Rambo while she pondered what Betty had just said. She liked the idea that God might still have a plan for Andy's film—and, consequently, for Jacob's list. But how could she reconcile what Betty called "choosing A" with Jacob's death?

Betty touched Pam's elbow. "I've got to get home in a few minutes, but I wanted to ask about Michael. I mean, we can't claim to have arranged for world peace if we don't run the gamut in both families," she said, forcing an attempt at humor.

"I don't really feel like I have a family to talk about anymore," Pam said. "As much time as Jacob spent at your house, I doubt it's any surprise if I tell you that Michael and I haven't been—all right—for quite a while."

"I suspected," Betty said. "But not because of anything Jacob ever said. He was very proud of you both. And in his eyes you are both terrific. He really didn't hint at anything else—at least not to me. And you are more than welcome to tell me to mind my own business right now."

Pam concentrated on pulling a cocklebur out of Rambo's fur while she talked. "It started a long time ago. I'd actually begun to think that once Jacob graduated from college I'd probably file for divorce."

"I'm so sorry."

"Me, too. I don't know if I ever would have really done it. Michael's provided very well for us. There's a lot of good in my life because of his hard work." She ran her palm across her forehead. "Before the accident, we were pretty much living separate lives. Then, for a while, things were actually a little better between us." She shrugged. "I think it was a survival mechanism. But he's gone back to work and back to his old ways. And I find I have very little tolerance for that now."

"It's very admirable for someone who's been through a profound loss to be able to look beyond their own pain and help someone else. Trying to handle the practice by himself had to be a great burden for someone Dr. Nolan Senior's age."

Pam cleared her throat to keep from snickering. It might not be the day to drag out all the Nolan dirty laundry, but she wasn't about to perpetuate the "Dr. Michael Nolan, dedicated physician" myth. "Michael's prime motivation for becoming a doctor was meeting his father's expectations. He talked about humanitarian service for a little while when he was in school. But his father's expectations were what got him through. Once he graduated, the topic of public service rarely came up." Briefly, she told Betty about Dr. Nolan Senior's Sunday evening appearance at the house. She motioned with her hands as she concluded, "So Daddy cracked the whip, and the son climbed back in the harness."

When Betty was silent, Pam continued. "As soon as that happened, it was business as usual again at home—long hours, late nights, missed dinners—all the stuff people who look at the big house and the fancy cars and the cruises don't see." She thought she'd stopped caring long ago. She'd explained the one night of lovemaking away as a weird way to express a jumble of emotions. But as she shared with Betty, loneliness and despair welled up and tears overflowed.

"Man," she said, brushing the tears away with the back of her free hand, "I hate being a crybaby." She jiggled Rambo's leash and he leaped to his feet. "Let's head home." They were quiet on the long walk home, and Pam was glad. She kept going over what Betty had said about the choices in life. A. God's in control. B. He's not. She had to be honest. Given the recent past, it looked to her like B was the right answer when it came to the Nolans.

––––––––

He froze. The kid on the table couldn't breathe, and all Michael could think of was how much he looked like a ten-year-old Jacob. Beyond that, his mind was blank. For a brief second, he stood just inside the exam room door, his own panic rising in concert with the child's mother's. Just when things could have really gotten out of hand, the door opened and Michael's father apologized for being in the wrong room.

Somehow Michael managed to grab the doorknob and pull his father in. He glanced at the child and the panic-stricken mother and back at his father, and as Senior strode forward and took charge, Michael backed out of the room. It took all of three minutes for him to get his car keys and jacket from his office, mumble something about a personal emergency to the nurse in the hall, and get to his car. He could hear the siren as an ambulance came roaring up the street. He started the Beemer and pulled away just as the ambulance rounded the corner and screeched to a halt at the front door.

He didn't remember what came next, but when his conscious mind kicked in again, Michael was parked on the familiar brick lane dividing two historic sections of Wyuka Cemetery, staring across the rows of granite to the black headstone with the name Nolan etched into its surface. It was a while before he felt like he could make it to the bench, and when he finally moved to get out of the car, his cell phone rang. He pulled it out of his pocket and winced when he saw the caller's number.

Michael Senior didn't even wait for him to say hello. "What is *wrong* with you?!"

"I—I don't know. The kid looked like Jacob. I just froze."

"Well, unfreeze yourself and get back over here. The boy will be fine. I had him transported to the hospital as a precaution, but it wasn't nearly as bad as it looked. We've both seen worse. Thankfully, the mother didn't pick up on what was really happening with you or we'd be looking a huge lawsuit in the face."

*The kid was all right.* Michael slumped against the car, relief making him feel weak-kneed.

"Did you hear me?"

"Yes, Dad. I heard you. Ryan's going to be all right."

"Is that all you heard? I also said you nearly got us involved in a malpractice suit. And I want you to pull yourself together and get back here. The delay has put us both behind. We'll be lucky to get out of the office before seven this evening."

Michael disconnected the call while his Dad was still venting and tossed it onto the passenger seat.

What was wrong with him? He'd left the cemetery, and then his mind had gone blank. When he realized where he was headed, Stan Novac's voice sounded in his head. *You could end this thing in that much time.* And he *had* ended it. So what the heck was he doing now? With a squeal of tires, Michael peeled onto a side street and parked. The maneuver had sent his cell phone flying, and now it lay on the floorboard, its message light blinking. For a few minutes Michael sat staring down at his hands.

He rubbed his sweaty palms dry on his dress pants and gripped the steering wheel. A quick U-turn headed him back toward home. *Where you belong.* If only that were true. If only the clock could turn back to the time in his life when his wife loved him and his son thought he could do anything.

By the time he was on the overpass that took him past the Huskers stadium, Michael was back in the present where he was smart— but dumb—and where home was the last place he belonged. A beer would be good. If he had two, maybe Pam would be asleep when he got to the house. Senior would probably have called her by now looking for him. Maybe he'd be waiting for him at home with yet another pep talk. Wouldn't that be great? Either way, his days of driving to the Highlands were over.

Much to Michael's relief, there was no sign of Senior's Town Car in the driveway at home. He slipped the Beemer into the garage, and leaving the cell phone in the car, went inside. At least the dog still liked him. Here he was, nudging his hand with a warm snout and wagging his tail.

"Hey, boy," Michael said quietly, glancing up the stairs. "Is she sleeping?" When Rambo stayed at his side, Michael took that for a yes. He headed up the winding stairs that led from the entryway up to the guest rooms. He wouldn't have to go past the master suite at all this way. But at the top of the stairs he could see light spilling out of Pam's door. Of course Rambo's behavior had given him away. The only reason the dog would have left Pam's side at this time of night was to check on a noise—in this case, his arrival. Good dog. Bad dog. Pam called his name. Yanking at his tie, he headed down the hall, pausing in the doorway and hoping she would get the message and make it short. She was reading in bed, a cup and saucer on the bedside table—it would be chamomile tea, he knew.

"Is everything all right?" she asked as she laid the book aside. "Your father's called a couple of times this evening looking for you. He sounded upset."

"When isn't he upset these days?" He leaned against the doorframe. "I'll talk to him tomorrow."

Throwing back the covers, Pam slid to the foot of the bed. "Can we talk?"

"Can it wait?"

"Does it have to?"

"I guess not," he said and crossed to the love seat. "What's up?"

"I know what I want us to do with the memorial fund," Pam said. "We should pay Andy's tuition at UNL. He's looking for seasonal work in addition to his regular job. He was counting on 'Xtreme Ten' to get him some extra financial aid. Without it he's going to have to delay applying to the film school he really wants to get into. If we could pay his tuition, it would take off some pressure and maybe even give him time to figure out a way to finish 'Xtreme Ten.'"

"Isn't the demise of that project a given?"

"Maybe not," Pam said. "He's hoping to come up with something. But it certainly won't be in time to help with school this year. The memorial fund is the perfect answer."

The enthusiasm in her voice was annoying. "Whoa." He held up both hands. "Could we at least pretend to have a discussion about this before you tell me what we're doing?"

Her voice echoed his annoyed tone. "You said yourself that a scholarship fund was the most logical thing to do with it."

"Yes." He nodded. "But I never said anything about paying some-one's entire college tuition. That kind of thing can ruin a person."

"It won't ruin Andy."

Michael shrugged out of his sport coat and settled back. "What brought this on?"

"Betty and I took a walk today, and she told me Andy is looking for a second job and he can't figure out what to do with the pieces of video he has and school is going to be—"

"Wait," Michael said. "Just. Wait." He frowned. "We can't give away several thousand dollars because Betty Novac told you a sob story."

Pam's shoulders went back and her chin lifted. "Betty Novac did *not* tell me a sob story. I was asking how the children are doing. It wasn't until later today that I began to think about how grateful I am that the Novacs are in our lives—"

"Look," he interrupted. "Betty has helped you. That's great. I'm glad. But it's a really *really* big leap from being grateful for someone's help to virtually putting their kid through college. I repeat—that kind of money can ruin a person."

Pam folded her arms and made a face. "You sound just like your father."

"What's *that* supposed to mean?" He scooted to the edge of the seat and sat up straighter.

"You know exactly what it means." She lowered her voice to mimic the elder Nolan. "'Throwing money at a problem is never the right answer.'" In her own voice she added, "Unless, of course, the money is being thrown into the coffers of something *he* cares about. Something that will enable him to call in a marker one day."

Michael knew she was essentially right, but the venom behind what she was saying surprised him. Had she always hated his father this much? What had Senior ever done to her? *What's he ever done* for *her?* With a sigh, he tried to soothe some of the negative emotion in the room. "I'm not saying you don't have the seed of a good idea. I like the idea of a scholarship. But couldn't we at least discuss something more long-lived than Andy Novac's education? What about endowing a scholarship *fund?* That would make it mean something for years to come." *Where did that come from?* He hadn't really given this much thought . . . but it was a good idea. So was the next thing that came to mind. "Maybe we could link a scholarship to Jacob's list somehow. Maybe it could be for some degree that would end up helping mankind in a unique—or extreme—way." He smiled and nodded. "I'm on to something. I like that."

"Of course you like it," Pam snapped. "You've just taken what I said and changed it to suit yourself."

"What?"

"You aren't listening to me. I don't want to establish a scholarship fund for strangers. I want to help Andy Novac."

Michael shook his head. "Look. I already told you that I agree with you—in essence." He leaned forward, resting his elbows on his knees and tenting his hands together with the fingertips touching. "Betty Novac has been a good friend. Making an education possible for kids who might not be able to pay tuition is admirable. Both are true. But that doesn't mean we have an obligation to those people."

"Those people? What do you mean 'those people'?" Her face was getting red. "The Novacs aren't 'those people' to me, and they weren't 'those people' to Jacob. And since when does there have to be an *obligation* for us to do the right thing?" She cleared her throat. "What could be more right than funding a way for Andy to be able to finish the project he and Jacob started? If Andy doesn't have to take on all these extra jobs, maybe he could finish 'Xtreme Ten' instead of leaving it in some closet."

"Did Andy tell you he plans to finish Jacob's list?"

"No. Betty did."

Michael stood up. "It won't happen."

"How can you say that?"

"Where's he going to find another jock with a list like that? Where's he going to find the money to fund it? It was hard enough for Andy to do his part of those stunts. He'll never find someone else willing to take it on."

"You can't know that," Pam insisted. "As a matter of fact, Rachel might do it."

Michael snorted. "Right. She's going to kayak the Colorado River."

"And why is that so unbelievable?"

"She's a sixteen-year-old girl, with toothpick arms, who probably has the upper body strength of a ten-year-old."

Pam bit her lip. "Could we please get back to the subject? We have the means to help Andy with school. It's the right thing to do. And I believe in him. He'll find a way to finish Jacob's list and 'Xtreme Ten.'"

Man. What was the problem with everyone today? First his dad and now his wife. He felt like a punching bag, and whether it was the beer or the fiasco at the office or his dad or something else, his brain was beginning to short-circuit. He knew she'd hate his tone, but it was the only one he could summon at the moment—pedantic, forced, calm. "All right, all right. I may be wrong about Rachel Novac. Maybe she'll set a new world record for female kayaking. But that is not the point. The point is that this should be a joint decision. The point is that in the matter of Jacob's memorial fund, it is not yours to dictate what the right thing is. And the name Novac is not necessarily the defining ingredient for doing the right thing."

Pam jumped to her feet. The afghan slid off the bed. "What is *wrong* with you? Every time the name Novac comes up, it's like you get a cocklebur under your belt."

"That's ridiculous." He reached for the sport coat and draped it over his arm.

"It isn't ridiculous." When the house phone rang, Pam went to the end table and snatched up the cordless handset. Checking the caller ID, she held it out to him. "Your father."

He headed for the door. "I'm not here."

"But—"

He wheeled around. "I said I'm not here."

"I won't lie for you." She tossed the phone on the bed.

He marched across the room and snatched it up, glaring at her as he listened to Senior scream. "Yes, Dad," he said. "Yes. Uh-huh. Yes. I know, sir. I understand. Yes, of course. Of course you're right." He blinked. This was embarrassing. The hand that held the phone was shaking. Happily, his voice didn't betray anything of the tears gathering behind his eyes as he continued to agree with everything his father said. He was a huge disappointment. Weak. Undependable. "Yes, sir. Yes, sir, I am. Ashamed. Yes, sir."

Finally Senior ran out of steam and that's when Michael was finally able to say no. No, he would not be coming back to the office on Monday. No, he wouldn't be able to make rounds tomorrow. *No. No. No.*

By the time he'd hung up the phone, Pam had pulled on her bathrobe. "What's happened?" she asked.

"I don't want to talk about it. Honestly, I'm just about past coherence on any topic."

"I—I'm sorry. I should have known something had happened when Senior kept calling. I shouldn't have pushed you. I could tell you were exhausted."

"Don't apologize. I deserve every negative thought you've had about me since the turn of this century." His voice wavered, but he fought for control as he said, "Long story short, I nearly self-destructed with a patient today. A ten-year-old who reminded me of Jacob for some reason. I froze. Thankfully, Dad was able to cover for me, the boy is all right, and the mother who witnessed my 'episode' is none the wiser."

"Oh, Michael—"

He couldn't stand her sympathy. Not now. He held up his hand. "Look. It's been a pretty awful day. Frankly, I feel like I've been hit by a truck." He winced as soon as the words tumbled out. Could he possibly make any more mistakes today? "I'm sorry. Sorry about fighting, sorry about everything. And I'm going to get some rest."

"I'm sorry, too," she said, crossing the room and putting her hand on his arm.

He wanted to reach for her. Instead, he patted her hand as he said, "You need to get over that. It'll destroy you."

"SO HERE'S THE DEAL," Rainelle said. "I know things have been weird between us, and I know it's my fault—"

"No," Pam interrupted her. She leaned her rake against the wheelbarrow and shifted the cell phone to her right hand. "It isn't anyone's fault. It's life. And I am not going to listen to you apologize for being human. It's good to hear your voice." Something *was* good. How wonderful to be able to say that and mean it. She walked up to the patio and sat down.

"So you'll give me another chance?"

"Stop that. You're the one putting up with a friend who has a nervous breakdown every few days. I tried to call you over Labor Day, by the way, but your phone was off. Is everything all right?"

"Everything's fine," Rainelle said. "Better than fine, actually." She lowered her voice. "Especially with me and you know who."

"You and Malcolm?"

"Uh-huh."

"And you're at work so you can't talk."

"Uh-huh."

"What time and where tomorrow?"

"Let's try that new seafood place down in the old Haymarket."

"Ex-cuuse me. I thought I had Rainelle Washington on the line," Pam joked.

"I know, I know—I don't like seafood. I'm trying to widen my horizons."

"Pretty radical behavior, Counselor."

"Eleven-thirty?"

"Can I at least have a hint whether this is about Good Malcolm or Bad Malcolm?"

"Good *and* bad," Rainelle said.

"Bad as in not good or bad as in baaaaddd?" Pam tried to mimic a rapper's voice.

Rainelle cracked up. But she didn't answer the question, just verified the place and the time and hung up. Pam went back to raking the early-falling leaves scattered around the backyard and tried to maintain the positive emotions Rainelle's call had resurrected. Inevitably, though, her mind betrayed her good intentions and careened toward worry. There was so much to worry about. Michael hadn't been back to the office. She didn't think he'd talked to his father, either. And all he would say was, "Everything's fine. Don't worry." That lie had become her mantra, too. "We're fine, thank you."

She also hated the way Eddie Lee Monroe controlled their lives. Sentencing was approaching, but between now and September 27 there would be meetings with their attorney, settlements to discuss with the trucking company's insurance carrier, and a Victim's Impact Statement to complete for the judge. *Victim's Impact Statement.* The idea of trying to translate the impact of losing a child into words on a piece of paper seemed almost blasphemous. How did any parent even begin to do that?

Their attorney was guiding them through the maze of legal details, but it never seemed to end. Eddie Lee Monroe was the shadow behind nearly every conversation. As Rainelle had initially warned, Philip Riley told them to be prepared for Monroe to receive a comparatively light sentence. There were mitigating circumstances. Monroe had a family who needed him. He was remorseful. He didn't have a record. His employer was supporting him.

During one meeting Pam had put her head in her hands and wept. "Stop, Philip. Please. Just—stop. This man killed my baby. He—"

Riley responded by suggesting that perhaps Pam should "see someone."

Michael spoke up. "My wife doesn't need to see a shrink."

"It's not a character flaw," Riley said. "I'm sure you've suggested it to your own patients in the past. Seeking professional help with something as devastating as a child's death is in no way a—"

Pam interrupted him. "I know that it's normal to go nuts for a while, Philip. And I know that Paxil is my friend." When Michael reached for her hand, she was grateful. But she was just as grateful when Philip Riley left, and she and Michael went their separate ways.

When, Pam wondered, as she bent to handpick some leaves caught at the base of a row of lilacs, had they perfected the public waltz that became a two-step of private avoidance and denial? Michael got up, she slept in. He stayed up late, she retired to her room. He showered, she slipped outside. She soaked in the hot tub, he took Rambo for a walk. She wondered how long they would be able to keep it up. She thought back to that night she had melted into his arms . . . and then recoiled. That one night had revealed a weakness she'd consciously denied for a long time. In spite of everything, part of her still longed for Michael and the happiness of their early years of marriage. Memories she thought long since dead rose up to taunt her with *what if*s and *if only*s.

"Okay with you if I let Rambo out?" Michael called from the back door.

Pam started and looked toward the house. He'd been gone when she got up, presumably walking the dog. But he'd shaved for the first time in days. And he was dressed more like his old self. "Where are you headed?" she asked. "Golfing today? Weather's perfect for it."

"Mind reader," Michael said. "Thought I might give it a go."

"Enjoy," Pam replied, almost wishing he would ask her to join him. He seemed about to do exactly that when Rambo crashed into the pile of leaves at her feet, sneezed, flopped down, and effectively destroyed her last few minutes of work.

"Rambo!" Michael scolded as he stepped out on the patio.

"Don't scold. He's just trying to make me laugh." And he succeeded, crouching down on all fours, thrusting his nose into the leaves, sneezing, and then standing up with a hat of leaves atop his head. "It's all right. I need the exercise anyway." When she took a swipe at the leaves, Rambo bounded off toward the back of the yard. Memories of Michael and her raking the huge backyard—often ending up in a leaf fight or a leaf pile together—while Jacob toddled about almost pushed her over the barrier between them today. She almost asked Michael to help. But then he said something about his tee time. And the yard.

"You know we can hire someone to do this if it gets to be too much," he said.

"And you know that the yard work is more or less my therapy." She forced a smile. "And so much more cost effective than pharmaceuticals." She waved good-bye. When he was back inside, she sighed, blinking back tears, glancing toward the back of the property, where there had once been a little boy playing in a sandbox or swinging on an old tire swing. She sobbed audibly. Remembered the comfort of Michael's arms around her that night. The scent of his aftershave.

Diva-Ray's voice sounded in her ear. *"You are one confused woman. Who you gonna be? Tough Mama or Baby-oh-baby-save-me?"* Taking a deep breath, she decided Tough Mama was more likely to survive the next few weeks. At least until Eddie Lee Monroe's fate was known.

———

Friday was sunshine and blue skies. Parking behind one of the historic buildings in the Haymarket district, Pam made her way up a cobblestone alley between two former warehouses—one an art gallery and the other remodeled into upscale lofts. Claiming a table on the patio, she savored hot chai while she waited for Rainelle, watching cars come and go, smiling at a couple photographing each other in various crazy poses on a jungle gym in a small park up the street.

Rainelle's blue convertible whipped past Pam and into a parking stall just across the street. The first thing Pam noticed was the shoes. Pumpkin-colored stilettos. "If you weren't my best friend," she teased as Rainelle glided across the brick street, "I'd have to hate you. How dare you look so sleek? And where *did* you find those fabulous shoes?"

"On the Miracle Mile in Chicago."

"Chicago?" Pam echoed. "You didn't tell me you were going to Chicago."

"I didn't know." Rainelle plopped her handbag on one of the extra chairs at their table for four and sat down. "Malcolm surprised me with tickets to a play last weekend."

"You . . . uh . . . went to Chicago . . . on a date?"

Rainelle nodded. "It's only a ninety-minute flight."

"Give me a break," Pam laughed. "That had to impress even Diva-Ray."

The waiter arrived, recited the daily specials, and departed with a promise to be back soon with Rainelle's latte. "So," Pam said as he retreated inside, "I'm thinking you may have more than just a few words to say about *Good* Malcolm."

Rainelle fluttered her eyelashes, smiled, and put her left hand to her right shoulder in a mock attempt to tuck in an errant strap—although there was no errant strap. There was, however, a rock the size of a jawbreaker on a previously unadorned finger.

Pam choked on her chai, grabbed a napkin, swallowed, coughed, took a sip of water, and coughed again while Rainelle smiled. And smiled. And smiled.

The waiter returned, and Rainelle ordered salmon, with a glance in Pam's direction and an explanation.

"Turnabout is fair play. I'm eating fish; Malcolm's going to try to learn to like Cicero."

"With white wine or red?" Pam joked.

"That's not funny," Rainelle said, even as she stifled a laugh.

"Maybe not, but it would have been fair revenge if I could have made you snort your coffee on that white blouse. I cannot believe you didn't tell me about this for almost a week." She lifted a piece of lemon out of her water glass and flicked it into Rainelle's.

"It just happened Saturday night." Rainelle sent the lemon back into Pam's water.

"Almost a week ago!" Pam repeated and threatened to squeeze the lemon in her direction. "Do you have a date?"

"Hey now," Rainelle said, shaking her finger at Pam. "This is no place to start a food fight." She glanced over her shoulder toward the kitchen. "I think these folks would be slightly less understanding than Mrs. Jeffers was. And we're waiting for the boss to adjust to the idea of us both being gone at the same time so we can plan a very *long* honeymoon."

"Good," Pam said as she admired Rainelle's rock. "So. Let's hear the long version of this momentous event. And please do tell me that you can take a long lunch."

"Honey," Rainelle grinned. "Long lunches are for business meetings. I took the entire afternoon."

Sharing a high five as their food was served, the two friends settled in. Pam drenched a bite of calamari in cocktail sauce as she said, "I want to hear every tiny detail from takeoff to landing."

"First things first." Rainelle reached for Pam's free hand and squeezed as she said, "This is the official request. Would you be my best woman?"

"Be your what?"

Rainelle grinned. "*Matron* of honor is so . . . stuffy. So . . ."

"Best woman," Pam said with a nod. "I like it."

As they rose to leave the restaurant, Pam realized that she had actually gone for nearly three hours without obsessing about her problems. Oh, sure, she'd teared up a time or two when nostalgia attacked and she thought back to her own engagement, but overall she had succeeded in making the time with Rainelle just that—time *with* Rainelle *about* Rainelle. It felt great, and as they left the restaurant and made their way to their cars she said so and gave Rainelle a hug, commenting on how much she was looking forward to making the next few months about "Wedding gowns and invitations, reception dinners, and dance bands, happiness, love, and life—amen."

Rainelle bumped into her. "Hey," she said and did a quick about-face. "Let's bop in here."

Pam looked up at the sign. "Since when do you like antiques?"

"You know the rhyme: 'Something old, something new, something borrowed, something blue.' Let's get the 'old' taken care of. It'll be a great memento of today." She pointed to something at the opposite end of the display window. "There," she said, touching Pam's elbow and pulling her along. "Let's ask to see that."

As they headed for the door, Rainelle bumped Pam again and blamed the new stilettos for throwing her off balance. Which was weird because Rainelle Washington had a closet full of stilettos. She wore them in court. She could walk blocks in the things and never complained that her feet hurt. With a shake of her head, Pam prepared to follow Rainelle into the store, but then something made her glance at the small park just beyond the shop door. A couple. Standing by the fountain. Embracing. The woman was shapely. A blonde.

Michael didn't see Pam.

––––––––

"I miss you," Michael said aloud. He shed a few tears and then leaned back on the wrought-iron settee they'd had installed next to Jacob's grave. Across the way one of the cemetery staff was mowing. Michael watched him walking in and out and around the graves, once in a while bumping the corner of a granite monument with the mower, stopping, correcting himself, then moving on. *There's your life*, he thought. For years now he'd been walking an erratic path rife with obstacles. It started with Pam's cancer, descended into marital problems, and then . . . then what Stan Novac would call terminal stupidity in the guise of women. With every jolt he'd tried to regroup and do better, but all he'd managed to do was walk blindly into something worse. And it had to end. Now.

*"For a smart guy you sure are stupid. Does having all the stuff make you happy? For a smart guy . . . you're stupid. You could end it like that.*

*She deserves a thousand percent more than she's getting. . . . Are you happy? Are you happy?"*

Stan Novac's comments had never been far from his conscious thoughts for weeks now, while Michael wandered the big house, newly aware of how careful Pam was to leave a room shortly after he entered it. They might be living under the same roof, but they weren't together in any real sense of that word. Instead of lingering over coffee, Pam jumped up from the dinner table and began to clean up. She spent long hours outside in the yard and never asked for help. She'd begun to close the bedroom door as soon as she retired every night. *No admittance* couldn't have been any more clearly stated.

In recent days, Michael had stopped resenting what Stan had said and admitted Novac was right. Increasingly, he'd begun to envy the guy. Betty was clearly nuts about him. His kids adored him. It seemed to Michael that when Novac had decided what was really important to him, "stuff" hadn't even appeared on the list. The guy was about all the corny "traditional values" talk the media sometimes mocked. And corny or not, Michael had to admit that Stan Novac seemed happy in his glorified double-wide across town, while Michael was beginning to think that if he didn't do something soon he was going to fall headlong into an early version of hell—absent the fire and brimstone but also absent of all the things and people he loved.

"I've got to make a change," he blurted out. And then, looking down at Jacob's grave, he began to talk. "There was this woman. I kept running into her at the hospital. She had a great sense of humor." He leaned forward, resting his elbows on his knees and staring toward the street on the other side of the high wrought-iron fence. After a minute he admitted aloud, "Okay, okay. She was great looking, too. Your mother and I—It had gotten to where it felt like the temperature dropped ten degrees every time I opened the front door at home. Kim was always glad to see me."

He sat back, rubbed his forehead, and without looking back at the grave, continued. "You just get caught up in it. Ego. Image. You get the big house near the oldest and most prestigious country club—

which your father makes sure you're invited to join—and then they start building mansions south of town that make what you thought was your dream house look outdated and small. But you don't let yourself realize that all you're doing is running a maze. Like a rat looking for the next meal. Eventually you start wanting distractions. Your kid grows up and isn't around as much anymore and you look at your wife and realize the two of you don't even know each other anymore. Things are always strained. So you buy her the Suburban she's always wanted and you send her for spa dates in Scottsdale, and while she's gone you—you take what's offered from women who make you feel like there's nothing wrong with you . . . when the truth is, most of the things that are wrong in your life begin and end with . . . you."

It felt good to be dumping it out. He shook his head. "This is . . . this is thanks to your buddy Stan, you know. He's the one who made me face it. At first I told myself to just blow it off. Thought I'd go back to work and get away from it. But it's not that easy." He sat quietly for a while, then said, "Maybe it's too late. I don't know. But . . . I hope not. I didn't plan it. I swear I didn't. But like Stan said, I didn't *un*plan it, either. And before I really knew what hit me, there I was into something I never intended to happen."

He looked across the cemetery and watched the gardener mowing for a minute. He started up again, crying as he talked. "After everything I've done to avoid your mom, I still need her. Just knowing she's in the house—even if she's in a different part of the house—she may not like me very much . . . but she's there." His voice wavered. "She's stronger than I am, you know. Always has been. She never wanted that house. Said she wanted me at home. But I didn't listen. And the cancer—the way she handled that. Oh sure—I did the doctor thing and insisted on second opinions, but when it came right down to it I was running scared, and she just calmly sat there listening to the list of chemotherapy drugs, checking off this list of questions she'd written down."

He broke off. "It's my job to handle bad news well. But it's one thing to be the guy in the chair handing it out and another thing entirely to be the one getting it. Do you remember how strong she was? Do you remember that night when she told us both not to worry?" Michael closed his eyes. "She joked about getting her skull tattooed and just letting people deal with her bald head. She *joked* about it." Of course he realized that was for Jacob's sake. She'd cried about it, too. He'd held her through those tears. One thing he'd done right.

"Your mom went somewhere with Rainelle today. I hate it when she's gone. The house feels a thousand times more empty without her. I told her I was playing golf again. But when I got to the clubhouse, Dave and Grant were just heading in. I'm tired of playing the 'I'm fine' game. So I drove off. Headed downtown instead of facing them. Figured there wasn't any chance I'd see anyone I knew down there. Thought I'd just hang out at The Mill for a while. Buy a latte. Pretend I was still in my right mind.

"I was headed out the door, and there she was. Kim. After we both stuttered around she asked me to walk with her. I told her I couldn't. That I meant what I said that night at her house. She said she knew. She's got her house on the market. Has a new job in Omaha. Said she hoped I could rebuild my life with your mom. She even hugged me good-bye." He leaned over and murmured, "'Rebuild my life.'" He raked his fingers through his hair and sat back up.

"I don't deserve your mother. I've been trying to figure out why she's put up with me. I finally realized why. She did that for you." He cleared his throat. "She wanted to see you finish that list, kiddo. You didn't know it, but she would have gone on that wilderness trek. She'd started working out at the gym. Trying to get her upper body strength back, so she'd be ready." His voice broke. "I was such a jerk to her about that. Told her she was crazy to think she could ever haul a loaded pack. Told her to face reality." He shook his head. "Face reality. As if I had any idea what I was talking about. I was too busy shopping for my BMW and hanging out at the country club to pay attention to what she was trying to do.

"You remember that trip to D.C. when we laughed about the guy on the bus? The one talking on his phone . . . talking about somebody he said was 'stuck on stupid'? That's me, Jacob. Stan Novac was right. I've been stuck on stupid." His voice wavered. "Things are going to be better now. I don't know how I'm going to do it, but somehow I'm going to find a way to make things right."

## {twelve}

BRINGING HOME A GOURMET carry-out dinner and setting the table had been the easy part. Deciding what to say was something else again. He didn't think a maudlin confession was necessary or particularly wise. Details would only cause Pam more pain, and she had been through enough. He would take responsibility for their troubles and make the case for healing. He worried a little that Pam would take one look at the lighted candles and yellow roses and think it was just another act. But then he'd come up with the perfect way to convince her. She might not believe the romantic dinner, but telling her his plan about Jacob's list and Andy's education? That would get her attention. In time, she'd see that he was sincere. About everything.

When he heard the garage door going up, Michael lit the candles. And then . . . Stan Novac came through the door followed by Betty . . . Rainelle . . . and, finally, Pam. The three women huddled together staring at the table with varied expressions, none of them good.

"What's this?" Michael asked.

Novac stepped back. Betty and Rainelle linked arms behind Pam.

"This," Pam said, "is me leaving you." She headed for the stairs that led up from the kitchen to the master suite.

"What? Wait!" Michael said, reaching out to her.

Pam paused on the stairs. Without looking back at him, she said, "I don't want a scene. I asked Stan to come so there wouldn't be one. Betty and Rainelle are going to help me pack."

"But I-I made . . ." Michael gestured toward the table. "I bought roses. Yellow ones."

"I won't take long," Pam said and continued up the stairs. Neither Rainelle nor Betty looked his way as they followed.

"You might want to put out the candles," Novac said.

"You put out the blasted candles," Michael snapped back. "I'm going upstairs to talk to my wife."

Novac blocked his path. "That's not a good idea, Doc. Not today."

Who did he think he was, anyway . . . coming between a man and his wife?

"Look," Michael said, lowering his voice. "You're the one who said I was an idiot. Well," he gestured behind him at the table and the flowers, "you were right. This is about making a change. So get out of the way and let me—"

Novac put a hand on his shoulder. "She needs time to calm down."

"What do you mean she needs time to calm down?"

"You really don't know?" When Michael shook his head, Novac told him. "She and Rainelle had lunch in the Haymarket today. Then they crossed the street to go into the antique store. That's when Pam saw you. With the blonde."

"It wasn't what she thinks," Michael protested. "We just ran into each other. And what she thinks she saw was good-bye. Nothing more."

"Yeah, well, for there to be a good-bye like that, there had to have been a hello at some point, didn't there?"

Michael backed away from the stairs. He ran his hands through his hair and began to pace back and forth. "I can't believe this is happening. Not now."

The women descended the front stairs and headed for the front door. When Pam called for Rambo, Michael grabbed the dog's collar and ordered him to sit. His hand still on Rambo's collar, Michael said, "Please just come back here so we can talk."

Pam didn't move from the door. Her voice was emotionless as she said, "I have nothing to say to you. Please let go of Rambo's collar.

He's the only thing left in this house I care about. And I want him with me."

Michael let go. When Pam repeated the command for him to come, Rambo hesitated. Michael looked down. "It's okay, boy. Go on." With an almost apologetic glance in Michael's direction, the dog went into the laundry room and emerged with his leash in his mouth. Again he whined and stood looking at Michael.

"It's okay, boy," Michael repeated. "Go on."

When Rambo reached her side, Pam attached his leash, opened the front door, and left. Rainelle and Betty followed, each one pulling a huge piece of wheeled luggage. Michael's heart sank. She'd packed a lot.

"I'll check in with you later," Novac said and followed the others down the hall and out the front door.

Michael sat at the breakfast bar. He heard the garage door close. When the candles began to sputter he blew them out and sat down at the table, listening to the house creak as a gentle breeze stirred, raining leaves on the patio.

———————

"He isn't worth all this," Pam muttered, pulling another tissue out of the box, blowing her nose, tossing it in the wastebasket on the floor beside Rainelle's couch. She glanced over at Rainelle, who was curled up in one of the leather club chairs with Cicero in her lap. "Thanks for letting me stay. I'll—I'll make some arrangements s-s-oon." She dabbed at fresh tears. "I just can't think right now."

"There's no reason to rush into anything." Cicero arched his back. His purr transformed into a low feral growl as he glared at Rambo, who had been lying prone at Pam's feet but just then sat up.

Pam waved a tissue at the cat. "Cicero would agree with me about our moving on as soon as possible."

"Cicero," Rainelle said, pulling the cat into her arms, "will adjust." She carried him down the hall to her bedroom, dropped him inside, and closed the door. As she came back into the living room she said,

"It's been less than a day." She gestured toward Rambo. "They'll work it out."

Pam sighed. "I can't seem to think past Monroe's sentencing the twenty-seventh. I cannot believe I have to sit next to Michael in court and . . ." She broke off.

"That's nearly three weeks away, hon. A lot can happen between now and then."

"You're right," Pam agreed. "Besides, it's just one last performance as 'the happy couple.' I've been doing that for years." She began to cry again. Rambo put his head on her knee as Rainelle moved to her side and took her hand.

"You've done everything a wife could possibly be expected to do."

Pam shook her head. "The one thing I swore was that I would never be like my mother. That I'd never stay with a man just to keep up appearances."

"You didn't," Rainelle insisted. "You stayed to preserve your child's family. That took more strength than I'd ever have. If Malcolm ever—"

"Don't say it. Don't even think it. You and Malcolm are going to have a long, happy life. You're perfect for each other." She got up and crossed to the wall of windows overlooking the city. "Maybe I should get something like this place," she said. "Maybe a fresh start—" She looked back at Rambo. "You wouldn't like this, though, would you?"

Rambo tilted his head and looked at her, whining.

Rainelle cleared her throat. "Hold on, girl friend. When things calm down a little, you need to make it clear to Dr. Nolan that *he's* the one looking for new digs—not you."

Pam turned around to face her. She sighed. "I don't know . . ."

"I know you don't know. That's why I'm telling you. *He* did this. And he's the one who moves out. You just say when, and I'll prepare the legal documents to tell him so."

"I can't do that to him. Not with everything else that's going on."

Rainelle stood up. "Listen to yourself, Pamela Sue. You can't do that to *him*? You aren't doing anything—except maybe surviving.

*Michael* did this." She crossed the room to stand beside Pam. Looping her arm around Pam's waist, she said, "Just think about it. Like I said before, you have a home here as long as you need it. But I wouldn't be a good friend if I let you give up your home because of that— that—" She pressed her lips together. "If I'd known when I introduced the two of you that things would turn out this way . . ."

Pam turned away from the window and took Rainelle's hand, shaking it lightly. "I've had those thoughts over the years. But they always ended up back at the same place."

"What place is that?"

"Not a place, really," Pam murmured. "A person. Michael gave me Jacob."

"And betrayal. And emotional pain."

Pam nodded. "Worth every tear."

———

By Sunday evening, Michael had convinced himself that things would be all right. After a few more days, Pam would let him apologize and explain. Well—at least apologize. There was no acceptable explanation for Kim. Still, he told himself, Pam would forgive him. She'd been doing it for most of their married lives. Just once more, and she'd never have to do it again. That would be a big part of what he would say when she was ready to listen. He'd promise, and she would come home. He'd go back to the practice after New Year's. By then Senior would be ready to take him back without a lecture. It wasn't a simple plan, but he would do whatever it took to make it a reality.

He kept the table set. And he called. When the roses began to wilt and drop petals on the table, he replaced them. He began sending flowers to Pam at Rainelle's. He ate at the breakfast bar or in front of the television in the media room. Carryout containers and boxes from pizza delivery began to accumulate. Caller ID finally said it was Pam about a week and a half after she'd left.

"You have to stop this," she said the minute he answered. "You're wasting your money."

"I'm not stopping until you come home."

"I'm not accepting any more deliveries," she snapped.

"Then they'll line the hall outside the door. I'm not giving up."

She took a different tack. "You're making Rambo sick. He's allergic to roses, in case you don't remember."

"If Rambo's sick, it's probably because he wants to come home. And when it comes to allergies, he's probably allergic to cats by now, too." He paused and consciously made himself speak calmly. "Come home, Pam. I'm a loser and a jerk and completely unworthy of you. I'll give you the long version as soon as you agree to have dinner with me." He added what he thought might at least put a crack in the wall of rage. "You want marriage counseling? We'll go to marriage counseling. You want me to be home more? I'll talk Senior into hiring a third partner. You want me to grovel? I'll grovel. And—" he paused before adding his best argument—"and we can do whatever you want about the memorial fund."

The long silence on the other end of the phone wasn't promising. Finally, Pam said, "What do you want me to say?"

"You don't have to say anything. I'll do all the talking you want. Any or none of the details and reasons. But I want to *see* you."

"If I agree to that right now, you'll talk yourself into believing everything's going to be all right. It isn't."

"Of course it isn't," he agreed. "At the moment our life is like one of those jigsaw puzzles we used to do with Jacob. Someone swept the blasted thing all over the room. Nothing makes any sense at all. Please, baby. Come home. We *can* put it back together. But we have to be *together*." He was pleading. He didn't care. "Please. Haven't we lost enough? Huge pieces of the thing will always be missing no matter what we do. But can't we manage to reconstruct at least part of it? I think we can. I think it's worth trying. If you could only forgive me."

"That's not an *only*, Dr. Nolan," she snapped.

"I didn't mean it that way. Of course it isn't."

"Look. Michael. To be honest, I don't even know if I want to try. It's all gotten very . . . tiring."

"I don't blame you for feeling like this. I deserve it. Honestly, it was a miracle you stayed as long as you did. But you did stay, and that has to mean something."

"Of course it means something," she retorted. "It means I was willing to make personal sacrifices for the good of our son. And for Jacob's sake, I don't regret it. His life was filled with good things because I was willing to hurt quietly. I knew what I was doing, Michael. And, to use your analogy . . . I was keeping the puzzle together on the table. *I* did that, Michael. With precious little help from you."

Something about her calm made the words hurt more. "You're right," he said. "I lost track of what was really important."

"No," she interrupted. "You never lost track of what was important to *you*. You always did what made you feel good." Her voice wavered. "It was the rest of us you forgot about. Jacob and me."

"That's not fair." Even as he said it, he knew she was right—in more ways than he wanted to admit. "I understand Jacob was a big part of what kept us going," he said. "And I know I've made horrible decisions. I've hurt you over and over again. But we can't give up." He snagged the only proof he could think of that, in spite of everything, Pam still had feelings for him. "That night together," he said. "That night in early July. It had to mean something."

"That night was about finding a way to relieve mutual agony. It didn't mean anything about you and me." She paused, then added, "And it's definitely not a reason to think there's something left for us to build a life on now."

"But that's what I want," he said. "I want us to be back together."

"Listen to yourself." There was a hard edge to her voice. "After everything you've said, it's still all about what *you* want. Are you even listening to what I'm saying? Because if you are, you should have picked up on this little bit of reality: I don't *want* to build a life with you, Michael. Right now I don't even like you."

"Well, I love you."

"Does that line play well on your planet, Dr. Nolan?"

"Tell me what you want me to do. I need you in my life. I want you to come home so we can work this out. We have a court date on the twenty-seventh. Please. Just tell me what you want me to do."

"I want you to leave me alone. Don't send flowers. Don't call. Give me time to breathe."

"But what about Monroe's sentencing?"

"What about it? Do you honestly think there is any way to prepare for something like that? You've got to let me untangle all of this without you looming over me."

"All right. I won't loom," he said. "But I'm not giving up."

"You do what you have to do, Michael. Right now, I have to go." She hung up.

———————

Sometimes at night he imagined he could hear Rambo galloping down the hall into Jacob's room. Sometimes he thought he heard Jacob laugh, and that didn't always happen at night. He consulted his medical journals on the topic of stress. He read a couple of books on what was often called "the worst loss." Everything he was experiencing was normal—an interesting fact that did Michael no good at all.

"You, my friend," he said to himself as he stared in the mirror a week after Pam had hung up on him, "are on the cusp of clinical depression. Better do something about that."

He knew he should seek out professional help, but he didn't.

He knew he should get back to the gym so he could handle stress better. But he didn't even care about shaving, let alone working out.

His father called and delivered a military-style pep talk from his self-appointed pedestal. It was clear all Senior really cared about was getting Michael back to the office. The man's self-centeredness hurt. *Never loses track of what's important to him*, Michael thought, and then realized that was exactly what Pam had said about him.

Stan Novac had said he'd be in touch, but that was . . . Michael wasn't even sure when that was. It was a while ago. A long while. This morning, as he stared at the bleary-eyed guy in the mirror, he tried to convince himself that that was for the best. "The last thing you need right now is a visit from a Bible-thumper."

*"We don't thump our Bibles, Dr. Nolan. We read them."* That's what Andy had said to him one time—how long ago was it?—when he'd walked by Jacob's room and looked in to see Andy and Jacob huddled up on the bed with Bibles open in front of them. Michael had made some snide comment, and Andy had given him that comeback. Which was, Michael now admitted, a pretty good one. Jacob had started going to the Novac's church not long after that. And had that ever annoyed him.

"So, all of a sudden your parents' church isn't good enough for you? Nolans have been members of First Church since its founding," Michael said.

"I know," Jacob replied. "And I don't want to make a big thing out of it, but . . . I want something different." He smiled. "You should come with me sometime. You and Mom. Just visit."

Of course that had never happened.

With a sigh, Michael headed out of the guest room bathroom—his bathroom now, he guessed. With Pam gone he could have moved back across the hall. But that would have felt like surrender. At the door to Jacob's room, he paused. The indentation from Rambo's many nights curled up on the bed was still there. Everything else in the room was just the way it had been the day Jacob died. Except for the dust.

Sitting down at Jacob's desk, Michael turned on the old computer, waited while it cranked to life and then spent a few minutes going from web site to web site, checking out Jacob's history. He'd been on some religious sites. Maybe a little more right wing than Michael would have preferred, but nothing crazy.

Turning his back on the computer, Michael got up and crossed the room to the book shelf. A couple of travel guides to help serious mountain bikers and hikers. Half a dozen books on fitness. Textbooks on veterinary science and a few worn paperbacks. Michael smiled remembering how Jacob had complained about his reading assignments in his senior high English class and then ended up loving a couple of the books. *Frankenstein* and *Crime and Punishment*. What a pair. And here they were, gathering dust just like the pile of children's books. *He kept those?* All their favorites were there, from *Ira Sleeps Over* to the Berenstain Bears books . . . all the ones Michael used to read aloud at bedtime back in the day before—before.

Blinking back tears, he went back to Jacob's desk and sat down. One of the articles tacked to the bulletin board was on something called *abseiling*. What had Jacob said that was? Here was an article with a photo. A guy standing at the top of a cliff, and a woman lowering herself over the edge. This was fun? Jacob had drawn a star beside one section of an article printed off the Internet titled "10 Greatest U.S. Adventure Vacations." The paragraph on "Llama Trekking the Hoover Wilderness Area" described California's High Sierra as a place of "solitude and spectacle." As he took the article down and read about the five-day trek in a wilderness "of lodgepole pine and red fir, arid desert, and U-shaped glacial valleys," Michael thought it sounded like something they all could have enjoyed together. *Oh yeah? You didn't even make time for the local sky diving on Father's Day.*

With a grimace, he laid the article aside and sat for a minute, clicking through some more web sites. Finally he opened the top drawer of Jacob's desk. Someone had had Jacob's name engraved in gold in the lower right corner of a Bible in the drawer. Lifting it out, Michael opened the cover and read, "Presented to Jacob Nolan by his second family." The old resentment flickered, and then Michael decided not to dwell on it. Why hold on to a stupid grudge against people who had done nothing but try to be good friends? *Face it. Novac isn't "holier than thou." He's honest. And the only reason you didn't like Jacob hanging with them was because it hurt your pride. Stan Novac was right about that, too. You bought toys, but what Jacob really wanted was time with a family.*

Stan Novac sat in his pickup staring at the Nolans' front door wishing that for once in her life Betty had just kept quiet.

"Pam has Rainelle. Michael doesn't have anyone," Betty had said. "He shouldn't have to walk into that courtroom alone."

"His father will be there."

"His father is about as supportive as a rock. Remember him at the funeral? Remember how Pam said he ordered Michael back to work?"

"I know, I know. You're right," Stan groused. "I'll go." He sighed. "But I'm telling you right now that I am the last person on earth he's gonna want to see at his front door."

"Then you'll be back home in time for dinner," Betty said with a big smile. "And you'll have done the right thing." She shoved him toward the door. "You're in a unique position to help Michael. You know the truth about him. And you know the only One who can fix him."

"He won't listen."

"I didn't say you should take out a gospel tract and try to convert the guy," Betty retorted. "I said you should try to be a friend."

She was right. About everything. But that didn't mean his heart wasn't pounding. That didn't mean his hands weren't shaking. *You coward. What would Ken Randolph think if he could see you now? What's got you so rattled? Greater is He that is in you than He that is in the world . . . remember?* Yeah, he remembered. He also remembered how he'd reacted the first time someone tried to tell him that Jesus was the answer. "You hear me asking any questions?" he'd said before slugging the guy.

Okay, so Michael Nolan wasn't likely to react that way. But Stan was pretty sure he also wasn't going to want advice or support from the guy who lived across the city in the trailer park. What was it the doc had said? Something about Betty having to garden to keep the kids from going hungry. The comment still rankled. Taking a deep breath, Stan stepped up on the porch. Even the doorbell was intimidating. A button in the mouth of a roaring brass lion. *Stupid doorbell probably cost more than I make in a week.*

---

On September 27, the day of Eddie Lee Monroe's sentencing, they all gathered in the hallway just inside the courthouse doors. Philip Riley had already checked the docket and knew which courtroom. He was there with Michael. So were Stan and Betty. Pam knew the Novacs were coming with Michael. Betty had called to tell her that Stan had gone to see Michael and that Michael would be riding to court with them. Pam didn't know what to think. She supposed she should be glad—as a human being—that Michael had someone besides his robotic father to be with him. On the other hand, she couldn't help but feel a bit betrayed. Betty and Stan were *her* friends. Michael had never had any use for them. And the idea of Michael climbing into the Novacs' minivan was nothing short of comical.

Today, he looked . . . haggard. It tugged at her heart, thinking she was the cause of most of it. *No. He did this.* That's what Rainelle kept saying. And she was right. But—he looked bad, standing there in his best suit. He'd lost weight. When he looked at her he barely made eye contact.

"This way," Rainelle said and put a hand beneath her elbow. They all walked through the maze of halls, Pam grateful for lawyers who knew their way around the place and feeling awkward about sitting next to Michael in the courtroom. Rainelle led the way along the benches. Michael followed, then Philip Riley, their attorney. Next came the Novacs—Stan, Betty, and Andy. Michael's father arrived separately and, after shaking his son's hand, elected to sit in front of them near the door. Pam wondered why he'd even bothered to show up.

Finally "the case of the State of Nebraska versus Eddie Lee Monroe, docket 06, page 204" came up. When the judge asked if the State had had "the chance to review the presentence," Malcolm Sutter said

yes. When asked if the State had any additions, corrections, or dele-
tions to the presentence, Malcolm made a valiant attempt to argue
why Monroe should face the most severe sentence allowed by law.
When Eddie Lee Monroe stood up and faced the judge, Pam clasped
her hands so tight she could feel her nails digging into her palms. All
she wanted was to get this over with and get out of there. She glanced
up at Michael. His focus was locked onto Eddie Lee Monroe. She
could almost hear his teeth grinding as he worked his jaw.

The judge asked Eddie Lee if he had read the letters from the
victim's family. Eddie Lee said he had. And then it was over. Just like
that. The judge read from a legal pad as he commented on the loss to
Jacob Nolan's family and the community.

Pam's heart began to pound. This wasn't going well. Somehow she
just knew it. She thought back to what Rainelle had warned them
could happen. Instinctively, she reached for Michael. When their
hands touched, he glanced down momentarily, then clasped her hand
in his.

"It would appear by all accounts that the defendant has accepted
responsibility for this tragedy. There has been no plea for leniency. No
attempt to plea bargain." The judge paused for half a heartbeat and
then read the sentence. Six months in jail. And he's already served
part of that because he hadn't made bail. Two years probation. A personal apology to Jacob Nolan's parents. Visit Jacob Nolan's grave on
June 19 for the next five years.

"What?!" The word exploded from Michael's mouth. He dropped
Pam's hand. The bailiff headed their way, but Philip waved him away,
grasping Michael's free arm and babbling in his ear.

Pam felt caught in the space between the judge's last words and
the reaction in the courtroom, as if she were an observer of the pro-
ceedings but not a participant. A flash of pink caught her attention
and as Michael leaned down to listen more intently to what Philip
was saying, Pam noticed Eddie Lee Monroe's wife and baby, the latter
a tiny bundle cradled in one of those shoulder bags that some young
mothers used to keep their babies close. Pam's throat tightened. Tears

threatened as she looked at the tiny bump of humanity close to his mother's heart. Eddie Lee was holding his wife. Pam couldn't see the tears on the woman's cheeks, but she knew they were there, because as he spoke to her, he reached up and cradled her face in his hands and, with his thumb, brushed them gently away.

The defense lawyer was smiling and nodding at them both. Then the next case was called. Just like that. The bailiff—who had been watching Michael after his one-word outburst—moved back to his place by the door. Pam could not take her eyes off Lisa Monroe, who could not take her eyes off the lean young man headed back to jail.

Once Eddie Lee was no longer in view, his wife stood looking at the closed door he'd gone through. Pam saw her shoulders slump, saw her look down at her baby and murmur something with her lips curved up in a weak smile. Then she glanced at Pam. Their eyes met for a scant second before Lisa ducked her head and hurried out of the courtroom.

*I wonder how often she visits him.* Pam raised her hand and pinched the bridge of her nose where a dull throb had begun.

"Are you all right?" Michael asked.

"What?" Pam tore her gaze away from the door through which Lisa Monroe had just left. "What did you say?"

"Are you all right?"

"Fine," she said automatically.

Once they were out in the hall, Philip offered a meeting "to answer any questions you might have."

Michael shook his head. "I can't believe it. Jacob's killer will be home for *Christmas*." The sound he made was something between a sob and a laugh.

"Don't think about it," Pam said. "It's done."

They were standing in an awkward group waiting for the elevator when a flash of pink caught Pam's eye again. Lisa Monroe stood up from the water fountain across the hall, wiping her mouth with the back of her free hand while the other arm cradled her baby. When she headed toward them, Pam realized the young woman must have been waiting for them.

Michael reacted first, grabbing Pam's arm and heading for the stairs. Stan Novac stepped in the space between the Nolans and Lisa.

"Please," she called out, trying to dodge Stan. Two guards came out of nowhere.

"You need to leave, ma'am," one said to Lisa and tried to herd her toward the elevator.

The other motioned for Michael and Pam to follow him down the stairs.

"Please," Lisa called out. "Please listen," she pleaded.

Pam turned around. The bundle in the carrier moved, and as Pam watched, a tiny hand appeared as the baby reached for his mother. "Wait," Pam told the others.

Lisa clutched the infant's hand as she spoke. "Please. We're both eaten up inside with sadness for you." Her voice warbled and then was joined by the soft mewing of the baby. "We—we—Eddie Lee—" Her voice broke and she looked down at the floor. "We'll pray for you every day for the rest of our lives."

Michael jerked the door to the stairs open. Pam and the others followed him. As they descended the stairwell, she could hear the baby's hungry wail echoing in the hallway above.

# {thirteen}

SHE'D PROMISED NOT to wear out her welcome at Rainelle's, but Eddie Lee Monroe's sentencing sent Pam into a tailspin that negated any intelligent decision making.

"How many times do I have to tell you I understand?" Rainelle said. "I advise clients all the time not to make major life decisions at times like these. So—" she clicked on the television and called up the classic movie channel—"sit back and relax while I make popcorn. And stop fretting."

"You're just hoping I'll see things your way and kick Michael out," Pam chided.

"I object to your choice of words," Rainelle said from the kitchen doorway. "It doesn't have to be that ugly. Michael's a smart guy. He has to know it's coming."

"He's still in denial. Betty said that when Stan was over there before the court date, Michael hadn't even cleared the table off yet. As if he's still waiting for me to join him for dinner."

"Well," Rainelle called from the kitchen, "he's stopped sending roses here. So maybe reality is starting to get through to him." She came back in and plopped down on the couch, positioning the stainless steel bowl of popcorn between them and handing Pam a can of diet soda.

When the movie was over, Pam collected a few magazines as she got up. Wishing Rainelle a good night, she called Rambo to her side and made her way down the hall to the guest bedroom. The instant she closed the door, she could hear Rainelle let Cicero out of her bedroom.

The doorbell rang. She heard Malcolm's voice. With a sigh, Pam put in a CD and turned the volume up. Rambo sat down beside the door. His eyes never left her face.

"I know, I know. Trading spaces isn't your idea of a good time." Rambo chuffed.

"We'll figure something out. Soon," Pam promised. "But for now . . ." She climbed into bed and opened a magazine. With a sigh, Rambo lay down.

---

"Good morning," Malcolm said.

He was standing in Rainelle's kitchen buttering toast as if it was something he did every Sunday morning. Shirtless. Wearing pajama bottoms that Pam thought were probably silk. He had a minor belly and a major tattoo that started right above his elbow and crept up over one shoulder and onto his back.

"Can I pour you some coffee?" Malcolm had finished buttering the toast and reached into the cupboard above the coffee maker. "Or make you a latte? The espresso machine is a little tricky—but then you probably already know that."

Pam was too distracted to answer right away. She'd known that Malcolm probably stayed over once in a while. Rainelle wasn't flagrant about it, but she definitely didn't hold to what she called Pam's old-fashioned rules. They'd agreed to disagree and avoided the subject. But Pam couldn't avoid the half-dressed man in the kitchen and she couldn't get past feeling awkward. When he turned around she couldn't help noticing that his tattoos continued all the way down his back . . . and beyond.

"Hawaiian petroglyphs," he said.

"What?"

"The tattoos."

"Oh . . . right . . ." Pam felt herself starting to blush.

"Sure I can't make you something?" he asked, then moved aside. "Or maybe you'd rather do your own thing."

She shook her head. "Haven't tried it. Too many dials and buttons. I just go to Starbucks when I walk Rambo."

"They let him in?" Malcolm tilted his head to where Rambo lay sprawled across the doorway.

"He waits outside."

"Really?"

"He's a very well trained dog. I say *stay*, Rambo stays."

"Rambo the wonder dog, eh?" Malcolm chuckled and went to work at the behemoth espresso machine, which, Pam realized, he operated like a professional barista.

As the smell of fresh ground coffee filled the air, Pam inhaled and murmured with appreciation. "Best aroma in the universe. If the offer's still open, yes. I'd love one—an espresso, though, instead of a latte—if you're taking orders."

"Don't trust him," Rainelle said as she stepped over Rambo to enter the kitchen. "He doesn't *take* orders. He *gives* them."

Pam glanced Rainelle's way. *Uh-oh.* She knew that expression. "On second thought," she said quickly, "Rambo's bladder is probably about to burst. I should be—"

Rainelle waved a hand in the air. "Rambo is still curled up on the floor. Don't run out on account of us." She forced a fake smile. "We're fine. Just fine. Really. Nothing to see here."

Malcolm wiped off the frothing spigot with a damp dishcloth and finished mixing his latte and making Pam's espresso before settling at the table with his toast. "Don't lie to your best friend," he said to Rainelle before turning to Pam. "Your dear friend *Miz* Washington has just informed me that she doesn't want to take my name after we're married."

"Don't be changing what I said," Rainelle said with a huff, "trying to make me sound all uppity. Putting negative spin where it doesn't belong." She put her hands on her hips. "I've worked hard to build a professional reputation," she told Pam, "and I don't see why I should have to change my identity. I've always been Rainelle *Washington*. Why does that have to change just because—"

"Just because you've promised to love, honor, and obey?" Malcolm interjected.

"For your information, Mr. Sutter, no one uses those old vows anymore."

"What does that mean?" He leaned back in his chair, a slight frown on his face. "And why shouldn't you want my name? Does it disempower one or more of those infamous alter egos of yours to be associated with me?"

"Look who's talking about being disempowered," Rainelle said, making a face and turning to Pam. "Explain it to him, girl friend."

"Explain what?" Pam frowned. "Those were the vows I took—along with my husband's name."

"And look what all that servility did for you." She turned to Malcolm. "The girl is a walking, talking impact statement for my side of this. No reason a woman should lose her identity in a man."

"I don't expect you to lose anything," Malcolm said. "I was rather hoping you'd look at our marriage—and the name Sutter—as a nice addition to your life."

"Now don't be like that." Rainelle walked over and put her hand on his shoulder. "Of course I think that, too, or I wouldn't have said yes. But I still don't see why I can't keep the name I was born with instead of taking on a man's." She patted his tattooed shoulder. "Even though, in this case, the man in question is truly fine."

"Inconsistent argument, Counselor," Malcolm muttered.

"Oh it is, is it?" Her voice went up a couple of decibels.

"Yes, and the reason should be obvious."

"Well, excuse me if I don't follow your sterling logic."

"It's inconsistent because the name you *have* came from a man you never even met. So explain to me why it is you're refusing to take the name of a man you allegedly respect in favor of a man who wasn't much more than a sperm donor." He folded his arms across his torso and waited.

Rainelle blinked. "It's not about whoever gave me the name. It's about what I've done with it." She sighed. "Malcolm. Darling. I love you. I want to marry you. But I don't want to obliterate who I am."

"No one's asking you to obliterate anything."

"Except a perfectly good name!"

*Whine.* Rambo was standing by the door looking anxious, his gaze moving from one human to the next. "It's all right, boy," Pam said and got up. "Looks like I'm outta here—" she forced a laugh— "although I hate to leave this scintillating discussion." By the time she'd changed into a running suit and tennies, Rambo was waiting at the door, leash in mouth.

---

"Well, the place is just too quiet, that's all. If you can believe it, I even miss Fur-face." Michael looked down, first at the grave, then at the book in his hand. This was a very slim hair shy of crazy. Heck, he probably *was* crazy. Nothing in his life made sense anymore. So what did it matter? If this took him back to the days when he was still a pretty good guy, who could say there was anything wrong with it? There wasn't anyone else around, unless you counted the guys raking up leaves two sections away. They were probably used to seeing odd things here in the cemetery. He looked over in the next section, where a bouquet of helium-filled balloons and a spinning garden ornament had been left at a grave.

Taking in a ragged breath, he began to read. "'I was invited to sleep at Reggie's house.'" His voice wavered. He gulped. "Okay, okay. I know. I can do better. You always wanted me to do voices." Michael cleared his throat and repeated it, only this time in the character of a thrilled six-year-old boy. "'I was invited to sleep at Reggie's house. Was I HAPPY!'"

---

"I'm not sure I should even bring this up," Betty said as she and Pam chugged along the bike path with Rambo and Reba in tow. "But a couple of churches in town are sponsoring a retreat next month. I've gone the last couple of years, and it's a very refreshing two days. Would you like to come this year?"

Pam shook her head. "Thanks, but I'm not good in groups. Not now. Maybe not ever."

"You don't have to be part of a group," Betty said. "A lot of women don't even attend the sessions. They spend the entire time alone, meditating, journaling, walking the trails at the retreat center. It's very do-it-yourself. Last year I spent practically the whole time in the chapel—either crying or journaling."

Pam looked at her in surprise.

"Don't be shocked. Beneath this exterior there's a half-crazed woman determined to get out and ruin my life."

"You're joking."

"I'm not," Betty insisted. "Everyone has their own issues. Mine's depression."

Pam frowned. "You're the most even-keeled person I know."

"Then it's working," Betty laughed. "Be sure and tell Stan that so he realizes the great return he's getting on his investment when he sends me to this thing."

"You said earlier you journal?" Pam asked. "Seems like that comes up all the time in some of the reading I've been doing."

"It's a lifeline for me. For others, not so much. But you should try it. I'm sorry I haven't mentioned it before."

"Maybe you did. Michael always said I'm pretty good at only hearing what I want to hear." *Michael again.* When was she going to stop defining her life by what Michael thought or said or did? "So . . . what's so great about this place?"

"It's one of the most peaceful places I've ever been. Lovely chapel. Tall glass windows that look out on the woods. It'll be gorgeous with all the leaves turning color."

Pam chuckled. "I'd hate to ruin it."

"What makes you think you'd ruin it?"

"Well, after I go in there and tell God what I think of Him, there's going to be lightning."

"Very funny."

"I'm not joking."

"You mad at God?"

"We've had words."

"Words are good," Betty said. "Even angry words."

"Right," Pam snorted. "Like the Almighty doesn't mind being told He's blown it."

"It's a pretty sure bet the Almighty knows you think that." They walked along in silence for a few minutes and then Betty said, "You could ask Rainelle to come, too. With her high-stress job, I bet she'd love a retreat. There's a decent restaurant attached if you don't want to do the group thing, and a spa."

"Well, now," Pam mused, "you didn't mention a spa. Where is this place?"

"Halfway between here and Omaha. Beautiful wooded area. Walking trails. Lots of wildlife. I've seen deer, raccoons . . . even a red fox once when I was hiking along the creek." She added, "You can drop Rambo at the house for the weekend. The kids will love it."

"I'm telling you right up front that I'm not interested in the Jesus-y part of this," Pam said. "But I could use some time away. Frankly, so could Rainelle. She's been great about it, but I know having me and Rambo around all the time has put a strain on her life."

———

"Who is that guy?" Eduardo said as he and Tomas raked leaves in section 12. "He comes every day. I checked one day after he was gone. Some poor kid is buried there."

"I think it's the boy's father," Tomas answered, stooping to pick up a pile of leaves, then dumping them in the lawn cart.

"Is he crazy? He talks to that grave all the time. He brings *books* to read."

Tomas shrugged. "I'd probably be a little crazy, too, if something happened to my Rosa."

"I'm staying away from that guy. He needs to see a head doctor or something."

Tomas bent over, and with a pair of garden shears began to trim back a peony bush damaged by the previous night's heavy frost. "He's got a lot more trouble than that grave. Yesterday while you were at lunch, a woman in a black Suburban drove in. I recognized the car— it's been here before. She was headed for that same grave. She's got a big black poodle that rides with her. Nice dog. But it was clear she didn't want to see that guy. Turned around the minute she saw him and headed for the gate. But the dog—whoosh!" Tomas motioned with his hands. "He was out the open window and charging toward that guy like a kid running to Santa Claus. The guy started laughing, he was so happy to see that dog. But the woman called him away. The dog didn't want to go, but finally he did."

"What happened then?"

"After a while the guy got up and drove away." Tomas lit a cigarette and took a drag on it. "I'm guessing they're married, but the boy dying caused big trouble. Or maybe they already had some troubles and this brought it all out." He shook his head and crossed himself. "I'm gonna light a candle for that guy at mass tomorrow. He's in bad shape."

"You've been working here twenty years, and now you're gonna start lighting candles?" Eduardo gestured around. "You're gonna go broke, man."

Tomas shrugged. "Something about him makes me feel like maybe he needs something special from God. He drives that fancy car but he dresses like a bum. Sometimes I think I'm gonna come to work and he's gonna be laying on that bench like—" He pantomimed shooting himself in the temple.

Eduardo flinched. "Aw, that's not gonna happen. It's gonna be too cold soon for people to be spending much time out here."

"Yeah. You're probably right. Though I wonder what he's gonna do then." He straightened and watched the man for a minute. "That's a guy who doesn't want to go home."

Eduardo slapped him on the back. "Maybe you could ask him over for a drink, eh?"

"Ask him to church is more like it."

"Oh, yeah, man," Eduardo teased. "That guy's gonna drive his fancy car to church with you. He's gonna kneel right there and cross himself and be your brother." He snickered.

"Hey!" Tomas said sharply. "If you don't wanna go to church, that's you. But don't be making fun of what you don't know anything about."

"I know there ain't no rich white guy coming down to our part of town looking for God."

"I'm still gonna pray," Tomas said. "Maybe it'll help, maybe it won't. I just feel bad for him." He gestured toward the grave. "If that was my boy laying there, you might as well put me in the hole right next to him."

"If that was your *boy* laying there, Josefina would probably dig the hole," Eduardo joked.

That was a good one. Tomas, proud father of six daughters, smiled. Together, the two men returned to raking, and as he raked Tomas did exactly what he had said he would do. He prayed for the guy on the bench.

# {fourteen}

ON HIS WAY HOME from the cemetery on Halloween, Michael stopped at Walgreens and bought candy. He might not know as much as he should about his son, but he knew Jacob had loved handing out treats to the neighborhood kids on Halloween. He didn't know if many kids would come by, but he'd put the porch light on and see what happened. What happened was hordes of Zorros and Frankensteins and cowboys and princesses. Spiderman was the one that got him, though.

"I miss Jacob," the voice said. The kid was about the same size as Michael visualized Jacob being while he read books to him at the cemetery.

"John William!" a voice hissed, and a guy dressed in a sweat shirt and jeans stepped from where he'd been watching—the Dad escorting the kid, Michael realized, with a pang of guilt. *Pam always did that.*

But John William Whoever was stubborn. "He taught me how to throw a football," he said.

Michael crouched down. "He did?"

Spiderman nodded and pointed to the top of the hill. "In my yard."

Michael had no idea which house he was pointing out. He didn't even know the names of most of the people on this street. *Pam would know.*

"We're the Blackwells," the dad finally said. "I'm John." He nodded toward Spiderman. "John William."

Michael grabbed a handful of candy and shoved it into the child's bag. "Well, John William Spiderman, thank you for telling me you miss Jacob." His voice wavered. "I miss him, too."

Spiderman leaned sideways to look past Michael as he asked, "Where's Rambo?"

"You know Rambo?" More kids were coming up the drive.

Spiderman nodded and held out his hand. A dog biscuit.

"I'm sorry," Michael said, "Rambo isn't here tonight." Swallowing the lump in his throat, he promised to give the biscuit to the dog later.

The dad offered an explanation. "One year Jacob had the candy in a basket with handles. Rambo actually held the basket while the kids took their treat. John William was only four, but he staged a huge campaign to get a poodle after that. It resurfaces every time he sees Rambo." He shook his head. "I keep telling him we don't have time for a dog, but . . ."

Michael put more candy in Spiderman's bag. As the next gaggle of trick-or-treaters made their way up the walk, Spiderman and his dad turned to go.

"Say?" Michael called out.

The two turned back.

"Get a dog," he said.

The dad looked down at Spiderman, then back at Michael. "Yeah," he said. "Maybe we will. Thanks."

Setting the bowl of candy on the porch, Michael told the kids to help themselves. Stepping inside, he closed the door. Dog biscuit in hand, Michael walked to the back of the house. Setting Rambo's treat on the kitchen counter, he headed into the media room and began to pull family albums down from the bookshelves.

---

"Well?" Betty asked as she continued to chop celery for that night's version of meat loaf.

"He wants to meet for breakfast." Stan grabbed a piece of celery off the cutting board and munched while he stared out the window at the trick-or-treaters approaching their neighbors' trailer.

"Praise the Lord," Betty whispered under her breath.

"I wouldn't be any more surprised if the last perp I arrested wanted to treat me to an ice cream cone over at Dairy Queen."

"Come on, sweetheart. He didn't throw you out when you went over to see how things were going before the court date. And I think he was happy to have us there on the twenty-seventh."

"Polite. He was so polite it was exhausting."

"Well, I think he was glad for the show of support." Betty cracked two eggs into the bowl and began to mix the meat loaf. She chuckled. "He rode in our minivan."

"Still freaks me out just thinking about that day."

"I'll admit I expected Pam to be more open than Michael, but God has a way of surprising people." She sighed. "I haven't heard much from Pam lately. She's nice when I call, but distant."

"But she's going to the retreat," Stan reminded her.

Betty nodded. "With Rainelle."

"Maybe she's afraid you're going to try to talk her into taking her husband back."

"Well, it worked out for me, didn't it?" Betty pressed the meat loaf into a pan and put it in the oven.

"Yes, but I have to admit I don't see Pam moving home anytime soon."

"More prayer required."

"Add your husband to that list," Stan said. "I told Dr. Nolan I'd meet him at Village Cafe in the morning."

Betty glanced at the calendar hanging above the sink. "I promised to help sort donations for the city mission tomorrow." She smiled at Stan. "Plenty of opportunity to pray while I fold sweaters and pair socks."

————

That evening Stan practiced several different speeches. He looked over the verses he had read at Jake's funeral, preparing answers to every question he imagined Nolan could have about faith and hope and heaven. He prepared a good argument for working at keeping a marriage together, and even readied himself to talk about his own failures. But for all his planning, Stan was not prepared for what Nolan brought up over breakfast.

"Come again?"

"I want to see that Andy finishes the project," the doc said. "If you're okay with my getting involved."

Stan didn't know what surprised him more—the overall idea or the fact that Nolan was asking his permission.

The doc opened the file folder he'd brought with him. "It would mean doing all this stuff. Do you think Andy can still make it work? Didn't someone mention that he was trying to come up with a way? Or did I dream that?"

"No. He's been working on it. But it's tough."

"I can imagine," Nolan said, looking down at the scribbled list. "I don't even know if this is the final version, but it looks like they were only about halfway there when the accident happened."

"That's about right," Stan said, taking the piece of paper Nolan offered. He perused the list. "I think the final list is a little different from what you have there." He looked up. "Seems to me there was something in California on it."

Nolan smiled and shuffled through the folder. He showed Stan the Internet article about the Hoover Wilderness llama trek.

"Yeah. I think that was it."

"Thought so. Do you know any of the details?"

Stan shook his head. "Can't help you there. All I know is Andy's stuck with some bits and pieces—" his voice gentled—"and it would be really great for him to finish . . . for lots of reasons." He shook his head. "But I honestly don't see any way."

"The money has to be at least part of your concern." When Stan nodded, the doc said, "Well, I've got plenty of that." He held up his hand. "Now, don't get your macho-man pants all tied up in a knot. Let me finish."

Stan almost cracked up. Dr. Nolan had obviously been watching *way* too much late night television.

"Pam and I discussed how to use the memorial money. To be honest, we fought more than we discussed. Pam wanted to pay for Andy's education. I didn't." Michael paused. "I know how that plays with you. No man wants to be reminded he can't provide for his own." He flinched. "Sorry again. I didn't mean that the way it sounded."

*Betty must be praying hard while she sorts clothes at the mission*, Stan thought. Because instead of acting on instinct and punching the guy out, he was still sitting here letting Nolan insult him. "Go on," he said, forcing himself to loosen his death grip on the coffee mug.

"Initially I told Pam it was a horrible idea. Told her that much money and an easy ride through college could ruin a kid."

"And you were right," Stan agreed.

Nolan cleared his throat. "Except, to be honest, that wasn't my motivation when I first said it. I was just hiding behind that because I didn't want—" He looked away, then back again. "I've never liked you, Novac. And that goes way back before I had to face you when you found me with Kim." He took a deep breath. "I've resented the time Jacob spent with you and your family. I was jealous."

"Jealous?" Stan didn't try to hide his surprise. "Of what? The fabulous laundry room I built onto the double-wide?" He snorted in disbelief.

"I felt threatened. By all of you. Jacob was so drawn to you—the perfect family with a great life. I thought it might change when he went off to KSU. But no—every time he was home from school he had one obligatory meal with the parental unit, but I could tell he couldn't wait until it was over and he could head out the door to your place. Heck, the *dog* practically waited by the door to leave with him. I hated it. I'd worked long and hard to achieve what I thought was success, and my own son preferred to spend his evenings at a trailer across town." He waited while the waitress put their plates in front of them. "So I was jealous."

"I knew you didn't approve of us," Stan said, "but I never thought of jealousy as one of the reasons."

The doc sat back. "Believe it or not, I used to be a nice guy. But somewhere along the way I lost my focus about what was really important in life. And then Andy and your family moved to town, and we all met, and I found myself haunted by someone on the opposite side of the financial universe who had exactly what I wanted."

"Which was?"

"A happy marriage. A thriving family. Good times." Nolan paused before adding, "And it didn't make it any easier that you were all so blasted *nice*."

"I see. You don't like us because we're . . . nice." Stan took a big bite of his hash browns. "Sure. Anybody could understand that. Nice can be the most annoying thing on earth."

Nolan reached for the list. "Well, you're the one who said that for a smart guy I was really stupid. I guess this is just more proof you were right." He paused.

Stan saw the guy's jaw working, and for a tense moment he thought there were going to be tears.

Nolan cleared his throat, glanced up momentarily, then focused on the list in his hand, took a deep breath, and continued. "My life is in shambles. My wife isn't speaking to me. Jacob was what held us together . . . and he's gone. My father isn't really talking to me, and even if he were, I know I can't practice medicine right now. I'm not competent—especially when it comes to children who remind me of my son." His voice wavered. "I'm looking at losing everything I've worked for all my life, and there's not one single thing I can do about any of it today. Except this." He tapped the list. "*This* I can at least try to make right."

He looked up. Looked Stan in the eye. "So. What I want to propose is that the two of us," he gestured between himself and Stan, "offer to help Andy finish." He lifted a shoulder. "Two middle-aged guys aren't much of a substitute for Jacob, but—you're in shape. And I could get there."

If Betty was praying for Dr. Nolan's soul, God was answering in a very strange way, because as far as Stan could tell, nothing spiritual was going on here. "Even if I could afford it, I can't get off work for all these stunts. I don't have enough vacation time."

"I bet if we put our heads together we could make it work."

Stan took the folder and flipped through some of the papers. He refilled his coffee cup. "You need to talk to Andy." He cleared his throat. "I'll see if Andy can stop by your place in the next day or two."

———————

Lisa Monroe picked up the pencil tied to the end of the string attached to the refrigerator door handle and drew an *X* on the home-made calendar. She knew the count by heart, but repeating the ritual every morning made it more real.

"Thirty-three days, Baby Lee," she said to the infant sleeping on the nearby couch. "Daddy'll be home in thirty-three days."

With Eddie Lee gone, she'd gotten into the habit of talking to herself. Some people might think she was crazy, but Lisa knew she'd *go* crazy if she didn't have company. She didn't really know any of her neighbors and she was afraid to introduce herself for fear they'd hear the name and know about Eddie Lee. It had been in all the papers, and Lincoln was a surprisingly small town when it came to gossip and news.

It had been Lisa's experience that people generally chose to think the worst about people who were on her rung of the social ladder. Once she'd gone into one of the small neighborhood grocery stores where rich people shopped. All she was doing was buying milk, but there was something about the way people looked at her. Like she didn't belong. Like she should go someplace else. Most people would never think someone like Eddie Lee could be a good man who had made a mistake. They wouldn't think he might be just as sad as everyone else about what had happened.

*Most people would be like that boy's parents.* Lisa had thought about them a lot since that awful day at the courthouse when she'd tried to apologize. If she had a way to get to the cemetery, she would put flowers on Jacob Nolan's grave. Maybe it would help them to know someone cared enough to bring flowers. Of course, they wouldn't know it was her. That was okay. Maybe it would be even better. But the truck wouldn't start, and she didn't have money for groceries, let alone flowers or a taxi. She'd had a breast infection and then the flu in the last few months. It was all she could do now just to take care of the two of them.

The scene at the courthouse all those weeks ago still bothered her. "What did you expect them to do?" she said aloud. "You know how you'd feel about the person who did it if your own baby had died that way."

Often when she looked down into Baby Lee's face she thought how Jacob Nolan's mother had done this very thing. Sometimes she woke at night crying from a dream that put her child in the cemetery and Jacob Nolan in the courtroom. She'd seen his picture in the paper with his obituary. Dark hair, square jaw. Probably had blue eyes like his daddy. He did in her dreams, anyway. Sometimes at night when she was huddled up on the bed with the baby and her stomach rumbled and she didn't know if she was going to make it, she would croon to Baby Lee, "It's all right. Only a little while longer and Daddy'll be home again. Mr. Hersh is going to give Daddy a different job. And things are going to be all right."

Lisa opened the refrigerator. One egg. A little milk that smelled suspicious. Two slices of bread. She could make an egg sandwich for breakfast. She wished she had some ketchup. She fried the egg and toasted the bread, serving the sandwich on half a paper towel. She was out of dish soap. But the water was on, and the electric company had agreed to keep things going until late December, when Eddie Lee would get a paycheck and they could start to get caught up. Mr. Hersh was paying the rent. She wasn't going to whine to him about needing anything more.

The thought of leaving the baby with someone else so she could go back to work made her feel panicky. Baby Lee needed her. How could she protect him if she wasn't there? They'd had it all figured out. She was going to open a little day care right here at home. But no one would bring her their kids now. Not when Eddie Lee had served time. They could lie about it and hope no one found out. But lying was the first step down a road Lisa had traveled before. A road she was never going down again.

She'd learned a lot of Bible verses as a child in that Baptist Sunday school in Mount Vernon, Illinois. They came back now in a steady stream while she chewed her egg sandwich, reminding her that the Lord was her Shepherd and Jesus loved her and would leave her no, never alone. Lisa wasn't quite sure which phrases were from hymns and which were really from the Bible, but it didn't matter to her because they all made her feel a little better.

"What time I am afraid, I will trust in thee," she said aloud. "Fear not: for I am with thee. I know the plans I have for you, plans for a future and a hope." Looking around her, Lisa realized that anybody in their right mind would be scared right now. She had a baby to feed, and she'd just eaten the last bit of food in the refrigerator. The phone was disconnected now, so she couldn't call a taxi even if she could afford to pay for one.

It was time to go back to the city mission. That was all right with her. The folks there were nice. They'd let her do some kind of work like sorting the donated clothes, and they wouldn't make her feel like something was wrong with her just because she needed a little help right now. They'd feed her and then she'd have good milk for nursing the baby. She'd head out as soon as Baby Lee woke up. It was a long walk, but she could do it if she took it in little bites.

"How do you eat an elephant?" she said out loud, repeating a silly joke Eddie Lee had told her once when they were still eyeing each other over pie at the truck stop. "One bite at a time." That's how she'd gotten by with Eddie Lee in jail. One day at a time. That's how she'd walk the few miles to the mission. One block at a time.

"They that believe in me will mount up with wings like eagles," Lisa said aloud. "They will run and not be weary." She smiled. She was glad for the part that said "they will walk and not faint."

"She didn't recognize you?" Stan asked as he shifted the telephone from one hand to the other.

"Why would she?" Betty said. "I was only in court that one time, and she had eyes for no one but her husband. I missed all the dramatics out in the hall because I was in the rest room."

"Forgot about that," Stan said. "So tell me again. How'd this happen?"

"I was in the donation room sorting clothes, and in she came with Marie. You remember Marie?"

"Plump. A little slow. Real friendly."

"That's her," Betty said. "Stan, the poor girl's a stick. I don't think her arms are as big around as Emily's. Something's wrong."

"So . . . did you talk to her?"

"I scooted out. It just felt too awkward. But I did do some sleuthing before I left."

"You mean you pumped Marie for information."

"Guilty."

"And?"

"Lisa spent some time at the mission a couple of years ago—before we started volunteering there. We have to do something. I don't know who her doctor is—or if she even has one—but she doesn't look well. If she's trying to nurse that baby—"

"So talk to the director," Stan said.

"I did."

"And?"

"He's going to get me the Monroes' address."

"Ninja Night at the Novacs'?"

"You've got it."

---

"You have got to be kidding me," Andy said. He got up off the couch, every muscle in his body tense. "No. I won't help with that. No way."

"Come back over here and sit down," Stan said, waving his son back to the couch, "and tell me why not."

"Because—because she—because her husband—" He glared at his dad. "You know perfectly well why not. And don't give me that 'What would Jesus do?' line."

Stan sat back. For a moment, he let the tension hang in the air between them. Then, quietly, with his deep voice as soothing as he could make it, he said, "If you don't want to participate, you can go talk to Dr. Nolan about your project while we make the delivery. But I think you'd feel a lot better if you came with us. And did what Jesus would do." When Andy glared at him, Stan shrugged. "It's a good line. And it applies." He leaned forward. "Mrs. Monroe isn't guilty of anything, Andy. And she really does need help."

"So call the director at the mission and tell him," Andy said. "Or call Pastor Garrison."

"I could do that. But that's not what I'm going to do. We've become aware of the need, and we can meet it. So we will."

"Then go for it. But count me out." He paused. "You tell Rachel who it is she'll be helping?"

"Of course," Stan said.

"And?"

"And she's going to help."

"Well, good for her," Andy said, and left the room.

———

As the Novacs sat around the dinner table that evening, Stan said, "It's been a while, but the giving jar is getting heavy. Time for a Ninja Night."

Rachel got up and retrieved a pencil and paper.

"A young mother and her new baby," Betty said. "The daddy's gone, so it's just the two of them."

"Baby food!" Maddy said.

"Not this time." Betty explained that the baby was still getting all his food from his mommy's milk.

"Diapers!" Megan suggested.

Betty nodded. Rachel wrote the word *diapers* on the grocery list.

"Fruit. Lots of fresh fruit," Rachel suggested. "And vegetables. So the mother's getting enough vitamins." When she glanced at Andy, her cheeks grew red.

"Vitamins!" Emily said. "We could get her some vitamins. And baby clothes." Her eyes shone. "Can I pick out a baby outfit?"

Andy asked to be excused.

---

"Sshhhh!" Emily raised her finger to her lips late the next afternoon. "We don't want the neighbors to hear us." Quietly, she tiptoed up onto Lisa Monroe's front porch, unstacking four plastic tubs with lids and lining them up along the edge of the porch. Once they were in place, the rest of the family—minus Andy—filled each tub with groceries and baby supplies, and Emily's contribution— tiny blue overalls. Once the lids were in place, Stan fetched four big rocks from the back of the van and weighted down the lids to keep what he called "varmints" out of the food until Lisa Monroe got back home from the visit to a free clinic downtown that Pastor Garrison had arranged.

"Hurry!" Stan said as a car started up the lane toward the Monroes' trailer. "That might be her."

The family scurried to the minivan and piled inside, barely rounding the corner at the end of the lane before the pastor's car stopped at Lisa's door.

"I wish we coulda seen her face," Emily said. "It would be fun just to see."

"I think we will some day," Betty said. "Someday in heaven Jesus will probably let us see the smiles."

"And they'll know we were the ninjas?" Maddy asked.

"Yep," Betty said. "They'll know."

Megan piped up. "But we don't want anyone to know now," she said, shaking her head back and forth, "'cause it's a secret."

Rachel chuckled. "Yeah. And it's a lot more fun being Grocery Ninjas than eating Ninja meat loaf."

## {fifteen}

THE DOORBELL RANG. When Michael peered through the peephole in the door, Andy Novac was standing in the pool of light cast by the porch light. He had his hands in his pockets and was rocking from side to side, shifting his weight and slapping the edge of one shoe against the other in a nervous little dance. The instant Michael opened the door, Andy thrust a DVD case into his hands.

"Dad said you wanted to see what I've got so far." He pointed to the sky diver on the cover. "A friend studying graphic design did that for me," he said. "You can't tell, but that's Jake. It's—it's as finished as I could make it. Not much good for the original purpose, but—still says something. At least I think it does." He forced a smile. "*Carpe diem* and all that."

"You changed the title," Michael said.

"*Jacob's List* is a better fit now."

"Have you eaten?" Michael asked abruptly. "We could order pizza."

"No, thanks. I'm not really hungry."

"Guys your age are always hungry," Michael insisted. He urged Andy inside, then retreated to the kitchen and set the DVD down on the counter.

When Andy reached for one of the books atop a pile on the kitchen island, Michael shrugged. "Jacob's favorites when he was a kid." Embarrassed, he grabbed the phone book. "Yia Yia's okay?"

"Yia Yia's is great," Andy said. "Expensive, though."

Michael flipped open his cell phone. "Should have them on speed dial by now." He hesitated. "Vegetarian? Pepperoni? Hamburger?"

"I'm good with whatever."

Michael ordered the largest pizza on the menu, half Hawaiian and half hamburger. "Twenty minutes. I'll drive, and you can hop out and pick it up. That all right?"

"Sure," Andy said, then perched on one of the bar stools. He grinned when he saw the dog biscuit.

Michael forced a laugh. "In spite of the evidence—" he gestured around him at the dirty dishes piled in the sink, the paper sack of empty Corona bottles by the door to the garage—"things haven't gotten that desperate yet. One of the trick-or-treaters seemed to think Rambo would be handing out treats."

"Yeah. It took Jake forever to get him to hold that basket in his mouth." He shook his head. "He could get that dog to do anything. Eventually." He picked up the dog biscuit. "Jake used to perch one on Rambo's nose and tell him to wait—" His voice trailed off. "But then you probably know that."

"Can't say that I ever saw that one."

Andy fiddled with the dog biscuit, clearly uncomfortable. Finally he said, "I'm sorry, Dr. Nolan. About everything."

What did a guy say to that? Michael wondered. He hadn't thought it would be quite this way. This strained. But then, why wouldn't it be? What had he ever done to get to know Andy Novac? He'd spent most of his time wishing Jacob would find another best friend.

He looked at Andy. Everything about the kid's expression and body language was negative. In what moment of insanity had he dreamed up the idea of working with Andy to finish Jacob's list? The kid sitting in his kitchen couldn't wait to get out of here. And he should just let him go. What had he been expecting, anyway?

"Look," he finally said, "you don't have to stay." He reached for his wallet and pulled out a couple of twenties. "You'd probably rather just pick up the pizza and head home." He forced a smile. "Tell your mom dinner's on me."

"My family's not at home right now. They're—doing this thing they do." He exhaled loudly.

"Without you?"

"I didn't want to go." Andy looked Michael in the eye. "I told Dad I wanted to come here instead."

Michael relaxed a little. "So . . . what's the thing they do?"

"It's called Ninja Night," Andy said. "It started when Rachel and I were little. It's a long story—but basically the family goes on a secret mission. Doing good without anyone knowing what they're doing. Tonight it's groceries for—" He broke off. "Groceries."

If Michael hadn't known better, he would think the kid was blushing.

"Sounds lame, huh?" Andy said.

"Not at all." Michael was suddenly aware of the size of his house, the condition of his cars, the balance in his bank account. Aware . . . and a little ashamed, mostly because he had always tended to grouse when it came time to write checks to charitable organizations.

"So you don't want a rain check?"

Andy shook his head. His stomach growled so loudly that Michael heard it and laughed.

"I'll get my car keys and coat and we can head out." Michael went upstairs to where his coat and keys lay on the floor outside the guest room. When he came back down, Andy had opened one of the books piled on the island and was looking at the illustrations, smiling.

"I *loved* this book." He recited the first page from memory. "We used to yuck it up when Dad read this. It was really funny when he tried to mimic Mama Bear."

Trying to imagine Stan Novac's deep bass imitating a woman made Michael smile. "I did voices, too, but I bet it wasn't nearly that entertaining."

"You did voices, too?" Andy ran his hand across the cover of the book, his voice wistful. "I never knew that. Kind of weird to find out about it now."

"I'll give you weird," Michael said. "I've been going over to the cemetery reading those to Jacob. I mean, I know I'm not really reading them to Jacob, but—" He laughed, embarrassed. "I hate cold pizza. Let's get going. We can pick up some Coke or whatever you like while we're out. And," he said, patting Andy on the shoulder, "how about you lose the Dr. Nolan and call me Michael."

---

Something strange happened over pizza. At some point the painful absence of Jacob receded, mostly because Andy seemed determined not to let sadness hover over everything. He told stories. The kind parents really don't want to hear until their kids are safely into a sane adulthood. Andy and Jacob were the ones who'd poured bubble bath in the fountain across from the Sunken Gardens. They were the ones who'd stolen all the flags from the country club golf course and planted them along Sheridan Boulevard.

"You have got to be kidding me," Michael said, laughing. "Does your dad know?"

"Oh, yeah. He knows. He didn't think it was quite as funny as you do."

"Oh, I bet he does. He just can't let on. He still has to—" The laughter died. He sighed. "He still has to parent you for a couple more years."

Awkward silence for a moment, then Michael said, "So . . . did your dad tell you anything about why he sent you over here?"

Andy nodded, but he didn't look Michael in the eye. "You think we can finish Jacob's list. With you and Dad doing the stuff."

"So what do you think?"

He shrugged. "I don't know. The funny thing is, a few days ago I called to check on sky diving down at K-State with the parachute club. As if this," he pointed at the DVD on the counter, "as if it isn't over."

"K-State has a parachute club?"

Andy held up the DVD and pointed to the sky diver.

"That's—You said that's Jacob," Michael said. "I just figured you put him in a photo of someone else. Computer generated stuff."

"Nope. That's really him." He sighed. "I told him he should tell you."

"Tell us what?"

"He was way into sky diving down in Kansas. I think he logged something like a hundred jumps last year." Sheepish grin. "He didn't want you to worry." He ducked his head. "I should have told you long before now. But I figured once you saw the DVD you wouldn't be so mad."

"Why would I be mad about that? I mean, sure, I wish he wouldn't have hidden it. But I never had any major problems with Jacob's list." Michael smiled. "It won't be the same. I know that. But if it could get you that scholarship—wouldn't it be worth it to try? I know the final product would be completely different from what you two had planned, but—"

"Maybe not as different as you think," Andy said.

———

Pam laughed as Rambo almost wiggled himself out of his fur with joy at seeing Andy. "Sorry to take Andy away," she said to the dog as she wrapped his leash around a bike rack. "But it's just too cold today for humans to think about al fresco dining."

"Ah, he'll be all right," Andy said. "Won't ya, boy?"

Rambo chuffed.

"You stay, and I'll bring you a treat," Andy said.

"From Starbucks?"

"Oh, yeah. The madeleines. He loves 'em."

"Madeleines," Pam murmured. "Didn't know about that one."

Inside, they ordered coffee and then sat opposite each other by the window, where Rambo could see them. "How is school going?" Pam asked.

"Okay, I guess." He stared back out the window at the dog.

"Do you have any plans for winter break? That must be coming up soon," Pam said, then gulped coffee. *Winter break. What on the list would he and Jacob have been doing over winter break?* Andy felt it, too, Pam thought. Jacob's absence. She reached across the table and patted his hand. "It's just me. I know it feels awkward. But I don't bite."

Andy forced a smile. "Yeah, well—"

"The best thing to do is usually to just spit it out," she said. "So—what's this all about? You called me, remember?"

"Did you get a chance to look at the DVD?"

"I did. And you did a wonderful job, especially considering what you had to work with." She smiled. "Thank you. I'll always treasure it. I assume you gave Michael a copy, too?"

Andy nodded. Shifted in his seat. Took a sip of coffee. Finally, he blurted out, "Dr. Nolan—Michael—he asked me to call him that—and Dad—they're going to help me finish it. The list. The film. Both."

He took a deep breath and then in more measured tones explained. "Michael took Dad out for breakfast and said he wanted to help."

*Michael initiated a meal with Stan Novac? He wanted Andy to call him Michael? He wanted to help with the list? Perfect. Just perfect.* He had done nothing but criticize the idea when she brought it up. Apparently he was open to it after all—as long as he got the credit. How very Nolan of him.

"Actually," Andy was saying while Pam stewed, "he said it was your idea—and that he'd finally realized it was a really good one."

"Horning in on the project was *not* my idea," Pam protested. "I have no desire to be the star of some adventure video. *My* idea was to fund your education."

"Yeah. That's what Michael said. That you wanted to help with my tuition." He paused. "But like I told him, I'm not going to need tuition because I won't even get into that school unless I can put together an impressive resume. And that requires a really good example of my work."

"Which was where 'Xtreme Ten' came in."

"Exactly." Andy nodded. "The DVD I gave you is a great

memento. But as a documentary?" He rolled his eyes. "Pathetic. And when I told Michael that, he said, 'So let's finish it.'" Andy grinned. "Apparently he'd already talked to my dad about it, and the two of them had this crazy idea that we'd use some of the footage with Jacob and tweak the topic a little and make it a film about a different kind of extreme living." He paused. "We don't have a catchy phrase for it yet, but the idea would be to show someone who takes on life and makes something positive out of it—out of all of it, even the garbage."

"And how do you feel about that?" She could just picture Michael waving thousands of dollars under his nose and telling him how he was going to do things. *Instead of "just do it," we'll tell people that when life hands them lemons . . . they can make lemonade.* She barely resisted the urge to smirk.

"Great."

Pam glanced up. "What?"

"Great," he repeated. "I love it."

"You do?"

"Yeah. It's a great idea. In fact, I'm going to pitch an article to *Geezerjock* as soon as we finish the first thing on the list with Michael and Dad."

"*Geezerjock?*"

Andy grinned. "It's a magazine for aging—"

"Jocks," Pam said, chuckling in spite of herself. Michael was not going to appreciate being called a geezer.

"Michael thought it was a great idea." Andy took a swig of his coffee, set the mug down, and said, "So . . . we—Michael and Dad and Mom and I—thought you should know what we're up to. I wanted Dad and Michael to come with me to talk to you, but Michael didn't think that was a good idea. So I told them I'd come by myself." He paused. "The thing is, Mrs. Nolan, I didn't want you to hear about this secondhand or think we were trying to leave you out."

*Except you have. You and the two geezerjocks.* She forced a smile. "I could never be upset with you, Andy. And I know Jacob would be thrilled to think you'd found a way to finish your film."

"I'm going to call it *Jacob's List*," Andy said. He cleared his throat. Shrugged. "Kind of a tribute thing."

Pam took a drink of coffee and asked Andy to tell her all about his plans. And all the while she was listening, she kept wondering who in the world this Michael guy was that Andy seemed to like so much.

---

"What is going on?" Pam let Rambo out into the backyard and confronted Michael, who was in the media room on the computer. He stopped clicking the keys and looked her way.

"Research," he said as he glanced up. "I didn't think you'd mind if I was here when you brought Rambo to play in the yard. You can have the rest of the house. I won't bother you."

She leaned against the doorframe and folded her arms. "You don't have to run for cover just because I came over to let Rambo enjoy the backyard," she said. "I'm not the enemy."

"I know that." Michael leaned back in the desk chair and folded his arms across his chest.

He was wearing jeans and a Harley T-shirt. And he looked great in a maddening sort of way. Nothing like a geezer. Pam cleared her throat. "Andy told me about your plans."

"I heard." He tilted his head. "And?"

"And I hope you follow through. He's a good kid. It would be really, really wrong not to keep your promises to him."

Michael cleared his throat. He waited a minute before responding, but when he did it wasn't with an explanation or a defense. Instead, it was with concern about her. "I'm glad you're not mad."

"Why would I be mad?"

"I don't know exactly." His mouth curled in a little smile. "Fact is, you were as much of an athlete as I was once. I was afraid maybe you'd feel like I was trying to take over, or do something behind your back."

"Are you?"

"No."

"Well, then," she said, "I guess it's all right."

"You—uh—you want to see some of the plans?" He pointed at the computer screen.

"Maybe some other time. I just need to pick up a few things. Betty invited Rainelle and me to go to this thing. Thought I'd take my hiking gear."

"The women's retreat?"

Pam nodded. "How'd you know about that?"

"I'm taking carryout over to the Novacs' place Friday night. But don't tell Betty." He smiled and winked at her. "She thinks Stan is cooking."

It wasn't until Pam had rounded up her gear and the dog and was backing out of the driveway that she let herself react. When she did, it was an explosive kind of anger that surprised even her. "He's taking dinner over? He's meeting with Andy? He's planning the list? He's—" Whatever was going on, it had to be a huge charade. She would not be fooled by it. As she sat at a red light she looked at Rambo and said, "Who is this guy pretending to be Michael? Michael isn't *nice*. I won't let him *be* nice."

She cried all the way back to Rainelle's.

---

Rainelle stretched out her arms and fell back on the lush bed. "Now *this* is what I call roughing it." She turned onto her side and propped up her head with one arm. "When does the maid bring our aperitif?" She fluttered her eyelashes.

"As soon as we pick up the phone and order it." Pam laughed and looked around her. "I had no idea something like this existed in Nebraska." She crossed the room and looked out the window to the grounds. Rolling hills studded with fall color faded into the distance. "It's stunning." She turned around. "Have you seen the chapel Betty was talking about?"

"*You* visit the chapel," Rainelle said. "I'm getting a pedicure."

"Can't we do both?"

"*You* can do both," Rainelle said, reading from the spa brochure. "The only spiritual experience I want this weekend is the lomilomi massage, orange blossom–peppermint salt glow, and seaweed body mask." She sighed and laid the brochure aside. "I'll have a manicure and pedicure, too—if I like what I see when I check out what products they use."

Pam picked up the retreat schedule and scanned the topics. *God's Pattern Book. How to Help a Grieving Friend. When Life Gives You Scraps.* "I might pop in on a couple of these," she said. "I wouldn't mind some enlightenment, as long as it doesn't get too freaky."

"Freaky as in . . . ?"

"Freaky as in a bunch of goody-two-shoes putting a nice little Jesus spin on tragedy."

"You sound so jaded." Rainelle was teasing, but when Pam met her gaze, she sobered up. "Really, honey. Please don't turn into a bitter old broad."

"I don't want to," Pam said, turning back around to look out the window. "Really, I don't." She glanced at her watch. "Let's head down to the registration desk and get that taken care of. We don't want you to miss out on sinking into the seaweed or the mudhole or whatever it was you were talking about."

"Not a mudhole," Rainelle said, quoting the brochure. "It's a 'state-of-the-art all-natural body mask guaranteed to rejuvenate and renew.'"

Pam chuckled. "I can just see the retreat director now. Spiritual rejuvenates on this side," she said, sweeping an imaginary group of women to one side of the hall, "body renewals over there." The two of them made their way down the hall to the elevator.

One floor down, two very proper gray-haired women got on.

"That's you and me in twenty years," Pam muttered.

The elevator opened and the older women got off. When the door closed again, Rainelle said, "Did you *see* those shoes? If I *ever* show up wearing something like that, just shoot me."

"Come on," Pam laughed. "You aren't going to be able to wear stilettos forever."

"Wanna bet? You can give me a trophy. *First Octogenarian Stiletto Champion.*"

"*First Woman Killed by Her Shoes* is more like it," Pam teased. "I'll put that on your tombstone after you fall off and break your neck."

Rainelle struck a fashion model pose. "But what a way to go, honey," she said, sashaying her way down the hall as if it were a Paris runway.

Pam followed, doing her best to mimic Rainelle. How very good it felt to laugh. It had been a long time.

———

She couldn't stay. The presenter was reading from someone else's journal about how it felt to lose her husband. The grief expressed was fresh and raw, and Pam couldn't bear to listen. Wishing she'd stayed with Rainelle for part two of the spa package, she slipped out into the hall. Taking a deep breath, she hurried away, hoping Betty wouldn't follow. And she didn't. So Pam decided to check out the chapel.

It was nice. Betty had been right about that. Peaceful. Candlelight, soothing music, high windows looking out onto an undisturbed landscape. When Pam sat down and closed her eyes, the sound of water washing over the stone wall at the back of the room helped her relax, eventually washing the tension from her body. *Maybe I could put a fountain like that in at ho—*. Home. She didn't even have a home at the moment, did she? So much for the comforting atmosphere in the chapel.

Back in her room, Pam pulled out the blank notebook Betty had given her that morning. *"Just try some stream-of-consciousness writing,"* Betty had urged. *"It can be very therapeutic to let your feelings spill out onto the paper. No one's going to ever see it but you. But once you've had a chance to express what's inside, sometimes it can be easier to deal with it. And sometimes you discover things about what's really going on."*

Wouldn't you know it? The first thing that tumbled out was something about Michael.

How do you ask a gorgeous man to accept a scarred, out-of-shape body? I can't imagine him ever wanting to make love to me again. He *said* it didn't matter to him. I think I joined the health club because I didn't believe him. In spite of being almost fifty, he is still gorgeous. He has a six-pack and broad shoulders and a full head of thick black hair that is graying, but in all the right places. And those eyes.

No surprises there. She had issues with Michael. Duh. She picked up the pen and scribbled another paragraph.

If it hadn't been for that infernal list, Jacob never would have been on that highway that morning. I hate that list and now Michael says he is going to *finish* it? Why couldn't Jacob have had a passion for fly-fishing? Why couldn't his list have been about trolling for some record size catfish or something? Michael and Andy and Stan Novac are going to continue with all this dangerous nonsense. And besides that, Betty and Stan are *my* friends and I don't want to share. I don't *want* Michael to change. I don't want him to be likeable. This is hard enough as it is. I am already terrified that something else bad is going to happen to people I care about.

And who, she thought, did she care about? Stan. Andy. *Michael*. She began to doodle around his name. Finally, she scratched through it and wrote,

Pamela Sue Nolan is one whacked-out woman.

She set the pen down. Closing the journal, she tucked it under her pillow and headed downstairs. Getting off the elevator, she hesitated. She could hear laughter coming from the meeting room down the hall. Apparently the speaker wasn't always making people cry. She looked the other way, toward the door that said *Welcome to the Spa*.

"I'M GOING FOR A JOG before I pick Rambo up from the Novacs," Pam said the Sunday morning after the women's retreat.

"Well, you go, girl," Malcolm said from his place on the couch where he and Rainelle had been cuddling since breakfast.

"Actually, it'll be more of a jog-walk-gasp kind of thing," Pam joked, "but it's a start toward getting back into some kind of shape other than round." *And it'll keep me from hiding out in the guest room all morning so you two can have some privacy.* She really did have to find alternative housing. It was nearly Thanksgiving, and Rainelle had been great, but things weren't any better between Cicero and Rambo, and the constant dog-cat management was getting on everyone's nerves. Of course the simple solution, Rainelle kept reminding Pam, was to put Michael on notice and claim what was rightfully hers. But for some reason Pam couldn't bring herself to do that. Kicking Michael out of the house seemed so . . . final.

"Why don't you let Michael have Rambo for a while?" Rainelle had suggested last week. One look at Pam and she'd backpedaled. "All right, all right. Not an option." She scratched the dog behind the ear. "I was just thinking of Rambo. You know he'd be happier with a yard."

Pam had been hoping for some revelation at the women's event that would somehow incline her toward an answer. But the only thing that happened at the retreat was her realization that, even after all these months, she was fixated on Michael and making little or no progress in handling Jacob's death.

Stepping off the elevator and into the street, she realized it was colder outside than she'd expected, even for November. She should have worn more layers. And gloves. About three blocks into her planned workout on the deserted streets of downtown Lincoln, she headed for her car, swearing softly as she pulled the parking ticket off the windshield and got in. Where to now? *Barnes and Noble.* She'd grab the local newspaper and check the classifieds.

After settling in at Barnes and Noble with coffee in hand and the newspaper opened before her, she hesitated, not knowing whether to look at living space for sale or for rent. There were other questions, too. *What part of town? How many bedrooms?*

When it began to rain, Pam glanced down at her watch. It was still too early for the Novacs to be home from church, and in weather like this there was no chance the dogs would be outside. She'd have to wait. She was really dreading it, anyway. Rambo was becoming increasingly reluctant to leave the Novacs—or anywhere—when the destination was Rainelle's condominium. It was especially bad on the days when she took him back to the house to play in his own back-yard. Tucked tail and ducked head, he practically crept back into the Suburban. The last time she'd almost left him with Michael. Almost.

Which took her back to the initial question about real estate and what to do next. With a sigh, she sat back in her chair and gazed out the window at the ominous clouds, finally admitting to herself that she didn't want to scour the classifieds or go to open houses or check out rental properties. She wanted to go home. As for what that meant when it came to Michael, she didn't know.

Laying the newspaper aside, she walked past the low iron railing dividing the café area from the magazine racks and began to browse. She found nothing to interest her until the cover of *Outside* caught her eye with a headline called "Hiking Hidden Hawaii." Grabbing the magazine, she headed back to the café area, took a seat at a table by a window, and began to read. The article reminded her of Jacob's list and the trek in Northern California she'd been researching for him. She'd have to Google that later. On a day like today, it could be ther-apeutic to mentally escape to California or Hawaii—even for just a little while.

Pam lingered until she was certain the Novacs would be home from church and she could retrieve Rambo and head back to Rainelle's. By the time she made a dash for the car, she had decided. She'd tell Rainelle today that she'd be gone by the end of the month . . . and then spend the rest of the day deciding exactly what that would mean.

All the way to the Novacs' she struggled with the idea of kicking Michael out. She couldn't imagine actually doing it. On the other hand, she also couldn't imagine returning to living separate lives under the same roof. *That* was one thing she'd figured out during her stay with Rainelle. She wasn't willing to settle for that anymore. Life was precious. Time was not a thing to be wasted, and today was not to be taken for granted.

*Whoa. You're beginning to sound like your son. Carpe diem and all that.* As she turned into the Novacs' neighborhood, she thought, Carpe diem? Carpe latte was more her style these days. She might have followed through and made a valiant effort at getting back into shape before Jacob died, but since the funeral, knowing there would be no mother-son wilderness trek had erased her short-lived interest. Her morning "runs" in downtown Lincoln were little more than a charade to get her out of Rainelle's condo and to burn off some of Rambo's energy. Now, as she pulled up at the Novacs' and glanced over at the magazine on the passenger seat, she realized that hiking was beginning to sound interesting again.

---

The trouble started when she and Rambo got back to Rainelle's. The instant Pam stepped inside, she heard a low yowl from the direction of the sofa. Rambo sat down. Cicero slithered down off the couch and stalked toward them on tiptoe, his back arched, his tail erect. *Oh brother*, Pam thought. As Cicero approached, Rambo inched closer to her. Expecting Rainelle to emerge from either the kitchen or the bedroom to retrieve her cat, Pam hesitated. That was when Cicero howled and sprung into the air, literally ricocheting off the hallway walls toward Rambo.

In the face of the feline attack, Rambo backed into the corner by the door, barking. Cicero flung himself forward, claws bared. With a yelp, Rambo tried to deflect the attack by rising up on his hind legs, but Cicero was too quick. He went after Rambo's front paws like a hunter stalking a mouse, sinking his fangs deep. Rambo went berserk, dancing and crying and yelping, trying to shake off the cat.

Pam rushed forward and grabbed Cicero, who let go of Rambo and turned his rage on her, raking his extended claws down both fore-arms and sinking his teeth into the soft flesh between her thumb and forefinger. Within seconds Rainelle and Malcolm had joined the fray, Rainelle trying in vain to get ahold of Cicero while Malcolm checked out Rambo's paw. Cicero's only response to Rainelle's attentions was to bite down harder.

Pam cried out in pain, and Rambo's hackles came up. Snarling, he came at the cat, who was still refusing to loosen his grip on Pam's hand. Finally, Cicero let go, ripping two deep cuts in Pam's flesh before climbing her like a tree and launching himself off her shoulder and up the hall toward Rainelle's room, with Rambo in pursuit.

At the door to Rainelle's room, all three humans screeched to a halt. Cicero had taken refuge under the bed. Rambo, his hindquarters up in the air, maneuvered from side to side along the edge of the bed, snarling and barking, completely oblivious to the paw that was bleeding on Rainelle's white bedroom carpet.

"You go, Rambo," Malcolm called out to the dog. "Put that bad boy in his place."

Rainelle slapped his bare chest with her palm and forced him back against the wall. "You stay out of it. I thought you liked Cicero!" She glanced at Pam. "Can you make him stop that racket?!"

"Rambo," Pam said. "No!"

Immediately, the dog turned toward her. He looked uncertainly back at the bed. "No," Pam repeated. "Leave it." With a sigh, Rambo obeyed and limped over to her, leaving blood spots as he walked.

"My carpet!" Rainelle said.

"I'll get something for it," Malcolm said and was back in a minute with a roll of gauze from the bathroom. Pam ordered the dog to sit and give her his paw and began to wrap it with gauze.

"That is one cool dog," Malcolm said.

"I thought you were bringing something for the carpet!" Rainelle snapped and brushed past them both. She was back in a moment, and kneeling down, began to pour hydrogen peroxide on the carpet and blot up the brownish foam that resulted.

"You're a mess," Malcolm said, looking at Pam's arms and hand. "We need to get you to the emergency room."

"I'll be fine."

"Sure you will," he agreed. "After a few stitches."

"Stitches?" Rainelle stopped tending the carpet and looked at Pam's arms. "Oh my—"

"You stay put," Pam ordered, "and work on the carpet. I know how you are around blood."

"But—" Rainelle protested.

"Take care of the carpet," Pam repeated. "I'll be fine." She was beginning to feel queasy. A cat could do a lot of damage.

Malcolm intervened. "Come on into the kitchen and let's get you washed up."

"What about Cicero?" Pam asked. "Did Rambo bite back?"

"Cold day in you-know-where before anything hurts that cat. He used to be a fighter. The ears tell all." Malcolm pulled her out of the room and into the kitchen.

"I thought his ear tips got frozen off back in his days as a stray," Pam said.

Malcolm arched his eyebrows. "That what Rainelle told you?"

"That's what I thought the shelter told her. I felt sorry for the poor thing, too. And I'm not even close to being a cat lover."

He smiled and shook his head.

Pam turned on the warm water and rinsed off her arms, then washed with soap and water, grimacing as she examined her arms and the deep cuts in the soft flesh between her thumb and forefinger. Rambo limped in, sinking onto the bare floor and beginning to gnaw at the bandage on his foot. As Malcolm stepped over him he told him to knock it off.

"I don't think 'knock it off' is in his vocabulary," Pam said.

"Really?" Malcolm looked pointedly at the dog, who had lowered his head to the floor and was looking up at them with an expression that could only be translated as misery.

Pam chuckled even as Malcolm handed her the bottle of hydrogen peroxide he'd lifted from Rainelle. Once the wounds were cleaned as well as she could manage, he helped her wrap both forearms, wrists to elbows, with gauze. "That'll have to do for now," she said.

"I'll get dressed and drive you to the hospital."

Pam reached for her car keys. "I'm taking Rambo to the vet first."

"The heck you are," Malcolm protested. "The dog isn't in bad shape at all. You need stitches."

"*I'll* take the dog," Rainelle said from the doorway. She looked down at Rambo. "That okay with you, Fur-face?"

When Rambo sat up, Rainelle waved Malcolm and Pam toward the door. "Go," she said, "get changed and get out of here before one of us faints. I feel bad enough as it is, moaning about my carpet like that. I'll come by the emergency room after I take Rambo to the vet—if you're still speaking to me."

---

It was Sunday morning, and as he stood looking out the back windows at the garden, coffee cup in hand, Michael noticed again how bad everything looked. A killing frost had laid everything low, and now Pam's flower garden was little more than a tangled mess of dead stuff. Fall cleanup was something she spent a lot of energy on every year. Opening the back door, he walked out onto the patio, shivering in the cold morning air. The rain that had fallen earlier this morning would be turning into snow before he knew it. Maybe if he called her, Pam would talk long enough to tell him what to do about the garden. They'd managed a couple of civil exchanges recently. Maybe if he promised to leave for a few mornings, she'd want to take care of things herself. He was beginning to think he should get a place to stay and let her come home. But he couldn't quite bring himself to admit defeat yet. Part of him still held a glimmer of hope that things would get better before too much longer.

Just as he turned to go back inside, Freaky Freddy next door interrupted his thoughts with a furious round of barking. Michael started to go back in the house but then decided to open the gate and walk along the side of the house to get the morning paper first. When he opened the gate, he was flattened by a black furball. Lying on his back while Rambo whimpered and moaned and licked, Michael started to laugh.

"Hey, Fur-face!" he said, sitting up and wrapping his arms around the dog and giving him a hug. "Have I missed *you*." He reached up and scratched the dog behind his ears, at once surprised by how happy he was to see Rambo and how nervous he was about seeing the female the dog would have in tow. But they could talk about the garden. Surely that was a safe topic.

"Where is she, fella? Did she go on inside?" He finally got to his feet, retrieved the coffee cup Rambo had knocked out of his hand, and went around front. The driveway and street were empty. That's when he noticed the leash dragging along behind the dog—and the limp. Kneeling down, Michael examined the paw, which was bleeding from a puncture wound of some kind.

"Where is she, boy? What happened?"

He didn't really expect an answer. Rambo whined and lifted his paw off the ground. If Michael didn't know better, he'd think the dog was trying to tell a sob story.

"Come on," he said, and patted the side of his leg. "Pam's probably going crazy wondering where you are."

With a sharp bark, Rambo limped to the front door and waited. As soon as he opened the door, Michael heard his cell phone ringing.

Running to the kitchen, he grabbed the phone off the table and glanced at the caller ID. Rainelle?

"What's happened?"

"Please tell me Fur-face came home," she said.

Michael looked at Rambo. "It's Rainelle," he said. "She wants to know if Fur-face came home. Can you say hello?" To his amazement, Rambo barked.

"Does that answer your question?" Michael asked. "He's limping, though. Tell Pam I'll have it checked out at the vet and call her later."

"I will. But, Michael, she's not here right now."

He paused. When Rainelle didn't say anything he spoke up. "Rainelle, this is me waiting for you to tell me what's happened."

"Cicero flipped out this morning. Jumped Rambo the minute Pam got back with him. Rambo fought back. Pam got in the middle, and Malcolm drove her to the hospital to get sewn up. I was taking Rambo to the vet for that paw, but the minute we got out on the street he bolted."

"Sewn up?"

"I know," Rainelle said, her voice miserable. "Cicero went bonkers. I didn't think a cat could—"

"What hospital?"

"What?"

"What hospital did Malcolm take Pam to?"

"Bryan West, I think."

He hung up and headed out the door, Rambo limping along at his side.

---

Just as Pam was escorted out of the waiting room and into an exam room, the quiet Sunday in the ER ended. Ambulances began to arrive with trauma victims from a multivehicle accident. Pam waited while the staff tore around trying to staunch bleeding, prep patients for surgeries, and respond to various codes. As she sat alone in the exam room listening to the bedlam on the other side of the door, her wounds began to throb. The longer she waited, the more they hurt.

What was she going to do now? She couldn't go back to Rainelle's with Rambo, and she couldn't imagine kicking Michael out. Or living with him. Dimming the lights, she retreated to the hospital bed and lay down, pulling a sheet up and closing her eyes. Her arms hurt. She was tired. Rambo was hurt. It would be nice to curl up on the big bed at home. To be back where she knew where the Tylenol was and she didn't have to worry about being a good house guest, where she could pad around in the night and not be hissed at by a silent creature lurking in the dark. Where she could get up in the morning and walk out the back door and see flowers and green—well, maybe not green. The frost the other night had probably left most everything brown. But there would be a lot of cleanup to do and Michael didn't have the faintest idea how to do that, even if he wanted to, which he never did. *"Hire someone"* was as close as he'd come to doing yard work in years.

Her arms weren't the only thing hurting. Life hurt. All of it. She just wasn't cut out to live downtown. Lovely as it was, Rainelle's condo felt claustrophobic. Pam didn't know how anyone could live without at least the option of growing a tomato plant or a flower. In the ground. "Potted plants and the farmers' market," Rainelle would say. That was great for Rainelle. But Pam wanted—no, she needed—to garden. It was as essential to her well-being as anything left in her life. Walking out on it had been a mistake. She wanted to go home.

Whatever else he might be a failure at, Michael was a fabulous nurse. And right now, lying in the hospital bed with her head beginning to throb in concert with the scratches on her arms and hands, she could do with a little TLC. She burrowed into the pillow with a groan. After weeks of refusing to talk to him and hours of telling herself that she was better off without him, she wished he were there.

*No, you do not want Michael,* she told herself. *You want some guy who doesn't exist anymore. You want the guy who used to plan family trips . . . who came home for dinner . . . who taught you how to make love.* She wanted the impossible. *You can't go back in time. It's over.*

Tears began to slide down her cheeks. She'd just started to look around for a tissue when the door burst open and in strode Michael, dressed in a lab coat.

"Things are a mess out there," he said. He came to the bedside and gently took her wrist and lifted her arm, whistling softly at what he saw. "That was one angry cat." At her questioning look, he explained. "Rainelle called me." He let go of her arm and tilted his head and smoothed her hair back from her face. "Hurts, doesn't it?"

She nodded. "More than I expected."

"Let's get this stitched up so you can get out of here." He hesitated. "You know I'm an excellent seamstress." He raised her hand and examined the deep slices. "And I'm guessing you'd appreciate not having bad scars."

She couldn't look him in the eye, but as he spoke, she nodded. "Yes," she said. "Please. Get me out of here. I just want to go home." *Home*. Had she really said that?

Michael rummaged through the cupboards. With a promise to return as soon as he'd collected everything he needed, he urged her to lie back down. "It won't take long once I get back," he said, "but you've had a major adrenaline dump, and I imagine you're going to feel exhausted before much longer."

"Already did before this happened," she said with a weak smile. "I'm not used to life with a nocturnal furball."

He left without comment, returning in a few minutes with the tray of supplies he'd need. Pulling on latex gloves, he went to work, directing her to lie on her back and position her right arm beneath the portable light. "So while I work, how about you entertain us both with this morning's series of unfortunate events."

Pam recognized his doctor voice and one of the phrases he often used to try to help children relax and tell him what he needed to know. Sometimes he even mimicked a character from a recent children's film. He did a hilarious not-so-wicked witch—and it usually helped calm them down so he could do his job more easily. She smiled and glanced over at him, almost disappointed when he didn't mug for her. When he met her gaze, she blushed. "I was waiting for the wicked witch to appear."

Michael shrugged. "Anything to help a kid calm down. Sometimes it works, sometimes it doesn't." He touched the edge of a cut. "Feel that?"

She shook her head.

"So," Michael said as he began to suture the wound, "tell me about this bad cat, Mrs. Nolan. Malcolm gave me a brief overview out in the waiting room, but I'd like to hear it in your words."

"Cicero isn't just a bad cat," Pam said. "He's the Prince of Darkness on a bad hair day. Rainelle simply can't see it. But this morning he let it show." She recounted the scene at Rainelle's.

"Well," Michael said while he stitched, "that's an even better explanation for why Rambo showed up at the house this morning."

"He—what?"

"Take it easy. He is, at this moment, waiting downstairs in my car for his own little trip to the doctor. Which," he said, raising his voice to keep Pam from saying anything, "I will oversee as soon as we're finished here. I looked at his paw, and I honestly don't think there's much needed in the way of professional attention. But I wouldn't appreciate a vet trying to stitch you up, and I know enough to extend Dr. Thomas the same courtesy when it comes to critters."

He went on to recount Rainelle's version of the morning's events. "She's out in the waiting room now. With Malcolm." He finished stitching up the hand and moved to a cut on her forearm. When he'd put a couple of stitches in, he moved his tray to the other side of the bed, brought over the light, and bent over her other arm. "These aren't as bad," he said. "Maybe a couple of stitches here." He touched one place and reached for a syringe.

While he worked, he said, "I want you to come home." He talked over Pam's mild protest. "Please let me finish. I am sorry to say that I've been down with a nearly terminal case of self-pity. Hence, your garden is a mess. As is the rest of the house. I can clean the house, but the garden—that's another story. Since that frost, I don't know what's weed and what's not, and I'm guessing that the way back into your good graces is *not* to mistakenly pull some prize perennial by mistake."

He tied off the last stitch and clipped the suture. "I am also fairly certain—given this morning's events—that neither you nor Rambo will be wanting to go back to Rainelle's. So. If you'll give me a little while to clean up the disaster and gather some stuff, I'll check into a hotel. Rambo can be at home, and Cicero can go back to being the undisputed ruler of his corner of the underworld." He sat back. "All right with you?"

Blinking back tears, Pam nodded.

He cleared his throat. "I'd appreciate being allowed to keep an eye on you—medically speaking—for the next week. Just to make sure there's no infection."

"All right."

"And I suspect the stitches in your hand will have to stay a little longer than a week. Hands are tough," he said. "I just wanted to warn you so you don't think it's a plot to hang around where I'm not welcome."

"Michael—"

"I could walk the dog." He motioned toward her bandaged right hand. "That slice between your thumb and forefinger is about the worst of the cuts. Rambo's a gentleman, but even he yanks on a leash now and then." He began to clean up the tray, discarding wrappers, moving the light back into the corner.

Watching him, Pam thought it was almost as if he felt nervous being around her. "Thank you for coming in and taking care of me," she said with an embarrassed laugh. "You always were a good nurse."

"Thanks." He stood quietly for a minute, and Pam put her guard back up, expecting him to try to recant some of his promises about their living arrangements. "I'll let Rainelle and Malcolm give you a ride home, if that's all right. I'll run Rambo to the vet, then head home to clean and pack. Shouldn't take long. Maybe a couple of hours. I'm not trying to tell you what to do. Just trying to . . . accommodate." He opened the door, then looked back. "I could get your things from Rainelle's. If it would help."

She shook her head. "Let us do it. None of this is her fault, but I imagine she's had just long enough to serve herself a big whopping mound of false guilt." Hopping down off the hospital bed, she reached for her purse. "Mind if I walk out with you? Otherwise I'll probably be here for another two hours waiting for paperwork to get done."

Michael paused at the main desk. "I'll take care of that for you," he said and pointed her toward the waiting room.

"Thank you."

He nodded. "Okay. See you at ho—at the house, then."

Pam made her way to the double doors that led out of the emergency room, which was quieter now. When she glanced back at the desk, Michael was bent over her chart, scribbling away. It was what he'd been doing the first time she'd ever seen him. He'd been the topic of conversation for more than a week—the "hunky" new intern with the fabulous smile. Some things never changed. What was the term for hunky these days? *Hot*. He still was. And she still noticed. *Pathetic. May I remind you . . .* She forced her mind away from the last hour, away from his compassion, away from his surprising decision to put her first and move out, and back to the hurtful things he'd done over the years. And her list was long.

———

Michael hurried from room to room filling a giant black trash bag with the evidence of his bachelor's existence. At least he'd eaten from mostly disposables. Coffee mugs alone filled the top tray of the dishwasher. And the kitchen sink looked awful. He had no idea what product Pam used on it, but he hadn't found anything under the sink, and besides there wasn't time now. He'd done better upstairs, but barely. He'd tell Pam he'd have someone come in tomorrow. She wasn't going to be able to do much in the way of housekeeping herself until the stitches came out in a week or so. He chased around behind the vacuum cleaner for as long as he dared before charging upstairs to Jacob's room.

Greeting Rambo, who was curled up on the bed, Michael turned Jacob's computer on. He needed to take everything possible with him so he could continue researching and planning with Andy and Stan. He was fairly certain he'd already visited most of the Internet sites Jacob had, but just in case, he began to jot down URLs from Jacob's history. Once that was done, he yanked open the desk drawer, grabbed Jacob's Bible, and using it as a folder, gathered the loose papers out of the drawer, stuffed them inside, and headed down the hall to pack. He'd wanted some of the stuff on Jacob's bulletin board, too, but there wasn't time. Besides, Pam would notice it was gone, and he didn't want to cause another fight.

"I LOOK LIKE I survived a suicide attempt," Pam said and shook her head, even though she was talking on the phone. "Honestly, Rainelle. I love you for thinking of me, but you and Malcolm deserve to have your first Thanksgiving together be a happy one. And if I was there, it would be just plain awkward. All this holiday is to me is the precursor for Eddie Lee Monroe's release. There's nothing for me to celebrate. I've stocked up on old movies, and I'm going to hibernate here at home and try to remain in a permanent state of denial."

An hour later when the phone rang and it was Betty Novac, Pam thanked her for calling and reassured her about the holiday. "Rainelle's invited me to spend the day with her and Malcolm. It's sweet of you to think of me, though." She anticipated the next question and answered it before Betty could ask. "I'm healing fine. Michael's coming over on Sunday to take the stitches out. You all have a good Thanksgiving. I suppose you'll be at the mission again? Well, you have a great day together." She hung up before Betty could offer any commiseration about December 5, lay back on the pillows, turned on her side, and closed her eyes. At least the part about the movies was true. She wondered what Michael would be doing Thanksgiving Day, but she wasn't going to call and find out.

———

"Dr. Nolan is unavailable. If this is a medical emergency, please hang up and dial 9-1-1. To contact one of the doctors on call, dial 402-0857." *One of the doctors on call?* Michael dialed the answering service. The flicker of guilt over what he'd put his father through these past weeks went out. Obviously, Senior was in Las Vegas.

With a sigh, Michael sat back and picked up the television remote. At least one Dr. Nolan was having a good holiday. Senior loved nothing better than cleaning someone's clock in a high stakes game of poker. After clicking his way through all sixty channels, Michael got up and went to the windows. He looked down on the city, visualizing Pam enjoying dinner with Malcolm and Rainelle just a few blocks away.

*Snap out of it. Norman Rockwell just doesn't happen anymore, and you know it. So stop feeling sorry for yourself and start being . . . thankful. Look around you, man. You're not where you want to be, but you're also not in a cardboard box under some viaduct.* He suppressed the resentment and anger he felt over the idea of Eddie Lee Monroe walking free down the streets in only a week. *He's already destroyed enough. Don't give him power over everything.*

With another sigh, Michael walked over to the desk and sat down. Pulling out some of the files he'd created about various things on Jacob's list and slipping his cell phone into his pocket, he grabbed his room key and headed downstairs to the business center. While the rest of America overindulged, he'd collect some more information. If today was any indication of what to expect for Christmas and New Year's Eve, he also needed to find someplace to go. There was no way he was going to slog through another holiday in Lincoln, Nebraska, alone. *Alone. Is this how it's going to be from now on? Chalk one up for Monroe.* He corrected his thinking. *No. Chalk one up for yourself. If she never comes back, you can blame* you.

As he stepped off the elevator, his phone rang.

"Did you get ahold of your dad?"

"No," Michael said. "He's out of town."

"So you're on your own today?"

"Yep." He forced enthusiasm into his voice. "I was just headed down to the business center to check online about that drop zone in Phoenix Andy mentioned. Later I'll hit the treadmill. And I'll probably end up at Wyuka sometime before sundown."

"Sure you won't reconsider and come with us?" Stan said.

"No, really. I'm fine. Thanks, though."

"Is that fine as in really fine or fine as in leave-me-alone-I'm-too-proud-to-admit-I'm-lonely-today fine?"

"You don't give up, do you?"

"Well, actually, I do. But I have this gorgeous woman staring at me with big brown eyes who seems to think you need a friend."

Michael could hear Betty's laughing protest in the background. And maybe he imagined it, but he also thought he could hear Reba barking and one or two of the Novac kids chattering away. And for some reason he didn't quite understand, Michael decided he wanted to be part of the noise. "Tell the woman she's not only gorgeous, but psychic, too."

---

Just inside the door of the city mission, the Novacs were greeted by an overweight woman dressed in purple sweat pants and a gray sweat shirt that said *BRAS*. Actually, it said *NEBRASKA*, but the way it was printed, only four letters were in view . . . unless she were to walk around with her arms held out like a garden scarecrow.

Shouting "Happy Thanksgiving!" she engulfed Betty in an over-zealous hug. Thankfully, when Stan introduced Michael as "Dr. Nolan," she just stuck out a pudgy hand for him to shake.

"Welcome," she said, "and Happy Thanksgiving. I'm Marcia. Are you helping today?"

"Yes." Michael forced a smile. Touring the facility with Stan and Betty was one thing. Getting to know the people was another. He really wasn't good at this.

She might be a little slow mentally, but Marcia wasn't clueless. "You don't need to be so nervous, Dr. Nolan. We don't bite here."

Stan laughed before telling Marcia that Andy was going to be filming them today. Her eyes shone. "Can I be in the movie?" she asked. "I'll comb my hair and put on lipstick." She hurried off in search of Andy.

Michael followed Stan and Betty through a maze of halls and into the kitchen, where a crew of people that included Rachel and Emily Novac seemed to be having a great time. Maddy and Megan were outside in the dining hall opening bags of disposable cups and plates and stacking them at one end of the serving line. Little Suzanne climbed up into the lap of a bearded old geezer sitting at one of the tables waiting. When he smiled down at her, his yellow teeth made Michael cringe. Suzanne giggled and tugged on his beard.

Betty stationed Michael behind the food counter to dish up mashed potatoes and gravy. As the moments passed, his smile became more genuine. He barely had time to think, and when concern for Pam came to mind, he reminded himself that she was spending the day with Malcolm and Rainelle. He would see her Sunday to take out her stitches. For now, he had other things to worry about. Like Betty moving him from mashed potatoes and gravy to pumpkin pie in spite of his protests that he had no idea how to carve a pie.

Emily took the knife out of his hand. "Okay, Dr. Mike—you don't *carve* it. Here—I'll show you." Shaking her head, she showed him how they wanted the pies sliced. She was bossy and a bit impatient, and Michael loved it because he was no longer being treated like a stranger.


"Isn't this your *third* piece, young man?" Michael scowled at the ten-year-old with mock ferocity.

"Chill, Doc," the kid retorted. "It's Thanksgiving, and Miz Betty said there's plenty of pie. More than we can eat today."

"You're out to prove her wrong, I see," Michael bantered. He started to dish up the pie, but just then someone out in the hall screamed for help. Dropping the pie, Michael launched himself toward the door and whipped around the corner to one of the small lounge areas, where a woman was holding an infant over her arm, beating on his back.

"Choking!" she cried. "He's choking!"

Marcia stood by crying, blubbering something about sharing with the baby.

"What'd you give him?" Michael asked.

"Peas," Marcia said. "Just some peas. For Thanksgiving."

"I'm a doctor. Let me—"

The woman handed over the infant, crying and sobbing. "He's a baby, Marcia." Her back to Michael, she got in the woman's face. "You don't give a baby grown-up food!"

Michael bent over the child, who was indeed choking on something, but when it finally came up, it wasn't a pea. Instead it was a tiny round bead—a faux pearl if he was correct—probably from a necklace.

Clutching at her throat, the young woman gasped. "I didn't even realize—I—I—" She slumped down onto the couch and began to cry. Reaching up to clutch Marcia's hand, she apologized. "I'm so sorry. . . . I didn't mean—"

"That's okay," Marcia said, patting the woman on her back with an awkward rhythm that Michael suspected was a little too hard.

Michael settled the baby down and then comfortably tucked him into the crook of his arm. Handsome baby. It felt nice to have a child in his arms again. When he handed the baby over and went back to the kitchen, he was almost overwhelmed by an emotion he hadn't felt in months. He felt *good*.

———

"Please," Betty said. "You haven't really had your own Thanksgiving dinner yet, and we'd love to have you."

Stan put his arm around his wife. "It's a tradition. After we help out here, we go home, where the menfolk eat until we're stuffed like the turkey itself and then crash on the couch while the womenfolk do all the work." When Betty looked up at him and arched one eyebrow, he recanted. "Okay, okay. The truth is," he said with a grin, "we all pitch in, and the guys do the dishes while the womenfolk knit and gossip."

"If you come, we could compare calendars and make some more concrete plans," Andy said, then glanced at his mom and added, "after we do the dishes."

"You could bring Rambo for a visit!" Maddy said.

"Hoorayyyyyy . . . Rambo!" Megan cheered. "Reba can share her turkey and dressing!"

Michael laughed. "Thanks, honey, but I doubt Rambo would want dressing. Although I know he'd love to see Reba."

"Rambo *loves* dressing," Megan said.

Michael looked around at the family, all of them nodding agreement.

"Reba taught him to like it," Maddy added. "Please please *please* you and Rambo come. We won't even make you mash the potatoes."

"We'll let you sit and put your feet up with Daddy."

Stan stepped in. "Hey, you guys. Quit ganging up on Dr. Nolan. He isn't used to a herd of hecklers." He laughed. "Come," he said. "Andy wants to talk Jacob's list, the girls like you, and they're right. Rambo loves dressing."

"It doesn't make him sick?"

"Not that I've seen," Stan said. "Can't explain it. I just go with it." He stepped closer. "We haven't explained the details of your situation the girls. You said Pam is with Rainelle. Will she be okay with you snagging Rambo? Don't do anything to make her mad."

Michael shrugged. "I think I'd be hard pressed to make her any more angry with me than she already is." He paused. "Actually, I've been granted parental visiting rights for Fur-face. And it so happens that I was supposed to go over later and check on him. So this will work out fine. And I'll leave Pam a note." He hesitated before saying, "One thing, though."

"Name it."

He told Stan about Emily showing him how to cut the pies, concluding with, "So could you please try and get your wife and the rest of the kids to call me Michael, too?"

"You lied to me," Michael said, pausing in the doorway with his hands on his hips. "You told me you were going to be with Rainelle and Malcolm for Thanksgiving dinner."

"I told you I was *invited*," Pam said without looking up from the magazine she was reading. "I didn't say I was going."

"A half truth is still a lie."

"You should know," Pam retorted, instantly regretting the nasty reaction to what she now realized was meant as an innocent kind of teasing.

He sighed. "Actually, I stopped by to get Rambo. Stan and Betty invited me over, and I thought I'd take him with me." He smiled. "Maddy and Megan insist that he loves dressing."

Pam made a face. "I hope you didn't believe them. I don't need a sick dog."

"I wouldn't do anything to make the dog sick. And neither would the girls."

"Fine, then. Try not to wake me when you let him back in."

"I'll do my best." He tilted his head and smiled at her. "Any chance you'd come along?"

"None."

He nodded. "Are we still on for Sunday? I mean—are you ready for the stitches to come out?"

"Of course."

"You look a little tired."

"I *am* tired. I don't know how to do holidays." She put the magazine down. "I don't know how to do *any* days."

"Yeah. Hard to believe December 5 is almost here."

She pressed her lips together. "It's just—wrong. So wrong."

He looked down at the floor. She could see his jaw working. Without looking at her, he said, "Jacob's list includes kiteboarding and scuba diving. I've been thinking . . . uh . . ." He cleared his throat. "I've been thinking it might be too much to stick around here over

Christmas and New Year's. Thinking of going somewhere warm. Where I . . . we . . . uh . . . where they do kiteboarding and scuba diving." He finally glanced up. "You love the beach. If you came, maybe you could do some snorkeling."

Before she knew what had happened, he'd bent to kiss her. It wasn't passionate. Just sweet. And, in some ways, very, very sad. She blinked tears back and turned her head away.

"Are you ever going to forgive me?" he asked, then added, "Don't answer that." He backed away and went to the back door and called Rambo in. "I'll have him home before it gets too late," he said and left quickly.

After he'd gone, Pam sat for a long time thinking. She didn't know what upset her more, the idea that he'd invited her on a trip or the fact that he'd assumed she wouldn't be up for anything particularly athletic. He was going to scuba dive. She could snorkel? What was up with that, anyway? He was going to try kiteboarding. She could sit on the beach?

Jumping up off the couch, she shoved in a movie and clicked the remote. Ten minutes later she was still coming up with good lines to throw at him the next time he brought up Jacob's list. At one point she almost drove over to the Novacs'. In the end, she convinced herself that was the worst idea she'd had in a long time. And if Michael wanted to be the star of *Jacob's List*, so be it. She didn't have anything to gain by horning in on two grown men trying to live out some macho fantasy.

---

Michael set the small bag that held what he'd need to remove stitches on the kitchen counter and glanced outside. "Care if I say hello to Fur-face?"

"Go ahead." Pam gestured toward the door. She stayed inside, watching as Michael stepped onto the back patio. Rambo came flying from the back of the property and nearly bowled him over. Pam turned away because the man-dog wrestling reminded her of Jacob.

Everything did. The instant she'd moved back home, the pain of loss had returned to flood stage, overwhelming nearly everything she tried to do. How could she have thought coming home would make things better? *Home*. This place wasn't home anymore. It was a monument to another time. All it represented now was brokenness.

Michael came back in and washed up. They sat at the kitchen table. He didn't make small talk, concentrating instead on her wounds. "They've healed nicely," he said, "except for this one. I don't like the look of that." He looked up. "Have you been feeling all right?"

"Tired. A little under the weather, maybe."

"Any fever?"

Pam shook her head. "You know I always feel exhausted when things aren't going well. That's how I do stress. Fatigue and lots of sleep. Nothing's changed." She looked around the room. "Coming back made it all fresh." She blinked away tears. Finally she said, "I think we should sell the house."

Michael considered. "You may be right. But all the experts say not to make any big decisions for at least a year."

"I can't take another year in this—mausoleum." She shivered and rubbed her arms.

He sighed and sat back. "I am so sorry. So sorry for everything."

He looked so sincere. She hated the fact that lately Michael was showing his best side and almost—almost—making her hope. "I'm not letting you come back, Michael. And I'm not going anywhere with you over the holidays, either."

He began to repack his bag. His voice was gentle when he said, "In case you notice, I took some things out of Jacob's room."

"I haven't missed anything. What'd you take?"

He shrugged. "Just a few of the old books I used to read to him and some things out of his desk drawer."

She frowned. "Why those things?"

"In a moment of insanity that first week after you left, I got those books down—remembering." He recited the first line of *Ira Sleeps Over*. "Remember how much he loved that?"

233

"I remember."

"Well," he said, forcing an embarrassed laugh, "I took them over to the cemetery and read them again. Out loud. I imagine the guys who work on the grounds think I'm certifiable."

She stared at him for a moment before asking, "Did it help?"

"Not really."

Pam nodded, then asked what else he had taken.

"Some things about the list out of the top desk drawer and a Bible he had in there."

"The one from the Novacs," she said.

"You knew about that?"

"I knew they gave it to him. He didn't make a big thing out of it."

"If you want any or all of it, I'll bring it back. It was just—something to have." He looked around the room, and if Pam hadn't known better, she would have thought he was getting emotional.

"Keep it," she said. "But thanks for telling me. I hadn't noticed." She paused. "I haven't been in there yet. I can't even watch the DVD Andy made all the way through." She peered up at him. "Can you?"

"I couldn't at first. But now—since we started planning a way to finish it—there's a strange kind of connection. Watching him so happy, hearing him laugh—it's awful, but it's wonderful, too." He reached for the tweezers he'd used to take her stitches out and tossed them into his bag. "I can't really explain it, but that list we were so worried about has ended up being a real gift to me." He rubbed his chin. "Do you remember how horrified we were that day when he first brought it up?"

"*We* weren't horrified," Pam corrected him. The last word caught in her throat. "I wish I'd been more like you that day. More supportive. I wish . . . he'd . . . known I came to see the sky diving after all." She began to cry. "I wish he'd known I came to watch him."

When Michael tried to comfort her, she pushed him away. Picking up his medical bag, he headed toward the door, then paused and said, "If you start to run a fever or if any of those scratches start to look infected, call me. Or Dr. Webb. I guess you'd prefer talking to your own doctor."

"You're a good doctor, Michael. I'll call you if there's a problem." Pam swiped at her tears and forced a smile. "You call back sooner than he does, anyway."

He nodded. "Right."

After he was gone, Pam opened the door to let Rambo in. He skittered to the front door and stood there, whining and wagging his tail. "He's gone," she called. With a sigh, Rambo padded back down the hall and settled at her feet. She reached down and patted him on the head. "You know what, boy," she said. "Part of me feels the same way."

*And the other part of me wants to strangle him.*

## {eighteen}

THERE SHOULD BE SUNSHINE, Lisa thought as she looked out the window. She had counted off the days, and she'd put the last *X* on the calendar yesterday. Pastor Garrison would be here any minute to give her a ride to the jail. For what seemed like the thousandth time she wondered what it was like to wake up in jail. Would it be different this morning? Was Eddie Lee nervous? Would he ever laugh and joke again like he had before the accident? Would he ever believe Pastor Garrison's assurances that every sin, every mistake, every single thing he'd ever done wrong was washed in the blood of the Lamb?

Lisa sighed. It was a hard thing they had to face together now. Eddie Lee might be free from jail, but he wasn't free from his guilt. It shone in his eyes every time she visited. Truth be told, she was a little afraid about today. "'What time I am afraid, I will trust in thee.'" She said it a dozen times, but her hands still trembled as she went through the morning's routine. She'd found an adorable baby outfit at the clothing bin at the mission. Sweet Baby Lee was going to look grand for his daddy.

Lisa hurried through her own primping and fussing so she'd look grand, too. *Dear Lord,* she prayed, *the day is here, and you got us all through. Now please get us through today.* She scrunched her eyes shut and willed the tears away to protect her eyeliner and mascara. *Give us our lives back. And help Jacob Nolan's parents today, too. I guess it'll be awful for them.* The baby cried. Lisa went to the bassinet and picked him up, crooning comfort and putting him to her breast. There wasn't much point to mascara and eyeliner these days, it seemed. Reaching for a tissue, she swiped at her eyes.

Eddie Lee's hands were shaking so badly he didn't think he'd be able to button the new flannel shirt that had just been handed to him by a prison guard. He couldn't get past wondering what it would be like now, living in a world with people who'd never done anything worse than getting a parking ticket. He'd paid his debt as far as the courts were concerned, but how did a person go about paying the debt to Jacob Nolan's parents? Eddie Lee didn't have an answer to that one. He didn't think there was one. One thing he did know. Lisa and the baby were the only things keeping him from planning a fast drive into a tree.

Pastor Garrison was bringing her and the baby to meet him because the truck wouldn't start. Lisa insisted she hadn't missed it and that folks had been kind and met her needs. She'd worked some over at the mission, and someone had been dropping off groceries on the front porch. Eddie Lee understood people wanting to help Lisa, because if ever there was an angel on this earth, it was her. Once she was connected to him again, he expected that would change.

He still had to face the parents. Apologize. What could a man say in a situation like that? The lawyer said he was working on arranging it, whatever that meant. Eddie Lee had come to the point where he figured he would just have to go through life feeling like a bowling ball was stuck in his craw right next to his heart. And he was flat out scared to go back to work. Mr. Hersh was being great, but sometimes folks being nice made things even harder.

He was scared to face Lisa today, too. She was the best thing that could have happened to him and he'd told her that a million times. But part of him couldn't help but believe that the minute he brought home a few decent paychecks, she would pack up and say good-bye. When that happened, Eddie Lee figured the show would pretty much be over for him.

Pastor Garrison and the chaplain here at the jail had tried and tried to convince him to forgive himself. The chaplain said it was a "damnable kind of pride" that made a man unable to forgive himself. *"Think about it,"* he'd said. *"You're telling the God who made you that you can sin bigger than He can forgive. Now what kind of nonsense is that, Eddie Lee? God said He forgives. You say He can't. Who's wrong?"* Eddie Lee couldn't argue with the man, but he knew what he knew. The chaplain could preach all he wanted to, but he wasn't going to preach Eddie Lee Monroe out of purgatory.

He wished the sun would shine. Warmer weather would make it a little easier for Lisa and the baby. *The baby. Lee Greenwood Monroe.* The idea of being a father was the scariest thing of all. How did a man go about telling his son he killed somebody? *"Don't worry over it,"* Lisa had said. *"That's a tomorrow trouble. We don't have to solve that today."*

When they came to tell him his ride had arrived, Eddie Lee was shaking so hard the guard asked him if he was okay. He nodded and followed him out to the front, where he picked up his stuff. Then the door swung open, and with a little cry of joy, Lisa flung herself into his arms. She kissed him, hugging him so hard that the baby in the little carrier over her shoulder started to wail. Oh boy. His little face was all crunched up. One instant Eddie Lee thought he looked like a leaky red raisin and the next he decided his son was about the most beautiful thing he'd ever seen—next to his mama, of course.

Pastor Garrison extended his hand and said, "Let's get you home."

---

Lisa had moved the baby's bassinet out of the bedroom before leaving that morning. She'd put clean sheets on their bed and even sprayed the last of her perfume on the pillows. But Eddie Lee had the truck started—said it was just the battery cable that needed cleaning off—and he wanted the three of them to go for a drive.

"A-all right," she said, trying not to show her hurt feelings. She went outside to put the car seat in the truck while Eddie Lee held his son. When she came back in, he was sitting on the couch looking down at the boy, crying. That scared her. She'd never seen Eddie Lee cry—not since their wedding day.

"They still sell flowers at Hy-Vee?" he asked.

"Sure," Lisa said. "But I don't have money for—"

"I do," Eddie Lee said. "Been sitting in my wallet since I got arrested."

Lisa stayed in the truck with the baby while Eddie Lee went in the store, her heart pounding. *Help me help me help me*, she prayed. *Help us help us help us. "What time I am afraid, I will trust in thee." I am no never alone.* She hummed fragments of hymns while she waited, trying to understand—but confused and a little afraid of—this man who looked like Eddie Lee but acted like a stranger.

He came out with the biggest bouquet of daisies she'd ever seen this side of their wedding. When he got back in the truck and put it in gear he said, "I looked it up while I was in jail."

Lisa pretended to understand and nodded as they drove off. Nothing made sense until they turned west on O Street. At the entrance to Wyuka Cemetery, Eddie Lee said, "I hope you know where it is."

"I called like you told me to." She pointed. "Straight ahead, just inside the gate. Left side of the chapel. Now up and around. There." She pointed to a black marble monument with a bench nearby.

"I need to do this alone," Eddie Lee said.

"All right." When he slipped out of the truck and reached for the bouquet, she touched his hand. "I love you," she said.

"I know you do. I just don't understand why." He left then, and went to stand by Jacob Nolan's grave, his back to the truck.

Lisa couldn't see anything but Eddie Lee's shoulders shaking. Then he put the flowers down one by one until they almost covered the grave. When he was finished, he crouched down and bowed his head for a long time.

"It looks beautiful," Lisa said softly when he got back to the truck.

"They said I have to come here every year for five," he said, then turned to look at her. "I'll probably do it a lot more than that. For a while."

"That's fine, honey. You gotta do whatever's right for you."

"I don't know what's right. I just know I gotta do more than the judge said." He took in a breath, half choked, then leaned his head on the steering wheel and cried.

———————

"I thought you'd be here," Michael said. "Mind if I sit down?"
Pam shook her head.

He pointed to the daisies spread over Jacob's grave. "It's comforting, somehow."

"How so?" Pam asked, wrapping her long scarf tighter around her neck and clapping her gloved hands together for warmth.

"Knowing someone else remembered. That someone else cares. That's a good thing, don't you think?"

She sighed. "I suppose so. I don't know. I can't seem to get past Eddie Lee Monroe at home with his wife and baby today . . . while we sit here." She leaned down and rubbed her temples with her fingertips. "It just isn't right."

"How's the hand healing?"

"All healed," she pulled her glove off and showed Michael the scar where the deepest wounds had been.

"Good." He tilted his head to one side and asked, "You feeling all right?"

"I'm fine," she said. Too quickly.

"Sometimes that's code for not fine at all," he chided.

"I don't want to talk about it."

He pulled something out of his dress coat pocket. "I was going to read this," he said. "Out loud. Do you mind?"

She shook her head.

Opening the piece of paper, Michael read, "Jesus said . . . I am the resurrection and the life.'" He continued even though his voice was trembling. "'He who believes in Me will live even if he dies, and everyone who lives and believes in Me will never die.'" He paused until he had regained control of his emotions. "'Do not let your heart be troubled; believe in God, believe also in Me. In My Father's house are many dwelling places; if it were not so, I would have told you; for I go to prepare a place for you. If I go and prepare a place for you, I will come again and receive you to Myself, that where I am, there you may be also.'"

Again he paused and took a couple of breaths. "'But we do not want you to be uninformed, brethren, about those who are asleep, so that you will not grieve as do the rest who have no hope. For if we believe that Jesus died and rose again, even so God will bring with Him those who have fallen asleep in Jesus. For this we say to you by the word of the Lord, that we who are alive and remain until the coming of the Lord, will not precede those who have fallen asleep. For the Lord Himself will descend from heaven with a shout, with the voice of the archangel and with the trumpet of God, and the dead in Christ will rise first. Then we who are alive and remain will be caught up together with them in the clouds to meet the Lord in the air, and so we shall always be with the Lord. Therefore comfort one another with these words.'"

When he finally finished, Pam looked down at the paper. "What was that all about?"

"It's what Stan read at the funeral."

"I know what it is," she said. "I just don't understand why you brought it out again. Today."

"Well . . . if anyone ever needed comfort, it's you and me." He glanced down at the paper again. "And it says we should comfort one another with these words."

"Are *you* comforted by that?"

He shrugged. "A little. In some way I can't explain." He pointed to the flowers scattered on the grave. "I know who brought those." He gestured down the hill, where two guys were climbing into a small Cushman. "I asked Tomas."

"Tomas?"

"He's one of the groundskeepers," Michael explained. "I drove by earlier and saw the flowers. Then I thought of doing this." He held out the paper. "So I went back to the hotel to get it and on my way out I asked him if he'd seen anyone putting the flowers out this way. He said it was a young guy in an old pickup. With a blond-haired wife. And a baby." He paused. "Eddie Lee Monroe. He must have come straight from jail."

"That doesn't make me feel any better," Pam said. "In fact, it makes me want to pick up every single one of those daisies and put them in the trash."

Michael nodded. After a minute or two he said, "You remember that ski trip we took when Jacob was little? How we were trying to beat a snowstorm and so we drove straight through from Aspen? You remember?"

"That has nothing to do with this."

"Maybe not for you," Michael said. "I'm the one who fell asleep at the wheel."

"You barely nodded off," Pam snapped. "And no one got hurt."

"But someone could have." He sighed. "It could have happened to anybody." As he folded up the paper and stuck it in his pocket, he said, "I can't see getting anything good—any comfort or hope—out of hating Eddie Lee Monroe." He laughed an embarrassed little laugh. "I'm working on forgiving him. I've made so many mistakes over the last few years. Who am I to judge anyone else?"

"Your mistakes didn't kill an innocent boy."

"Maybe not," he said. "But they've pretty much killed everything I cared about. All the stuff I used to dream about having and being when I was Jacob's age." He turned to look at her. "I want to change, Pam. Deep down at the core of who I am. And I want you to love me again. I know it would take a miracle, but I'm beginning to hope that maybe—if I ask Him—God might do that."

Pam pulled away and glared at him. She wanted to slap the smile right off his gorgeous face. How dare he pretend to be so good? "Miracles? You're asking for a miracle? Since when is God interested in doing miracles for a Nolan? Did God stop cancer from disfiguring me? Did God intervene when you were fooling around with that blonde? Did he wake Eddie Lee Monroe up?" She was crying now, sobbing. "Don't talk to me about miracles. And don't you dare pretend to have gotten religion." With a final very unladylike comment, she marched to the Suburban and drove away.

———

By the end of the week, Michael had given up the idea of Pam agreeing to spend Christmas or New Year's anywhere near him and called his father. "All I'm saying is if you want to do your usual thing over the holidays, I can cover for you." Senior's response was predictable.

"And what if another child who reminds you of Jacob happens to be in crisis? You said yourself it doesn't take much to make you think of him."

"I've been working with children off and on since Thanksgiving, and—"

"You have? Where?"

"At the city mission. Sort of a free clinic thing. Lots of sniffles and sneezing this time of year in a dormitory situation like that. Some flu. We've just—"

"We? Define *we*, if you please."

"*We* as in the staff at the mission and me. What I started to say was we've just been doing basic hygiene and contagion-fighting things."

"You mean you're teaching them to wash their hands?" he sneered.

*You aren't that Michael anymore. You don't have to snarl back.* "So. Do you want me to come back to the practice or not?"

"If you think you are ready to return to your profession, I would welcome a respite from the last several *months* of 24/7 stress. It's been difficult, Michael. I'm not a young man."

"I know, Dad."

"No. You don't. You have no idea."

The ice in the man's veins never ceased to amaze him. "I'm sorry. I don't know what else to say. I fell apart. I couldn't do it. But I'm better now. So, I repeat: do you want your usual two weeks off over Christmas and New Year's?" It took all of Michael's will power not to tell Senior exactly what plans he, Michael, was sacrificing to do this. He'd really enjoyed the idea of going to Hawaii with Pam. And it hadn't been easy to let the fantasy go—however impossible—and reach out to his irascible, unforgiving, pompous ... to his dad, who was, apparently, not finished making things difficult.

"Plane tickets will be impossible to come by at this late date."

"Call Silverhawk," Michael said. "Charter something. The practice can afford it."

"Don't be so sure," Senior said. "I'm not certain it's wise to be flaunting our success in light of your upcoming divorce. There's no need to give that lawyer friend of your wife's visions of grandeur when it comes to a settlement."

Michael's heartbeat ratcheted up. Pam was filing? How did Senior know that? She'd actually told Rainelle to file? He cleared his throat. "Uh ... Dad. Has Rainelle Washington been in touch with you?" *Rainelle wouldn't do that, would she? She practiced criminal law ... but ...*

"No. I'm just saying ..."

Michael breathed a sigh of relief. He'd been doing his best to give Pam both time and space since the scene at Jacob's grave. But as far as he could tell, nothing between them had thawed one degree. He wouldn't be surprised if she *had* talked to a lawyer. And he had no idea where either of them was spending the holidays. He was suddenly very glad that he'd called his father. He wanted to be busy. Very, very busy. Too busy to think.

Senior was still talking. About Michael's failings. "Uh, Dad," Michael interrupted. "Could we stick to the topic at hand? Do you want the time off? Do you want me to cover for you?"

"Yes. Thank you." That was all.

"Do you want me to call Silverhawk and arrange the charter?"

"No."

"All right, then," Michael said. "Just have Laura let me know when you scheduled office hours."

"Laura is no longer with the practice."

"What happened?"

"Well-l-l," he drew out the *l* sound, "unlike myself, she had a choice. When the stress level got too high, she gave notice."

"I didn't know."

"Would you have come running in to help with the filing?" Another sneer.

*Fine, Dad. Have it your way. Be a jerk.* Michael took a deep breath and told himself that the best way to defend himself in this instance was . . . not to. "I'm sorry for what I've put you through," he said.

"The new office manager's name is Brooke Sperling. Lovely girl. Quite proficient. I'll have her contact you."

Michael waited for Senior to say something more. Like he was glad to have his son back as a partner. But Senior was silent.

"Have a good Christmas, Dad. You've earned a breather."

"Indeed," Senior said. "Happy holidays to you, too." *Click.*

————————

A week after Eddie Lee Monroe was released, Pam was standing before the full length bathroom mirror with quaking knees, telling herself she was imagining things. She raised her left arm and began the exam she despised. Once. Twice. Again. She wasn't imagining things. Backing away from the mirror, she slumped onto the little bench where she usually sat to put on her makeup. She wasn't imagining anything. They were there. Not one lump, but two . . . right— she touched them again—*there.* She inhaled sharply. *Maybe it's nothing.* Her mind tumbled back to the nightmare from ten years ago. Flashes of diagnosis, treatment, and the aftermath. She'd survived, but her marriage hadn't. She'd survived, but Jacob had died. And now . . . what was left to be wrecked by cancer now?

With a moan, she leaned her head back and thunked it against the wall. Once. Twice. "Why?" she whispered. "Why ... God ... why?"

From the other side of the closed door, Rambo whined. Reaching up, Pam turned the knob to let him in. "Hey, boy," she said. "Good boy," she choked out. And let the tears roll.

# {n i n e t e e n}

Ten days after Eddie Lee Monroe was released, Pam and Michael sat across from one another at Philip Riley's conference table. Dressed in a sweater and wool pants, Pam couldn't seem to get warm. She sat with her hands locked together across her lap, trying to avoid meeting Michael's gaze. Finally, Philip came in.

"Frankly," he said, "I was surprised when you both said you'd come in to talk about this. On the other hand, I suppose there is something to be said for starting a new year without this looming over your heads." He looked from Michael to Pam and then back again. "We set the ground rules for the court-ordered apology. We say where and when. So," he said as he sat back in his chair, "tell me what you're thinking."

"I just want to go ahead with it," Michael said, then glanced Pam's way. "Whatever you want. You tell Philip what you want, and we'll go with it."

Pam directed her next comment to Philip. "I'm here to talk about the meeting in general terms. To get your insights on how best to handle it. But—" she motioned toward Michael—"didn't he tell you he's going on vacation over the holidays?" She sighed. "And besides, there is no way I'm going to be ready to do this thing anytime soon." She paused. "He's looking at two years' probation. Eddie Lee can wait."

Michael gave a little shrug. "When I realized it was foolish to think you'd go anywhere with me, I called my father and offered to cover for him. I'm not leaving town."

Pam didn't try to hide her surprise. "You're going back to work?"

He nodded, then looked back at Philip. "Monroe covered Jacob's grave with flowers the day he got out of jail. He spent money he could have used to feed and clothe his family. He obviously feels terrible about what happened, and—" he glanced at Pam—"I say we let him fulfill the adjudication and get on with his life. I don't think anyone gains by putting him through any more pain."

Pam shook her head. "I can't."

"There's no rush," Philip said. "His attorney just conveyed Mr. Monroe's request to set a date as soon as possible."

"You won't have to say anything, Pam," Michael urged. "You just have to be there and let him talk. You don't even have to *look* at him if you don't want to."

"It's December," Pam said.

"Exactly. All the more reason to get it done. Like Philip says, there's something to be said for not starting a year with that looming over it."

"It's December," Pam repeated. "And Eddie Lee Monroe and his wife are going to be spending Christmas with their new baby." She bit her lower lip. "You remember what that first Christmas with Jacob was like, don't you, Michael?" Her voice broke. "I will not listen to any apologies from the man who ruined my life."

Michael asked Philip to give them a minute. As soon as he closed the door, Michael leaned forward and said quietly, "Eddie Lee Monroe didn't ruin your life, Pamela. *I* did." His eyes filled with tears. He swallowed. "*I* betrayed you. *I* systematically destroyed our family." A tear slid down his cheek. "I've spent hours on my knees begging God to forgive me for that, and if I thought you would listen, I'd spend hours on my knees in front of you begging you to forgive me. But whether or not you ever forgive *me*, sweetheart, you have to reclaim your life. And meeting with Eddie Lee Monroe is a step toward doing that."

"How can you just—do that?" Pam glared at him. "How can you forgive him . . . as if nothing . . . as if what he did doesn't matter?"

"Of course it matters," Michael said. "It's ripped us both to shreds." He leaned toward her as he talked. "Do you remember that prayer you learned as a kid? 'Forgive us our trespasses, as we forgive those who trespass against us'? I bet I've rattled that thing off a thousand times over the years without ever thinking about what I was saying. 'Forgive us . . . as we forgive.'" He sat back. "The whole idea of forgiveness baffles me. Stan Novac has told me a dozen times that it's there—a free gift—and all we have to do is ask for it." He lifted his hands, palms up. "How can that be? The list of my trespasses is *so long*. How could anyone, least of all God, forgive all that?"

Pam looked up at him. He'd never believed in God. Not really. What was he up to?

"I know what you're thinking," Michael said. "I never believed in God before. So what's going on? You're wondering if it's just another performance to get what I want." He hesitated, then looked at her with an intensity she hadn't seen in years. "It isn't. I really have been changed."

He looked her straight in the eye. "The guy made a mistake, Pam. He didn't mean to hurt anyone. Me? I didn't make mistakes. I made bald-faced, self-centered, pre-meditated wrong choices." He didn't look away. "But I asked, and according to Stan Novac and his pastor and Jacob's Bible, when I asked, God gave free, unending, eternal forgiveness—which I don't pretend to understand. Except to say that part of what it means is that I have to forgive Eddie Lee. If I don't, I'm hurting myself just as much as him."

"You have it all figured out," Pam said. "Well, good for you. I'm glad you've found your happily-ever-after."

"Sweetheart. Don't you see? If you and I don't find a way to get past June 19, then death wins. You *hate* what it's done—the way it's destroyed your future. And yet, you're letting it win. Please, Pamela. Take your life back," he pleaded. He clenched his fists and pulled them toward himself, illustrating what he was saying. "Listen to his apology. Forgive him."

"I don't know how. I can't."

Michael crouched down beside her and took her hands in his. "Of course you can. You kept our family together. You survived breast cancer." He tilted his head and teased, "You hiked the Appalachian Trail long before it was the cool thing to do. You can pretty much do anything you set your mind to, Pamela Sue Nolan."

She shook her head and looked away. "I'm too tired to think about this right now. I—I need to go home."

He squeezed her hands. "I want you to call Dr. Webb and make an appointment. Tell him how you feel. Let him help you."

"Ah yes," she muttered, "the wonders of modern medicine." Which couldn't fix what was wrong with her . . . not without more surgery. Maybe not at all. *Maybe that wouldn't be so bad.*

"There's no shame in asking for something mild to help things get balanced again."

She sighed. "I suppose not."

"That's my girl."

"I'm not your girl," she reminded him.

Without commenting he stood up. "I'll tell Philip that Eddie Lee Monroe will have to wait. We're just not ready."

They parted ways in the outer office. Pam dragged herself home and up the stairs to her bedroom, where she pulled an afghan over herself and fell asleep. In her dream, she was hiking across a flowering meadow. There were cliffs in the distance, and a lake reflected a sky of impossible shades of pink and purple—colors never seen in the real world. As she walked along, an ornate staircase raised up from the earth. Jacob stood at the top of it, calling for her to come with him. She wanted to, but there was another hiker behind her, and when she tried to head for the stairway, he kept holding her back. When she struggled free and spun around to see who it was, it was Michael.

———

Pam stood leaning against the front door, regretting she'd answered the doorbell. She hadn't washed her hair in several days . . . she knew she had dark circles under her eyes . . . and here Michael was, looking great. Rambo was beside himself, prancing with joy, lick-ing Michael's hands. "Get back!" Pam ordered. Rambo backpedaled instantly and disappeared into the family room.

The air outside was frigid. When had it gotten so cold?

"Can we talk?" he asked.

"That depends."

"On what?"

She coughed. "On whether *we* are going to talk or *you* are going to preach so I can be impressed with your new righteous wisdom."

"Touché." He hunched his shoulders and looked behind him at the snow-covered landscape. "Can I please come in?"

As soon as she shut the door, she turned her back on him, irritated by the sight of Rambo peeking around the corner at them. She didn't have to see the tail to know it was wagging. Ignoring the dog-man reunion, she returned to the couch, where she'd been snuggled up drinking herbal tea and trying to read a book called *Time Lottery*. Betty had dropped it off a few days ago, saying Pam could probably relate to the topic. Could she ever. The novel was about people who were able to go back in time and change a decision and live a different life. Pam knew just which decision she would have changed. And he was petting her dog right now. Pulling the afghan up around her shoulders, she said, "So. What's this about?"

He seemed nervous. Almost self-conscious. Finally, he cleared his throat and said, "I wondered if you would let me send you and Rainelle for a spa date in Scottsdale. To unwind and—" he shrugged—"I don't know, to run away from home until after the first of the year." Before she could dodge the gesture, he'd reached over and tucked an errant strand of hair behind her ear, caressing her forehead as he did so. "You're worn out. I thought maybe time away would be a nice reprieve."

"Thanks," Pam said, shaking her head. "But no."

"You didn't call Dr. Webb."

"Have you been checking up on me?"

He shook his head. "I saw him in the hallway at the hospital and mentioned it. He didn't know what I was talking about."

"I don't need you hounding me," Pam said, coughing again. "The fact is, I'm too sick to go to the doctor." She forced a laugh.

Instinctively, Michael laid his hand on her forehead. "You have a fever," he said. "A fairly high one."

"I just took some aspirin. I'll be fine."

"Flu symptoms?"

"Back off," she said, moving away when he reached up with both hands to check for swelling under her neck.

"Pamela." His voice was taut as he met her gaze. "Do you have any lumps under your arm? I've been thinking about you so much . . . and worrying. . . . I've tried to call, but you never return my calls. I've tried to send messages through Rainelle, but she won't talk to me, either." He sat down on the couch. "I remember how long you ignored the lump on the left side because you were too terrified to face the C word."

She couldn't hold the tears back. He *knew*. Only God knew how, but he knew. And here he was offering comfort she didn't want. Except maybe she did—but she couldn't let her guard down. But she couldn't keep the tears in. She breathed deep to try not to cry. But he moved closer and he smelled so good . . . and she was so scared and in no condition to resist his arms around her . . . so she didn't.

"Sweetheart," he said, stroking her greasy hair as he talked. "Listen to me. When I talked to Brandon in the hallway that day, he reminded me of something. And, while it's not very common in adults, I think you have it. Brandon will definitely want to do a biopsy because of your history—but honey, listen to me." He pulled away and held her by both shoulders and looked straight at her. "I am 99.9 percent certain you have something called cat scratch disease. Not cancer. Cat scratch disease."

She sniffed. "Cat scratch disease?"

"Yes." He squeezed her shoulders. "The lymph nodes swell up a week to a month after a scratch. And you didn't just have a scratch."

"Why didn't you tell me about this!" Now she was angry. He should have known. He should have told her. He should have—

"Because it's rare in adults. Because there was no reason to think you'd get it."

"Then why are you here? What made you . . ."

"We've been married for over twenty years, Pam. I may be the worst husband in human history, but give me credit for knowing a few things about my wife. You weren't yourself when we met with Philip, and honestly, you haven't been yourself for a while now."

"How would you know whether or not I've been myself?" She was indignant. It felt like he'd been spying on her.

"I haven't dropped off the planet. And we do have mutual friends. And, okay," he teased, "sometimes I hold a Novac hostage until they tell me something about you. And lately, they've all had the same things to say. You aren't yourself."

She was still trying to process what he'd said about what she thought were malignant lumps. Her hand went to her side and she grimaced.

"Come on," he said, holding out his hand. "I'll show you what I'm talking about on the computer in the media room."

She let him pull her off the couch. With a few clicks of the mouse she was looking at text that described exactly how she'd been feeling and photographs of lumps that made hers look minor. Which was, Michael explained, part of the reason she was so terrified. "If you'd had a full-blown case like this—" he pointed at a particularly gross looking lump on the screen—"you would have automatically known it wasn't cancer and hightailed it to Brandon's office. But I'm guessing your lumps don't look that bad."

She shook her head. "Just a little swelling and tenderness."

"And you know enough about breast cancer to know that tenderness doesn't mean no malignancy." He reached up and ran his finger along the edge of her jaw. "Call Dr. Webb's office, honey. Tell him your symptoms. He'll want you to come in—probably right away if you tell him when Cicero attacked you—and he'll probably schedule a biopsy just because you'll need the peace of mind. I think there's a blood test now, too. But I'm telling you, forty-eight hours on the right antibiotic, and you won't believe the difference."

Michael pulled his cell phone out of his pocket and handed it to her. "Make the call." He walked over and petted the dog while she called her doctor. Relief washed over her in waves. She mopped up tears and then went to find Michael. "Don't gloat," she said, trying to suppress a smile. "I'm going in at eight in the morning."

"Not trying to tell you what to do," he said, "but you might also consider a bubble bath or a stint in the hot tub to work out some of the knots in your shoulders." When she dropped her hand away from the muscles she'd been kneading, he winked. Moving quickly, he pecked her on the cheek before she could avoid him.

———————

Later that evening, when Pam descended the stairs to dish up Rambo's dinner and to return to the fireside and her book, she paused at the bottom of the stairs and smiled—once again in spite of herself. A tray boasting a carafe of hot tea, her favorite cup and saucer, cream and sugar, and a package of Pim's cookies, her favorite. He had to have hurried to manage it, but the gesture was touching. Annoyingly touching.

## {twenty}

WITHOUT DISCUSSING IT, Michael and Pam found a way to coexist. It was tricky, but it worked. Michael stopped by every day to check on her progress. He was almost disappointed the day she said she hadn't spiked a fever that afternoon because it meant he didn't have an excuse to come by as often. While other physicians groused about their senior partners on holiday and having to be on call, Michael was grateful for the opportunity to lose himself in the world of medicine.

On Christmas Eve he and Pam went to church with Stan and Betty. Not together, but they were both there. Maddy and Megan were shepherds in the children's pageant, and Emily played Mary. Pam made a point of sitting beside Betty and urging Andy to sit next to her. Halfway through the program, Suzanne scrunched past Pam and Andy to climb into Michael's lap.

———

They'd gotten through the holidays and now ... now it was becoming increasingly difficult for Michael to think up excuses to stop by the house. Virtually his entire winter wardrobe was across town at the hotel. He'd brought what he needed from Jacob's room long ago. Still he wanted *home*. The joke was certainly on him. For years he'd been a champion of avoiding home, and now when every part of him longed for the place, he wasn't welcome.

Some nights he lay awake missing things he didn't even know he'd consciously noticed. Things like the way the house smelled when there was a fire going in the family room fireplace. The view from the family room window, especially the way the light tan bark of the river birch trees they'd planted at the south end of the property contrasted with the pine trees behind them. And Rambo. He really missed that dog.

———————

The January morning had dawned clear, although a little colder than normal. By noon the temperature had plummeted and sleet had begun to fall. Pam looked out the family room window as the afternoon light waned and evening approached. It looked like they might be in for a full-blown blizzard. Tree limbs already coated with ice hung low to the earth, and there was no sign things would let up anytime soon. Around ten that night she let Rambo out. While he wallowed in snowdrifts and took care of business, she went around the main floor pulling drapes shut and locking doors. When the dog came back in, she grabbed a towel from the laundry room and rubbed him dry.

"You've been having *way* too much fun out there," she laughed. He kissed her cheek. "Bedtime," she said, and together they headed upstairs, where Pam turned on some soft music and slipped into bed with another one of the novels Betty had loaned her.

Apparently serving up leftovers in the guise of meat loaf wasn't Betty's only "ninja" behavior. The woman had a way of slipping faith into the weirdest places. Lately it was in the reading material she loaned out. Pam hadn't known there was such a thing as fiction with a "Christian twist," but this book used Bible verses as chapter headings. Feeling a bit wary, a few nights ago she'd decided she should at least give it a try. One paragraph into the first chapter and she was drawn into the story of a woman facing a personal crisis not that different from her own. More than once, she'd fallen asleep with the book in hand. More than once, she'd had to apologize in the middle of the night when the book fell off the bed and bonked Rambo on the head.

It was taking much too long to feel better. Michael kept telling her that given her emotional state before cat scratch fever took up residence in her body, she had to expect it to take a while before she felt like doing much. Still, she was beginning to feel claustrophobic staying at home all the time. And she was thinking way too much, analyzing the past and second-guessing the future, ad nauseam.

As for the past, she realized she'd kept herself safe from being hurt by putting on emotional blinders, seeing only the good doctor, good provider, loving father part of Michael and refusing to consciously face the rest. *He says you're strong. But you're not. You're a coward. If you'd been strong you'd have left him long ago.* Jacob's death and seeing Michael in broad daylight with another woman had combined to rip off the blinders. In fact, the light of knowledge had been so bright at first that she hadn't been able to see anything but the glare of Michael's offenses. But just when she began to be strong enough to honestly analyze events—to be willing to look past her version of reality and try to find some truth—that was when Michael began talking about changing "at the very core of who I am." He apologized. He accepted blame. He talked about forgiveness. But it went further than the things he said. It showed up in the things he did.

Michael had always been good with children because it was required for him to be a successful pediatrician. But that had nothing to do with Suzanne Novac clambering into his lap on Christmas Eve and settling back against him—as if she did it often.

He'd always done the community service required to put the practice in a favorable light, but now he was volunteering as a physician at the city mission on a regular basis.

He'd always gone to church, because spirituality was part of the image he wanted to create in people's minds. But now he was going to church with the Novacs, and Pam didn't think there was any way that being connected to that church could possibly help build an image. She'd heard that pastor interviewed on the radio, and if there was an unpopular stance to take about an issue, he took it. All, of course, because of "what the Bible says."

The church thing was the hardest part of Michael to understand these days. The man who had, less than a year ago, openly sneered at

Stan and Betty Novac's evangelical faith actually seemed to have adopted it for himself. In fact, when Pam thought about it, she realized that Michael was starting to talk more and more like Stan these days. Like someone whose faith was more than a Sunday obligation.

The worst part about the whole thing was that she was feeling drawn to this new Michael, even though she wasn't sure she even knew who he was. The uncertainty of that was terrifying, given his history. And so, when he was around, she was careful to keep her distance. She needed to be that strong woman Michael claimed she was. She kept reminding herself of that. *You're a survivor. You don't need Michael. You don't need religion.*

———————

The sound of the garage door opening woke her up the next morning. Apparently Rambo had already shot downstairs to investigate. Pulling on her bathrobe, Pam walked toward the front of the house and looked down on the drive. Michael's BMW was parked out at the street. She could see his tracks leading up to the garage. From the depth of those tracks, she guessed that at least six inches of snow had fallen in the night. With a sigh, she drew the drapes and went to get dressed. By the time she went downstairs, Rambo was prancing at the garage door, whining to be let out. She opened the door for him and then went to pour herself a cup of coffee. On a whim, she pulled a package of muffin mix down from the cupboard and turned on the oven.

"Whew!" Michael said when he stomped inside. "Thank God for snowblowers." He hung his coat in the laundry room to drip dry and pulled off his boots and gloves before kneeling down to dry Rambo off. "Do I smell cinnamon?"

"I threw some muffins in the oven," Pam said. "Thanks for coming over to do that, by the way."

"No problem," Michael said. "I assumed you wouldn't mind my coming in and warming up before I leave."

"I don't mind."

"I can see you're feeling better. The color's back in your face. No more fever?"

"None. Although I wouldn't mind an infusion of energy." She waved him inside. "Come to the kitchen and have some coffee. The muffins should be ready any min—" The oven timer went off.

Michael inhaled with appreciation while he slathered butter on a muffin. He gestured outside. "It's a good day to be safe at home," he said. "They've canceled school."

"Are you going in to the office?"

Michael shook his head. "The office assistant Dad hired went in early. I couldn't believe she was already there when I phoned at seven-thirty, calling people to cancel their appointments. Most of them were relieved."

"But you'll still go in because there are always one or two who won't listen," Pam said.

"Actually, I'm meeting the 'one' at the hospital in about an hour." He looked down at his watch. "Which means I should be going." He stood up. "You stay warm and safe, and call me if you need anything."

"It's the nineteenth," Pam said. "I'm going to the cemetery."

"There's a layer of ice about two inches thick under that snow."

"I've got four-wheel drive. I'll be fine."

Clearly unhappy with her insistence, he did something unusual. Instead of driving his point home, he changed the subject. "It'll be spring before we know it," he said. "You started any seedlings yet?"

"Way too early," she said, then sighed. "Don't know if I'll bother anyway. There doesn't seem to be much point."

"Growing things is part of who you—" He stopped in mid-sentence. Then, with a shrug he said, "Whatever you think," and left.

Pam poured herself another cup of coffee, regretting that she hadn't bagged up a couple of muffins for Michael to take with him.

———————

Michael had been gone a couple of hours, and Pam was still sitting in the kitchen nook, her journal open before her, looking out on the backyard winter had transformed into a wonderland of fine silver and whipped cream. She hadn't used the journal in the way Betty intended. Instead, she'd started taking it with her to the grief support group meetings and writing down things people said so she could remember them later. It wasn't authentic journaling, but it was helping. So were the meetings, although she'd resisted the idea mightily when Betty had first brought it up. Now, she was glad she'd started going. She supposed it proved that Betty had been right when she said that married couples would find individual ways to survive. Michael was apparently turning to religion. She was finding her comfort in others like herself.

*There is a way out of grief, a way of surviving, that is positive.* The day she had written that down, she hadn't believed it. Now she was beginning to. Michael had called her a survivor so many times. And every time he said it she wanted to slap him. What did he know about any of it? He'd left emotionally the minute her breast came off. *Did he? Did he really? Or were you the one who built that wall?* She didn't really know the answer. But she did know that blaming Michael for everything that was wrong was too simplistic. *So is blaming Eddie Lee Monroe.* She ignored that thought and returned to the journal.

*Nothing can ever be the same again. Through grieving you will have to rebuild a world where you can live.*

She was just now getting to the point where she believed she could do that—find a new world where she could live. The question was, what from the old life would she take with her into the new? Would she sell the house? Would she still have Michael? That was the biggest question of all.

Someone at a meeting had said most parents sense a shift in things around four months after a death. It had taken longer for her. Nearly seven months.

Her therapist had taught her to set aside a piece of time every day, fifteen to twenty minutes, where she could be by herself uninterrupted. That was her time to think about losing Jacob. Whatever came up or wherever her thoughts went was fine. It was like fencing off a space in the middle of an endless prairie; there was no difference between what was inside the fence and what was outside. But after a while, her therapist assured her, there would begin to be a difference.

Pam had followed this advice, and going to Jacob's grave every day had become her time to wallow. And she wasn't going to let a snowstorm stop her. She had a four-wheel-drive Suburban, and even if the gates at the cemetery weren't open, she could still park in the funeral home parking lot and walk back through the grounds. She needed to go.

The television and the radio both verified what Michael said. Schools were closed, emergency routes the only thing plowed this morning, and everyone was being urged to stay home. But it was the nineteenth. She had to go.

"You ready, boy?" she said to Rambo. What a great companion. He always said yes.

---

"Holy moly," Pam said aloud as she navigated the side street that led up to Sheridan Boulevard. Surely that had been cleared by now. Guiding the Suburban across the first set of double lanes, she turned north. Or, rather, slid north. Michael said there was a layer of ice beneath the snow, but she hadn't anticipated it being this bad. Rambo sat on alert in the seat beside her as they crept along toward South Street, which thankfully was plowed and sanded. Kids were out everywhere, pummeling each other with snowballs, building snowmen, having a great time on their day off from school.

Pam wondered aloud what the Novac kids were doing today. "Probably building an igloo or something." Talking aloud helped her loosen her death grip on the steering wheel. She rambled on until she reached O Street and turned right, driving slowly along the perimeter of the cemetery and finally sliding into the entrance and a parking place at the funeral home.

"Just like I thought," she said. "The gates are closed. Come on, Fur-face." She didn't bother to attach Rambo's leash. The place was deserted except for a couple of workers already out trying to clear the winding lanes that led from the entrance back into the cemetery proper.

––––––––––

Tomas nudged Eduardo and nodded toward the woman trudging through the deep snow. He held out his hand. "I told you she'd come. Pay up."

Eduardo slapped a five dollar bill into his friend's hand. "Both those people are crazy," he said. "How long has it been?" He counted on his fingers. "Seven months." He shook his head. "I feel bad for them." He looked at Tomas. "Are you still praying?"

Tomas nodded.

"Well, it's not working."

"You can't say that," Tomas insisted. "Praying always does some good some way." He fastened the last bolt that held the snowplow on the four-wheeler and stood back up, motioning for Eduardo to climb on and get started. "I'll be right behind you soon as I get the truck warmed up."

"How come," Eduardo asked, "you get the pickup and I'm out freezing on the four-wheeler?"

Tomas grinned. "That's life, man. You don't always get what you want, you know?"

As Eduardo drove off, Tomas climbed into the pickup. He sat for a moment, watching the woman standing at the boy's grave. She was bending over reaching for one of the red flowers the other guy had brought out earlier.

"Whoever he is," Tomas whispered to the heavens, "I pray for him, too." Crossing himself, Tomas asked for comfort for the three people who came—the two who visited day after day, and the other guy who came only once a month . . . when he covered the grave with flowers.

––––––––––

It made Pam angry to think that Eddie Lee Monroe had actually beat her out here in this weather. She bent down to pick up a red carnation just as Rambo tore off after a black squirrel that had descended halfway down a nearby oak tree and hung suspended upside down, chattering fiercely at Rambo, who circled the tree, barking happily.

As she stared down at Jacob's grave, the wind chapped her dampened cheeks. "I'm better, Jacob. At least I think I am." *Yes. You are. No shrieks. No loud displays. Just quiet grief most of the time now.* Turning around, she brushed the snow off the bench and sat down. She didn't have much to say, but she was glad she'd come. When her cheeks began to feel numb, she called Rambo to her side. Dropping the carnation, she headed for the gate—walking this time on the slippery surface left by the snowplow that had cleared away the snow, exposing the ice beneath.

She drove carefully—always had. It happened so quickly she didn't have a chance to react. One minute she was driving down Sheridan Boulevard—almost home—and the next the Suburban was fishtailing. Things got worse when she overcorrected. Thankful that there weren't any other cars nearby, she tried to control the slide. She was helpless. The street might as well have been a frozen pond. That's when she heard the high-pitched screech. Saw the snow fort. And felt the impact.

*God help me. God help me. God help me.*

Shaking, she fought her way out of the deflated air bag. Opening the car door, she stumbled to the front of the Suburban, which was buried up to the hood in what remained of a wall of snow. Built by kids. Having a snowball fight. And they were . . . they were . . . She stumbled over what was left of the wall, her heart racing, her hand to her chest.

"Hey, lady," someone called. "Are you all right?"

Children appeared from every direction.

The door to the house opened. "Christopher!"

"It's okay, Mom," the tallest of the children hollered back. "We're all okay." He turned around and looked at the remains of the snow fort. "The fort's trashed, though."

"I thought . . ." Pam choked out the words. "I saw . . . I heard."

"You heard Ashley," the boy said. "That's my sister. Thinks it's fun to give grown-ups a heart attack." He pointed toward an evergreen and out stepped a beautiful girl, her face red, her breath rising in the frigid air like silken threads.

"Oh, gosh, ma'am," Ashley gushed. "I'm sorry. I'm sorry. I didn't think you'd freak out. I just—"

Pam leaned against the car trying to catch her breath. That's when she thought of Rambo. *Never put him in the front seat, Mom, unless you disable the air bag. It'll kill him if you're ever in an accident.* She was sobbing before she even got to the car, but her sobs changed quickly to laughter when Rambo launched himself at her, raised up on his hind legs, put his paws on her shoulders, and began to lick her face— all the while moaning and making such a commotion it sounded like he was delivering a lecture on her pathetic driving skills.

"Christopher Jonathan Miller," an adult woman's voice said. "Get inside. Now. And bring your sister with you."

The gaggle of children dispersed, and Christopher and his sister lumbered toward the English Tudor-style house.

"Are you really all right?" the woman asked.

"I'm fine," Pam said. "I just—when I thought—" Her voice broke off. *You will not cry you will not cry you will not cry.* "I'm fine," she said.

"At least the snow fort did some good, although I told the kids they couldn't play behind it. Too close to the street. Guess they'll see their mom isn't as stupid as they think sometimes." She paused, then said, "I'm sorry Ashley scared you so badly. You can be sure she's going to get a lecture when I get back inside. And she won't be playing out in the snow anymore today."

"Don't," Pam said. "She didn't mean anything by it. Kids do stupid things sometimes."

"Let me count the ways," the woman said. "You must have some of your own."

Pam swallowed. Are you still a mother when your child is dead? "A son," she said. "He's grown up now. But he had his moments." She barely choked the words out before she had to turn away.

Finally back home and parked in the garage, she checked the Suburban for damage. Not a scratch. She wobbled into the house and sank onto the couch, holding Rambo and crying with relief . . . and, eventually, with other emotions, too. In the blink of an eye she'd almost . . . she could have . . . been in the shoes of the man she blamed for ruining her life.

What was it Michael kept saying? *"He didn't do it on purpose. He made a mistake. Something we all do."*

––––––––

"Man," Michael huffed, "this was easier when I was twenty." He planted his ski poles and forced himself across the snow, certain he looked more like a battery-operated robot than an athlete. "This is humiliating," he said. "I used to be good at this!"

"If it's a contest, I win," Stan said, rubbing his arm and shoulder. "I thought I knew the meaning of the word *burn*. I was wrong."

"Listen, you two geezerjocks," Andy joked as he came up between them, "it doesn't feel all that great at twenty-two, either." He laughed. "Can we stop and breathe?"

"Finally!" Stan said.

"At the blue spruce up ahead," Michael called as he took off. He could hear Stan sigh and then start to follow.

When the three men finally stopped to catch their breath, Andy said, "We'll be glad we did this when it comes time to film the kiteboarding this summer."

"Kiteboarding?" Stan protested. "I'm not even going to *be* there for kiteboarding." He dropped his ski poles in the snow. "I did this for *kiteboarding*?"

Michael laughed and headed out. "Nah, you did this because you didn't want to miss out on all the bragging about how sore we are later."

Burning lungs and aging muscles aside, it was a gorgeous day. The blue sky and the pine trees laden with snow made Pioneers Park look like a greeting card. Even the requisite bright red cardinal was on tap to perfect the scene. It was, Michael realized, a good day to be alive. The Jacob-shaped hole in his heart would never close up, but as Betty and Stan had promised, some amount of recovery was beginning. It came in flashes, with moments like this one where being alive felt good. More often than not, just as quickly as the happiness came, a shadow followed. Sometimes he was thrust back to the bottom of the well of grief and had to claw his way back out. Sometimes his longing for Pam got tangled up in the battle. At other times, he could distract himself and move on without such a terrible struggle. But the raw edges of his sorrow *were* beginning to heal, and the time between struggles was gradually lengthening. He was nowhere near feeling like he was going to "overwhelmingly conquer," as the Bible said, but he was beginning to see the horizon of a land where that might be possible.

When the three men had loaded their rented cross-country ski gear into the back of Stan's pickup and were on their way to the Novacs and a promised chili dinner, Stan turned on the radio, groaning when the weather report predicted more snow. "You have got to be kidding me," he said. "Six to ten more *inches*? Below zero temperatures? For several *days*?"

"Hey," Andy said, "it's not all bad. Maybe I'll get a couple of extra days off school before I have to turn in my psychology paper. And maybe I can earn some bucks shoveling walks for people."

"Ah, the enthusiasm of youth," Stan said. "You wouldn't be so excited if you were the one who had to scrape ice off all the car windows and then spend your day driving all over town helping stranded motorists and working fender benders."

Andy leaned his head back and closed his eyes. "So . . . just keep focusing on summer." He smiled. "I'm seeing beaches and waves and . . . bikinis. Lots of bikinis."

"Yeah, well," Stan groused, "if wishes were horses beggars would ride."

"You always say that," Andy said. "And I'm never exactly sure what it means."

"It means," Stan said, revving the cold engine, "that if wishes could make it happen, we'd all be on a beach somewhere instead of shoveling snow and scraping ice. But wishes don't make things happen. Wishing won't conjure up a horse for a beggar so he doesn't have to walk, and wishes won't conjure warm weather in January. At least not for those of us living in Nebraska."

"Hey," Michael said, "at least there's a bowl of hot chili in our future. And I don't know about you two, but I'm starved." He was quiet on the ride to the Novacs', his thoughts busy with wishes and horses and beaches and sand and . . . talking to Pam.

## {twenty-one}

IT WASN'T THE REACTION Michael had expected. After coming up with his great idea, he knew he wouldn't sleep until he talked to Pam, so he arrived unannounced at the front door. She let him in, albeit with an increased level of wariness. This was not the muffin-baking woman who'd thanked him for coming home to snowblow the drive only a couple of days ago. That woman had smiled in such a way that Michael was able to imagine a reunion someday. There was no such softness in the woman who stood leaning against the kitchen counter tonight.

She repeated his idea without expression. "You want to take the Novac family—the entire family—to Hawaii. For two weeks."

He nodded. "Like I said, what are we waiting for? Here we are in sub-zero Nebraska when we could be taking diving lessons and swimming with dolphins. Why wait until summer? And then I realized the reason we were waiting was so Andy could work and save his money. But . . . we have Jacob's life insurance and the memorial money—and that's not even counting the trucking company's settlement. Why not use some of it? Who deserves to share in that more than the Novacs, anyway?"

"I can't believe I'm hearing this," Pam said, plopping down at the kitchen table. She looked up at him. "I suggested helping Andy with that money months ago, and you threw a fit. Now all of a sudden you want to take the entire family to Hawaii?" Angry tears gathered in her eyes and her cheeks flushed. She pressed her lips together.

"What—what's going on? Why are you crying?"

"Because I'm angry," she spat out. Her voice was a thread shy of a

screech. "What's *going on* is this . . . this . . . mess you've left me with."
She gestured around her. "All this kingdom building. I stood by you
and played the part. And then it all falls apart, and what do you do?
Just start another one. Get religion. Be the nice guy. Forgive Eddie
Lee. Take the Novacs to Hawaii. Make it all better."

He could almost see the steam coming out of her ears.

"In case you haven't noticed, Dr. Nolan, while you've been out
making things better for everyone else, I've been here at home trying
to remember how to breathe."

"I'm aware of that," Michael said quietly. "Nearly every minute of
every day. And I want to change it, but you won't let me."

"So I should smile and pretend everything's fine now, because the
great Michael Nolan is going to make it all better?"

"That's *not* what I'm doing." He sat down opposite her.

"You are so right. That is *not* what you're doing. And you know
why? Because I'm not playing charades anymore."

"It isn't a charade," he said quietly.

"Oh no? Then how is it you've suddenly taken over Jacob's list like
*you* thought it up? How is it you're suddenly the one doing the planning and the deciding? How come *you're* the one hanging out at the
Novacs while I sit—here—in the wreckage of our life with Jacob's
ghost all around me?" The words faded into a sob. When he reached
out to her, she waved him away.

Rambo rattled the back doorknob with his nose. Pam got up and
let him out, then stood watching as he trotted to the back of the
property and disappeared around a berm. Without looking in
Michael's direction, she began again.

"I almost killed someone a few days ago." She paused. "It wasn't
really all that close, but I could have." In short bursts she told him
about the snow fort and the Suburban spinning out. "I'm beginning
to get it, Michael. At least when it comes to Eddie Lee Monroe. I
don't *want* to get it, but the truth rose up and slapped me in the face
and you were right. It was a mistake. An awful, gut-wrenching, life-
changing mistake, but a mistake—no more, no less. But *you*,

Michael . . . you didn't just make a mistake. You knew exactly what you were doing every time you betrayed me." She muttered, "Every single time. And now . . . now you want to be the good guy." She shook her head. "Honestly, Michael, it makes me sick." She opened the door and called the dog in.

"I should go," Michael said. "We can talk another time."

"No." Pam put her hand on his shoulder to keep him in his chair. "We'll talk now." She sat back down. "Here's how this is going to work. I'm not so self-centered as to let my issues deny something wonderful for the Novacs. I love them, they deserve this, and this is something Jacob would want me to do. Heaven knows those kids are never going to get another opportunity like this one."

"Is that a yes?"

"That's a yes."

"Do you think Stan will go for it? I mean, without insisting they pay something?"

"It's Jacob's money, not ours. Stan may have to strut his feathers a little to preserve his manhood, but he won't want pride to be the reason his kids miss out." She leaned forward. "What's Senior going to say about you leaving for two weeks when you just returned to the practice?"

Michael shrugged. "Hank Morgan did a great job picking up for me last summer. Frankly, I think Hank would probably jump at the chance to join the practice. Senior likes him. It'll work out."

"And what about Stan? Is he going to be able to get away on such short notice? Will Andy be able to miss that much school?"

"Stan's been the go-to guy for the entire department for a long time—the one everybody asks when they need someone to work for them. I bet he'll be able to work it out. I don't know about Andy's school. We'll just have to see."

"So if it all works out, we'll go to Hawaii, and I'll stick with Betty and the girls while you guys go do whatever it is that makes you feel macho. But—" she tapped his arm—"I will *not* pretend to be your little woman and I will *not* sleep in the same room with you." She paused. "You see to that. And I'll see to it that Betty and the girls have the time of their lives."

———

Pam's first view of Hawaii was not very encouraging. The terrain around the Kona Airport was black asphalt and lava. Only a cluster of palm trees around the airport buildings hinted of a tropical paradise. And the hint was faint. Things changed quickly, though, as they headed north toward Waikoloa and the resort Michael said had won awards as a great family vacation spot.

Sleeping arrangements weren't a problem. Michael had booked adjoining suites, and as soon as they arrived, he suggested Pam and Rachel take the bedroom while he and Andy bunk on the pullout couch in one suite, with Stan and Betty and the younger girls in the other. Pam thought she saw meaningful glances exchanged, but she chose to ignore them and concentrate on the breathtaking view from the balcony.

It took most of their first day just to tour the resort itself. No one even thought about leaving the grounds as they wandered along meandering waterways discovering lagoons, waterslides, waterfalls—even Jacuzzis and hidden grottos in freshwater pools.

"Talk about a place that has everything," Pam said early that evening as she and Betty lounged on the beach watching Maddy and Megan chase the waves as they went out, then screech and backpedal up the beach when the next wave came in. "Did you see the spa offerings? And a day camp and . . ." She opened her arms wide.

"Michael did good," Betty said with a smile.

"Yes," Pam agreed. "He did."

Over the next four days, while the men attended scuba diving classes, Pam and Betty and the girls explored the island. Pam had read a guidebook on the plane. "The Big Island has it all . . . pristine rain forests, lava deserts, beaches, snow-covered mountains."

They saw Kilauea Volcano at night, gasping at the sight of fire falling into the sea sending great plumes of steam skyward. At Kealakekua Bay when spinner dolphins leaped out of the water and cork-screwed through the air, Pam shrieked with joy right along with the children. Almost as thrilling, and certainly less expected than dolphins or whales, were the Hawaiian cowboys they saw moving cattle through a gate on the Parker Ranch.

"Whatever I expected Hawaii to be, this wasn't it," Pam said, gesturing at the rolling grassy hills extending in all directions. "It looks like home."

And that was how it went. Delight in the unexpected, amazement at the diversity on the island, and a renewed appreciation for creation. Everything was going smoothly until Stan brought the sad news that the girls wouldn't be getting their promised chance to swim with the dolphins.

"It has to be booked six *months* in advance," he explained. "I'm so sorry, girls."

As tears of disappointment welled up in the twins' eyes, Betty reached for their hands. "Let's ask Jesus," she suggested. "Maybe He'll decide that He wants you two to meet the dolphins after all."

Pam thought the woman was nuts. Why would anyone set her kids up for that disappointment? What was even more confusing, why would Betty tempt fate that way? The Novacs wanted their children's faith to be strong. What was she going to say to Maddy and Megan when their wish didn't come true?

That evening Andy and Rachel offered to stay with the younger girls while the four adults enjoyed the sunset on the beach. As they lounged and talked, laughing at the men's tales of their mistakes as they shared the highlights of their underwater experiences, Pam broached the topic.

"I mean, get real. Stan said the thing is booked six months in advance. You can't really believe saying a few words to Jesus is going to change that."

"Well," Betty said, "maybe not, but I believe it *could*." She smiled. "I've heard you exclaim several times over God's creation since we've been here, Pam. It's not a very big step to go from believing God created it all to believing He can handle something like a dolphin quest list."

"And what do you say to the twins when Jesus doesn't give them what they want? How do you keep them from getting mad at Jesus?"

"I wouldn't think of trying to keep them from getting mad," she said. "Of course they'll be mad and disappointed. Things don't always go our way. God isn't some genie who grants every wish. And I don't believe He expects us to deny our feelings. If the answer is no, then we'll talk about that, including all the reasons why Jesus might say no."

"Which are . . . ?"

Stan spoke up. "Maybe the kids already on the list needed it more. Maybe there's something even better that Maddy and Megan would have missed if they'd been in the lagoon. It could be any number of a million things, and maybe the girls won't know exactly. Maybe they simply need to learn to accept disappointment without throwing a fit. But whatever happens, their faith is stronger because we include Jesus in every part of our lives."

Pam sat quietly, pondering what Stan had said. It wasn't preachy or superior. She had known them both long enough and well enough to know they were sincerely sharing what they truly believed. But she couldn't get past the idea that they were setting their girls up for disappointment.

And then, the next morning, the hotel concierge called to say there had been a last-minute cancellation—and if the two girls still wanted to swim with the dolphins, they could.

———

Hawaii was filled with small miracles like that. Sunsets beyond belief, every single one a different set of breathtaking colors. Mesmerizing ocean life, from dolphins to whales to sea turtles. And yet, it wasn't in the sites that Pam found her lasting memories. It was in the little things she began to notice when she was with Betty and the girls. The simplicity of their faith. The way they always thanked God for their food. The way they always thought of Him first when they saw something amazing. Maddy even prayed for an injured bird. When Megan scoffed, Maddy said, "God cares about the sparrows, and He cares about that fancy bird, too."

After a while, Pam felt like she was being chased around the island, not by a fire-breathing volcano god, not by a war god, but by a gentle wind that kept incessantly caressing every raw place in her heart.

On the last afternoon before they were to pack up and leave, while Betty and Stan and the girls went shopping and Michael and Andy were going over some of the video Andy had shot, Pam slipped away by herself to return to a site called Place of Refuge. In spite of her several days' worth of attempts at understanding some of Hawaiian history and culture, she didn't quite understand all the details of this place. Still, she was drawn to the idea that there was a place in that long-ago world where people could go to make restitution and to receive forgiveness for things that otherwise would have been punished by death. She stayed until sunset and, as the setting sun gilded the coconut trees and turtles munched on greenery near the canoe landing, she started to cry.

"All right, God," she whispered. "If you really are there, and if you really do want to help me make sense of all this, I'll listen. I'll try." There wasn't much to it beyond that. She cried for a little while longer, and then as the colors were fading from the sky, she returned to the hotel and joined everyone at their farewell luau.

---

It was dark and Pam was leaning against a palm tree on the beach listening to the ocean when Michael joined her and asked, "You all right?"

"Hard to believe we're heading back into winter. Andy said he checked the Weather Channel, and the high at home tomorrow is going to be about twenty-two degrees." She shivered.

"Oh, I don't know," Michael said. "This has been great," he said, gesturing around him, "but that's home. And as wonderful as all the whale watching and volcanoes and beaches and luaus have been, I think the Novacs are ready to leave." He shrugged. "Truth be told, so am I."

It hung between them, almost palpable on the warm breeze—the waiting, looking away, knowing one of them should say something . . . the right thing . . . but who knew what the right thing was? A hundred times in the last two weeks Pam had caught Michael watching her. A hundred times she'd smiled at him, all the while knowing her reaction wasn't what he wanted. She was being polite. Friendly. He wanted more, and he took no pains to hide it. He didn't overstep and he didn't force himself on her, but still, he was there. And now he was here. And they were alone.

"You did a wonderful thing, Michael," Pam said. "Andy babbles about his documentary like he's already won that scholarship. And the children. I will never forget the look on Maddy's face when that dolphin swam up to her. Or Megan exclaiming over the sea turtle sunning on the beach." She chuckled. "Or Stan charging across the sand after Rachel when he thought she was flirting a little too much with that guy from South America."

"He was hot," Michael said. "Stan—not the Latin lover."

They shared a quiet laugh, and then Pam said, "Thank you, Michael."

"You don't have to thank me. This was as much your doing as mine."

"No . . . I don't mean for the trip. I mean for respecting the boundaries. For not crowding me." She paused. "I think—I think maybe it's time to close some doors and move on."

"What—exactly—does that mean?"

"When we get back I think we should have Philip set up the meeting with Eddie Lee Monroe."

# {twenty-two}

IT WAS EVENING WHEN the plane approached the landing strip in Lincoln. The sunset sky was mildly colorful, but as Pam peered down at the city below, the browns of the dormant landscape did nothing to make her feel good about returning to reality. She wanted to believe that something profound had happened to her in Hawaii, but as the plane touched down, she wondered if her moment at the Place of Refuge was nothing more than wishful thinking. God didn't really answer people who threw challenges at Him, did He? Nothing had *really* changed. At least nothing that would spare her from having to face the empty house and Jacob's room alone. She couldn't even pick up Rambo until the next morning.

When Michael dropped her off at the house, she blurted out an invitation. "Come in for coffee?"

"I'll help you in with your luggage," he said. "But I can't stay."

"Can't? Or won't?"

"Wasn't it only last night you were thanking me for respecting your boundaries?"

"It's just coffee."

Michael shook his head. "You don't get it, do you?"

"Don't get what?"

"How hard this is for me." He yanked a piece of luggage out of the back of the BMW, pulled the handle upright, and reaching for her carryon, slung it over his shoulder and headed for the front door.

Pam followed him, unlocked the door, and stepped inside. "Thanks for the ride," she said.

"You're welcome."

Michael had turned to leave when she called his name.

"You—uh—if you want to stop by and see Rambo tomorrow, I should have him back home around nine in the morning."

"I'd like that," Michael said.

"Maybe you'll want coffee then."

He stared at her for a minute. "Maybe I will." Then, before she could close the door he strode back up on the porch, pulled her into his arms, and kissed her. The only thing that bothered Pam about it was that he apologized and left before she had a chance to kiss him back.

---

"Oh, all right," Pam said, "you win." She patted Rambo on the head and glanced over at the kennel attendant. "I can't stand the look on Reba's face. Care if I take her, too? We'll wait outside until the Novacs get here."

"Sorry," the attendant said, "but we can't release a dog to anyone but the owner."

"I know they'll be here in a few minutes. How about if I take both dogs out to romp in the play yard until Betty and the girls get here?" She motioned to Reba, who was standing at her kennel gate looking forlorn. "I just can't walk off and make her think she's being left. Look at her," Pam said. "Another minute and she'll conjure up tears."

Glancing at Reba, the attendant smiled. "Such a baby," she scolded, albeit in a tone of complete affection. Reba's tail moved back and forth in an almost imperceptible response. The young woman looked back at Pam. "If you're willing, I'm sure that will be all right."

---

"Whoa!" Pam hollered as Rambo strained at the leash. When she let go, he lunged for the car, racing around it with glee, prancing about in an undignified dance that made Pam laugh out loud. "All right, all right, boy. Settle down. You'll be home soon." Of course he couldn't settle down, and she didn't really care. Reba was doing the same kind of dance around the Novacs' minivan.

"Makes me think we'd better never leave them again," Pam said.

Betty grinned. "It *is* good to be home, isn't it?" She tilted her head and looked at Pam. "I prayed for you last night."

"Thanks," Pam said. "It was . . . all right." She patted Rambo on the head. "But it'll be better with Fur-face back at home." She bent down and spoke to the dog as she opened the door. "And Michael's coming by this morning to see you." Rambo chuffed and climbed in. When Pam looked back at Betty, she was smiling.

"What?" Pam said.

"Oh . . . nothing."

Pam felt herself blushing and changed the subject. "While Michael's playing with Rambo I'm going to the garden center and pick up some supplies to start some seeds." She gestured around her. "All this brown is so . . . *brown* compared to the Big Island."

"Can we do that?" Emily leaned out of the minivan window and spoke to her mom. "Can we start some flowers?"

"There's no room for that kind of thing at home, honey," Betty said. "And you know how I am with flowers." She glanced at Pam. "I can grow blue-ribbon vegetables, but anything that has to be started in those little pots never works for me."

"If your mom says it's all right," Pam told Emily, "you could help me this afternoon." She gave a quick look in Betty's direction. "There's plenty of room on the windowsill in the family room for several trays of peat pots. In fact, each of the girls could have their own tray if they want. If it sounds like something they'd like to do."

Maddy spoke up. "I wanna grow *red* flowers." Megan wanted yellow. Emily said something about daisies.

"You sure you want to do this . . . today?" Betty asked, raising her eyebrows and muttering, "With Michael coming by?"

"I'm sure. In fact, it'll be great. Unless you and Stan had plans for the girls?"

Betty laughed. "The only plan we have is to do laundry. *Mountains* of it."

"Well, then," Pam said, "drop them off whenever."

"When did you say that other person was coming over?"

"I have no idea. And it doesn't matter. He's coming to see Rambo. In fact," she said, "why don't the girls just ride home with me now?"

---

Pam sat at the kitchen table staring out the window as shadows lengthened and darkness swallowed up the last views of her garden. When Freddy next door began to yap, she got up and called Rambo in, then headed upstairs. She had expected the adjustment to living alone after being around the Novacs all the time to take a while, but it had been two weeks, and she wasn't getting any more comfortable with the empty house. Turning the radio on, she headed into the master bath for a long shower, then crawled into bed and picked up a book. When the story line failed to interest her, she got up again, eventually wandering down the hall to Jacob's room, surprised that tonight she could face it with dry eyes.

She lay down atop the Rambo-rumpled bedspread, her hands clasped behind her head, looking up at the glow-in-the-dark universe she'd brought back from a long-ago trip when she was still accompanying Michael to conferences, remembering a night in Hawaii when she had taken Maddy and Megan and Emily for a walk on the beach. They had all been mesmerized by the night sky, with one significant difference. While Pam exclaimed over the view, the Novac girls thanked Jesus for creating it. Emily had even recited a Bible verse about a man looking up and considering the heavens and wondering why a God who could create all that would bother to pay attention to people.

As she lay on Jacob's bed looking up at the plastic stars on the ceiling, Pam thought back to the moment at the Place of Refuge when she'd told God that if He wanted to speak to her she would listen. Whatever she had expected, nothing dramatic had happened in the two weeks since she'd been home. *Maybe it doesn't work that way. Maybe all the dramatic stuff is in the movies. Maybe He's answering right now, right here. Maybe it's God reminding me that He made the stars overhead, that He hung them in the sky just as surely as I put these on Jacob's ceiling years ago.*

"But if you hung the stars . . . if you have the power for that kind of thing . . . why didn't you save Jacob?" She whispered the question aloud, knowing there would be no answer and wondering again how people like the Novacs could live with no answers and still love God so much.

"But we have answers," Betty had said once when Pam asked her the question. "They just aren't the answers we want." She had smiled softly. "His ways are not our ways, but He loves us, and He always does what is best. He promises that heaven is real. He promises so much." Betty's eyes had clouded over with tears, and she'd blinked them back and squeezed Pam's hand. "And I *so* want you to know Him."

Pam sat up, remembering how she had smiled and patted Betty's hand and said that while she couldn't accept the same answers that seemed to comfort Betty, she did love her for caring. Tonight, even though she still wasn't ready to believe everything the Novacs believed, Pam realized that something was different. She didn't know when it had happened, but at some point in the recent past she had gone from observing the Novacs' faith with a distant kind of that's-great-for-you-but-it's-not-for-me appreciation to consciously acknowledging that she wished she could trust God that way. Feeding bitterness and hate took a lot out of a person. She was beginning to wonder if forgiving Eddie Lee Monroe would do as much for her as everyone seemed to say it would. As for forgiving Michael . . . part of her had already decided that wouldn't be so bad, either, but the other part was terrified by the idea of trusting him again. With a sigh, Pam got up.

Back in her room, she stood at the patio doors looking down on the moon-silvered lawn that would, in a few weeks, be green again. Opening the door, she caught her breath at the blast of cold air rushing into the room, then stepped out onto the deck. As she gazed down at the garden, she realized how much she was looking forward to the first crocus . . . and the daffodils and the tulips that would line all the curving flower beds. It would be Easter soon. She smiled as she remembered Jacob and a few friends hunting for Easter eggs in the backyard. Spring. Renewal. New growth. Puppies and bunnies and fresh starts for the drab brown world.

"I don't want to hate people anymore," she said aloud. "If you could help me with that, I'd really appreciate it." Retreating back inside, she crawled into bed and fell asleep.

---

Pam had spent hours envisioning how things would work when it came time for Eddie Lee Monroe to deliver his court-ordered apology. For a long time she'd wanted to make him page through all the photo albums that showed Jacob growing up. She wanted him to visit Jacob's empty room. And she wanted him to have to stand at Jacob's grave when he apologized. Planning it and playing it over in her head had occupied a lot of time . . . and accomplished nothing beyond dragging her downward into an ever deepening hole of helpless anger and depression. She was ready to be free of it. She'd told Michael that in Hawaii, and she felt even more certain of it now. There was only one problem. Michael was out of town.

"Phoenix?!" Pam exclaimed into the phone. "What on earth are you doing in Phoenix?" *And why didn't you let me know you were going?*

"I'm getting some stuff together that has to do with Jacob's list," was all he would say. "I'll be back around the third, so if you want to call Philip and arrange the meeting, I can be there anytime the first week of April."

Pam said she would do that and hung up, her heart pounding. What if he'd met someone down there? What if . . . *Stop it. You kicked him out. You can't blame him if he's looking for a new life.* And, she realized, she didn't blame him. She might not have served divorce papers, but she'd gone to a lot of trouble to remind him of his faults and to insist that it was over between them. She hadn't even kissed him back that night after they got back from Hawaii. She hoped she'd get another chance.

————

As promised, Michael got back to Lincoln on April 3. The morning of the sixth he picked Pam up at the house.

"Have a nice time in Phoenix?" Pam asked as she slid into the passenger seat of Michael's BMW.

He nodded.

"You aren't going to tell me what you've been up to, are you?"

He shook his head. "Let's just get through this morning, okay?"

————

Eddie Lee Monroe and his attorney were waiting in Philip Riley's conference room. Monroe stood up when Pam and Michael entered, his thin fingers laced together, his knuckles white. Only when it was time for him to speak did he finally manage to look them in the eye.

"I was afraid I would forget something important, so I wrote it first, and I been working on memorizing it. So if it sounds like I'm just reciting something, it don't mean—" He looked away and cleared his throat. It seemed to take forever before he looked up again. Taking a deep breath, he continued. "It doesn't mean I don't mean what I'm saying."

Pam couldn't help but notice the way the suit hung on his thin frame. He was clean-shaven. Some would say even nice looking. She wondered about his wife and baby, thinking back to the slender blond woman so passionate in her defense of her husband, so obviously in love with him.

"I don't expect you'll care about the why," Monroe continued. "But if you would just listen—"

"We'll listen," Pam said, gripping the back of the conference chair in front of her, surprised that now that this moment had arrived, she was glad she hadn't demanded any more of this terrified man than what was happening right now.

Monroe cleared his throat. "There is no excuse," he said. "But there is a reason." He glanced at Michael. "The most important thing in a man's world is his wife—that is, when he loves her. And I love my wife more than I ever thought I could. When she called from the hospital to tell me the baby was coming early, I was so far away and so afraid something bad would happen." As he spoke, he picked up steam until finally he blurted out, "I should have stopped and rested, but I didn't think I was that tired and I wasn't over the limit." His voice broke.

Finally, he looked at Michael. "I am sorry for what happened." Monroe turned to Pam and repeated it. "I am sorry for what happened." He swallowed. "I don't deserve for you to forgive me," he said. "But I am sorry. And I thank you for listening and letting me say it."

That was all. Pam and Michael moved away from the door and Philip Riley opened it so that Monroe and his attorney could leave.

As they stepped through the door, Michael spoke up. "Eddie Lee," he said.

Monroe hesitated. Pam thought he moved like an old man as he turned back and faced them.

Michael cleared his throat. "You're forgiven. By God. And by me."

When Michael spoke the words, Pam realized that God had answered one of her prayers. She didn't hate this young man anymore. In fact, she almost felt sorry for him. Slipping her arm through Michael's, she said, "*We* forgive you."

Monroe stared at them. His eyes filled with tears. "Thank you," he croaked, and was gone. When the door closed behind him and his lawyer, Michael and Pam clung to one another weeping.

———

As she watered the flourishing seedlings on the windowsill, Pam leaned closer and inhaled the aroma of moist soil and life. *Life*. Rambo lay curled up in the sun on the patio on the other side of the window. Looking beyond him to the garden, Pam surveyed the greening lawn and the flower beds, smiling at the sight of a cluster of purple and yellow crocus blooming along the fence. Daffodils would not be far behind . . . then tulips . . . and then things would start to leaf out and bloom so quickly it would be hard to keep up.

It was getting harder to convince Megan and Maddy that they didn't dare plant their flowers outside yet. But Pam was insistent. "They're very tender right now and frost would kill them." She was looking forward to helping the girls plant their flowers at the Novacs'. Her own seedlings would go into the pots waiting outside the back door. On Mother's Day, the official "safe from frost" date for Lincoln.

*Mother's Day*. Even the term made her cringe. Thank God for the Novacs, who were already counting on her to come over and help with the gardening. As for Father's Day . . . somehow she would help Michael. She didn't know how. But she would find a way.

"WELL, IF IT ISN'T the right reverend Dr. Nolan," Rainelle said as she left her office and sashayed past Michael, briefcase in hand. "I've got to get to court. You should have made an appointment."

"I've tried," Michael said, following her down the hall and toward the elevators. "I've called you at least a half dozen times since the first of the month. You don't answer my messages."

"Imagine that. Now why would I want to avoid you?"

"I need your help," Michael said.

"You've come to the wrong office," Rainelle retorted and pointed upstairs. "Divorce lawyers are upstairs. That isn't my bailiwick."

"It's about Pam."

"It usually is," Rainelle said. "And you have to know that I don't care what she says, she's better off without you. And all that stuff I hear about Hawaii and church and community service doesn't change my opinion one bit. You don't deserve another chance."

"You're right," Michael agreed. "I don't. But like I said, this isn't about me. It's about something Jacob wanted to do for his mother. Something I want to see finished."

"Ah yes," Rainelle said, lowering her voice like an announcer as she said, "the list." She looked him up and down. "What's that got to do with me?"

"You aren't listening," Michael repeated. "Andy and I want to finish something Jacob was planning *for his mother*. This wasn't really part of his list—although planning the list probably inspired this stunt."

"All right," Rainelle said. "You've got my attention."

"We need your help getting Pam to an event. It would mean a lot."

"To who?"

"To Pam. This is completely *about* her and *for* her."

The elevator arrived. Rainelle stepped back and set her briefcase down. "You've got three minutes. And this had better be good."

He talked as fast as he could. When he finished he said, "So . . . what do you think? Like I told you, this isn't about me."

She looked around the hallway. "Where is Dr. Michael Nolan, and what have you done with him?"

He smiled. "So you'll answer the phone when I call with directions?"

Rainelle nodded. Together, they stepped onto the elevator. At the street, Michael wished her good luck in court.

"I don't need luck, honey," she said, holding her head high. "I'm good."

As Michael made his way back to the parking lot, he replayed part of the conversation. *"I don't care what she says, she's better off without you. You don't deserve a second chance."*

---

Pam recognized Rainelle's voice, even though she was purposely muffling it, trying to sound mysterious.

"At precisely five-thirty Friday evening, there will be a knock at your door. You will greet Andrew Novac and turn over your dog. One half hour later, you will be standing on your front porch, dressed for an evening of live music and dancing, suitcase in hand. If you do not comply with these instructions," Rainelle said, "the Bellini brothers will have to complete their mission. And you do *not*, I repeat you do *not* want to tangle with the Bellamy brothers."

"I thought you said it was the Bellini brothers," Pam said, laughing.

"Whatever," Rainelle said. "Dark suits, dark shirts, white ties, sunglasses. You get the picture."

"Any instructions as to what exactly should be *in* the suitcase?"

"Jammies and a toothbrush. You can buy the rest in Kansas City."

"We're going to Kansas City?"

"Oh yeah. Barbecue, jazz, and blues. All night long, girl friend."

"That's Friday. What about the rest of the weekend?"

"I have the inside scoop on the best shoe stores in town. So you might want to bring your husband's credit cards." She accented the *s*.

"Multiples, eh?" Pam laughed. "What's Michael going to say about that?"

"Not a word and you know it. You've got him right where you want him—ready to let you have anything you want and begging for mercy."

Pam ignored the dissing of Michael. "Really," she said. "Give me some idea of what I should bring. Is this a spa date, shopping date, casino date, or—?"

"Yes. And that's all I'm going to say except we have a suite at the Raphael and I took Monday off."

"You rock," Pam said.

"I know."

Pam hung up and looked down at Rambo, who was standing at the family room window extending his nose toward the young plants growing there. "Not edible, Fur-face," she said and shook her finger at him. Rambo sat down and cocked his head sideways, looking at her as if asking for more information. "It would seem that you are going to Reba's for a visit." The dog only needed to hear *go* and *Reba* to start a happy dance around the family room. Pam laughed and hugged him. "You're a good old dog," she said, and headed upstairs to pack for the weekend. It might only be Tuesday, but you could never plan too far ahead to run away from Mother's Day.

---

"It's all arranged," Rainelle said.

"Thank you," Michael replied. "How exactly are you going to get her out there without letting on?"

"That's easy. I say get in the car, the girl gets in the car." She hesitated. "I'm picking her up on Friday evening. We'll do all the usual stuff in the city, and then on Sunday morning—earlier than I care to think about—I'll drag her into the car and head out. How long did you say the drive would take?"

"Close to two hours," he said. "And you'll call—"

"Stan Novac's cell phone as soon as we're getting near the turnoff. Calm down, Michael. It'll go fine. She'll love it. She'll cry and all that, but she'll love it." She paused. "You're in danger of getting in my good graces again, Michael Nolan," Rainelle said. "It's more than a little unsettling."

"Which Rainelle would this be on the line?" he joked. "Because unless they all agree, it's going to be a lot harder to get my wife back. Not that I'm going to give up, mind you, but since you were the one who introduced us in the first place—"

"Don't remind me. Times change."

"So do people."

"I'm thinking about that. And I'm watching."

"And what are you thinking?"

"Not sure. But it's not all bad."

Michael's voice was gentle. "Thank you. That means a lot. Now you make sure Diva-Ray and Tough Mama know how you feel."

His laugh sounded forced. Was he actually nervous about talking to her? "Michael?"

"Yes. I'm listening."

"Is it true what I heard from Malcolm? That you're breaking off from your father's practice and setting up a free clinic downtown?"

He cleared his throat. "It's more in the 'think and pray' stage at the moment. I didn't know Malcolm knew about that."

"Word gets around." She paused. "It's good stuff, dude. Really good stuff."

"Well, it's not that big a deal. And it hasn't happened yet. Besides, *Jacob's List* is the really big effort."

Rainelle nodded, even though she knew he couldn't see. "Maybe you should hang around on Sunday. See it for yourself."

"I'm riding up at dawn," he said. "That's my part. The rest is for Pam. I don't want to mess it up for her. Andy's promised to take lots of film. I'm sure I'll see it the minute he gets back to town."

"All right then," Rainelle said, "I'll be seeing you."

---

Before dawn on Mother's Day, Rainelle shook Pam awake. "And now," she said, mimicking a TV announcer, "for something entirely different." She stood up. "Time to get dressed."

"What?" Pam said and lifted her head off the pillow. Rainelle was dressed. "What time is it? Are you nuts?" She scrunched the pillow beneath her head and turned back over.

"We have an appointment out of town, and we've got to get going. I'm packed. I'll go get us some more coffee—I already drank what the housekeeper left. I'll be back with some fresh brew, and you had better be dressed and in your right mind when I get here."

"UNNNHHHHH!" Pam moaned and burrowed down into the pillow.

Rainelle cleared her throat.

"All right, all right," Pam said and sat up. "This is *not* funny."

"It's not supposed to be funny."

After Rainelle left, Pam got up and dressed. What was she supposed to wear? What was Rainelle wearing? She hadn't noticed. Jeans had better be good enough. Fumbling in the dim light, Pam showered and dressed. True to her word, Rainelle arrived with Starbucks for them both. They checked out and hit the road.

"West?" Pam said. "We're going west?"

"You want I should head into the sun and blind us?" Rainelle mugged. "Just sit back and relax. Here," she said, handing Pam a CD case. "How about a little Keb Mo for the ride? Maybe some Vance Gilbert. It's a two-CD ride."

---

"Oh, this is great," Pam said as they drove through a small town. "I've always wanted to visit the Oz Museum in . . . Where are we?"

"Waumego, Kansas."

"It's not open. So what's the plan? A gourmet breakfast at the truck stop while we wait?"

When Rainelle drove through town and headed back east on a two-lane road, Pam shook her head. "Curiouser and curiouser."

Rainelle was silent, obviously unfamiliar with the road. Suddenly she flipped open her cell phone, pushed a speed-dial number, and said to whomever answered, "We're here."

Something pink was tied to a road sign in the distance. Balloons. Streamers. They pulled off at a gravel road. Someone had tied a sign to a concrete railing. It said *Jump for Jake*. Pam looked at Rainelle. Back at the sign. Up ahead, cars lined the narrow gravel road winding south through farm fields. Every car adorned with pink balloons. Signs. Banners. And people. Lots of people. Rainelle honked. Once. Twice. Dozens of strangers began throwing pink and white confetti onto the road, clapping, whistling, watching as Rainelle drove slowly down the road.

"What—is—this?"

"You'll see," Rainelle said.

At the end of the road stood three tiny metal buildings. A field full of campers and tents. A plane. No, two planes. And just now, coming down out of the sky, half a dozen parachutes. And pink everywhere Pam looked. Rainelle pulled through the crowd and up to the largest of the three buildings. The sign said it all.

Jump for Jake
In memory of Jacob Michael Nolan
1983–2005
Celebrating the Survivors
Funding the Research
Finding a Cure

"What the—?" Pam looked at Rainelle through her tears. "Who?"

"Jake was planning it. Michael and Andy saw it through."

Pam covered her face with her hands and leaned over, sobbing. Andy came to her side of the car and opened the door.

"I know you'll need a minute," he said. "But my family's here. And when you're ready, there are a lot of other people I'd like you to meet." He turned aside and pointed across the parking lot to where the rest of the Novac family waited. And Rambo and Reba, both of them sporting huge pink ribbons around their necks. Turning back toward Rainelle, Pam noticed for the first time. She muttered. "I should have suspected you were up to something. A pink manicure?"

"I always try to dress for the occasion." Rainelle handed Pam a pink tissue. Pam blew her nose and scooted out of the car, hugging Andy as they were surrounded by members of the KSU Parachute Club—Jacob's friends she'd never met. They had all collected pledges—every jump earned a specific amount of money for breast cancer research. Andy explained that there was a swap meet set up on the field next to the runway, and a silent auction, and lunch was being served inside the building. Proceeds from everything would go to the cause.

"Michael should see this," she said as she walked with the Novacs and Rainelle toward the runway to watch a takeoff.

"He was here earlier," Betty said.

"He arranged for the second plane," Stan told her. "More jumps, more money."

Andy spoke up. "We had a memorial jump at dawn," he said. "Both planes went up. We learned it's a tradition for that to be a silent jump. They wear black armbands and try to exit the plane just as the sun pops up above the horizon. It was . . . great," he said, his voice wobbling. "Just great. And Michael made a perfect landing. He even had a pink parachute. Said he might start going to more fund-raisers."

Had she heard that right? "Michael . . . jumped?"

"Oh yeah. Impressed the heck out of everyone. They thought he was just the moneybags old guy." He grinned. "So now you know what he was up to down in Phoenix."

"Phoenix?"

"Yep. Great drop zone. Fabulous weather. Best place ever to get licensed." He held up his video camera. "I'll show you some of what I got—but that guy over there will have better footage."

Pam followed Andy's nod to where a guy with cameras mounted to his helmet was retrieving his parachute.

"He's a pro. Promised some awesome footage for *Jacob's List*."

"Where *is* Michael?" She scanned the crowd.

Rainelle spoke up. "He said he didn't want to take anything away from it being your day. Your day from Jacob."

Andy held up an envelope. "He said to give this to you."

———

"You're gonna wear out the hinge on that cell phone, girl," Rainelle said.

Pam glanced at her friend's profile and then back at the stretch of two-lane highway before them.

"Why don't you just call him and get it over with? Even I would agree that Michael did something wonderful today. So call Mr. Wonderful and say thank-you." She paused. "Unless, of course, you have some sweet nothings to say you don't want me to hear." She chuckled.

Pam shook her head and looked out the side window. It had been a surreal day. Planeload after planeload of sky divers taking to the air and floating back down over and over again. They didn't have a final total, but Andy said a few thousand dollars would be going to the Susan Komen Foundation for breast cancer research. Pam's hand went to her side as her mind replayed Michael touching the tip of her scar and swearing that it didn't make any difference to him.

Pam reached in her purse and pulled out the card Andy had handed over just before she and Rainelle drove off. It was one Jacob had given her for Mother's Day years ago. A horse's head on the cover and then a joke inside that had sent her into gales of laughter . . . and birthed one of those secret family chuckles that could be brought on by a one-liner that made no sense to anyone but the family. To think that Michael knew she'd kept it and had gone looking for it in their photo albums was touching. As was the sweet note he'd added to the inside. There was no doubt about it. The man had changed.

She wished he had stayed around today. She smiled, trying to imagine him gliding through the sky attached to a pink parachute. The man was . . . different. No doubt about it, he had changed since Jacob's death. So had she.

"I heard that sigh," Rainelle said. "And so did Fur-face."

Back in the moment, Pam realized that Rambo was resting his snout on the back of her seat.

"I'm okay, boy," Pam said and reached across her shoulder with her right hand to pat his head. He responded with a soft kiss to her fingers and a brief snuggle.

At an intersection south of Lincoln, Rainelle turned right to skirt the southern edge of the city. "So make the call," she said. "The wait is killing me."

"I don't know what to say."

"Yes, you do," Rainelle coaxed. "You just don't want Diva-Ray or Tough Mama to hassle you." She paused. "Neither of them will say a word," she promised. "Get it over with, girl friend. Make the call."

Pam slid the phone into her purse. "I'm not going to call," she said. "This—this has to be done in person."

---

In the end, Pam couldn't find Michael. She had to call. "Where the heck are you?" she asked, more than a little frustrated that things weren't going according to plan.

"Just leaving the office," Michael said.

"Is everything all right?"

He paused before answering. "Yeah. In a weird kind of way, everything is . . . really great. I suppose I can tell you . . . the practice is going to be changing. Actually, it's—uh—it's over. I tracked my father down over here tonight to talk about coming back to work, and he let me have it with both barrels."

"Oh, Michael. I'm sorry."

After a long minute she heard him exhale. "I should have done it years ago. Maybe things would have been different."

Pam agreed. "Maybe." She cleared her throat. "I don't know how to thank you for today."

"Don't thank me," he said quickly. "It was all Jacob's idea. I'm just glad it played out so well. Andy said they raised a good amount of money. And Betty said you had a good time."

"I did. Except . . . Michael. You should have stayed."

He disagreed. "It played out exactly the way it needed to."

She forced a joke. "But I want to see your pink parachute." Awkward silence. She cleared her throat. "Can I at least come over and give you a hug to say thank-you?" *Lame. That is so lame.* "Or maybe you'd want to stop at the house? I should be there in a few minutes."

"You aren't home yet? I figured Rainelle's blue rocket would have slid into the driveway hours ago."

"We stopped for dinner and . . . I've been looking for you. Rambo's doing his I-gotta-go dance or I'd come to you. Will you come home?"

––––––––

A thousand things charged through his mind on the short drive from the office to the house. This was it. She was going to ask for a divorce. But she'd used the word *home*. He scolded himself. *Don't read anything into that. It doesn't mean anything.* She was going to hug him, and they'd be friends. She said she wanted to see the parachute. What did that mean? Of course she'd still want to be part of finishing Jacob's list. How was he going to manage that . . . having her around and not having her? *Help me help me help me help me.*

She was waiting on the front porch with the dog at her side when he drove in. When he got out of the car and headed for the house, Rambo bounded over to him first. Of all the thousands of possibilities that his imagination had played in his mind on the way over here, Michael hadn't dared to imagine the one that played out in actual time and space. In the end it wasn't even all that dramatic. She simply walked up to him and into his arms. At first he told himself this was just the promised thank-you hug for what had happened today. He felt awkward trying not to take it past a friendly hug. But then . . . then she looked up into his eyes and said the three words he would cherish for the rest of his life.

"Don't let go."

"Therefore if any man is in Christ,
he is a new creature;
the old things passed away;
behold, new things have come."

2 Corinthians 5:17

# {afterword}

MOST NONFICTION BOOKS on the subject of grieving a child's death indicate that recovery is usually only beginning two *years* after the child's death and that, in many ways, parents never recover. For a long while after learning this, I didn't think I could possibly write the book I had promised my wonderful publisher. My thoughts ranged from a panicky *No one will want to go here with me* to *No one will stay in this place long enough for it to be even minimally realistic.* In the end, I dealt with this challenge in the only way I knew how. I used the "novelist's privilege" to shorten the time for Pam and Michael's recovery—by a lot. I wish, therefore, to beg the understanding of those parents who have endured what many call the worst loss in human experience and to express my admiration for those who have not only found the courage to survive but who have, through organizations like Compassionate Friends, extended a hand to those who follow along the same path.

*Jacob's List* has been, in many ways, the most difficult book of my writing life. Remaining in what Pamela Nolan calls "this broken place" for all the months of writing and rewriting was a heartrending challenge. In the end, of course, I finally made my writer's way toward healing and hope, not because I believe in fairy tales but because personal experience has taught me that the worst moments of our lives can eventually birth the brightest moments.

When my husband of twenty-eight years died of cancer, I never expected to be happy again and I certainly never expected to be excited about my future. But here I am, several years into widowhood, remarried and learning to apply the lessons I learned in my own "broken place," surprised to have discovered that I love riding a motorcycle, that blues music festivals are fun, and that old ladies really can learn to dance as if no one is watching.

It is my sincere hope that you, dear reader, will be given strength to endure your broken times until healing begins and you can believe that tomorrow does hold promise.

Thank you for taking time to read this Stephanie Whitson novel. Thank you for writing me, for telling your friends about my books, and for all you do to encourage my writing life. *May the Lord of peace himself give you peace at all times and in every way* (2 Thessalonians 3:16 NIV).

Stephanie Grace Whitson
3800 Old Cheney Road
#101–178
Lincoln, NE 68516

# {acknowledgments}

SPECIAL THANKS TO . . .

Bethany House Publishers, for giving me the honor of working for them.

Shirley Dworak, sister in Christ, for painting the picture of Thanksgiving dinner at the Lincoln City Mission.

Michael D. Gooch, attorney-at-law, for enlightenment regarding the legal system.

The Kansas Eight writers, for brainstorming and encouraging.

Deputy Scott R. Lanagan of the Woodbury County, Iowa, Sheriff's Office, for explaining law enforcement protocol.

Jesse Magana of the KSU Parachute Club for making it possible to write about jumping out of an airplane without actually doing it.

Nancy Moser and Deborah Raney, peerless peers, for not letting me quit.

Joseph Reinhard, award-winning freeflyer (and son-in-law) for suggesting and brainstorming "Jump for Jake."

My fellow Lincolnites, for allowing me the novelist's license to adjust reality as it applies to Jacob's hometown.

And as always . . . Chi Libris . . . let me count the ways.

For a full menu of *Jacob's List* discussion questions for your reading group, book club, or writers' critique group, visit the author's Web site at *www.stephaniegracewhitson.com* or *www.bethanyhouse.com*.

Stephanie Grace Whitson would be delighted to visit your group via conference call. To arrange a "speaker phone" visit, contact her directly at stephanie@stephaniewhitson.com.